Acknowledgments

A great big heaping mountain of thank-you to everyone who lent a helping hand in the development of this book: my family, friends, beta-readers, proof-reader, avid readers, feedback givers, reviewers, hand-holders, muses and many more.

To name only a few: Michelle Chenoweth, Monique Taken, Zan-Mari Kiousi, Tray-Ci Roberts, Vicki Goodwin, Denise Boutin, Elizabeth Greenwood, Corinne Lehmann, Lynn Herron, Karen Semones, Maria DB, Kim O'Shea, Tricia Toney, Deborah Montiero, Keti Vezzu and Patty Michinko.

RUINED

and

Redeemed

THE EARL'S FALLEN WIFE

BY
BREE WOLF

This is a work of fiction. Names, characters, businesses, places, brands, media, events and incidents are either the products of the author's imagination or used in a fictitious manner.

Any resemblance to actual persons, living or dead, or actual events is purely coincidental.

Cover Art by Victoria Cooper

Paperback ISBN: 978-1546518310
Hardcover ISBN: 978-3-96482-119-5

www.breewolf.com

To My Great-Aunt

RUINED
and
Redeemed

Prologue

England, spring 1804 (or a variation thereof)

Three Years Ago

Ahand curled around a glass of water, Lady Charlotte Frampton stood by the refreshment table. Doing her best to drown out the cheerfulness of the many attending guests to her father's rather impromptu ball, she forced the clear liquid down her throat, hoping it would somehow clear her mind and ease her heart.

"You look lovely tonight, my dear," Lord Northfield whispered from behind her.

His breath brushed over the bare skin on her neck, and she gritted her teeth as a wave of nausea rolled over her. Swallowing, she turned around, eyes hard as she regarded him with all the repulsion that burned in her heart. "I'd appreciate it if you'd refrain from calling me that, *my lord.*"

Instead of being offended, Lord Northfield chuckled. "How endearing," he said, then glanced around the large ballroom before leaning closer. "You did not object the other night."

"I did object," Charlotte forced out through gritted teeth. "However, how was I to know that you are anything but a gentleman?"

Amused, Baron Northfield laughed. "Be that as it may," he continued, "Your father will make the announcement within the hour," his unrelenting eyes held hers for a moment before drifting lower to linger on more intimate places, "and then I shall have every right to call you *my dear*." A triumphant sneer drew up his lips as he held her gaze, daring her to fight him, knowing that she could not win.

As his threat echoed in her ears, Charlotte felt her body grow rigid with dread and repulsion and the utter hopelessness of her situation. Her fingers tightened around the glass in her hand until her sinews stood out white and her hand began to ache. And yet, Charlotte welcomed the pain for it was far better than the torturous despair that ate at her soul.

Brushing a golden lock of his meticulously groomed hair behind his ear, Lord Northfield smiled at her, clearly amused with the struggle that coursed through her.

Once, she had thought him handsome with his clear blue eyes and symmetric features. He was tall and striking, and women flocked to him. However, on closer inspection, Charlotte now knew that he was a wolf in sheep's clothing, a predator who preyed on the weak.

For a reason Charlotte could not fathom, his choice for a target had fallen on her.

And he had taken her down.

The memory of a nightmare flashed before her mind's eye, and her hand convulsively clenched around the delicate glass in her hand.

A moment later, a soft crack reached her ears, and then the opposing pressure vanished. Cold water ran over her hand as tiny shards of crystal dug into her fingers and palm, others falling to the floor.

Lord Northfield's eyes narrowed slightly as his gaze shifted to her hand.

Blood welled up between her clenched fingers and dripped to the ground. However, no one seemed to notice. The music continued to play. Couples continued to dance. And the world continued to turn.

Why didn't anyone notice?

From a distance, a voice echoed to her ears. "Charlotte!"

Hearing his voice, Charlotte's muscles instantly went slack with relief. Her hand opened, and the remaining shards fell to the floor as she fought the growing dizziness that threatened to knock out her legs from under her.

As she turned her head, she found him rushing toward her, his kind face clouded with concern as his eyes shifted from her face to her bloodied hand.

He was her friend, her protector, her saviour. He always had been, and yet, today, he could not help her.

"Kenneth," she gasped as he reached for her hand, his watchful eyes examining the small cuts.

"Are you all right?" he asked, pulling a handkerchief out of his pocket. "What happened?" His eyes drifted to Lord Northfield, and she noticed the slight tension that always came to his jaw whenever he wanted to say more than he dared.

"I'm fine," Charlotte said, allowing his strong arms to hold her upright as white lights began to dance before her eyes. "I'm fine," she repeated although the meaning of that sentence was lost on her.

"It is nothing," Lord Northfield interjected, a disapproving frown on his face as he glanced from her to Kenneth. Then he held out his hand to her. "Allow me to escort you to the terrace for some air."

Staring at her own hand as though he'd just threatened to cut it off, Charlotte took a step back and then shook her head. The mere thought of being alone with that man terrified her to her very core.

At her rejection, Lord Northfield's jaw clenched and his eyes hardened, revealing the unfeeling heart that beat in his chest. "You will do as I say," he snapped, advancing on her.

"That's enough, Northfield," Kenneth commanded, stepping in front of her, shielding her with his body. He glared at her enemy. "Leave. Now."

A snarl on his face, Lord Northfield took a deep breath as the glare in his eyes promised retribution. Squaring his shoulders, he raised his head, looking down at them with unconcealed disgust. Then he turned on his heel and walked away.

Closing her eyes, Charlotte took a deep breath. Although she held no hope in her heart for herself, she prayed that Kenneth would not suffer for his gallant heart. Who knew of what else Northfield was capable?

"What is going on, Charlotte?" Kenneth asked, his warm eyes searching her face as he held his handkerchief pressed to her wounded hand. "What just happened?" The look in his eyes told her that he was not referring to her bleeding hand.

Swallowing, Charlotte forced a smile on her face. "Nothing." She shook her head, unable to look him in the eyes and lie. "Everything's fine. Let me just go and take care of this." Withdrawing her hand from his, she stepped around him and hastened toward the door before he could object.

Tears burned in her eyes, but she held them back until the solitude of the corridor engulfed her. Then the dam burst, and all the pain and misery of the past fortnight poured down her cheeks.

Unable to hold back the agonising sobs that tore from her throat, Charlotte fled through the first door she could find and retreated to the very back of the library, hoping that the distance would drown out her sobs. With hands curled into fists, she leant back against a tall bookshelf, resting her head against its precious volumes, before her knees gave in and she sagged to the ground.

Then she heard the door open and footsteps approach.

Instantly, Charlotte froze, her sobs stuck in her throat as images of that one fateful night flashed before her eyes and her heart doubled over in pain. *Not again!* Her mind screamed, and she pushed herself to her feet. Had he come after her as he had then?

"Charlotte? Are you in here?"

For the second time that night, Kenneth's voice washed over her strained nerves and put them at ease.

Taking a deep breath, Charlotte swallowed as her heart hammered in her chest. "I'm here," she whispered, all strength gone from her body.

Footsteps echoed closer, and then Kenneth stood before her, his dark eyes searching her face. "Tell me what's going on? What did he do?"

Averting her eyes, Charlotte shook her head. "Nothing," she

insisted in a feeble voice as she could not bear the thought of him looking at her the way her parents had. Not him. Not Kenneth. She needed him to look at her the way he always had. Only then did she stand a chance to come out of this with her soul intact.

As she tried to step around him, his hand settled on her shoulder and held her back...and Charlotte loved him for it. For knowing her so well. For being able to tell that something was wrong. For wanting to help her.

His other hand settled under her chin and gently tilted up her head. "Look at me," he whispered, and when she finally did, a soft smile curled up his lips. "Tell me, and I will protect you."

Wishing with all her heart that he could, Charlotte felt herself begin to tremble. "You cannot. There's no way. You have to let me go."

The expression in his eyes hardened. "Let me be the judge of that," he said, his voice insistent. "Tell me. Did he say something to upset you? You've been acting strange for the past fortnight. Ever since the night of Lord Radcliffe's ball, you've been..." His voice trailed off as his eyes narrowed in suspicion. "The way he spoke to you..." His eyes drilled into hers. "What did he do to you?"

Blinking back fresh tears, Charlotte shook her head. "That doesn't matter now. I-"

A strangled growl rose from Kenneth's throat as he stepped back, his hands balling into fists. Pacing the floor in front of her, he clenched and unclenched his hands, occasionally running them through his hair as though trying to pull them out by the roots. His eyes were dark and threatening, and the pulse in his neck hammered with such speed that Charlotte feared for him. Never had she seen him in such a rage.

Then he stopped his frantic pacing and came to stand in front of her, holding her gaze for a long time as though needing one final confirmation. Then he spun around on his heels and stormed toward the door. "I'll kill him. I swear to God I'll kill him."

At his words, panic seized Charlotte's heart and she rushed after him. "No. No. No. Please, don't," she pleaded, reaching for his arm and pulling him back to face her. "Please, I beg you. Don't do this."

Looking down at her, his eyes searched her face, confusion

mingling with the rage so clearly edged in his features. "Why not? Give me one good reason why I shouldn't go out there and challenge him."

"Because he'll kill you," Charlotte sobbed, knowing her words to be true. "Believe me. He doesn't fight fair. If you get in his way, he will kill you. And I'd rather marry him than lose you. You're the only one who-"

"Marry him?" Kenneth's eyes bulged. "Are you out of your mind? After what he did to you, why would you even consider-?"

"Because my father insists on it." Swallowing, Charlotte looked into his eyes, remembering the moment she had gone to her parents for help, certain that they would protect her.

She had never been more wrong.

"What?" Disbelief written all over his face, Kenneth stared at her. "Why?"

As her hands began to tremble, Kenneth reached for her and pulled her into his arms, holding her tight until her body began to still. "He said," Charlotte began, remembering the look of disappointment on her father's face, "that I should not have allowed him to take advantage of me." As fear surged to the surface, she lifted her head and looked at him, her eyes pleading. "But I...I didn't. I tried to stop him. Believe me." Agonising sobs tore from her throat as she pleaded her case. "Please, believe me. I tried. I-"

Once more, Kenneth lifted her head and made her look at him. "I never thought I'd say this," he forced out through clenched teeth, and Charlotte's heart stopped, terrified to see him turn against her...just as her parents had, "but your father is not the kind of man I thought him to be." He swallowed, raw emotions underneath his calm exterior. "You," he looked deep into her eyes, imploring her to believe him, "have done nothing wrong. Do you hear me? This is not your fault. None of it!"

Closing her eyes, Charlotte sagged against his shoulder, and once again, his arms held her tight.

Until that moment, she hadn't realised how desperately she had needed someone to believe her, to not accuse her of wrongdoing, but to stand by her side...even if there was nothing he could do to help.

"Look at me," he said once again, and she opened her eyes. Holding her gaze, he smiled, "Marry me."

Charlotte's eyes opened wide. "What?"

"Marry me," he repeated, "and I swear I'll protect you. That man will never lay a hand on you again."

At his offer, a faint hope began to blossom in her heart, but Charlotte immediately crushed it. "No, I can't let you do that. You can't-"

"That is for me to decide," he insisted, his gaze unwavering. "Your parents demand that you marry him to avoid a scandal, is that not so?"

Swallowing, Charlotte nodded.

"Then marry me instead," Kenneth said, his warm hands wrapped around her chilled fingers. "If all they care about is to avoid a scandal, then marry me." Holding her gaze, he nodded. "This is the choice you have: either I go out there and kill that bastard," the muscles in his jaw tensed, and he swallowed, "or you marry me and give me every right to protect you from him."

"But-"

"It's either or," he interrupted. "And don't for a moment think that you can talk me out of it."

Surprised beyond comprehension, Charlotte stared up at him; yet, deep down, she had known that he would be her only hope. She had been so afraid for him to find out, not because she'd feared he wouldn't believe her, but because she'd known that he would sacrifice himself to save her.

A soft smile tugged on the corners of his mouth. "Marry me," he said once again, and Charlotte wished she had the strength to refuse him.

Chapter One

SMOKE & FOG

England, spring 1807 (or a variation thereof)

Three Years Later

L ike a monster advancing, smoke curled out from under the closed door, reaching out its talons for her.

As though in a daze, Charlotte stood alone in the middle of the long corridor, eyes fixed on the nightmare slowly materialising before her. Could this be real? She wondered. How ought she to know?

Ever since … she couldn't remember. Ever since when? It had been a long time since a clear thought had occupied her mind. All she could remember was the strange fog that hung about her, keeping her separate from the world around her, keeping her safe.

Inside the fog, it was dim and cushioned. There were no loud noises or bright lights. No pain or regret. Nothing. It was as though she were floating in water. There was nothing sharp or hard, but simply a liquid essence of life, carrying her wherever it chose.

Charlotte blinked as distant screams reached her ears. Shaking her head, she closed her eyes, stumbling backwards until her back collided with the hard wall.

A touch of pain shot through her. It wasn't much, but rather unexpected. She couldn't remember the last time she'd felt pain.

An image of a moon-lit night flashed before her eyes. Then, there had been water, too. Cold water. Icy cold. It had threatened to engulf her, but someone had pulled her back to the surface.

Frederick.

A moan escaped her lips as a deep ache bit at her heart, and she almost toppled over. Sinking to the floor, Charlotte hugged her knees, willing away the memories that had left her at peace for so long.

With her head resting on her knees, she tried to fight down the rising panic, taking one long breath after the other.

Then she began to cough.

Lifting her head, Charlotte found herself not surrounded by fog... but by smoke. It stung her eyes and burned in her throat, tearing ragged coughs from within her. Her body convulsed, fighting the invading presence, forcing her out of the place in her mind where no pain existed.

Deep down, a part of her knew she couldn't stay. If she did, she would be lost.

Get up! A familiar voice whispered, and her eyes went wide, searching up and down the corridor. *Save yourself!*

"Kenneth?" she asked, holding her sleeve before her mouth and nose. "Kenneth?"

For a moment, a short precious moment, Charlotte was certain that he had come for her, the way he always had.

But there was no one there.

Only smoke.

Get up or die! His voice snarled at her. *It's either or.*

Pushing herself to her feet, Charlotte shook her head, trying to clear away the last remnants of the fog that dulled her senses. Where was she?

Winham Institute, her mind supplied.

Charlotte nodded. Yes, that sounded correct. But why was she here?

Then she shook her head. No, that question could wait until later.

Once more looking up and down the corridor, Charlotte realised that she was alone. That was strange. After all, she was never alone. Not when they allowed her out of her cell and took her to see Dr. Watkins. Someone was always with her lest she ...

Again, screams reached her ears, mingling with frantic shouting and the incessant ringing of a bell.

Stumbling onward, Charlotte reached for each door on her way down the corridor, only to find them all locked. After a while, she realised that some of the loud noises drilling into her mind came from inside those rooms as though someone was banging on the door, screaming at the top of their lungs.

Were there people in there?

Again, the bell rang, its shrill sound a warning that echoed in her bones.

More coughing shook her body, and she stumbled farther down the corridor, eyes squinted against the smoke, but fixed on the door at the opposite side of the long hallway. Would it be locked, too?

Fear sneaked into her heart as her body fought to survive, pushing her onward. Then the door was within reach; yet, Charlotte hesitated.

Right then and there, she still had hope. However, once she found the door to be locked, it would vanish, leaving her to die alone.

Am I not ready to die? She wondered.

While her mind and heart screamed in confirmation, her body refused to surrender, fighting for supremacy.

Finally, as the smoke nearly took her sight, her hand reached out, slowly inch by inch, searching for the door handle. Finding it, she stood for a moment, uncertain what outcome to hope for.

Then her hand moved as though of its own accord, ... and the door sprang open.

Shocked, unprepared for the new decisions that were now forced on her, Charlotte stood and watched as the smoke curled around her legs, reaching out its arms to claim the new space she had opened to it.

Move! Kenneth's voice snapped, and Charlotte flinched.

Taking a tentative step toward the back staircase, she glanced around, but there was no one there. Screams, however, echoed to her ears like a stampede, hammering at her eardrums with such force that she feared they would burst.

Step by step, Charlotte descended the stairs to the ground floor, then turned around a corner and came face to face with the real-life nightmare that had forced her out of her own. Through the window, she could see into the inner yard of the circular building, its right wing swallowed up by flames, stretching out its arms, hungering for more. Here and there, she saw people running, shouting to each other. Although Charlotte did not recognise them, she knew that very few of them were patients.

Squeezing her eyes shut, she tried to ignore the screams of those trapped in their cells, unable to free themselves. Ought she to go back for them?

Get out now! Kenneth's voice screamed above the roaring of the fire. *Move!*

Startled, Charlotte spun on her heel, relieved to leave the fire behind her, and started for the door and the freedom it promised. However, the moment her hand came down on the handle, luck abandoned her.

It was locked.

Instantly, panic rose, and Charlotte scanned her surroundings with frantic eyes. Was there another door she could try? Or were they all locked?

The window!

Charlotte's head snapped up. Yes, she could smash the window. If only she had...

Glancing around, Charlotte's eyes fell on a spindly looking chair, an abandoned walking stick...and then she saw the potted plant. Sitting in a ceramic pot filled with dirt, it ought to have the needed weight to break through the glass.

Determined, Charlotte strode over, her hands reaching for the key to freedom.

Lifting it, she groaned. The inactivity of the past few weeks? ... months? ... years? ... had robbed her of all the strength she'd once possessed.

Approaching the window, she stood sideways at the best angle for her to aim, took as deep a breath as she could without coughing her lungs out, and hurled the potted plant at the window.

The second the glass burst into a million pieces, her heart rejoiced.

Was she truly ready to die?

Scrambling through the window, Charlotte felt small shards dig into her hands and legs. As the blood ran down her skin, a memory of long ago resurfaced.

Once again, she saw Kenneth's face before her, his kind, warm eyes looking into hers. "Marry me, and I swear I'll protect you," he'd said, and he had meant it.

Lost in her past, Charlotte flinched when shouting reached her ears. Somewhere to her left, people were running about, arguing.

"We have to do something. They're all going to die."

"Do you truly want to go back in there? Don't be an idiot!"

"But-?"

"Forget it! I'm not risking my life for those bedlamites!"

As the harsh world around her came knocking on the door to her soul, Charlotte shrank back. Receding little by little, her fog disappeared, leaving her vulnerable and burdened with a life she didn't deserve. Why was she not locked in her cell, waiting for death? After all, no one deserved it more than she!

But she wasn't dead. So, the question remained: what now?

Taking a tentative step forward, Charlotte swallowed as she proceeded toward the angry shouting. Her skin crawled with the apprehension she felt at encountering the man who had spoken so harshly. But had he been wrong?

Confusion entered her mind, and Charlotte felt reminded of the struggle that had been her daily bread not too long ago. What was right or wrong? For a long time, she had not been able to tell them apart, and she was not certain if she ever would be able to again.

Stopping in her tracks, Charlotte inhaled deeply, and her body rejoiced as clean air filled its lungs. For a moment, she closed her eyes and then peeked around the corner.

As the flames began to devour more and more of the building, the doctors and orderlies stood on the front lawn, watching as most of their patients were trapped inside, with death waiting to claim them.

Even years later, Charlotte could not say what happened in that moment. But her feet refused to carry her any further. She knew she ought to return. She knew she belonged there, not among decent people. And yet, she turned around and walked away.

Chapter Two

LIFE & DEATH

At what point she'd lost her shoes, Charlotte did not know. Stumbling through the underbrush of the dense forest surrounding Winham Institute, she simply kept walking as stones and twigs cut into her feet. It was an old, familiar kind of pain, and yet, a part of Charlotte felt as though she was experiencing it for the first time.

Occasionally, a small voice would claim her attention. Unfortunately, it was not Kenneth. She hadn't heard him since leaving the asylum's grounds hours ago. No, this voice came from deep within her, incessantly asking a question she had stubbornly chosen to ignore: *Where are you going?*

As the sun began to set, she sighed, cursing the nagging voice. Finally, she decided to answer if only to silence it. However, her only response was, "Onward."

What else was there? After all, she had nowhere to go. She had no family, no friends. She was dead to the world, and if she didn't return, even her parents would believe the lie. They would finally be free of her, and the scandal she had brought down upon them.

But even so, she had to go somewhere. If going back was not an option, then where?

"Onward," Charlotte mumbled as her fingers trailed through the tall-stemmed grass spreading out before her. Leaving behind the forest, she welcomed the day's last rays of sunshine on her face, warming her chilled skin and bathing her in a glowing light that pained neither her eyes nor her soul.

After crossing the field, she looked around as the sun slowly disappeared behind the horizon. Night was falling fast; soon, she would be blind, unable to see the ground in front of her. Her eyes began to droop as though suddenly realising how long she had gone without rest. As though objecting to being neglected, her stomach rumbled and churned demanding to be fed.

But there was nothing. Nothing but the open land.

Sinking down onto a soft patch of ground, flanked by a bush with gentle leaves, Charlotte ripped out handfuls of stalks of the tall grass around her and used it as a pillow to bed her head.

The moment her eyes closed, her stomach ceased its protest and her body relaxed, abandoning all hold on reality and drifting off into a world where time had no meaning.

It was in that place that Kenneth came to her again.

With his warm, kind eyes looking into hers, he whispered promises she knew he'd never meant to break. But he had, and his loss had sent her down a path she could never undo. She had become a monster, allowed her own pain to change who she was, and there was no turning back.

When she awoke the next morning, Charlotte for a moment expected the white walls of her cell, the strange smell of confinement and the confused mumblings of others like her. Instead, she found a clear blue sky touching green pastures, all set aglow by a warming sun.

Never in her life had Charlotte seen anything so beautiful.

And it scared her.

How could she live in such a world? For years, all that she had known had been pain and loss, agony and regret. Was there even anything left of her old self? Or had her soul long since been consumed, eaten alive little by little ever since that one fateful night years ago?

Again, an image flashed before her eyes, and Charlotte cringed.

This man's eyes were neither kind nor warm. Instead, they promised pain and humiliation. The sneer on his face told her that he cared for no one, only himself, only his wants and desires. The memory sent a chill down her back and turned her stomach upside down.

Although filled with very little, it churned and rumbled, and a sickening sensation spread through her body. Drawing in ragged breaths, she could barely hold herself propped up on her elbows before her stomach expelled its final contents.

Wiping her mouth with the back of her hand, Charlotte dragged her tired limbs away until the stench that assaulted her nostrils had finally vanished. Her eyes filled with tears, and she rolled over onto her belly and buried her face in her hands.

There she lay for a long time as her life slowly caught up with her.

Bit by bit, her memories returned and she wept for all that had happened, all that had been done to her and all that she had done to others. How could she blame Lord Northfield for his misconduct if she herself had done far worse?

Rolling onto her back, Charlotte closed her eyes, hoping to give her mind a moment of peace. However, the second she did, she found herself looking at Kenneth once again -- Kenneth and his smiling eyes and his heart of gold. She also saw the disappointed look on her father's face as he had shaken his head at her for what she had done. She saw Frederick's solemn eyes as he had gulped down one drink after another. Then she saw Leopold on the floor, writhing in pain, his wife's sobs filling the air as she watched her husband die.

Charlotte knew that she had crossed a line that there was no coming back from such a heinous deed. Then what ought she to do now?

For a moment, she thought to simply lie there in the early morning sun and wait for death to claim her. However, her body instantly protested. Her mouth felt dry, and her stomach churned. Her eyes burned, and her throat was parched. Her limbs ached, and her head throbbed. And yet, it was her heart that hurt the most.

Where had all this pain suddenly come from? Charlotte wondered. How had she not felt it before?

Lying still, Charlotte tried to calm her frantic thoughts, and before long, a soft sound reached her ears. It had probably been with her throughout the night, only her mind had been too occupied to hear it.

Pushing herself up, Charlotte began to crawl through the tall-stemmed grass until she reached another side of the field that led down into a sparkling green valley, here and there dotted with groves. Hesitantly, she stood up, her knees wobbly, and scanned the land before her.

There, not too far away, a small stream trickled through the ocean of grass.

Licking her cracked lips, Charlotte strode forward as fast as her body allowed.

When she finally reached the small bank, she almost dropped to the ground, her hands eagerly reaching for the nourishing liquid. Scooping it up with her cupped hand, she forced herself to drink slowly, aware of her stomach's delicate state.

It felt heavenly.

After drinking her fill, Charlotte sat down in the shade of a large oak tree, resting her back against its huge trunk. The world around her looked so beautiful, yet, -

No!

Shaking her head, Charlotte forced the thoughts away. Kenneth had been right. She had to make a choice. Live or die? For a reason she couldn't name, maybe simply an innate desire to survive, she hadn't been able to choose death. Therefore, her only choice was to live, and if she had to live, then she couldn't entertain these thoughts. She had to lock them away and only think about what her body needed to stay alive.

Everything else didn't matter.

Food! Her stomach screamed.

Craning her neck, Charlotte let her eyes sweep across the land. Maybe she ought to follow the stream. Then at least, she would have water and maybe find some berries growing near.

With her mind made up, Charlotte forced herself back on her feet and continued onward.

At some point in the afternoon, she finally came upon a bush that held a few red berries that she'd seen before. However, in that moment, their name eluded her. Once more forcing herself not to rush, she picked as many as she could, sat down by the stream and slowly ate one. Then another. And another.

At night, she once more curled up on the ground near a bush with soft twigs and leaves. In the morning, she woke up chilled as the temperature seemed to have dropped that night. However, as soon as the sun came up and she began to walk, her body warmed up.

For days, Charlotte simply continued onward, following the stream, eating what she found. Her mind remained detached from the past, only focused on what to do next. Her limbs, however, grew more and more slack with each day. Sometimes the lack of food made her dizzy, forcing her to sit or lie down.

After what seemed like an eternity had passed since she had left the asylum, Charlotte came over a small hill and spotted a grand house in the distance.

The reminder of civilisation, of people, hit her with such force that her knees gave in and she sank down. Hitting her head on a small rock, she sagged into herself before rolling down the hill.

Bruised and exhausted, Charlotte tried to open her eyes, but the effort was too much. Her mind protested, forcing them closed, and she abandoned all thought.

Chapter Three

A BROTHER'S LOVE

With anger in his heart, Sebastian Campbell, only son to the Earl of Weston, urged his horse onward. Clinging to the back of his chestnut gelding, he gritted his teeth as the blood boiled in his veins. For a moment, he closed his eyes, but not even that allowed him to shake the image of his sister's face as pain and misery edged into her beautiful eyes.

Cursing under his breath, he guided his mount down the slope and toward his father's estate, Hartridge Hall. When he finally reached the front stoop, he jumped to the ground, not bothering to toss the reins to the stable boy who came running toward him. Instead, he climbed the few steps in a single bound and threw open the door before the footmen even had a chance to reach for the handles.

"My lord," they greeted him, inclining their heads.

Sebastian, however, ignored them. "Where is he?" he demanded, a snarl on his face. "Where's my father?"

"In the study," one of them replied, his face tense with discomfort.

Striding onward, Sebastian tried to force his muscles back under control, lest he strike his father on sight. Not that the man didn't deserve it!

Before he had reached the hallway leading to his father's study, a soft voice called from the upstairs landing. "Sebastian, you're home."

Stopping in his tracks, Sebastian looked up and saw his mother hurrying down the stairs, a glowing smile on her face as she came toward him. "Hello, Mother."

"I didn't expect you home so soon," she said, wrapping him in a soft hug. "How was the continent? Did you enjoy yourself?"

With hard eyes, he glared at her. "Why didn't you tell me?" he hissed, and her face instantly changed.

Gone was the delighted smile, replaced by an expression of haunted guilt. "I'm sorry, Sebastian. I pleaded with him but ..."

Gritting his teeth, Sebastian nodded, knowing only too well how unrelenting his father could be. "You could have written to me," he said, shaking his head. Again, his hands balled into fists as his anger boiled hot in his veins. "I'll kill him for this," he snarled, then stormed off.

"Sebastian!" his mother called after him, her dainty footsteps echoing behind him on the parquet.

Not bothering to knock, Sebastian threw open the door to his father's study, bursting in like a madman bent on carnage.

Instantly, his father's head snapped up, disapproval marking his face at the intrusion. However, the moment he recognised his son, the corners of his mouth curled upward, and he slowly set down the quill he had been holding. Then he rose to his feet. "I see you have returned."

"How could you?" Sebastian snarled, glaring at his father, fighting to keep control. Never in his life had he been this angry...or this miserable. "Is this why you sent me away? So, you could do as you please?"

A hand on his rounded belly, his father laughed, "I always do as I please. It's a prerogative of my station."

"Then why didn't you tell me?" Sebastian demanded. "Why did you marry her off the second I left the country?"

Shrugging, his father sighed. "I didn't tell you because-you have to admit-you're a bit of hot-head, and I didn't wish for your personal feelings to complicate the matter."

"Complicate the matter?" Sebastian echoed, staring at his father in disbelief. Although he had known all his life that his father was prob-ably the most unfeeling man in England, a small part of him had always hoped that he was wrong.

Now, he knew.

All the while, his mother stood by the door and watched ... as she always had ... and didn't utter a single word.

"Yes," his father said, shaking his head in disapproval. "Look at yourself. I wager everything I own that the second you found out about this, you've been riding non-stop, only to throw your hatred in my face. Am I not right?" His eyes narrowed, and his lips pressed into a thin line before he continued. "You act like a child, rash and impul-sive, and that is precisely why I thought it best not to give you an opportunity to interfere and ruin everything."

"Ruin everything?" Taking a deep breath, Sebastian gritted his teeth. "How dare you speak of her as though she were a horse you can sell?"

His father snorted. "Please do not be overly dramatic. I did not sell her. I merely married her to an esteemed gentleman who will give her a good life. If you would calm down, you'd see that this is a most advan-tageous marriage. Although he is merely a baron, his family is vastly wealthy and of high standing in society. He is everything we could hope for."

Now, it was Sebastian's turn to snort. "We? Or you?" Holding his father's gaze, Sebastian stepped closer. "I just saw her," he forced out through gritted teeth, and for a second, he thought to see his father's careful mask of indifference slip. However, it may have been a trick of light. "Of course, after I heard what you had done to her, I went to see Victoria...first. Although she tried her best to put on a brave face, it was clear that she's miserable. She didn't agree to this marriage, did she?"

His father sighed. "No, she didn't. But women generally tend to be a little skittish when it comes to married life. She'll settle into her duties soon enough."

In an instant, Sebastian's hands snapped forward and grabbed his father by the collar.

"What are you doing?" With wide eyes, his father tried to keep his composure. "This is not the way of a gentleman."

Bringing him closer, Sebastian's voice dropped to a freezing low. "Neither was yours, and yet, you had no scruples."

"Are you truly surprised that I should marry my own daughter to whom I please?" his father asked, struggling to free himself from Sebastian's grip. "Isn't it a father's duty to find a good husband for her as well as for the family?"

Sebastian inhaled slowly as his mind argued that his father was not wrong. However, where Victoria was concerned, Sebastian had never been able to remain rational.

Born into a loveless marriage, Sebastian had spent the first ten years of his life alone while his father had been busy pursuing *other* matters and his mother had retreated from life altogether, only seeing her own misery. But everything had changed the day Victoria had been born.

From the moment, Sebastian had laid eyes on his little sister, he had loved her with all his heart and soul, vowing to protect her until the end of his days.

Now, he had failed her.

Releasing his father, Sebastian stepped back, his anger replaced by the misery he had seen in his sister's eyes.

"Now, come, come," his father said, straightening his collar. "Do not forget that this will ultimately benefit you as well. After all, you are the heir to my title and fortune. Does that not please you?"

Closing his eyes, Sebastian shook his head, then met his father's gaze once more. "None of that matters to me."

"How can you say that?" his father demanded, eyeing his son through narrowed eyes. "You've always been strangely attached to your sister, but-"

"I love her," Sebastian interrupted, staring at his father. "Do you truly not know what that means? Is there no one in this world whom you love? Whom you would give your life for? Whom you would relinquish your fortune for?"

Staring back at him, his father seemed to be at a loss. "That is not the point. I-"

"That is precisely the point," Sebastian argued as his anger surged through his veins once more. "I know I can't undo what you did, but I will not rest until I see her smile again."

His father snorted, "You're a fool."

"And you're a monster," Sebastian snapped, pleased to see his father's eyes open wide. "And I swear I'll make you regret this. You will pay for what you did to her."

His father shook his head. "Almost thirty years of age and you act like a child."

"Say what you will," Sebastian replied, stepping backwards. "But don't for a second believe that this is the end of it." Then he spun around and left.

Chapter Four

LOTTE

When the blackness receded from her heavy mind, a new cold spread through her body, freezing her limbs and chilling her bones. Every part of her being ached, inside and out, and Charlotte wondered if this was hell. However, the absence of tormenting agony led her to believe that she was still alive after all.

Trying to open her eyes, she cringed when a blinding light pierced her skull, and she immediately closed them again, squeezing them shut. Through the drumming in her head, another sound slowly found its way into her mind, and Charlotte held her breath, listening.

Hoof beats.

Ruling out the unlikelihood of a runaway horse, Charlotte determined that a rider must be approaching. Had they found her? Was she still close to the institute? After days out in the country, she had lost all sense of time and place.

The hoof beats slowed down, and she dimly noticed someone jumping to the ground just as her head began to spin once more. Then a warm hand settled on her chilled shoulder.

"Miss, are you all right?" a stern voice asked, a hint of annoyance unmistakable. Clearly, the man was displeased with the inconvenience of her appearance in his path. "Blasted woman, what are you doing out here?" he grumbled when she failed to react.

Strangely annoyed with his manners-considering her situation-Charlotte inhaled deeply, trying to muster the strength to open her eyes and meet his anger. However, her mind refused to cooperate, welcoming the fog that returned, wrapping her in a comforting warmth.

Slowly, everything receded. The cold. The blinding light. As well as the warm hand on her shoulder.

A moment later, she fell into a dark nothing.

As unconsciousness abandoned her once again; the memory of the icy chill that had gotten a hold of her returned, and Charlotte instantly gritted her teeth, awaiting its onslaught. However, instead she found herself wrapped in a comforting warmth, and she carefully moved her hands over the soft ground that held her. Was she in a bed? How had she gotten-?

Then another memory returned.

The memory of hoof beats and a man, displeased to have stumbled upon her.

Instantly, Charlotte's eyes flew open.

The dimly lit room she found herself in was barely furnished. Three simple beds stood along the walls, a closet in one corner and a chair as well as a table with spindly legs had been placed beside Charlotte's bed. Its glass slightly smudged, a modest window at the back wall allowed for a small beam of bright light to filter into the dark interior. Everything about the room spoke of simplicity, and yet, the walls whispered of a strong foundation, built with money, and not one erected quickly out of necessity.

Charlotte took a deep breath. How long had she been unconscious? Was it still the same day? How much time had passed?

Panic began to rise, and Charlotte closed her eyes for a moment, trying to fight it back down. At least, she was not back at Winham Institute - those walls she would remember for the rest of her life-which meant that the man who'd found her had not belonged to a search party looking for her. But then who was he? And where had he taken her?

Opening her eyes, Charlotte glanced around the room, but couldn't discern anything more than she had on her first inspection. However, through the door, dim voices and the shuffle of feet drifted to her ears.

Brushing a hand over her head as it began to feel dizzy with the many thoughts that suddenly rushed to the front of her mind, Charlotte found her hair to be coarse and knotted. Her face, however, felt clean, a little raw even as though it had been scrubbed to get the dirt and grime off that had undoubtedly accumulated there after spending days out in the country. Only her fingernails still showed remnants of the time she had spent outside, a dark line running along their chapped edges.

Where was she? Charlotte wondered again. Dimly she recalled seeing a stately manor in the distance mere moments before she had collapsed. Was it possible that the rider who had come upon her had taken her there? Was he a gentleman of the upper class?

At that thought, Charlotte's stomach churned. What if he had recognised her? What if ...?

The throbbing in her head returned, and Charlotte groaned. However, a moment later, her faculties seemed to return as she reminded herself that if she was indeed at the manor house she had glimpsed these were definitely the servants' quarters, which meant that he had not recognised her after all.

Carefully pushing herself up, Charlotte felt the strain of such a simple task in every muscle of her body and immediately sank back down.

In the next instant, the door opened, and Charlotte's heart almost jumped out of her chest as she stared at the young woman's face who'd stuck her head in through the small gap in the door.

"You're awake," the young woman gasped, and a gentle smile came to her face. "I'll be back in a moment."

Then the door closed, and footsteps hurried away, a distant echo of voices drifting to Charlotte's ears.

Long moments passed, and Charlotte felt her skin crawl as she waited for whatever was to come. Where had the young woman disappeared to? Who was she alerting?

As the minutes stretched on, Charlotte wished she could simply rise from the bed and search out those who could provide answers. However, she doubted that she could make it even two steps toward the door in her weakened condition.

Moments later, a battery of footsteps echoed from down the hall and then a middle-aged man accompanied by another young woman as well as the one Charlotte had seen before burst into the room. Approaching the bed, the man smiled at her, his kind eyes calming the rapid beating of Charlotte's heart. "Good morning, my dear," he said in a quiet and steady voice. "You had us quite worried. Can you tell us what happened?"

Overwhelmed by the situation at large, Charlotte stared at him, unable to form a coherent thought. What was she to say?

"It's quite all right," the doctor said, seeing her distress. "We can talk about that later. Allow me to introduce myself. I'm Dr. Procten." Then he gestured to the other young woman, who had entered with him. "This is my daughter Evelyn, and I suppose you've already met Betty," he concluded, glancing at the young woman, who had discovered Charlotte's wakeful state only moments earlier. Then his eyes turned back to her. "Can you tell us your name?"

Never in her life had Charlotte been asked a more complicated question!

Swallowing, she opened her mouth. What was she to say? Giving them her name would ultimately take her back to the asylum, and although Charlotte wasn't certain of much these days, she knew she never wanted to see that place ever again. "My name ...," she croaked, frantically searching her mind. "I mean, I'm ... I'm Lotte."

"Lotte," Dr. Procten repeated. "It's nice to meet you. How are you feeling today?"

"My head hurts," Charlotte answered, relieved that he didn't press for more details about herself.

Feeling her forehead and checking her eyes, he nodded. "That was to be expected. From what Lord Ashwood said you must have taken quite a fall. Although you're in need of rest as well as nourishment, there's nothing else wrong with you except for a few scrapes and bruises. You were quite lucky, my dear."

"Thank you," Charlotte whispered, worrying what would happen next. From what Dr. Procten had said, it was reasonable to assume that after coming upon her, Lord Ashwood had reluctantly taken her to his estate rather than letting her freeze to death. However, where would she go from here?

"Do you have any family living nearby?" Dr. Procten asked, a gentle smile on his face as he looked at her the way her father used to when she had been young. "Can we send a message?"

With wide eyes, Charlotte stared at the kind man standing beside her bed as her heart hammered in her chest. What was she to do? If her family knew where she was...

Once again seeing her distress, Dr. Procten shook his head. "Do not worry, child. All shall be well." Then he stepped around the bed and spoke to his daughter in hushed tones. After a while, she nodded. A moment later, Dr. Procten stepped toward the door, gesturing for Betty to follow.

When their footsteps echoed down the hallway, the doctor's daughter approached the bed and then sat down on the chair. "Hello, I'm Evelyn," she introduced herself once more. "Do you need anything?"

Shaking her head, Charlotte stopped. "Maybe some water," she whispered, watching the tall dark-haired woman as she rose from the chair and carefully poured a glass from the jug on the nightstand. "Thank you," Charlotte mumbled as Evelyn handed her the refreshing liquid. How long had it been since she'd last drunk anything?

Returning to the chair, Evelyn smiled at her. "My father often allows me to help when he is taking care of female patients," she explained. "Although I'm not a doctor, he has come to realise that it is often easier for women to speak to another woman." Sitting back, Evelyn looked at her expectantly. "Is there anything you would like to say? Anything we should know to help you?"

Taking a deep breath, Charlotte shook her head.

"All right," Evelyn relented. "Can you tell me what happened to you? Do you remember how you got here?"

Remember? Charlotte wondered, realising that it might be far easier to plead memory loss than to form a complicated lie for her to explain her whereabouts as well as her identity. Hoping that the young woman would believe her, she shook her head. "I don't remember."

"I see," Evelyn nodded. "Do you have any questions?"

Charlotte took a deep breath as relief eased her heart. "Where am I?"

"This is Farnworth Manor," Evelyn explained, "home of Lord Ashwood, his mother, the dowager viscountess, as well as his sister Claudia. From what my father told me, Lord Ashwood came upon you not too far from the manor. It seemed you had fallen down a slope to the side of the path leading up to the estate. Do you remember how you got there?"

Again, Charlotte shook her head. How much longer would this woman believe her if she did at all?

"But you remembered your name," Evelyn observed, her watchful eyes lingering on Charlotte's face. "Do you remember if you have any family nearby?"

Charlotte swallowed. "I don't have a family," she said, hoping that would keep them from asking around and maybe arousing suspicions. "They died a long time ago."

"Then you do remember something?" Evelyn asked, the tone of her voice free of suspicion but instead laced with curiosity.

"Not much," Charlotte lied, hoping that Evelyn would soon give up. "I've always been alone, worked as a maid here and there."

"But you cannot remember how you came to be out here all by yourself?"

Yet again, Charlotte shook her head.

"Very well," Evelyn said, a kind smile on her face. Then she rose to her feet. "You rest now, and I will have something to eat brought up to you shortly."

"Thank you," Charlotte mumbled, relieved to be finally left alone. "And please thank your father for tending to me. After all, there is no way for me to repay him for his kindness."

Evelyn smiled at her. "Do not worry yourself. My father has an innate desire to tend to those in need, and besides, he was at Farnworth Manor anyway in order to see to the dowager viscountess." Holding Charlotte's gaze for a moment, the young woman nodded before turning to go.

When the door closed behind Evelyn, Charlotte sank back into the pillows, her mind spinning. What would happen now?

Chapter Five

UPON MEETING MISS DAVENPORT

After a long nap as well as a bowl of chicken soup and some bread, Charlotte felt unexpectedly well. Her body seemed to be on the mend, and the exhaustion that had been her constant companion in the past few days receded. However, as her mind was no longer occupied with concerns for her physical needs, it constantly spun in dizzying circles around the one question she couldn't answer: what now?

Charlotte knew she ought to be thankful for the viscount's hospitality. Instead of letting her freeze to death, he had taken her into his home, fed her and allowed his mother's doctor to see to her injuries. In return, she suspected he would at the very least demand some answers. Or would he not?

Considering the impression he had likely gained when he'd stumbled upon her, he probably thought her a simple maid. Come to think of it, she herself had said something of the kind to the doctor's daughter Evelyn.

Therefore, Lord Ashwood might already have forgotten about her. However, none of these considerations answered her question: what now?

Maybe she could ask to be employed in the viscount's household.

Maybe she could work as a maid or in the kitchen. Maybe the family would be kind enough to help her.

If not, then what?

After she'd sufficiently recovered, would she be allowed to leave? To go where? Try her luck at another estate and beg for work? Or make it to Town and see how her chances were there?

Although her hands trembled with the uncertainty of her future, Charlotte welcomed the distraction for it kept her mind busy and focused on something other than her own heart-breaking past where only guilt and shame waited to engulf her once more.

For a long time, Charlotte lay in her bed and stared up at the window, imagining the green hills in the distance, wondering how best to proceed, when suddenly footsteps came hurrying down the hall toward her chamber. Expecting Betty, one of the two maids who kindly shared their room with her and tended to her whenever they could, Charlotte swallowed as a young woman, dressed in one of the finest gowns she had ever seen, burst into the room, eyes sparkling with excitement.

"Oh, how wonderful! You're awake," the young woman exclaimed, clapping her hands together in delight. "I've come by a few times, but you were always sleeping. I was ready to give up, but then I thought to myself, 'No, one more time. I'll go and see her one more time.' And here you are, wide awake." Dancing across the small room, the young woman came to sit on the chair still standing by Charlotte's bed. "Betty tells me your name is Lotte and that you don't remember how you got here. Oh, what a marvellous story! It must be so exciting! Tell me, is there anything you do remember? What is it like not to remember? I cannot ever imagine not remembering what I did yesterday or the day before. It must be quite strange indeed."

Overwhelmed by the woman's rapid speech, Charlotte merely stared at her, uncertain how to respond. Apparently though, a response was not at all necessary for the young woman continued unimpressed, discussing all by herself the strangeness of memory loss.

After a while, Charlotte began to relax and watched her visitor with a sense of appreciation. It had been a long time since she'd had a reason to smile.

"Dr. Procten said there's nothing much wrong with you," the young woman continued, occasionally jumping off the chair and dancing around the room in her need to move before returning to a seated position, "except for your memory loss, of course. Do you remember anything now that you didn't before?"

Again, before Charlotte could even attempt an answer, the young woman bounced off the chair and around the room. "How exciting your life must be," she sighed, and a hint of sadness came to her glowing eyes. "Quite unlike my own. Out here in the country, it is dreadfully boring. Oh, how I long for the next season! London has so much to offer." Again, she sighed. "But here I have nothing to do but sit and read or embroider or paint. It's all very dull to tell you the truth."

"I'm sorry to hear it," Charlotte said when the young woman remained quiet for the barest of moments.

A hint of surprise on her lovely face, her visitor turned from the window and smiled at her. "Thank you," she said, then walked over and sat down on the chair once more. "My brother does not understand what it is like to have nothing to do. He has this estate to take care of, but I, what do I have?" Again, she sighed rather theatrically. "I spend all day with Mother. However, since she's been ill, she sleeps for hours and hours on end." Then her visitor looked up, and her eyes sparkled with delight. "But now, you're here."

"Are you Lord Ashwood's sister?" Charlotte asked, relieved to finally have an idea who the young woman was.

"Yes, my name is Claudia Davenport," she replied, a hint of puzzlement on her face. "Did I not say so? I apologise. Sometimes, my mouth runs away with me and I forget my manners." Her countenance darkened. "An attribute my brother dislikes in particular and never fails to criticise me for." Appalled, she shook her head. "Do you believe that he dragged me out here so that I would have less of an opportunity to embarrass myself?" Huffing, she paced up and down the room. "I tell you the only thing he is afraid of is that I embarrass him."

"I'm glad you came to visit me, Miss Davenport," Charlotte interjected when Claudia paused for air. "You are very kind to spend your time brightening my day."

A deep smile came to Miss Davenport's features, and once more, she hurried over. "How sweet of you to say that! I just couldn't stay away. To tell you the truth, you're the most exciting thing to happen in over a fortnight."

An apologetic smile on her face, Charlotte said, "I'm afraid my story is far from exciting. Since I do not know what happened to me or how I came to be here, there is nothing much I can tell you."

"That truly is a pity," Miss Davenport exclaimed, a disappointed frown drawing down her brows. "I had hoped for some excitement." Then she angled her head in a thoughtful way, eyes slightly narrowed. "Maybe you've been robbed. Yes, maybe a highwayman took all your possessions and left you for dead."

Not wishing to indulge her host's imagined adventure, Charlotte shrugged. "I do not believe I had any possessions worth stealing. I am just a simple maid with nowhere to go."

"Nowhere to go?" Miss Davenport asked, eyeing Charlotte closely. "What about your family?" Then her gaze narrowed, and a thoughtful expression came to her face. "A maid?" she repeated, a doubtful tone to her voice. "Do you truly believe you're a maid?" She shook her head, her curls dancing across her shoulders. "The way you express yourself is quite unlike a maid's, I must say. Truly, I feel quite comfortable speaking with you. Maybe you're even a gentleman's daughter. After all, why would a highwayman rob a maid." Shaking her head yet again, Miss Davenport turned to Charlotte, determination edged into her face and a spark of excitement lighting up her clear eyes. "No, we need to find out who you are and who your family is."

As the blood drained from Charlotte's face and her body grew cold, she felt panic seize her. "But...no...I'm certain I'm not a gentleman's daughter. I'm merely...Lotte. I mean, I do remember my name, and although I do not recall much more than that, I feel certain that I have no family." Seeing a spark of compassion in her visitor's eyes, Charlotte gave her a sad smile. "I have none. Truly," she whispered, feeling a pang of guilt for exploiting the young woman's kindness for her own purposes. However, what choice did she have? If Miss Davenport felt compelled to seek out her true identity, all would be lost. And if she was sent from this house with no way to support herself, then she might as well have died in the fire. Maybe Miss Davenport could put in a good word for her with her brother, the viscount, and help her procure a position as a maid after all.

"I'm sorry to hear that," Miss Davenport answered, honest regret shining in her dark blue eyes. "I recently lost my father." Charlotte cringed inwardly. "He died after a long illness. Shortly after, my mother took to her bed. Dr. Procten says that there is nothing much wrong with her. It's her spirit that was broken when my father died." Taking a deep breath, she looked at Charlotte. "This has been a sad house ever since."

"I'm sorry," Charlotte said, cursing herself for bringing new pain to such a kind heart. "I did not mean to intrude."

"Oh, I don't mind," Miss Davenport assured her with a shake of her head. "I do not believe in hiding away from the world. I loved my father, and I'd rather remember him fondly than with regret." A gentle smile lifted the corners of her mouth. Then she reached out her hand and placed it on Charlotte's. "Then it is settled. You'll stay here with us and be my companion."

"What?" Gawking most unbecomingly at the young lady in front of her, Charlotte thought her ears certainly had deceived her. "You wish for me to be your companion?"

"But of course," Miss Davenport exclaimed, once more clapping her hands together in delight. "This is the perfect solution to all our problems."

"I fear Lord Ashwood would object," Charlotte pointed out. After all, she had no family ties, no education to speak of, nothing to recommend her. "I'm certain he would wish for his sister to have a more suitable companion."

A frown on her face, Miss Davenport snorted. "You are most certainly right," she admitted grudgingly. "Have you ever met my brother? Indeed, Richard can be most unpleasant, always sitting atop his high horse. Nothing and no one is ever good enough for him." Shaking her head in annoyance, she rose from the chair and once more began to pace the short length of the room. "What can be done? What can be done?" she mumbled to herself, her quick blue eyes flitting here and there as fast as the thoughts that coursed through her head.

"Please, don't trouble yourself on my account," Charlotte said, wishing she had never even suggested anything of the like.

"On the contrary, my dear Lotte," Miss Davenport said, a sparkle in her eyes. "This is the most fun I've had in a long time. I shall go and speak to my brother immediately. We'll have this all sorted out straight away."

"But-"

"Don't you worry," Miss Davenport insisted, heading for the door. "I shall take care of everything."

And then Charlotte was alone, wondering if Lord Ashwood would be kind enough to allow her to fully recover before sending her from his home. For surely, a nobleman would care very little for a nobody inciting his sister to rebel against him.

Oh, what had she done?

Chapter Six

A PROMISING NOTE

T he sun was setting by the time yet another stampede of footsteps echoed toward her chamber.

Pushing herself up into a sitting position, Charlotte stared at the door with dread and fear curling into a heavy ball resting in her stomach. She clasped her hands together to keep them from trembling and nervously gnawed at her lower lip. All the while, she stared unblinkingly at the door, wishing it would open, and yet, fearing that it would.

By the time, Miss Davenport and her brother entered her chamber, her eyes stung and burned, and a single tear rolled down her cheek, that she quickly wiped away.

"May I present my brother," Miss Davenport said, a hint of annoyance in her voice as she gestured to the tall, dark-haired man next to her. "Richard Davenport, Viscount Ashwood. Brother, this is Lotte."

"Lotte?" he asked, his dark grey eyes looking at her as though he could see into her soul. There was something deeply unsettling about this man. Clad in dark colours, he didn't seem to know the use of a smile or kind word. His voice sounded harsh and commanding, and the way he stood before her clearly stated who was in charge.

Charlotte disliked him on sight. "Yes, my lord."

His eyes narrowed as he regarded her. "What is your family name?" he demanded, displeasure in his tone for having to ask.

Forcing her heart to slow as it hammered in her chest, Charlotte swallowed, then took a deep breath. All the while, the viscount's penetrating eyes never left hers. "Ferris," she finally blurted out, using the cook's name at her father's house for inspiration. She could only hope the dear old lady would never find out.

"Where are you from?"

"Town."

"How did you get here?"

Charlotte's breathing quickened as he bombarded her with questions. "I don't know."

"So you say," he growled, not bothering to hide his disbelief. "And yet, here you are asking to be my sister's companion. Would you not consider that suspicious behaviour?"

"But I-"

"It was my idea, Brother," Miss Davenport interfered, and Charlotte almost fainted with relief.

Slowly turning his head, Lord Ashwood regarded his sister with disapproval. "Yours?" he asked, his voice menacingly low.

"Do not fret, Brother," Miss Davenport chided him, obviously completely unimpressed by his threatening demeanour. "You have to admit this is a splendid idea."

"Do I?"

"Yes," Miss Davenport insisted, stepping up to the bed and coming to stand next to Charlotte. "She has been through a lot, and she needs our help. And I," resting her hands on her hips, she met her brother's penetrating gaze, "need someone to talk to or I shall go mad in this house."

"Is that so?" Lord Ashwood asked before his eyes shifted back to Charlotte, almost squinting as though to look even closer and possibly ... or rather very likely ... discover her secrets.

Although she wanted nothing more but to sink into oblivion, Charlotte took a deep breath and raised her chin. "My lord, I apologise for trespassing on your hospitality."

He grumbled low in his throat, but made no other reply. His eyes, however, were trained on her as though trying to glimpse the truth he knew she kept from him.

"I assure you I would never presume to offer myself as a companion to your esteemed sister." Had she been mistaken or had he just given a faint snort? "However," she continued, wondering if his reaction was an insult to his sister or to her, "Miss Davenport was kind enough to offer, and I must admit I am in need of your assistance, my lord."

"If that is indeed the case," Lord Ashwood began, his calculating eyes watching her every move, "then tell us about yourself."

Charlotte swallowed, then opened her mouth, but Miss Davenport came to her defence. "Were you not listening? She suffers from memory loss. How can she tell you something she doesn't know?"

Ignoring his sister, Lord Ashwood held Charlotte's gaze, a demand burning in them that did not allow for excuses.

"My name is Lotte Ferris," Charlotte began, hoping the few lies she could give him would be enough. "I have no family to speak of, nor do I have anything to recommend myself besides my own words." She swallowed, not knowing what else to say. "Should you decide to give me a chance, I shall promise to do my best and always be truthful." Charlotte could've sworn she'd cringed on the last word. Had he noticed?

Even if she longed to know, she didn't dare meet his eyes.

"There," Miss Davenport exclaimed. "What more could you want, Richard? I must say that I'm quite satisfied with her answers. She's a lovely, young woman, and we shall have a good time together." When her brother remained quiet, she huffed in annoyance. "Do you truly begrudge me the company of another woman, someone to talk to and confide in? For if that is indeed the case, then I shall inform you that without her company I do not know what I will do."

The viscount's eyes narrowed as they shifted to his sister's pouting face. "Is that a threat, dear Sister?"

"Not at all," Miss Davenport replied as she lifted her chin, eyes raised to the ceiling as though he was too lowly for her to look at. "I am merely stating that you yourself often complain about my improper pursuits. Therefore, this arrangement ought to benefit us all."

"So, it would seem," the viscount mumbled as his glance shifted back and forth between Charlotte and his sister. Then he took a long breath, rolled his eyes in sheer annoyance of life and cleared his throat. "If I have your word that you'll behave the way you were brought up," he said, holding his sister's gaze with a penetrating one of his own, "then I shall grant you your wish."

As Miss Davenport rejoiced, clapping her hands together before flinging her arms around her brother, who seemed most uncomfortable by such a display of emotions, Charlotte merely sighed as relief washed over her. Finally, she realised how afraid she had been of the future that lay ahead.

"Only until next season," Lord Ashwood insisted, disentangling himself from his sister's embrace, "for then I shall do my utmost to find you a suitable husband and have him deal with your theatrics. Agreed?"

"Agreed," Miss Davenport rejoiced, sinking onto the bed beside Charlotte. "Oh, I can't wait for the next season."

Shaking his head at the dreamy look in his sister's eyes, Lord Ashwood grumbled something under his breath, then turned on his heel and quit the room.

"Don't mind him," Miss Davenport said, dismissing her brother with a wave of her dainty hand. "He doesn't know the meaning of fun." A deep smile came to her face. "But we shall enjoy ourselves." Almost crushing Charlotte in a tight embrace, Miss Davenport sighed. "When I got up this morning, I wish I'd known this day would end on such a promising note. Isn't life mysterious?"

At a loss, Charlotte merely nodded.

"I shall leave you to your rest," Miss Davenport said, taking her leave. "Until tomorrow."

Sinking back into her pillows, Charlotte couldn't help but wonder what would await her in Miss Davenport's company. However, the young lady was definitely the lesser of two evils. After all, where else could Charlotte have gone?

Chapter Seven

A PRICE TO PAY

Once Charlotte had sufficiently recovered to leave her room, she was moved upstairs to a somewhat finer bedchamber only for herself as her new status as Miss Davenport's companion demanded.

With her days now occupied, the weeks flew by in a blur of Miss Davenport's monologues. For although the young lady had pronounced her desire to converse with another woman, mostly she needed someone to listen. Day in and day out, she complained about everything that came to mind: the food, the fact that her brother refused to employ a seamstress, the weather, the shrill singing of the birds in the gardens, the lack of company, her brother's sullen face and watchful eyes … to name only a few.

Charlotte, however, didn't mind.

Although the first few days sent her to bed with a drumming headache behind her temples, she soon found herself enduring Miss Davenport's chatter with ease, like the sound of the wind rustling though the trees or a babbling brook in the distance.

Her own thoughts kept her busy enough, and yet, even after a few weeks, she still did not know what to do, watching the end of the year approach with dread. Once the new season began, she would be on her own, and what then?

One cloudy afternoon, Charlotte descended the large staircase upon retrieving Miss Davenport's sketches from her chamber and found the viscount standing at the bottom of the stairs, his dark grey eyes fixed on her face. Was he waiting for her? Charlotte wondered, unable to hold his gaze.

"A moment, please," he demanded, then gestured to the drawing room. "I wish to speak with you."

Charlotte nodded. "Certainly, my lord."

Following her into the large room, Lord Ashwood closed the door, then turned to her. For a moment, he remained quiet, his eyes searching her face as though he was trying to solve a puzzle. "Were you able to recall anything about your past since you've come here?"

Swallowing, Charlotte took a deep breath, forcing herself to hold his penetrating gaze. However, before she could answer, he opened his mouth once more.

"Your presence in these parts is still a mystery," Lord Ashwood continued, and his eyes seemed to narrow even more. "Although I've made enquiries, I have not heard of a young lady missing."

Again, Charlotte swallowed as her pulse thudded against her veins. "I'm no lady, merely a maid. No one would have noticed my disappearance."

Inhaling deeply, Lord Ashwood eyed her with a touch of dark humour in his gaze and the corners of his mouth twitched as he said, "For someone who claims not to remember who she is, you are fairly certain to be no more than a maid."

Knowing that another lie would only make things worse, Charlotte decided to change the subject and hope he would not press the matter. "Is there anything I can help you with, my lord?" she asked, praying that he would never even guess at her secrets, much less unravel them.

Lord Ashwood cleared his throat, then stepped toward her the curiosity in his eyes suddenly gone. "I am pleased to see that my sister has been rather docile these past few weeks," he observed; however, the tone in his voice was far from complimenting. "As you might have noticed, she has always had a remarkable lack of self-control and consideration for others, always doing as she pleases."

"I think you misjudge her, my lord," Charlotte objected, surprised at her own boldness.

The viscount, too, seemed to be taken aback. At her words, his mouth closed and his eyes narrowed, and he looked at her as though she had just sprouted another head. "Do you?" he growled. "Would you care to elaborate?"

Taking a deep breath, Charlotte raised her chin. These past few weeks had been a struggle for her. Brought up as a lady of the upper society, she had never bowed her head to anyone, at least not in the way it was expected of a servant. However, as Miss Davenport's companion she had to adapt, forcing herself to be submissive when her own desires urged her to speak her mind.

"I mean no offence, my lord;" she began, trying to be diplomatic, "however, I do not believe that your sister does what she does out of malice. She has a zest for life and dreams of adventure since her own life appears relatively uneventful to her, which is why she longs for the next season to begin. Quite frankly, she is bored."

"That I am aware of," Lord Ashwood grumbled, inhaling deeply as he regarded her through narrowed eyes. "However, if my sister is bored, she ought to find something to entertain herself," he held her gaze, then lowered his head a fraction, "but in an orderly, appropriate fashion for she is not a child any longer. She ought to know that actions have consequences. However, most days I fear that she does not, and that one day she will pay for her carelessness. Pay dearly, Miss Ferris."

Charlotte nodded, remembering the price she herself had to pay. Had she been careless? "You're quite right, my lord. I admit I share your concerns, and I have often tried to counsel your sister regarding her impulsiveness."

Straightening his shoulders, Lord Ashwood nodded. "Thank you. I appreciate your support."

"I apologise for my outspokenness, my lord," Charlotte said, seeing that he was merely driven by concern for his sister. "I only meant to point out that she does not have bad intentions. She does not set out to break the rules or go against your wishes."

Lord Ashwood swallowed, then shook his head. "Miss Ferris, good or bad intentions are ultimately irrelevant. If my sister finds herself compromised, if her reputation is ruined, it won't matter why she did what she did. The price to pay will still be the same."

Charlotte nodded, knowing only too well that even the innocent sometimes had to pay.

"Therefore, I ask you to keep a close eye on her," Lord Ashwood continued. "Although her behaviour these past few weeks has surprised me, I live in constant fear of the moment when her impulsiveness, as you call it, will lead her astray once more."

"I promise to do whatever I can to protect her, my lord."

"I appreciate that," Lord Ashwood said, then he turned on his heel and left.

Chapter Eight

A STRANGER AT THE GATE

One afternoon, Charlotte sat in the parlour, reading yet another Gothic novel to Miss Davenport. During the past week, temperatures had dropped considerably, forcing them to spend most of their time in the house, which had not improved Miss Davenport's mood.

Quite the contrary.

"Have you read this book to me before?" Miss Davenport asked, sighing rather theatrically. "I feel as though I've heard the story before."

"Not that I recall," Charlotte answered, finding her own mood waning at the sight of such melancholy. "Do you wish to do something else? We could play cards or finish the embroidery on the cushions."

Again, Miss Davenport sighed, staring at the half-finished stitches. "I'd rather not."

Taking a deep breath, Charlotte put the book down, raking her mind for something to do, anything to lift Miss Davenport's spirits as well as her own. Unfortunately, nothing came to mind that would find approval from the lady sitting across from her.

Glancing out the window, Charlotte blinked. Had her eyes deceived her? Rising to her feet, she stepped closer to the glass, narrowing her eyes. "Miss Davenport, look," she exclaimed, feeling her heart thudding in her chest. "It's snowing."

"It is?" Instantly, Miss Davenport's head snapped up, and a moment later, she stood beside Charlotte, gazing at the tiny snowflakes dancing through the cold winter's air. "Isn't it a bit early for snow?" she asked, open delight on her face.

"I suppose," Charlotte agreed, grateful for the distraction. "However, it has been unusually cold this past week."

"How beautiful!" Miss Davenport exclaimed, clapping her hands together in excitement. It had been a while since Charlotte had last seen it.

"It is," Charlotte agreed. "It's a pity that it doesn't settle on the ground. I suppose it's still not cold enough."

Spinning around, Miss Davenport turned to her, eyes lit up with excitement. "Let's ride out!"

"What? In this weather?"

"Yes! It'll be wonderful, I promise. Let's hurry!" After pulling Charlotte up the stairs, Miss Davenport vanished into her chamber.

Resigned to her fate, Charlotte hurried to change into her riding habit and then rushed down the stairs lest Miss Davenport left without waiting for her. Charlotte wouldn't put it past her. Caught in her excitement, Miss Davenport tended to overlook minor details.

As they trotted through the soft snowfall less than half an hour later, Charlotte had to admit it had been a splendid idea. Although the cold had shocked her at first, biting her cheeks and pinching her nose, now she felt invigorated, refreshed and exhilarated.

In a word: alive.

"Isn't this delightful?" Miss Davenport called out as she closed her eyes and lifted her face to the sky. Tiny snowflakes danced all around her. Some caught in her hair while others landed on her face, giving her cheeks a rosy glow.

Charlotte smiled. There had been a time when she had been this carefree herself. Now, she barely remembered it.

"I'll race you to the gate," Miss Davenport suddenly challenged, mischief sparkling in her eyes.

Instantly, the smile vanished from Charlotte's face. "I doubt your brother would approve of this. Especially in this weather." Glancing around, Charlotte lifted her hand to shield her eyes. Was it snowing heavier than when they had set out? Turning her head to the ground, Charlotte noticed with some concern that here and there a few snowflakes remained visible upon touching the path and surrounding meadow.

"Oh, he'll never know!" Miss Davenport called, then spurred on her mare and they flew off.

Not having a choice, Charlotte followed, squinting her eyes against the snow as it settled on her eyelashes, chilling her even more. "We should return to the house," she called against the wind, doubting that Miss Davenport could hear her. Oh, she didn't dare imagine Lord Ashwood's reaction if anything happened to his sister on her watch!

Racing down the winding path that led to the front gate of the estate, Miss Davenport threw all caution to the wind and urged her mare on to even greater speed.

Charlotte's stomach turned and twisted as she worried not only for her own well-being but also for that of Miss Davenport as well. It was reckless to be riding this fast with such low visibility!

"Miss Ferris!" Miss Davenport called. "Are you still there?" As she turned her head for a moment to glance back at her companion, Charlotte saw the joy on her face, and her own anger receded.

Maybe this was exactly what Miss Davenport needed to endure the coming weeks until the new season would finally begin.

Just as they neared the short brick walls that held the entrance gate to Farnworth Manor, a looming shadow appeared out of nowhere, hidden by a thick curtain of snow.

The breath caught in Charlotte's throat, and she reined in her horse.

At least two horse lengths ahead of her, Miss Davenport screamed in alarm and her mare reared.

"Miss Davenport!" Charlotte called, watching in terror as the young woman clung to her mount's back, struggling to keep from falling off. Again, and again, the mare reared, her ears flattened in panic.

Then a dark figure appeared on the path, approaching the terrified horse cautiously. Lifting his hands, he reached for the reins, but the horse shied away. Nervously, it pranced backwards as the man kept advancing.

Over the wind and snow, Charlotte could barely see him much less understand what he was saying. However, after a long while, Miss Davenport's mare seemed to decide that no threat emanated from the stranger after all. She allowed him to take her by the reins and rub her nose.

Urging her horse closer, Charlotte looked at Miss Davenport's ash-white face. "Are you all right? Are you hurt?"

"I'm fine." After taking a couple of deep breaths, Miss Davenport quickly regained her composure, turning to the stranger still holding her horse's reins. "Thank you, kind sir. I owe you my life."

Although the situation was far from amusing, Charlotte was stunned to see an overjoyed smile on Miss Davenport's face. How could she be smiling in a moment like this? Shaking her head, Charlotte realised that this was likely the very adventure Miss Davenport had dreamed of all her life.

Patting the mare's neck, the stranger lifted his head, his face still hidden under the cloak he wore. "Such reckless behaviour is not advisable and certainly not suitable for a young lady," he observed in a stern voice.

Instantly, the smile slid off Miss Davenport's face.

"I'm fairly certain your brother would not approve," the stranger continued. "He will be very displeased."

Miss Davenport snorted. "I care very little for my brother's opinion as I am certain he does for mine." Her eyes narrowed as she regarded the stranger with suspicion. "Are you acquainted with my brother?"

"I am indeed," he answered, a sudden hint of humour in this voice. Then he threw back his head and the hood slid off, revealing a smiling face with strikingly blue eyes that sparkled with mischief.

"Sebastian!" Miss Davenport exclaimed, joy chasing away the suspicion that had been there a moment before. "How wonderful to see you! What are you doing here?" Suddenly, her eyes narrowed just a little. "Surely you do not plan on speaking of this to my brother, do you? That would be most ungallant, and I refuse to believe that of you. After all, we've known each other these past two decades and I would hate to have been so mistaken about your true character."

"Has it been that long, Miss Davenport?" the young man asked, glancing at Charlotte for a split second, a question in his eyes. "I scarcely believe it."

"Indeed, it has," Miss Davenport insisted. "Well, almost two decades for my birthday will not be for another six months. What brings you here? I was surprised not to see you at your sister's wedding. Oh, how beautiful Victoria looked in that dress. However, from the expression on her face, one would have thought she was not at all delighted with it."

Listening intently, Charlotte watched the conversation between Miss Davenport and *Sebastian* with curiosity. He seemed to be an old family friend, well acquainted with Miss Davenport's endeavours, and yet, delighted to see her. However, upon her mentioning his sister, his face changed, became solemn, with a hint of guilt edged in his eyes.

Charlotte's heart skipped a beat as she recognised the familiar emotion.

Swallowing, the young man forced a smile back on his face. "May I ask what you're doing out here in this weather?"

"We needed some fresh air," Miss Davenport defended herself, her eyes instantly narrowing at the implied accusation. "Forced to spend your days indoors, even you would go raging mad, dear Sebastian."

"We?" He asked, once more glancing behind Miss Davenport at Charlotte.

"Oh, I forgot my manners," Miss Davenport exclaimed, turning in her saddle and gesturing at Charlotte. "This is my companion, Miss Lotte Ferris. Lotte, this is Sebastian Campbell, Viscount Huntly. Although his character is far more amiable than my brother's, he is a good friend of his. For what reason, I do not know."

Lord Huntly laughed, "Do not be so harsh, Miss Davenport. Your brother does have good qualities," he grinned, "although I have to admit he hides them well." Then he took a step forward, and his eyes shifted to Charlotte. "I'm pleased to make your acquaintance, Miss Ferris."

"As am I, Lord Huntly," Charlotte said as his sparkling blue eyes slid over her in a way that reminded her too much of her past. Turning away, she urged her horse forward, keeping Miss Davenport and her mare as a buffer between them.

With a hint of confusion in his eyes, Lord Huntly turned back to Miss Davenport. "Allow me to escort you back to the house." He whistled, and his horse came running, waiting patiently as he got into the saddle.

"If you insist," Miss Davenport relented, a hint of annoyance in her voice.

"I'm afraid I must," Lord Huntly replied, a good-natured smile on his face. As he met Charlotte's eyes once more before turning his mount toward the house, whatever she had seen before had vanished. Maybe it had just been her imagination. Ever since that fateful night years ago, she'd felt rather skittish around men who'd shown even the mildest interest in her.

The moment they arrived at the manor as though out of spite, the snowfall began to ease up.

Due to the excitement, none of them had noticed how the continual snowfall had slowly seeped through their clothes, and so while Lord Huntly sought out his old friend, the two ladies returned upstairs to change into something drier.

Chapter Nine

A MOST UNSUITABLE BRIDE

Glancing over his shoulder, Sebastian took a deep breath as his eyes followed Miss Davenport's companion up the stairs. Something about her called to him. Indeed, she was beautiful, even in the comparatively simple riding habit she wore, and yet, it was something far beyond physical attraction that stirred his heart.

The second their eyes had met, he could have sworn he'd heard her thoughts.

Thoughts not unlike his own, their echo resonating within his heart and soul as he knew only too well how crippling they could be.

Guilt.

Remorse.

Pain.

Yes, he knew them only too well. As did Miss Ferris. Lotte.

"Sebastian, my friend," his old classmate greeted him, rising from the heavy chair behind the humongous mahogany desk in his study. Long strides carried him across the floor, and he embraced Sebastian with a warmth he rarely showed to others. "It is indeed good to see you. How was the continent?"

Sebastian sighed as he stepped back.

His friend's eyes narrowed. "Is something wrong?"

Gritting his teeth, Sebastian shook his head. "I'd rather talk of something else." Instantly, Miss Ferris image flashed before her eyes. "I see you've found a willing companion to your sister's escapades."

Throwing up his hands, Richard rolled his eyes. "Willing? I'm not certain. Although I admit, she seems rather fond of Claudia. However, the reason for her presence here is far from ordinary."

"Pray tell," Sebastian urged his friend, realising how desperately he desired to know more of this elusive woman.

Richard snorted, a hint of displeasure in his dark eyes. "I found her injured and unconscious near the gate to Farnworth Manor."

Sebastian's eyes opened wide, and a hint of concern stole into his heart. "Had she been robbed?"

"I doubt it," his friend continued, "for she seems to be a mere servant." Again, he snorted. "At least as far as she remembers."

"As far as she remembers?" This Miss Ferris did indeed prove to be a fascinating woman!

"She claims she has no knowledge of how she came to be there," Richard explain, suspicion clear in his voice, "or how she sustained the injuries she had. However, at the same time, she could *recall* her name as well as the fact that she does not have any living family for us to contact. However, she does speak like a woman of noble birth or at least like a woman raised in the presence of one." He shook his head. "Maybe she was a governess. However, at present, we do not know more than she is willing to reveal, which is very little. The whole situation was most unusual."

"You don't believe her," Sebastian stated, but his friend merely shrugged. "Then why is she still here? Why did you make her your sister's companion?"

Pouring himself a drink, Richard turned to look at him. "You know Claudia," he said almost accusingly. "You know how...wild and irresponsible she's always been. And now that my father is dead, it falls to me to keep her from ruining herself as well as her family." Shaking his head, he began to pace the room. "I had hoped bringing her out here would eventually break her spirit, but with each day that passes, she just becomes more and more ... unpredictable in her anger."

"Well, she's bored," Sebastian said with a smile, remembering the countless times Claudia's escapades had infuriated her brother to no ends. He could not remember it ever having been any different.

Richard scoffed. "You sound just like Miss Ferris."

"I do?" Surprised at the touch of pleasure this small comparison brought to his heart, Sebastian smiled.

"She, too, observed that my sister does what she does out of boredom and not malice," he explained, a hint of displeasure in his voice. "As though that mattered." He shook his head. "I tell you, Sebastian, count yourself lucky that your own sister is so well-behaved. Believe me, not even you would care for the trouble a headstrong woman causes, especially one as careless as my sister."

At the mention of Victoria, Sebastian slumped down in his seat. How was it that he could feel so enchanted one second and then utterly depressed the next?

"Is something wrong?" his friend enquired, taking a sip from his glass. "You seem uncommonly subdued. Has something happened?"

Meeting Richard's gaze, Sebastian rose from the chair, a touch of anger boiling in his veins. "Victoria was married. Did you not know?"

His friend nodded. "I did, yes. However, I fail to see how that is cause for melancholy. If I were you, I'd celebrate. After all, your father's health is not the best either, and should he die, it would have fallen to you to find her a suitable husband. From experience, I can tell you it is not a task to be envied."

Gritting his teeth, Sebastian cursed his friend's detachedness. Although he knew ... or at least suspected ... that his friend was not as unfeeling as he often appeared, Sebastian sometimes couldn't help but wonder how they had ever become friends. "You know my father," he said, willing his tone to remain free of the anger that burnt in his heart. After all, none of this was Richard's fault. "He married her off to an upstanding gentleman of title and fortune," he bit out, sarcasm dripping from his tongue. "However, he failed to take into consideration said gentleman's character as well as the way it would influence my sister's life."

"Come now," Richard said, trying to appease his friend. "He did what he thought best for her. After all, it is common practise to choose a spouse based on such factors. I am certain your sister will come to see that eventually and thank him for it."

"She's miserable!" Sebastian snapped. Taking a deep breath, he forced his hands to still as the blood boiled in his veins. "I know that you see things differently, and that you and your sister do not share the same bond that I have with Victoria, but you should have known that I would have opposed the match. You received a wedding invitation, did you not?" His face still, Richard nodded. "Then why didn't you write to me? Why didn't you tell me? Why didn't you give me a chance to come home and ...?"

"And what?" his friend asked, shaking his head. "It is your father's right to choose her husband, not yours. Even had I known that he chose not to inform you of your sister's nuptials, I would not have written to you and risked a scandal. Where your sister is concerned, you're too much like mine. You act reckless and without thought and consideration. Who knew what you would have done?" Again, he shook his head, this time vehemently. "No, I would not have told you, and I apologise if you consider that a betrayal, but I am your friend, and I do what I must to ensure your well-being."

Meeting Richard's unwavering gaze, Sebastian exhaled, and his anger slowly quieted. "I know," he admitted, "and yet, I wish you had told me." He took a deep breath, remembering his sister's solemn face as he had called on her upon returning from the continent. "I've seen her, and she's just not herself anymore. It's as though she's in mourning, grief-stricken and inconsolable, and yet, she forces a smile on her face and pretends that her life wasn't just ruined by my father's greed. I fear for her." Closing his eyes, he shook his head. "I truly fear for her, not just for her happiness, but for her life."

"What are you saying?" Richard asked, a deep frown on his face.

Sebastian shrugged, then met his friend's eyes. "I honestly don't know. All I can say is that she is no longer the woman I knew to be my sister. Something has changed. I can no longer say what she might do."

"You're not truly afraid she might harm herself, are you?"

Again, Sebastian shrugged. "I don't know. I hope I don't need to be." Then his eyes hardened, and the muscles in his jaw clenched. "I swear if something happens to her, I will end him."

"Her husband?" Richard asked, deep concern in his voice.

Sebastian nodded. "And my father. I'll end them both."

Shaking his head, Richard poured another glass and handed it to his friend. "You must not talk like that. Yes, your father was wrong not to inform you, but you cannot allow your anger to get the better of you. Give it time, and you'll see that your sister will be fine. I believe it is common for women to need some time to adjust to marriage. However, before long she'll be a mother, and according to my own, children are a woman's pride and joy."

Sebastian scoffed, then downed the drink in one gulp. "The thought of her bearing that man's children is sickening."

"Have you lost your mind?" his friend demanded, anger now clear in his voice. "You act like a child, whining and pouting, not like a man of your age." Stepping closer, he looked into Sebastian's eyes. "This is the way the world works. I suggest you'll reconcile yourself to it or you'll go up in flames."

"I know you're right," Sebastian said, shaking his head, "and yet, I cannot help how I feel. You cannot understand because you and I have always been so very different. All I can say is that I envy you. Although your father always proved a decent man, now you're free to ensure your sister's happiness yourself. You do not have to stand by and watch how others make decisions for her, unable to interfere. To tell you the truth, I had hoped that my father would join yours before long and leave my sister's future in my hands."

"Do you truly believe that she would have been happier with a gentleman you would have chosen for her?"

A sad smile came to Sebastian's face. "No, but I wouldn't have. I would have let her choose for herself."

Richard scoffed. "A love match is generally the worst way to begin a marriage. Emotions quickly change or fade, and then you're tied to someone who is not your match in any other regard. No, Sebastian, your father did right."

"Believe so if you will," Sebastian said, knowing that he wouldn't sway his friend's mind any more than Richard could sway his. "It doesn't matter now. However, my father will pay for what he did."

"What do you mean?"

"All the man cares about is the good family name and the fortune and titles attached to it," Sebastian said, disgust clear in his voice. "Well, if that is so, then I swear I shall do my utmost to ruin that which he holds dearer than his own daughter's happiness: his reputation."

Richard's eyes narrowed, and a hint of suspicion came to his eyes. "What are you saying?"

"I'm saying that I will make my father's life a living hell for all he cares about is the advancement of the family name," Sebastian snapped, a sneer on his face as he imagined his father's shocked face. "I will bring shame to his family. I will-"

"*Your* family!" Richard interrupted, clasping him by the shoulders and meeting his eyes. "It is also *your* family. Don't forget that. Everything you do to him, you also do to yourself, your mother and ultimately your sister as well. Do you truly want to add to her misery? Is that what a brother does?"

Shaking off his friend's hands, Sebastian stalked around the room, rubbing his hands over his face. "Then what am I supposed to do?" he demanded, feeling helplessness engulf him like a heavy blanket, slowly suffocating him. "Tell me! Please! For I have no idea. I cannot just sit idly by and let him get away with what he did. I-"

"Yes, you can," Richard insisted. "You're a gentleman, an earl's son, and despite your lack of foresight, you are a good man as well. Live your life, Sebastian, and let your sister live her own. She is not your responsibility any longer. Find yourself a wife and start your own family. You don't have to follow in your father's footsteps, but neither should you condemn him for making the choices that he sees fit."

Feeling utterly defeated, Sebastian stared at his friend. Somewhere in the back of his mind, a voice whispered that Richard was right, and yet, Sebastian's heart ached with the need for vengeance. Torn between desire and duty, he closed his eyes, hoping that he would find a way to go on.

In that moment, Miss Davenport's voice echoed through the closed door, followed by soft laughter.

Miss Ferris.

Instantly, Sebastian's eyes darted to the door, and his heart warmed, melting the ice that had held it captive. A smile came to his face as an idea slowly took root.

"What?" Richard asked, eyeing him with concern. "What are you thinking?"

"I'm thinking you're right," Sebastian proclaimed with delight, listening intently as Miss Ferris' faint voice echoed through the door. "I should find myself a wife."

Seeing the expression on Sebastian's face, Richard's eyes narrowed before they shifted to the door as well. "Are you out of your mind? You cannot -! That is most unsuitable. She is just-We have no way of knowing who she truly is!"

"Exactly!" Sebastian rejoiced. "She would be a most unsuitable bride." And yet, she was the most bewitching woman he'd ever met.

Chapter Ten
QUALITIES TO RECOMMEND

"He is very dashing, is he not?" Miss Davenport exclaimed the following day as they sat in the parlour. With a visitor in the house, the indoors had acquired a certain allure that it had lacked before. "I've always thought so." Leaning in conspiratorially, she whispered, "When we were young, Victoria and I would jest that one day I would marry her brother and she would marry mine. However, Victoria never seemed so very taken with the idea. Considering my brother's unpleasant character, I cannot fault her for desiring a different husband."

A smile on her face, Charlotte nodded. "Yes, I suppose your brother is a fairly acquired taste. However, Lord Huntly seems to see favourable qualities in him." Delighted that Miss Davenport's mood had finally improved, Charlotte didn't mind the topic of their conversation. However, she did fear that the gentleman in question would happen to come upon them at any moment for he never seemed to be far away. More than once she had caught him *lurking* nearby as though wishing to join them. But if so, why didn't he?

"I have to admit it is a mystery to me," Miss Davenport exclaimed. "They are quite unlike one another, and I've often envied Victoria her brother. They've always been rather close. I was surprised not to see him at her wedding. I would have thought nothing short of death could have kept him from her side. It was most unusual."

"What qualities recommend Lord Huntly to you?" Charlotte asked, curious to learn more about the gentleman with the piercing blue eyes. Sometimes she feared he would take one look at her and see the secrets hidden in her heart. It was unsettling!

"Oh, he's very gallant," Miss Davenport mused, a deep smile on her face. "He's a wonderful dancer and knows how to treat a lady. Unlike my brother," she added with a grumble. "He's been to the continent recently." Miss Davenport sighed longingly. "Oh, what he must have seen! I wish I could go as well. It is quite unfair that young ladies are not awarded the same liberties as gentlemen. After all, do we not all hunger to know the world and see its wonders?"

"I suppose so," Charlotte mumbled, finally understanding that Miss Davenport's fancy with Lord Huntly stemmed from her unsated hunger for adventure rather than a deep love for the gentleman himself.

"Excuse me, my ladies."

Looking up, Charlotte found the very gentleman they had just been discussing standing in the door, a good-natured smile on his face as he glanced from Miss Davenport's delighted face to Charlotte, his eyes lingering on hers for a moment too long.

Instantly, Charlotte's breath caught in her throat.

"Sebastian," Miss Davenport exclaimed. "Would you not join us? You haven't yet told us anything about your adventures on the continent."

"I came for that very reason," he said, then took a seat across from them. "What would you like to hear?"

While Miss Davenport queried Lord Huntly on every detail of his travels; Charlotte concentrated on the embroidered cushion in her hand. Slowly, she moved the needle through the delicate fabric, her eyes cast down. And yet, she could almost feel Lord Huntly's gaze as it travelled over her face, lingering here and there as though seeking to familiarise himself with her image.

Did he recognise her? Although she remembered hearing his name mentioned, Charlotte was certain they'd never crossed paths. However, that did not mean that he had never seen her, had been told who she was, even without her knowledge.

The thought sent a jolt of panic through her being, and her hand began to tremble, dropping the needle. Leaning forward, she retrieved it, and her eyes met his for a bare instant.

What she saw there terrified her, not only because she feared her identity might be revealed but also because she remembered such a look from an old life.

Back then, she had cherished the admiration and hidden passion shining in a gentleman's eyes when he had kissed her hand or escorted her onto the dance floor. Now, however, she knew only too well what it could lead to, and that thought terrified her like no other.

"Oh, I've only ever been to London or Bath," Miss Davenport exclaimed with a sigh. "Nothing exciting."

Listening, her gaze still focused on the cushion in her hands, Charlotte heard Lord Huntly shift in his seat and knew even before she heard his voice that she could not escape his attention forever.

"And you, Miss Ferris?" he asked, a hint of honest curiosity in his voice. "Have you ever travelled anywhere exciting?"

Lifting her eyes, Charlotte swallowed when they met his gaze, looking back at her with such intensity that a shiver ran down her back.

Yes, he was indeed dashing with his cinnamon brown hair strangely off-setting his piercing blue eyes. It was an unusual match, and yet, it was the way he held himself that spoke of an honest and kind man. There was nothing hidden in his eyes or his bearing, no hint of deceit or falsehood lurking in the slight curl of his lips, and her heart responded with a warm sense of comfort.

However, the moment passed quickly as the first flames of desire lit up his eyes, open and without pretence, and yet, terrifying to someone like Charlotte.

"I have not," she said, surprised at the rudeness in her tone.

His eyes widened slightly, but his lips curled up in amusement. "Do you desire to go?" he asked, a hint of teasing in his voice.

"Not at all," Charlotte replied, quickly returning her gaze to the safety of the cushion in her hands.

"How could you not want to go?" Miss Davenport exclaimed, throwing up her arms. "Oh, how I long to see the world. Believe me, after being trapped in this house for weeks on end without anyone to speak to, you, too, would find yourself dreaming of the world outside."

"I certainly agree," Lord Huntly said in a tone matching Miss Davenport's enthusiasm. Then, however, he cleared his throat and a more serious note came to his voice. "Have you never seen the world, Miss Ferris? Or did you simply find it lacking and have no wish to return to it?"

Her needle froze midway through the fabric, and slowly Charlotte lifted her head, eyes wide as she stared at the man who seemed to read her like an open book. What did he know? Was this a game? Did he know who she was and was he trying to lure her out?

"Why would you ask that?" she whispered, her voice weak and unable to hide the tremor that ran through her.

Holding her gaze, he leant forward and a gentle smile came to his face. "I merely speak of the way you arrived here. Although you may not remember what happened," for a bare second, a question lit up his eyes, "it must be terrifying to imagine the atrocities committed against you. I suppose that alone is reason enough for anyone to avoid the world at large." For a long moment, he held her gaze, and she thought to see a flicker of understanding.

"Yes, indeed," Miss Davenport exclaimed, and the moment was broken. "It was most horrifying." She turned slightly widened eyes to Lord Huntly. "Do you think we are in danger here? Surely, whoever attacked her has long since left the area, don't you agree? Oh, to think of him somewhere here on the estate would just be so terrifying! I shall not sleep another wink until he's been apprehended."

Although Miss Davenport's words suggested her displeasure with the situation, Charlotte noticed the slight flutter in her voice as she spoke, betraying her excitement with a new adventure lurking just around the corner. Miss Davenport was indeed unfamiliar with the world for only someone who had never come face to face with another who wished to hurt them would deem such a prospect desirable.

Relieved that Miss Davenport once more drew Lord Huntly's attention, Charlotte returned to her needlework. In the future, she would have to take better care to avoid him for he unsettled her greatly, and she could not afford to let even a single word slip that might shatter the life she had built here ... as short-lived as it might be.

Chapter Eleven

A PROPOSAL AND ALL THAT IT ENTAILS

Throwing open the door to his friend's study, Sebastian grinned. Today proved to be a splendid day, indeed.

Richard looked up from the ledger in front of him, and his eyes narrowed instantly. "I see trouble walking toward me," he observed, then put down the quill. "Why are you here?"

"I came to ask for your assistance," Sebastian said, almost dancing in his step. As he came to stop in front of his friend's overly large desk, he added, "I intend to ask for Miss Ferris' hand in marriage."

Rolling his eyes, Richard groaned. "Are you mad?" Rising to his feet, he rounded the desk. "I had hoped you would abandon that silly idea. Sebastian, marrying an unsuitable girl to punish your father is truly the worst idea you've ever had."

Sebastian smiled. After all, in his eyes, she was most suitable, indeed. There was something in the way she looked at him that felt incredibly familiar as though they had known each other for years, and after having known her for only a few days, the thought of being without her already pained him. Why? He could not say. Never had he experienced anything like it.

"You'll ruin your life," Richard continued, a hint of exasperation in his voice. "What kind of marriage do you believe to have with a girl like that? She has no family connections, no breeding, no fortune."

Sebastian frowned. "You have to admit she is cultivated, and her manners are impeccable. In every way, she reminds me of a society lady. If you hadn't told me that-" His eyes narrowed, and he wondered if Miss Ferris was truly who she claimed to be.

"What?" Richard enquired. "What I believe is irrelevant! Do you truly believe society will accept her? The daughter of ... well, no one." He sighed. "You're being foolish." Throwing up his hands, he shook his head. "Not unlike my sister."

Sebastian laughed, "Are you now my big brother as well, seeking to save me from ruining my reputation and disgracing my family?"

"Well, it does feel awfully familiar," Richard said. "I'd rather not have to lock you up as well."

Laughing, Sebastian stepped forward, then met his friend's eyes. "I am determined to have her as my wife." Richard's head sank. "You may not agree with me, but I ask that you respect my decision." He took a deep breath, and a smile came to his face. "I never thought I'd say this, but she's the one."

"Again, you sound like my sister," Richard cursed, shaking his head in disbelief. "I've never known you to be such a fool for love. All this romantic nonsense is just-"

"It's not nonsense," Sebastian objected. "And I do not merely choose her because her background and standing would displease my father. To me, she has a multitude of appealing qualities."

"You've known the girl for a mere few days, Sebastian," his friend objected. "How well can you possibly know her?"

"Well enough to not want her to slip through my fingers," he stated, nodding his head for emphasis. "So, will you help me?"

"Help you? How?"

Sebastian grinned. "Distract your sister."

"My sister?"

"I wish to speak to my future wife in private, and your sister is making that exceedingly difficult."

For a long moment, Richard merely stared at him, possibly considering alternate arguments to persuade him from his path. However, after a while his shoulders slumped. "Fine. When?"

"Now."

"Now?" he gasped.

Again, Sebastian grinned. His friend could be truly entertaining at times. "They are in the drawing room."

Richard inhaled deeply. "Fine. Do as you wish," he mumbled as he headed for the door.

Following his friend, Sebastian realised that he was indeed a little nervous. What if she refused his offer? Although he suspected that she had experienced the same sense of recognition when their eyes had met, he had sensed hesitation on her part, even a hint of fear. Maybe it would be advisable to approach her from a rational perspective.

Standing back, half-hidden behind the door, Sebastian waited as Richard asked his sister to follow him back to his study. Although annoyed with the interruption, she did so without argument, merely grumbling under her breath about her brother's lack of good manners.

When they were out of sight, Sebastian took a deep breath and stepped up to the door just as Miss Ferris was about to leave. When they almost collided, her eyes widened in surprise before she swallowed. He could see a hint of fear in her hazel eyes. Her hands curled into the fabric of her dress, and she took a few steps back. "Lord Huntly," she mumbled, almost shying away from him.

Closing the door behind him, Sebastian stepped forward, careful to keep his distance. "I wish to speak with you, Miss Ferris. Do you have a moment?" he asked politely, seeking to put her mind at ease.

Miss Ferris, however, seemed tense as she nodded, eyes fixed on the door that barred her escape. Then she returned to her seat on the settee while Sebastian took the armchair across from her. "I came here to enquire about your plans for the future," he began, noting the hint of surprise that came to her face. "Lord Ashwood tells me your position here is only for the remainder of the year until the next season begins."

"It is," she confirmed, her eyes studying his face, clearly seeking to understand why he would ask such a question.

"Do you have another offer to be a companion?" Sebastian continued, hoping that logic would be his ally. "Anywhere to go once the family returns to London?"

Miss Ferris swallowed, her hands digging deeper into the fabric of her dress. "Not at present."

"I see," he said, trying his best not to appear too threatening despite his line of argument. "I thought as much." He shifted in his chair, leaning forward, his eyes fixed on hers. "See, I came here to make you an offer."

Her eyes narrowed. "An offer, my lord?"

"You see, there has been a bit of upheaval in my family recently, developments that could and should have been avoided but now only serve to endanger the happiness of one close to my heart."

"Your sister?" she asked, and yet, a hint of understanding shone in her eyes as though she understood the misery of Victoria's fate better than anyone.

"Yes, my sister," Sebastian confirmed, feeling his spirits temporarily subdued at the thought of her hopeless situation. "In my absence, my father forced her into a marriage to a gentleman who does not deserve the word." He swallowed.

"I'm sorry to hear that," she said, honest regret in her voice as she held his gaze for the first time without a sign of anxiety in her lovely eyes. "But what does that have to do with me? Do you wish for me to be her companion?"

A gentle smile came to Sebastian's face. Maybe she was right. Maybe he ought to find a companion for his sister to lift her spirits. "That's not what I had in mind."

Again, her eyes narrowed as she searched his face.

He took a deep breath. "I mean no offence, but you're precisely the kind of woman my father would object to."

Her eyes went wide. "Excuse me?"

"Therefore, I would like to ask for your hand in marriage," he stated calmly as his heart hammered in his chest.

With her heart pounding against her ribs, Charlotte sat in shock, staring at the man in front of her who had just made her an offer of marriage because his father would deem her unsuitable.

Had she misunderstood him? Never had she heard of such a line of thinking. Certainly, it was not unheard of that a son sought to rebel against his father, but never in such a way. Was he serious?

"I assure you, Miss Ferris, that I do not share my father's opinion," he added when all she could do was continue to stare at him. "You are a beautiful woman of infallible character, graceful manners and most importantly you have a kind heart. All these qualities recommend you to me."

Knowing that at some point she would have to respond, Charlotte swallowed. "You cannot be serious, my lord."

"I am," he assured her. "I propose a marriage of convenience, which after all is the usual way to conduct the marriage business. However, where such dealings are usually influenced by title and fortune, ours shall be based on other attractions." A teasing note came to his voice as he spoke the last word, and Charlotte couldn't help but wonder whether the reasons he stated were true. "I offer you a secure life. After all, I am the heir to my father's title and fortune. In return, you help me exact revenge on my father for the cruelty he bestowed on my sister."

Shaking her head, Charlotte struggled to find words to express the tumult raging in her heart and mind. "I mean no offence, my lord, but surely you must be jesting. Surely, for a grown man of your years to act like a little boy whose favourite toy was taken away, there can be no other explanation."

He laughed then, and Charlotte relaxed a little, relieved that he did not seem prone to uncontrolled fits of anger.

A frown came to her face. Was she truly considering his proposal?

"I appreciate your honesty, Miss Ferris," he said, smiling at her in approval. "I myself tend to call a spade a spade. Titles and fortune may hide those of questionable character, but in the end, they are always revealed for who they are."

As footsteps echoed closer, Lord Huntly rose from his seat, then stepped forward and held out his hand to her. Reluctantly, Charlotte took it and allowed him to pull her to her feet. For a long moment, his hand held hers, his thumb gently brushing over her fingers as his eyes considered hers, allowing her to see the true nature of his character.

At the closeness, the breath caught in Charlotte's throat, and for a moment, she feared she would faint. However, somewhere in the back of her head, she recognised that no threat emanated from this man, and slowly, her hammering heart calmed down.

"Think about it," he whispered before he released her hand and stepped back.

In the next moment, the door flew open and Miss Davenport rushed back in. "Oh, Sebastian, there you are. I haven't seen you all day; I feared you might already have left."

"I would not dream of it," Lord Huntly replied, his eyes darting to Charlotte, an amused smile curling up his lips.

The rest of the day passed in a blur as Lord Huntly's words echoed in Charlotte's mind, *Think about it*.

Charlotte knew she ought to disregard his proposal without further thought, and yet, lying in bed, wide awake, she couldn't help but do as he'd asked.

Right here, right now, her life was almost perfect. As Miss Davenport's companion, she was well taken care of, spending her days in peace far off any resemblance of the society of London and the life she had left behind. And yet, soon it would end, leaving her with no means to support herself. She would have no roof over her head and no food in her belly. Likely, on her own, she would soon fall prey to a shadowy creature roaming the streets or end up back at Winham Institute, locked in her cell, tormented by images she couldn't banish from her mind.

Gritting her teeth, Charlotte closed her eyes. "I can't," she whispered into the dark. "I can't. It wouldn't be right."

Should she ever be found out, the scandal would surely ruin his family as much as it had almost ruined hers. From a conversation between two nurses, she had caught a few snippets here and there, concluding that her parents had sent her to Winham to satisfy Lord Elmridge. After killing his brother, it was not an unreasonable demand, and she could not fault him for it. However, to avoid a scandal, her parents had proclaimed her dead in an accident, knowing that she would never be released.

Realising the finality of her situation, Charlotte had retreated into a world far away from pain and regret.

Until the fire.

Now, suddenly, her life was back in her own hands, and the decision was hers.

Rolling over, Charlotte buried her face in the pillow as her hands clawed at the soft mattress in frustration. What was she to do? If she agreed to his proposal and was found out, he would never forgive her. Or would he? After all, he desired nothing more but to bring shame to his father. Maybe he would even welcome her past. At the very least, she ought to warn him about the skeletons in her closet before accepting his proposal.

Accepting his proposal? And all that it entailed?

At the thought of being Lord Huntly's wife, images of her past resurfaced, and Charlotte swallowed as bile threatened to rise up her throat. Again, she felt Northfield's hands on her body, his hot breath on her skin as she had struggled against him ... to no avail.

Curling up into a ball of misery, Charlotte hugged her knees to her chest, shaking as the memories ravaged her soul once again. "I can't," she whimpered as tears streamed down her face, soaking her pillow. "I can't."

Chapter Twelve

A FITTING PUNISHMENT

T he next morning came much too soon, and by the time Charlotte left her own chamber and headed down the hall to see to Miss Davenport, her heart and mind still ached with the situation she found herself in. While her mind encouraged her to accept Lord Huntly's proposal, stating that there was no alternative, her heart twisted in agony at the mere thought of it.

Entering Miss Davenport's bedchamber, Charlotte noted that to her surprise the curtains were still drawn. "Is something wrong?" she asked the maid hurrying in after her, carrying a tray with tea and biscuits.

"Miss Davenport has taken to bed," the maid whispered, glancing across the dimly lit room at the shadowy figure resting against a myriad of pillows.

"Is it serious?"

"No, just a cold." Then the maid crossed the room with quiet footsteps, deposited the tray on the nightstand and poured some tea for the poor invalid.

As Charlotte approached the bed, the shadowy figure stirred. "Oh, Miss Ferris," Miss Davenport exclaimed, her voice hoarse and lacking the exuberance it usually possessed. "I feel rather poorly. Maybe riding out in such weather was rather unwise after all."

A gentle smile came to Charlotte's face at the childish behaviour of her charge. "It may not have been the best of ideas," she said, "but it was a day I'll never forget."

Closing her eyes, Miss Davenport smiled. "Neither shall I. I can still feel the snowflakes on my face," she mumbled as her voice grew quieter. A moment later, she had fallen asleep, snoring slightly.

Turning to the maid, Charlotte said, "Send for me the moment she awakes," then left the room. As she headed down the stairs, she glanced left and right, expecting Lord Ashwood to approach her. Surely, he was not pleased with his sister's condition, most likely blaming Charlotte for allowing her to ride out in a snowstorm.

However, the man who stepped out of the drawing room, eyes fixed on her face and a teasing smile on his lips, was none other than Lord Huntly.

Taking a deep breath, Charlotte descended the last few stairs. "My lord."

"Miss Ferris," he said, slightly bowing his head to her. However, the smile remained fixed in place. "May I speak to you?" Stepping aside, he gestured behind him at the drawing room.

Swallowing, Charlotte nodded, then stepped inside.

As he closed the doors behind them, she took a deep breath, willing her trembling hands to still. Being alone with him reminded her too much of...

She shook her head. There was no use in entertaining such thoughts.

"I've heard that Miss Davenport is ill," Lord Huntly began, then stepped back as though understanding her need for a certain distance between them. "I hope it is nothing serious."

"It is merely a cold, my lord," Charlotte said, finding her own voice feeble and without strength. "I'm certain she will have recovered in a few days."

"That is good news," he said, an honest smile on his lips as his eyes held hers, studying her face. Then he took a step toward her, and his eyes narrowed as her own widened, watching him with apprehension.

Again, he seemed to be studying her, gauging her reaction, before he said, "Have you thought about my proposal?"

Charlotte took a deep breath, then nodded, noting with surprise the tension in his shoulders. Did he truly fear she would refuse him?

"May I ask if you've come to a conclusion?"

"I have," Charlotte said, trying to speak with as much confidence as she could muster. "I would ... accept," a smile lit up his face, "your proposal ... under one condition."

"You have a condition?" he mused, then nodded. "I should have expected nothing less of you. Name it, and if it is within my power, then you shall have it."

Gnawing on her lower lip, Charlotte fought the overwhelming desire to avert her eyes and forced them to remain steady as she spoke. "While it is within your power, and yours alone, I doubt that you will agree, my lord."

His eyes narrowed slightly, intrigued, and a curl came to his lips. "Are you proposing something indecent?" he teased, approaching with measured steps while his eyes observed her reaction.

Clasping her hands together, Charlotte tried to ignore her hammering heart. "I wouldn't call it indecent, my lord, rather ... unusual."

"Unusual?" Coming to stand before her, his eyes shifted from hers to her trembling hands before returning to her face. "Now, I'm intrigued, Miss Ferris."

Charlotte swallowed, forcing the words out without another thought. "I'll accept your proposal if you give me your word that you will never visit my bed." Heat crept into her cheeks, and she quickly averted her eyes.

With her gaze fixed on the tip of her shoes, Charlotte could not see his reaction to her condition. However, for a long moment, he remained quiet, almost immobile as he stood before her. Then she sensed him shift, and a moment later, he reached out his hand.

Instantly, Charlotte tensed, forcing herself to remain still.

However, she must have flinched ever so slightly for his hand stopped in mid-air before it fell back to his side. Then he cleared his throat. "Will you look at me, Miss Ferris?"

Swallowing the lump in her throat, Charlotte lifted her eyes and found him looking at her with such compassion and understanding that the pain in her heart began to subside. "If this is truly what you desire," he said, his gaze steady, "then you have my word that I shall never lay a hand on you," he lowered his head a fraction, "unless you invite me."

A jolt went through Charlotte and she took a step back, shaking her head. "That I never will."

He nodded. "Nevertheless, you have my word."

Taking a deep breath, Charlotte eyed him as doubts clawed at her resolve. "Can I trust you?"

"Never have I broken a word given," he said earnestly before a dark cloud passed before his eyes. "At least not willingly."

"Not willingly?"

Gritting his teeth, he swallowed. "The day my sister was born, I vowed to protect her, to not let any harm come to her." He sighed. "But I failed. I broke my word, and every day, it pains me to see her so miserable." For a moment, he closed his eyes and a contemptuous smile curled up his lips. "A fitting punishment."

Seeing the pain and guilt over his failure in his eyes, emotions she knew only too well, Charlotte felt herself relax. As far as she could tell, he was an honourable man. A man who would keep his word. She could only hope he would not come to regret the day he had given it.

Tearing his eyes from the inner thoughts that tormented him, Lord Huntly looked at her once more. "I would not fault you for doubting my word."

Charlotte nodded, wondering if she ought to reconsider. "I see no reason to do so, my lord." To her surprise, the words left her mouth without another thought.

A soft smile came to his lips as he held her gaze. "Thank you," he said, and she could see how much her trust meant to him. "I shall speak to Lord Ashwood, and we'll be off in a day or two."

"Off to where?" Charlotte asked in a shaky voice as the reality of her new situation came crashing down around her.

A smirk came to his face as he stepped back. "To Gretna Green."

Turning to the door, he glanced over his shoulder. "For my father would never approve of such a shameful wedding."

Three days later, Charlotte found herself in a carriage on her way to the little border village in Scotland to wed a man she had met a mere fortnight ago.

Keeping her thoughts fixed on the here and now, Charlotte still could not help the occasional jolt of panic that would course through her veins at the thought of what was about to happen. Once again, her life had changed abruptly, not giving her even a single moment to catch up with it. And yet, had she had a month, Charlotte would have doubted that she had been more prepared.

"Life is strange, is it not?" her betrothed asked, seated across from her. "Sometimes a mere moment changes it in such a fundamental way that it leaves one struggling for breath."

Swallowing, Charlotte nodded, wondering how he knew her thoughts. "It does indeed, my lord. Sometimes I wonder if it will ever stop."

Once again, his eyes lingered on her face as though seeking to look deeper. "Your life has changed direction before, has it not?" he asked in a tone that was not a question. "More than once."

Again, Charlotte nodded. "Sometimes it is difficult to remember … who I am, who I once was." Taking a deep breath, she returned her gaze to the green landscape passing by outside her window. She ought not to speak to him in such a way. Too easily would things be revealed that could not be taken back.

The sun was already setting and the promise of snow danced on the air as they arrived in Gretna Green. They immediately proceeded to the Inn where her betrothed spoke to the innkeeper announcing their intention of being married that very night. After coins exchanged hands, the innkeeper summoned the local anvil priest and before Charlotte even knew what was happening, she was asked a question that would change her life forever.

"Do ye take this man to be your lawful wedded husband, forsaking all others, as long as ye both shall live?"

As her heart hammered in her chest, Charlotte once more stared at the man standing beside her, a gentle smile on his face, promising that all would be well. Would it? Charlotte wondered as her head began to pound with the enormity of the decision she was faced with.

And yet, there was no choice, was there? For the alternative terrified her to her very core.

"I will," Charlotte mumbled, and moments later, she was married.

Married!

Sitting at a table near the large stone fireplace, Charlotte picked at her supper, eyes staring into the distance. Never in her life had she thought that her destiny would take her to Gretna Green.

"Are you all right?" her husband asked, his eyes full of concern as he looked at her. When she remained quiet, he nodded knowingly. "You should eat. These past few days have been quite tiresome. A room is being readied for us upstairs. A good night's sleep will do you good."

Unable to eat more than a few morsels, Charlotte allowed her new husband to escort her upstairs to their room before he left to take care of...something. Shaking her head, she realised that she had barely heard a word he'd said to her as her mind had retreated into a familiar fog, shielding her from the harsh reality around her. However, when she stepped into the room she was to share with her husband and her eyes came to rest on the bed situated at the back wall, the fog vanished in an instant.

Panic gripped her heart as painful memories returned. Memories that felt real, so real, that her teeth began to chatter as her body trembled at their onslaught.

Rough hands had yanked up her skirts, then pushed her down. One hand wrapped around her throat, squeezing slightly until she had seen stars dance before her eyes. Hot tears had streamed down her face as her own fingernails had dug into her palms. But no matter what she'd tried, she hadn't been able to block out the feel of him. Nothing had been able to take her mind off the here and now, and even three years later, she remembered it as though it had happened yesterday.

Stumbling across the room, Charlotte sank down in front of the window, gripping the leg of a chair so tightly that her hands shone white in the silvery light that streamed in from outside. As her teeth continued to chatter, she bit down hard, forcing them to still, and her jaw clenched painfully. Tears fell onto her hands, and she realised that she was crying.

Resentment grew in her heart at the sight of her own weakness. How could she allow him to have such power over her? Even now, after all this time? She ought to be able to put the past behind her and only look to the future. But she couldn't. She wasn't strong enough. Maybe she didn't deserve to be free of her past. After all, she was far from innocent. Maybe this was her punishment.

A fitting punishment. Her husband's words echoed in her mind, and she wondered if they were more suited to each other than she had thought.

Then she shook her head. No, he deserved better. For all she knew he was a good man, who had spent his whole life protecting a sister he loved, only to fail her when she had truly needed him. And yet, she could not blame him for he had done everything in his power to keep his word.

Would he keep the word he had given her? Charlotte wondered, hoping that her judgement had not been misguided, that he would not fail her, too.

Only intentionally this time.

As footsteps echoed to her ears from down the corridor, Charlotte pushed herself to her feet, quickly brushing the tears from her face. She must not let him see her like this. If he sensed weakness, maybe he …

Again, she shook her head. Somehow it had become second nature to her to doubt people. However, he had never given her any reason to doubt him. Maybe he was truly honourable. Maybe he would protect her the way Kenneth had promised.

Swallowing, Charlotte turned to the door. As it slid open, she drew in a deep breath, steeling herself for what was to come. She could only hope she hadn't made the biggest mistake of her life by accepting his proposal.

Chapter Thirteen

HONESTY

Taking a deep breath, Sebastian pushed open the door to their bedchamber. His wife stood at the opposite end by the window, her hands clasped together, her eyes meeting his with a defiant, unflinching look to them that spoke of bravery rather than curiosity.

Did she fear him? He wondered as his gaze slid over her tense features. His stomach turned into knots at the thought that she might think him capable of breaking his word so easily, and he realised how much her opinion mattered to him.

"Everything is taken care of," he said, closing the door behind him. "Tomorrow, after breakfast, we shall return home." He took a step into the room, then stopped as her shoulders tensed and she all but shrank back from him. Holding her gaze, he frowned. "Are you all right? Is there anything that you need?"

"Where will you sleep, my lord?" she asked, her voice trembling ever so slightly as her eyes darted to the bed before returning to meet his. Still trembling, she lifted her chin like someone sentenced to death, but determined not to beg.

Unable to understand the fear that held her in its clutches, Sebastian pointed to the floor. For a long moment, he held her gaze before the corners of his mouth drew up into a gentle smile. "Unless you would consider sharing the bed," he said, a teasing tone to his voice as he tried to lighten the mood.

However, he immediately cursed himself as her features darkened and she took a step back, drawing in a shaky breath. "I'm sorry," he said, striding forward, then stopped when her eyes widened. "I'm sorry. I didn't mean to-"

"Do men truly not care who they bed?" she asked unexpectedly. "Do you not mind sharing something so intimate with a stranger?"

Taken aback, Sebastian studied her face, trying to understand what she was asking. Although he understood that women were generally nervous on their wedding night, his wife seemed far beyond nervous. Even *afraid* would not do her justice. She seemed terrified, and he couldn't help but wonder why. "You're not a stranger," he said, hoping to find the right words. "You're my wife, and-"

"And yet, you don't know me," she interrupted, a touch of hysteria to her voice. "We've barely said two words to each other, and yet, we're married." Closing her eyes, she shook her head. "I should never have agreed to your proposal," she whispered, then met his gaze once more. "It was foolish of me to think that I could ..." She took a deep breath. "I suppose there is a reason why it's a man's marital *right* to bed his wife and a woman's marital *duty* to share her husband's bed. From my own experience, I'd say these are fitting terms."

Sebastian's eyes narrowed. "Your own experience," he mumbled as a growing suspicion took hold of his heart.

No, her behaviour was not that of an innocent woman afraid of her wedding night.

Suddenly, everything fell into place. Her condition that he not share her bed. Her fear to be alone with him. Her panic when he came too close. No, she was not an innocent.

Her innocence had already been taken.

Without her consent.

He was certain of it.

Again, his stomach twisted into knots, burning red hot with rage, as he couldn't help but picture the very moment in which her fears had been born. Had she been married before? Had her husband ...?

Sebastian wasn't sure if he wanted to know; yet, meeting her eyes, he knew that she would continue to walk through life with fear clutching at her heart if he could not find a way to restore her trust...at least in him. He needed her to trust him.

More than that. He *wanted* her to trust him.

The thought that his wife feared he would force himself on her stung like nothing else he had ever experienced. It was an insult to his decency, his honour, and yet, he could not fault her for it.

Collecting his thoughts, Sebastian took a step forward, holding up his hands, trying to assure her that he was no threat. "You're right," he said, and a hint of surprise came to her hazel eyes as she watched him. "We are strangers. We know almost nothing about each other." Holding her gaze, he stopped an arm's length away from her, waiting for her to grow accustomed to his nearness. When she took a deep breath and her shoulders relaxed, he continued, "But we're also husband and wife."

Instantly, she tensed.

Gritting his teeth, Sebastian forced himself to stay calm. "I want you to know that I did not ask for your hand merely to punish my father." A soft smile came to his lips as he nodded, hoping that she would believe him. "When I first saw you that day out in the snow, I thought I saw something in your eyes that...that reminded me of myself. I thought there was a connection between us. I thought I'd finally found someone who could understand me." He took a deep breath, feeling his own muscles relax as the expression in her eyes softened. "We may be strangers now, but I am hoping that we won't be for long."

Gnawing on her lower lip, she looked up at him, her eyes studying his face, trying to determine if she could believe him. Then she took a deep breath and nodded.

A relieved smile came to his face. "Good." Raking his mind, Sebastian wondered how to begin. Should he ask about her past? Her family? How she came to be near Farnworth Manor? Did she truly not remember? However, all these questions seemed much too intrusive and would certainly push her even farther away. Therefore, he decided to leave the choice to her what to tell him and what not.

"You can ask me anything you wish to know," he said, "but for tonight, I would only ask you to tell me one thing about yourself. Anything. Just one detail."

Still gnawing on her lower lip, she blinked before her eyes became distant. Then she met his gaze once more, fear and pain in her beautiful eyes. "I was betrothed once," she whispered, her voice barely loud enough for him to hear. "He died in the war."

So, not a husband. Sebastian thought. But a fiancée. Had he forced himself on her? Judging from the saddened expression in her eyes, Sebastian doubted it, but he could not be certain.

"I'm sorry," he said, feeling encouraged that she would share such an intimate aspect of her life with him. "How long has it been?"

Tears welled up in her eyes. "Three years," she whispered, swallowing hard. "Three years."

Seeing her misery, Sebastian's heart ached to hold her, and before he knew what he was doing, he found himself reaching out for her.

Instantly, her eyes widened, and she shrank back, back pressed against the window.

Dropping his hands, he cursed his foolishness. "I'm sorry. I didn't mean to scare you. I ..." Raking his hands through his hair, he tried to think of a way to ease the tension between them. She believed that he wanted to bed her, and she was right. However, he would never do so without her consent, and she needed to know that. She needed to believe that.

Honesty, then.

"Listen," he began, refusing to back away but equally standing his ground. "I want you to trust me, and so I will be honest with you. Completely honest."

He held her gaze until she nodded.

"I gave you my word," he reminded her, "that I would not lay a hand on you without your consent, and I need you to believe me that I will not break it. Not every touch is fuelled by passion. Some are meant to comfort, to ease pain. I swear I had no intention of betraying what little trust you might have in me."

Again, her body relaxed and her breathing evened.

"However," he continued, wishing that he didn't feel the need to, "to be honest, I ..." He took a deep breath, and her eyes narrowed, suspicion in them as she waited for him to go on. "I will not deny that I desire you." She tensed. "You asked whether men did not care who they took to their beds, and I suppose many do not or at least not always. I can only speak for myself, and I need you to know that you're not just anyone to me. We may not know each other well, but I do feel like there is something between us or at least like there could be. I will not risk the future we could have for a moment of pleasure."

Shaking her head, she averted her eyes. "Pleasure," she scoffed, then swallowed before her eyes returned to his face. "I want to believe you, and I want to trust you."

"Thank you," Sebastian said, relief echoing in his voice. "I promise I will do what I can to prove myself worthy of your trust." And maybe one day, she would trust him enough to allow him to show her that her marital *duty* could be pleasurable after all.

Chapter Fourteen

A HARSH TRUTH

T hat night, Charlotte slept like a log until the early morning light streamed in through the drapes, gently luring her away from the blissful nothing of slumber. When she opened her eyes and found herself back at the inn, reality came rushing back and she sat up with a start. Seeing her husband's blanket neatly folded on one of the chairs by the window, she glanced around the room.

It was empty. He wasn't there.

Quickly, Charlotte jumped out of bed and hurried to slip on her gown lest he return and find her undressed.

By the time footsteps could be heard from down the corridor, Charlotte was brushing out her hair, eyes fixed on the window and the calm street below.

The door creaked open, and she felt him enter the room as though a burning heat emanated from his body, reaching out to her.

A shiver went down her back, and then the door closed.

"Good morning," he said, a hesitant touch to his voice as he stepped closer. "I hope you slept well, my lady."

"Surprisingly so." Keeping her back turned, Charlotte continued to run her brush through her dark auburn hair. If she didn't look at him, maybe she could pretend they weren't alone in the room.

Although his honest words the night before had calmed her nerves, she couldn't help the nervous jitter that jostled her whole being whenever he approached. Nor could she banish the fear that clawed at her heart, threatening her with a repetition of the atrocity she had suffered.

"I'm glad." Standing behind her, he waited, then cleared his throat. "Would you look at me?" he asked, his tone pleading rather than holding a demand.

Taking a deep breath, Charlotte raised her chin, then turned around and met his eyes.

Even in the dim light of the room, they shone piercing blue as they travelled over her face, searching, asking. Then his lips curled up, and he nodded to her. "I assume you're hungry," he began. "I've taken the liberty of ordering a hearty breakfast for the two of us. Then we'll be off. Everything is prepared."

"Thank you, my lord," Charlotte said, once more averting her eyes as the intensity of his gaze became unbearable. It felt as though he was slowly peeling back layer for layer of her assumed identity, getting closer and closer to her true self. And whatever happened, she could not allow him to see her true self.

She was certain she would regret that for the rest of her life.

After following him down the narrow stairs, Charlotte allowed him to pull out a chair for her at the very table where they had shared their supper the night before. Always watching her, always noting even the smallest change in her movements, he was there as though he feared an attempt on her life and was ready to give his own to protect her.

And all the while, he took special care not to come too close, not to touch her.

While her husband exhibited an open curiosity about her, his eyes constantly watching, Charlotte mostly ignored him, keeping her attention fixed on the food on her plate. Only if asked a direct question did she speak to him, and only in short, clipped sentences.

After a while, she noticed the fascinated glow in his eyes dim.

Good. She thought. It would be better for them if they continued their lives separate from one another. After all, she could never be a true wife to him. To punish his father, her presence was not required.

At least not after being presented to the earl upon their arrival at his estate.

If she were lucky, she could retreat to a small country estate and spend the rest of her life regretting her past, waiting for death.

Once they had both eaten their fill, her husband had their bags brought down from the room and loaded onto the carriage. Then he pulled back her chair and escorted her outside. He walked beside her, but did not offer her his arm.

As they came to stand before the open carriage door, he turned to her, his eyes alert as he held out his hand to help her inside. "This is an offer," he said, glancing at his hand. "You are free to accept it or refuse it. My only intention is to assist you in whatever way I can."

For a moment, Charlotte was speechless at the consideration he showed her. Never would she have expected him to keep his word in the strictest sense. He would not lay a hand on her without her permission.

Grateful, she nodded at him, then lifted her hand and slowly placed it in his.

As his fingers closed over hers, she took a deep breath. The pulse in her neck began to quicken and before long it felt as though she had just run all the way from London.

His eyes held hers before they momentarily darted to her thudding pulse. Then, without delay, he guided her up the step and into the carriage, immediately releasing her hand.

Taking his seat across from her, he smiled. "If we press on, it should take us no more than two days to reach my father's estate."

Charlotte nodded in acknowledgement, then turned her gaze out the window as the carriage rumbled down the narrow street.

For a long time, silence settled over them, the only sounds coming from outside. The churning wheels. The howling wind as the end of the year approached on fast wings. The sound of hoof beats carrying them farther and farther south.

Then her husband shifted in his seat, and she could feel his eyes once more studying her face.

Taking a deep breath, Charlotte bit her lower lip, then turned to look at him.

A teasing smile played over his features as his gaze continued to search hers with such frankness that Charlotte felt her hands begin to tremble. Why was it that he seemed to see beneath her mask so easily? Could he tell that she wasn't who she said she was? Did he know more than he admitted?

"You look suspicious, my lady," he observed, his eyes darting to her clamped hands resting in her lap. "Have I given you any reason to be concerned?"

Although her eyes narrowed, Charlotte shook her head. "Not yet."

"Not yet?" Despite the good-natured curl to his lips, there was a hint of disappointment in his eyes. "Do you generally distrust people?"

"I didn't use to," Charlotte admitted, remembering years of levity before the harsh truth forced her into a reality she'd rather not have known existed. "There was a time in my life when I believed that all would be well, that people were good."

As his eyes narrowed and he regarded her more closely, Charlotte swallowed. Why had she said that? Why was it that he made her feel as though she could tell him anything?

Seeing the tension that had come to her posture, he sat back and his eyes softened. "I remember such a time myself." He sighed, then shook his head. "Maybe only the young have the luxury of such innocence. Maybe once we outgrow childhood, we are bound to be disappointed by the rules that govern the world."

Charlotte frowned, her eyes fixed on his face. "Do you speak of your sister?"

His shoulders slumped, and he exhaled deeply.

"I'm sorry. I didn't mean to pry." Although reluctant, Charlotte turned away. The devotion and unconditional commitment he always portrayed for his sister warmed her heart, and she realised listening to him speak of her in such ways eased the pain in her soul. After all, the world couldn't be such a bad place if devotion like that existed, could it?

"My sister has always been the one good thing in my life," he whispered, his head resting against the wall of the carriage, his eyes staring into nothing. "My father is probably the most cold-hearted man in England, and trapped in a marriage to such a man, I suppose my mother died a little more each year. I remember sometimes I would speak to her and she would look right through me as though I wasn't even there, as though she couldn't see me." He took a deep breath. "Remembering it now, I feel as though I lived the first ten years of my life in darkness." A soft smile drew up the corners of his mouth. "And then, Victoria was born, and the sun began to shine on my world."

Seeing the glow on his face, Charlotte smiled as she could feel its warmth reach across and touch her chilled skin.

He blinked then, and lifted his head. "Do you have a sister or a brother?"

"I had a brother once," Charlotte whispered, remembering the tiny infant she had barely gotten to know. "But he died within his first year. My parents were heart-broken." She looked up and saw nothing but sympathy in his eyes. "I often wondered what it would have been like had he lived."

"I'm sorry," he said, blinking back tears. Then he took a deep breath and cleared his throat. "Maybe I should not speak of this to you." A question rested in his eyes as he looked at her. "It will only cause you pain."

"No," Charlotte said, shaking her head. "I enjoy hearing about your sister. It reminds me of-" Breaking off, Charlotte turned away, forcing her gaze away from the man who knew how to draw out her secrets and to the safety of the rolling hills outside the window.

"Who does it remind you of?" her husband asked, shifting forward in his seat.

Again, she could feel his eyes on her as though he could simply read the answer on her face without her even speaking a word.

"I'm sorry," he said after a while. "I suppose for one day, we've shared quite a lot with each other, and I'm grateful that you would trust me with your secrets."

Her secrets? Charlotte wondered. If only she could. Deep down, she had never been someone to keep secrets. However, the past three years had changed all that. It had been so long since she had spoken to anyone openly, without fear of betraying her secret, without holding back. Sometimes her head throbbed with the effort it took to navigate her way through the lies she hid behind.

If only her brother had lived. Yes! Would he have stood by her side? Or would he have been disappointed as well, demanding that she marry the man who'd ruined her to avoid a scandal? Sometimes Charlotte didn't know what was the worst thing that ever happened to her. The night Lord Northfield had cornered her in the library? Or the moment her parents had turned against her, betraying the trust she'd always had in them?

Within days, her world had come crushing down around her so many times she had lost track. And then Kenneth had died, and with him, all hope for a future.

He had always been her protector, her support, her friend. And then he had been gone, and she had lost more than just the man she was to marry. Without him, she had lost herself. Her sense of self-worth. Her belief in right and wrong. Her sanity.

And it had made her do things she would regret for the rest of her life.

That night, they stopped at an inn half-way to London, and Sebastian was relieved to find that he could rent two rooms instead of just one. His wife, too, looked grateful to be able to lock him out and spend the night in safety.

Sebastian tried hard not to take her reaction personally; yet, it ate at him that she would still doubt him. Again, he reminded himself that she had suffered greatly and that such pain could not be overcome overnight. He needed to be patient if he ever wanted her to trust him ... unconditionally and without doubts.

The next morning when they set out again, he took great care not to step too close, keeping his distance and only offering his assistance wherever he deemed necessary, leaving the decision to her whether to accept it or not. Like the day before, she took his offered hand and allowed him to help her into the carriage, the ghost of a smile on her lips as her eyes lingered on his for a moment.

Suppressing a grin, Sebastian took the seat across from her, hoping that they could continue their conversation from the day before.

At first, she seemed disinclined, keeping her gaze out the window, her eyes distracted by inner thoughts. However, after a while, as the carriage continued to rumble down the country lanes, he noticed her gaze drifting to him every now and then. Not turning her head in his direction, she glanced at him through slightly lowered eyelashes.

Sebastian cleared his throat, and she quickly dropped her gaze.

Amused, he smiled, then turned to look at her. "I seem to remember you saying that you've never travelled anywhere," he began, hoping to draw her into a conversation. "Have you ever been to London?"

Meeting his eyes, she nodded. "Yes, I grew up there. At least during the season. My mother would-" Suddenly, she clamped her mouth shut, and he thought to hear a silent curse as her hands dug into her coat.

At least during the season. Her words echoed in his mind, confirming the growing suspicion he'd begun to have. However, pretending to ignore her slip of the tongue, Sebastian asked, "Have you ever wished to see more than just England? The continent maybe? Or even America?"

Swallowing, she lifted her eyes, a hint of relief in them that he didn't press for an explanation. "I never thought about it much. Every now and then, we would hear stories or my father would receive a visitor who'd been travelling and share his adventures at the supper table." She shrugged. "And you, my lord, what made you travel to the continent?"

Sebastian sighed, realising that naturally he could not ask a question without expecting one in return...but hating it nonetheless. "My father," he admitted. "In his opinion, it was the mark of a gentleman to have travelled the continent. He insisted, and I ... I allowed myself to be persuaded." He shook his head, remembering the moment he had received news of his sister's marriage. "I suppose I never truly believed he would trick me like that. He wanted me out of the country so that my sister would be defenceless against him. It is one decision I will regret for the rest of my life."

"It is truly sad," she said, her voice clouded with emotion as though she herself had just shared a deep, personal memory. "For so many reasons."

Meeting her eyes, Sebastian saw understanding and compassion in her warm gaze. For what reason, he could not say, but she knew the meaning of guilt, of regret. Her sympathy was one born out of personal experience and not a platitude voiced because of convention.

"Had you been there," she asked, holding his gaze, "what would you have done to prevent it?"

Taking a deep breath, Sebastian swallowed, then nodded. "Anything."

A soft smile came to her face. "You're a good man," she whispered, a touch of surprise in her voice as her eyes studied his face. "Your sister is fortunate to call you her brother."

Despite the warmth in her eyes, guilt once more clawed at his heart, and he wondered if he would spend the rest of his life with this ache in his chest. "I cannot help but disagree, my lady," he mumbled, uncomfortable that she should think of him that way when the truth was far from complimenting.

"You did not know what your father would do," she counselled, her gaze lowered to her folded hands. "People's intentions are not always written on their faces. One might seem gallant and honourable, but then prove to have no conscience, no decency, no respect for others." She took a deep breath. "It is a harsh truth. One not easily learnt."

Watching her, Sebastian frowned. "You speak from experience, my lady?"

For a second, her eyes flickered upward, meeting his, before they returned to her folded hands. "I suppose few can walk this world without seeing darkness at least once."

Sebastian took a deep breath. "How did you encounter it?"

Instantly, her jaw clenched, and she turned away, eyes fixed on the landscape outside, unblinking, until tears welled up, spilt over and ran down her cheeks. And yet, she remained quiet. No sob escaped her throat. No strangled moan was torn from her lips. Her heart suffered in silence.

And yet, Sebastian could hear her pain as though she was screaming at the top of her lungs. The agony he witnessed felt like a knife plunged in his gut.

Gritting his teeth, he forced air down his lungs. Although they had barely known each other a fortnight, her pain was now his, and he knew in that moment that he would walk through hell and back again to see her safe.

Not since Victoria had been born, had he felt such an overwhelming desire to protect someone ... no matter the cost.

Chapter Fifteen
WELCOME TO THE FAMILY

T he remainder of their journey, they spent in silence. However, Charlotte was acutely aware of her husband's watchful gaze as it lingered on her face, tracing the tears that spilt from her eyes.

Ashamed, she had turned her head away, and yet, there was nowhere to go. Trapped in a carriage, she was forced to endure the humiliation at having him witness her breakdown. Rarely in her life had she felt so mortified.

Fortunately, he remained where he was. At one point, he had shifted in his seat, leaning forward, his hand rising as though he intended to offer comfort. Then, however, he had stopped himself once again, allowing her the space she needed to force her emotions back under control.

When his father's estate came into view, Charlotte was once more in possession of her faculties. Stone-faced, she allowed her husband to assist her down the step and out of the carriage.

"Welcome to Hartridge Hall," he said, a soft smile on his face as he gazed down into her eyes. His hand closed over hers more tightly for the barest of seconds, stealing Charlotte's breath and sending a shiver through her body.

Seeing the shock on her face, her husband immediately released her hand. "I apologise, my lady," he mumbled, his eyes unable to meet hers. "Allow me to escort you inside."

This time, he did not offer her his arm, but merely walked beside her as they climbed the few stairs leading up to the front doors. As they approached, they swung open, allowing them to enter a large hall.

A balding man stepped up to them, bowing his head. "Welcome back, Lord Huntly."

"Thank you," her husband said, a frown still drawing down his brows. "Please summon my parents to the drawing room."

Although the butler looked mildly taken aback as his eyes darted to Charlotte, he nodded. "Certainly, my lord."

Feeling herself tremble at what was to come, Charlotte clasped her hands together, once again doubting the wisdom of her decision to accept her husband's proposal. What had she gotten herself into?

"Do not worry, my lady," her husband whispered by her side, his head slightly bent forward in confidence. "You have nothing to fear from my father. I admit, he will be furious, but other than that he is no threat to you." Holding her gaze, he nodded for emphasis. "I assure you I will always be by your side."

A soft smile came to her lips as she stared at him, at the seriousness and devotion that lay in his eyes. It had been a long time since anyone had spoken to her like that. Not since Kenneth.

Swallowing, she nodded, then lifted her hand, and although looking mildly surprised, her husband quickly offered her his arm. He drew in a deep breath as she hesitantly slid her arm through his; she could feel the strength he possessed like a shield around her. It had been a long time since she had felt safe. Not since Kenneth.

Acutely aware of the man by her side, Charlotte followed him across the hall and down the corridor into the drawing room. Everything around her reminded her of a life she had left behind a long time ago, and yet, a part of her felt as though she had finally come home.

Then the doors swung open, and a dignified woman, presumably her husband's mother, walked in, arms wide as though wishing to embrace him. "I'm so glad that you've returned," she beamed, joy marking her features as she approached her son.

As she beheld Charlotte, the woman stopped, a frown drawing down her brows. Her eyes darted to her son, a question resting in them, before she looked at Charlotte once more. "I apologise. I do not believe we have been introduced."

Her husband smiled, and his arm tightened on hers ever so slightly. "Mother, may I pre-"

"What is this nonsense?" a booming voice echoed from the hall, interspersed by racking coughs. "If my son wishes to speak to me, *he* ought to come to *me*, not the other way around. I am not a bloody servant who can be summoned." In the next instant, the door flew open, and in walked her husband's father, his massive belly straining against his jacket as red spots rose on his neck and cheeks. Sweat beaded on his forehead, and he dabbed a handkerchief to his face, eyes glaring at his son. "So, you have returned," he snapped, wheezing as he stepped forward. "I hope you have come to your senses and-"

In that moment, his eyes fell on Charlotte, who sincerely wished the earth would open and swallow her whole. While her husband's mother had seemed nice enough, although a little cold, his father glared at her with such open hostility that she could not help but cringe under his gaze.

"Who is this?" Lord Weston demanded, turning accusing eyes on his son. "What have you done now?"

A slow smile curled up the corners of her husband's mouth. His eyes, however, had turned to stone, cold and calculating as she had never seen them. "This, dear Father, Mother, is Miss Lotte Ferris." He drew out every word, slowly and menacingly. "Or at least she was until two days ago. Now, she is Lady Huntly, my wife."

Sebastian barely registered the surprise on his mother's face as his eyes were fixed on his father.

Standing before him, his father looked like the picture of waning health. While his head was already red from the exertion of walking to the drawing room, it now turned even darker, and his eyes snapped open as though he had just received a crippling blow to his midsection.

Then his gaze narrowed, and a sly grin drew up the corners of his mouth. "Don't even try to play me for a fool," he snapped, his eyes shifting to his new daughter-in-law, disgust clearly visible in them. "Not even you would be dumb enough to marry a woman of no standing."

A short laugh escaped Sebastian before he shook his head. "I assure you that I'm not jesting, Father. We were legally married two days ago in Gretna Green." The grin vanished from his father's face, replaced by a sudden paleness. "Would you like to see the marriage license?"

Beside him, Sebastian was barely aware that his wife's arm trembled as her gaze shifted around the room, avoiding his father's angry stare.

"You lie!" his father spat, and once again, his head turned as red as a tomato. With wild eyes, he took a step forward, gaze shifting back and forth between his son and his daughter-in-law, willing them to admit that it was indeed a lie. "You wouldn't dare! You-"

"Of course, I would!" Sebastian snapped as all his bottled-up anger since he learnt of his sister's marriage exploded within him, forcing its burning fire into every fibre of his being. "You married Victoria to the devil! You did not consult me when you chose her husband! Far from it! You tricked me and sent me out of the country, knowing she would be defenceless against you!" Shaking his head, Sebastian glared at his father. "Are you truly surprised that I would not consult you on who I marry? Do you truly believe that your counsel has any meaning to me?" Hands balled into fists, he leant forward, then whispered, "I promised I'd make you regret your actions, did I not?"

With lips pressed into a thin line, his father stared at him as the muscles in his jaw convulsed. Hatred burned in his eyes as they slowly shifted back to his son's wife. "You," he snarled, his hands clenched by his sides. "You, Harlot," he hissed, then suddenly stormed forward, hands raised as though wishing to strangle the woman presented to him as his son's wife.

Terrified, Charlotte shrank back as her father-in-law came toward her like a raging bull, eyes narrowed and nostrils flaring. Never had she seen such unadulterated hatred, and the blood froze in her veins at the thought of what a life her husband and his sister must have endured, only able to turn to one another for comfort.

"Don't you lay a hand on her!" her husband commanded, stepping into his father's path. "I could not protect my sister, but I will protect my wife!"

An image of Kenneth flashed before Charlotte's eyes as her husband did not hesitate to shield her from his father's wrath. Tears stung her eyes, and a soft smile came to her features at the familiar feeling that had seized her heart so unexpectedly.

For so long she had been alone. Only able to depend on herself. Facing the world with no one by her side.

Now, there was ... Sebastian.

Stopping in his tracks, the earl looked lost for a moment before his gaze focused on his son once more. Eyes locked, they stood facing one another, neither one uttering a word for what seemed like a small eternity.

Then the earl's features revived, and the muscles in his jaw convulsed once more. "You'll regret this," he wheezed, one hand clutched to his chest. "For you've not only ruined me, but also yourself. Are you too much of a fool to see that?"

Sebastian snorted. "Do you truly believe I care about the family's reputation?" he snarled. "I'd rather see my sister happily married than suffering in a *suitable* marriage."

Shaking his head in disbelief, the earl retreated, ragged breaths tearing from his lips. Then he turned around and stormed off. "You've doomed us all!"

Exhaling, Charlotte looked at her husband, who stood watching his father's retreating form. His shoulders were tense and his eyes narrowed. However, a hint of relief rested on his features as he turned around to look at her. "Are you all right?" he asked, his voice soft and caring as his eyes studied her face as though looking for injuries.

With her heart thudding in her chest at the sight of her husband's tenderness, Charlotte nodded.

"Well, now you've done it, my son," the countess whispered in hushed tones. Then she stepped forward, and her eyes travelled back and forth between Charlotte and her son, wondering, assessing. "Is it true?" she asked then, her gaze focused on her son. "Are you married?"

Her husband nodded. "We are. Does that shock you, Mother?"

"It does surprise me," his mother admitted, a soft curl to her lips. "A part of me wondered if you would ever marry. For you seemed determined to spite your father and never give him the heir he desired. Your father feared that you would be the last of his line."

Gritting his teeth, her husband nodded. "I did consider it," he confessed before his eyes travelled to Charlotte. "But plans change."

Watching them, the countess nodded, a faint sparkle in her eyes. "I'm glad they did for I do wish for you to be happy."

"Thank you, Mother."

"Well, then," the countess said, turning to look at Charlotte. Reaching out, she took her hands in hers and gave them a gentle squeeze. "For whatever it's worth, welcome to the family."

Chapter Sixteen

EXTRAORDINARY WOMEN

S ilence.

A looming, deafening silence hung over the breakfast table the next morning.

Seated next to her husband, Charlotte kept her gaze focused on the food on her plate or the tea cup in her hand, afraid to meet anyone's eyes, especially her father-in-law's.

Residing at the head of the table, he bore an expression that spoke of his hatred and disappointment at what his son had done to the family. Occasionally, he would glare in Sebastian's direction, and his face would turn a darker shade of red. Then he would cough, reach for his cup and sip its contents, hands shaking.

His wife, on the other hand, seemed to be unaware of any kind of misgivings between her husband and her son. A passive, rather disinterested expression on her face, she buttered her muffin, sipped her tea and refrained from interacting with anyone at all.

Glancing at her husband, Charlotte wondered if this was a normal occurrence within the family. Were they used to such open hostility? Did it not pain them to be at war with one another?

With a sigh, Charlotte remembered her own family. Their meals had always been a pleasure. Laughing and chatting, they had shared their plans for the day over breakfast or discussed the events that had transpired that day over supper. Never had she felt unwelcome or unappreciated. She had always loved her parents dearly, and they'd loved her. Always had she considered herself lucky to be treasured by them.

Until one night had changed it all.

Clearly, her husband did not have any such expectations. On the contrary, he generally seemed to be expecting the worst and was rarely disappointed.

For a moment, Charlotte thought that he might be far luckier than she ever had been. For when her parents had finally turned against her, she could hardly believe it. Never would she have seen it coming. Their betrayal had hit her with such force that it had brought her to her knees, panting for breath.

What had remained intact of her heart and soul after Lord Northfield's attack on her had crumbled into a million tiny pieces upon her parents' breach of trust. She had lost herself that day, abandoned sanity, allowed her heart to retreat from the pain around her.

Until Kenneth.

He had been her saviour. And then he had died, and her heart had stopped caring.

Hand on his chest, her father-in-law turned red as another coughing fit shook his body. His family, however, remained still as though nothing out of the ordinary was happening.

Clearly not expecting any support from them, the earl rose from the table and left the room.

The moment the door closed behind him, his wife came to life. "I have to say I am so delighted that you're here," she said, smiling at both. "I feared it would be another dreary Christmas, but now that you are here and Victoria is coming, I-"

"Victoria is coming?" her husband interrupted, his cup frozen halfway to his mouth.

Again, his mother smiled, then nodded. "I received a letter from her only last week."

Taking a deep breath, Sebastian swallowed before the ghost of a smile came to his features. "When? For how long?" The tea cup met its saucer with a loud *clink*.

"I'm not entirely certain," his mother said, a slight frown on her forehead as she tried to remember the contents of the letter. "She merely wrote that she planned on coming for Christmas. Surely, she will stay at least a fortnight."

"I truly hope so," Sebastian mumbled, eyes distant. Then he stopped, and his gaze narrowed, shifting back to his mother. "What about her husband?" he forced out through gritted teeth, and Charlotte could see the tension in his shoulders.

"Apparently, he has business in Town," his mother said, "and is, therefore, unable to accompany her."

Sebastian scoffed, "That's a lie."

"Quite obviously," his mother mumbled, sipping her tea. "Nevertheless, it saves us from having to endure his presence in this house ... especially over Christmas."

Sebastian nodded. "That is indeed good news."

After breakfast, her husband showed Charlotte around the estate. They started with the manor and then took a quick ride through the surrounding fields. The air was crisp and cold, but no snow was in sight. Instead, the landscape sparkled in the blinding sunshine, warming Charlotte's cheeks. It was a splendid day, and Charlotte enjoyed being out in the fresh air.

For a long while they rode side by side, not speaking, each lost in their own thoughts. Then Charlotte turned to look at her husband, trying to understand the dark cloud that had settled on him ever since his mother had mentioned his sister's impending visit. "You seem troubled," she observed, and he flinched as though he had completely forgotten her presence. "Are you not happy that your sister will be visiting?"

Meeting her eyes, he sighed. "Yes, and, no," he said, shoulders slumped. "I would love nothing more than to see her every day, and yet, seeing her in pain is simply ...," closing his eyes, he shook his head, "... is simply torture." Again, he met her gaze. "If she's not here, I can at least pretend that she is happy. I know I'm being selfish. After all, it is not I who was forced into a marriage with someone without scruples." A soft smile came to his face as he guided his gelding closer to her. "I consider myself very fortunate in that regard."

Taken aback by his bold statement, Charlotte averted her gaze as the breath caught in her throat at the intensity in his eyes. When he remained silent, she swallowed and cleared her throat. "I look forward to meeting her," she said, urging her mare onward. "After hearing so much about her, I must admit I'm curious."

Catching up with her, her husband smiled. "I'm certain the two of you will be the best of friends before the year is out. After all, you two are the most extraordinary women I've ever had the pleasure of knowing."

In the afternoon, Charlotte found herself aimlessly wandering around the manor. Her husband's words echoed in her mind, and she could not deny the warmth that came to her heart when she remembered those piercing blue eyes looking into hers with such devotion.

Long ago, she had given up on the dream of marrying for love, of becoming a mother and having a family that was her pride and joy. And although her conscience forbade her from ever even contemplating such a possibility-after all what right did she have to happiness?-a tiny spark of hope had ignited in her heart that day. And no matter what she did, how reasonably she argued that it was not to be, she could not silence it.

"You seem distracted, my dear."

Spinning around, Charlotte stared at her mother-in-law. Seated on the settee in the drawing room where they had first met, the countess worked a needle through a piece of fabric with skilled ease, her eyes barely glancing at the items in her hands.

"I'm sorry," Charlotte mumbled, glancing at her surroundings, unaware that she had ventured here. "I was ... lost in thought."

Her mother-in-law chuckled. "That much was obvious," she said, her eyes narrowing-not unlike her son's-looking closer. "The more interesting questions is: what thought distracted you so that you didn't even notice me sitting here?"

Warmth rose to Charlotte's cheeks, and she quickly averted her gaze.

The countess laughed. "There's no shame in that, my dear," she observed. "After all, he's your husband."

Mortified, Charlotte was rooted to the spot. Clasping her hands together, she tried to think of an excuse to quit the room.

"Why don't you come and join me?" the countess invited her, glancing at the armchair opposite her. "There's only so many cushions a woman can embroider without losing her mind." A sad chuckle echoed through the room. "Unfortunately, I passed that limit a while ago."

Hearing the loneliness in her mother-in-law's voice, Charlotte took the offered seat. "Thank you."

"It's my pleasure," the countess said, setting aside her needlework. "I admit I was very surprised when my son presented you as his wife. . However, I want you to know that I never felt any objections against you as my husband did. Despite your lack of pedigree, you have proved yourself a well-mannered and sensible young woman, and I believe you can make my son happy." Holding Charlotte's gaze, the countess nodded. "I hope you can believe me. Although I may not always have been the best mother, I do love my children and wish them nothing but happiness."

Charlotte nodded, hearing the sincerity of her mother-in-law's words. Herself trapped in a marriage to a man she never wanted, the countess probably had been a kind and loving woman ... once. "I cannot fault your husband for thinking as he does," Charlotte said, remembering that she was no longer an earl's daughter.

The countess' features darkened. "But I can," she said, shaking her head. "Although he is my husband, I have long since moved past the notion that I see it as my duty to support his every whim and excuse his heartlessness even toward his own children." She sighed, openly meeting Charlotte's gaze. "I myself have made mistakes. In the early years of my marriage, I felt too ... miserable about my own fate for me to see how much my son and daughter suffered. Thank God, they had each other." A hint of pain came to her eyes before she reluctantly went on. "Only when my husband ... lost interest in me did I find a way to be the mother I wanted to be. Unfortunately, by then, it was too late for my son. He had grown into a man all on his own without his mother's help and despite his father's influence. But my daughter," a sad smile curled up her lips as tears welled up in her eyes, "she was still young, so young, and I cherished the few years we had together. It broke my heart when my husband married her to *that man*."

Initially surprised that the countess would share such intimate details of her life, Charlotte soon came to understand what compelled her mother-in-law to speak as the same desire echoed within Charlotte's own heart. More than anything, she wished she could speak honestly to someone, anyone, to share her thoughts and feelings, confess her wrongdoings and reveal her hopes and fears ... and have someone listen and maybe, just maybe, understand.

"Your son is tortured by that as well," Charlotte said. "He believes it to be his fault for he promised to protect her, and then when she needed him, he couldn't." Although her husband was a grown man, maybe the relationship to his mother could still be mended. Maybe it was not too late for them.

"I know," the countess said, shoulders slumped as though unable to bear the weight resting on them any longer. "When I found out about my husband's intentions, I wrote a letter to Sebastian, hoping that he would be able to help." She sighed. "However, my husband discovered what I intended to do and prevented me from ever mailing the letter."

"Does your son know that?" Charlotte asked, wondering.

The countess shook her head. "It doesn't matter. He has every right to be angry with me for I failed them both as a mother. I will never forgive myself for allowing my husband to turn me into such a cold and heartless ghost, oblivious to my children's needs, for so many years." Looking up, a soft smile came to her lips. "I'm so glad that he found you." Swallowing, Charlotte froze. "I can see how much he cares about you. At first, I feared he had only married you to punish his father. I mean no offence, but my son often seems willing to do his utmost to spite his father ... even before Victoria was married."

Charlotte didn't know what to say. Of course, she couldn't openly contradict her mother-in-law and reveal her husband's plan.

"Although not unburdened," the countess continued, unaware of

Charlotte's turmoil, "he seems ... cheerful at times. I haven't seen him like this in a long time. Pray tell, how did you meet?"

Charlotte swallowed as the thoughts buzzed in her head. Did he truly care for her? Of course, she had noticed his kindness toward her, but did it speak to more than just his amiable character?

"My dear?"

Charlotte's head snapped up. "I'm sorry," she mumbled, remembering that her mother-in-law had just asked her a question. "I was the companion to Lord Ashwood's sister at Farnworth Manor when your son came to visit his friend."

The countess' eyes began to glow. "When was that?"

Charlotte swallowed. "About a fortnight ago."

Her mother-in-law's eyes grew round, and the corners of her mouth strained upward into a beaming smile. "And then he whisked you away to Gretna Green? Oh, how romantic!" she exclaimed, and for a moment, Charlotte could barely remember the reserved woman she'd seen over breakfast. "I've never experienced anything like it, but always hoped that my children would. At least, my son was fortunate enough to marry for love."

Marry for love? The words echoed in Charlotte's head as she stared at her mother-in-law's beaming face.

"I couldn't be happier," the countess exclaimed, sighing with relief. "Have you written to your own mother? I'm certain she will be equally delighted."

Charlotte tensed. What was she to say? That her mother believed her dead? That even if she knew Charlotte was alive, she'd shy away from acknowledging any connection to her daughter for fear of a scandal? "I haven't seen my family in years," she heard herself saying, unable to lie when her mother-in-law had just confided in her so openly. "Something happened that sent us in opposite directions. I'm afraid she would not be pleased to hear from me."

"I'm so sorry, my dear," the countess said, honest regret in her blue eyes as she looked at Charlotte's bent head. "I can see how much it pains you. Do you not think you should write to her nonetheless? Give her the chance to be happy for you? After all, a mother's heart never forgets."

Tears stood in Charlotte's eyes as she looked at her mother-in-law, wishing with all her heart that what she said could be true. Oh, how she missed her own mother! All her life, she had been Charlotte's confidante, a loving hand to guide her through life, and her heart ached for the unquestionable safety that only a mother could provide.

Only her mother hadn't.

As the tears began to run down her face, Charlotte suddenly found herself pulled to her feet and propelled into her mother-in-law's arms. Holding her tight, the countess mumbled soothing words of comfort in Charlotte's ear while stroking her back the same way her own mother had a million times.

Unable to resist, Charlotte's arms closed around her mother-in-law as she rested her head on the woman's shoulder. And for a moment, just a moment, Charlotte allowed herself to pretend that her own mother was holding her.

Chapter Seventeen
TRULY HAPPY

A frown on his face, Sebastian walked down the hallway toward his father's study. If he didn't know any better-and he did-he would have thought this a game!

After taking affront at being summoned to the drawing room by his son, his father had now summoned Sebastian to his study. At first, Sebastian couldn't remember the last time his father had wanted to see him. Only to recall a second later, that it had been to encourage him to tour the continent.

Instantly, Sebastian's mood darkened, and a scowl replaced the frown on his face.

Cursing himself, Sebastian shook his head. He should have known! After all, he could count on the fingers of one hand how many times his father had wanted to see him in the past three decades.

Of course, he'd had an agenda! And Sebastian had allowed himself to be tricked, to be manipulated.

Never again! He vowed, pushing open the door to his father's study without bothering to knock.

Seated behind his large desk, his father ignored his son's entrance, keeping his head bent over a stack of papers. However, Sebastian thought to have seen a slight flinch in the man's shoulders, and it pleased him greatly.

"You *asked* for me?" he said, his tone full of sarcasm.

His father cleared his throat. "I see your manners are severely lacking these days." Lifting his head, he met his son's eyes, his own filled with disapproval. "I suppose a tour of the continent was a bad idea after all, considering the negative influence such an experience has had upon you. I raised a gentleman of the upper class; now, look at you," he grumbled, his narrowed gaze sliding over Sebastian's features. "If you cannot conduct yourself in an appropriate way, society will shun you before long. Is that truly what you want?"

Sinking into an armchair, Sebastian shook his head. "For one, allow me to clarify that it was not my experiences on the continent which brought forth these *severely lacking* manners. On the contrary, I acquired them right here under your tutelage. And two, I've told you before-although I suppose I haven't made myself clear-that I care very little for society's opinion ... and even less for yours."

His father's eyes narrowed. "Do you still insist that your *marriage* is ... real?"

"Of course, I do," Sebastian scoffed. "After all, it is the truth."

Shaking his head, his father took a laboured breath. "I had hoped after presenting your chosen bride, you would have come to your senses. After all, it does not seem reasonable to ruin your life simply to annoy me, now does it? Was the expression on my face truly worth throwing your life away?"

Sebastian chuckled. "That and more," he said, leaning forward and meeting his father's eyes. "Allow me to be frank, Father. I despise not only what you do, but also who you are." The muscles in his father's jaw tensed. "Marrying Victoria to *that man* was the final straw. So, allow me to assure you that I do what I do merely to spite you, to cause you pain, in the hopes that this world will not have to suffer your harmful presence much longer." Then he leant back in his chair, a satisfied smile on his face as he watched his words turn his father's face ash white.

Swallowing, his father cleared his throat, his hands wrapped tightly around one another. "Is this how a son speaks to his father? What-?"

"If the father is you," Sebastian interrupted, "then, yes, it is."

Mumbling something under his breath, his father shook his head. "What did I do to deserve such disloyalty? You're my son, heir to my title. Have I not always done everything within my power to give you a good life? A privileged life?"

For a moment, Sebastian stared at his father, dumbfounded. Then he broke out laughing. "Are you serious, Father?" he asked, wiping a tear from his cheek. "Is this truly how you see yourself and all you have done?" He shook his head in disbelief. Did the man truly not see what was right in front of his eyes?

"Then allow me to instruct you, Father." Sitting up, Sebastian cleared his throat the way his old tutor had always done when imparting a new lecture. "Loyalty, dear Father, is based on respect, on admiration and love. I have none of those for you. Everything you've ever done was to look out for your own good, for what you wanted, no matter who you ruined in the process." Rising to his feet, Sebastian took a step toward his father's desk, then leant forward and rested his hands on the desktop, meeting his father's eyes. "You've brought this on yourself. And now, even should you wish it-and I can see that you don't-it is too late to make amends." Straightening, Sebastian stepped back, shaking his head. "You've chosen your path, and I've chosen mine." He stepped toward the door. "We're done, Father." Then he turned on his heel and walked out the door.

Walking down the corridor toward the front hall, a smile came to his face as he remembered his father's shocked face. Good! He thought. It was about time the man experienced the meaning of pain, of loss, of regret! And maybe, just maybe, it would be enough ... and soon he would be no more.

After all, his health was far from good. Even since Sebastian's departure to Farnworth Manor not even three weeks ago, his father's symptoms had increased. The coughing. The paleness. The shortness of breath.

His time was running out. Fast.

As Sebastian stepped into the hall, he saw the two footmen reach for the front doors. In the next instant, they swung open ... and Victoria walked in.

His breath caught in Sebastian's throat, and he stopped in his tracks, staring at her.

In that first moment, all he could see was the little auburn-haired girl, who had followed him like a shadow all his life. He remembered the trusting smile on her beautiful face, yet untouched by the world's harsh truths. He remembered how her azure eyes had sparkled whenever he'd found her high in a tree or on a bucking horse. Always, she'd been certain that he would catch her should she fall.

And he always had.

Pulling off her gloves, Victoria turned her head, her gaze gliding over the familiar surroundings until they fell on Sebastian. Instantly, a deep smile came to her lips that lit up her whole face, making her glow like the sun she was to him.

In that moment, as they looked at each other the same way they had a million times before, everything was as it always had been.

As Sebastian hastened toward her though, he couldn't stop himself from noticing the slight differences in her face. The deep blue of her eyes failed to sparkle the way he remembered. A strain rested on her lips as they curved upward. And small lines creased her face that spoke of pain and sadness.

Involuntarily, his steps slowed, and the coward inside wanted nothing more but to turn and run. For if he looked at her, he would see what he'd done to her by breaking his promise.

"Sebastian," Victoria called, an emotional hitch in her voice as she threw herself in his arms. "Dear Brother, it is truly good to see you."

Feeling as though in shock, Sebastian slowly closed his arms around his sister, feeling her small body rest against his. So fragile. So innocent. So in need of protection. Closing his eyes, he inhaled her scent and was once more transported back in time.

How was it that some things changed in such a way that they could unhinge the world while others stayed the way they were down to the most minuscule detail?

"I've missed you, big brother," Victoria said, stepping back, her eyes gliding over his face. "You look good." A soft laugh escaped her, and yet, to Sebastian's ears it sounded strained. "But then again, you always have." Handing her coat to one of the footmen, Victoria grasped his hands. "I feared you wouldn't be here," she whispered, her eyes full of concern. "After the way you left, I thought you'd break with Father for good and never set foot in his house again. I feared I'd never see you again."

Sebastian swallowed. "I'm sorry, dear Sister. I should not have left the way I did. I was angry, furious, and I did not consider your feelings the way I should have. I hope you can forgive me."

"Of course." Holding his gaze, Victoria shook her head. "Please, do not for a second believe that I said what I did out of anger. I was just ..." Her voice broke, and for a moment, she closed her eyes. "You've always been the one constant in my life, and ...," a soft smile came to her lips as she shrugged her slender shoulders, "I'm simply lost without you. Please promise me that you will never leave me."

"I wouldn't dream of it," Sebastian said, his voice choked as he fought back tears, "for you're like the sun to me, and I cannot live without you either." A radiant smile came to his sister's face, and impulsively, he pulled her into his arms, hugging her tight. "Nothing in the world could ever sway me from your side."

"Good," Victoria mumbled into his shoulder.

For a moment, they simply stood in the front hall, holding each other. Then Sebastian cleared his throat and stepped back, knowing that he couldn't escape reality much longer. Looking deep in her eyes, he asked, "How are you, dear Sister?"

Instantly, her features darkened before she could force a smile back onto her face. "I'm fine, Sebastian. Truly. There's no reason for you to worry."

"Your husband?" Sebastian growled out.

Victoria took a deep breath. "I admit he's not the husband I would have chosen, but..."

"But what?" Sebastian demanded as her voice trailed off and her gaze dropped from his.

Again, she swallowed, and although she forced her eyes back up, they wouldn't quite meet his. "Please, Sebastian. You know as well as I do that a marriage of convenience is the normal way to go about conducting these affairs. This is nothing out of the ordinary. Please, do not act as though Father sold me off to a slave trader."

Sebastian scoffed, knowing how true her off-hand remark was. "Let's not debate the normalcy of an arranged match," he said, still holding her hands in his. "What I want from you is honesty." A tremble went through his sister's hands as she swallowed. "How are you?" he asked again. "And please, do not pretend that I cannot see the truth on your face."

"All right," she finally relented. "If you insist. No, I am not happy." Sebastian tensed. "But neither am I miserable. Please, you must believe me, and do not blame yourself for neither do I."

Gritting his teeth, Sebastian remained still for a moment, waiting for his hammering pulse to slow. "I know this to be a lie, dear Sister, for you've never been able to hide anything from me. Again, I ask you to be honest and not spare me the guilt that is rightfully mine."

Pain shone through her eyes as she shook her head. "Please, listen, Sebastian, and know that I do not blame you. You could not have prevented what happened. It was not your place." She took a deep breath and gently squeezed his hands. "I do not wish for you to mourn me as though I've died. I want you to be happy. Please, do not add to my misery by being miserable yourself for I know that I am the reason why."

"But-"

"No," Victoria interrupted. "I *need* you to be happy; do you hear me? I need you to smile and laugh and find love. I need you to find a woman who is your match. I need at least one of us to be truly happy." She swallowed. "Can you do that for me, dear Brother?"

A soft curl came to Sebastian's lips as Charlotte's image unexpectedly appeared before his eyes.

"What is it?" Victoria asked, speculation lighting up her eyes. "What don't I know?"

Holding her hands safely in his, Sebastian met her eyes and smiled. "I'm married, dear Sister."

Eyes going wide, Victoria gawked at him.

Chapter Eighteen

BROTHERS & SISTERS

As a knock sounded on the door, Charlotte tensed, immediately dropping her arms and lifting her head off her mother-in-law's shoulder.

An apologetic look in her eyes, the countess brushed a strand behind Charlotte's ear. "Are you all right, Dear?"

Wiping the tears from her cheeks, Charlotte nodded, then turned to the window as her mother-in-law called for whomever to enter.

"Pardon my intrusion, my lady," Hartridge Hall's butler mumbled, giving a quick bow, "but your daughter is arriving this very minute."

"Thank you, Coleridge," the countess said, a hint of excitement in her voice. Once the door closed behind the butler, she turned to Charlotte, who was dabbing a handkerchief at her swollen eyes.

"I must look dreadful," she said, her voice still thick with emotions. "I apologise for-"

"Nonsense!" the countess objected, placing her hands on Charlotte's shoulders and looking her in the eyes. "We're family now. Your pain is my pain. Your joy is my joy." A soft smile on her face, she nodded. "I cannot change the past, but it is within my power to shape the future, and I refuse to allow the opportunity to pass me by. Do you understand?"

"I think I do," Charlotte sighed as her heart felt lighter than it had in a long while. It truly had been too long since she had been able to confide in someone, to allow herself to be vulnerable. Until a moment ago, Charlotte hadn't known how desperately she'd needed a shoulder to lean on...if only for a short moment.

"Come, Dear," the countess said, drawing Charlotte's arm through her own. "I want you to meet my daughter. I'm certain the two of you will have much to talk about."

"I'd like that," Charlotte said, a grateful smile on her face. Never would she have thought to find anything even resembling a family again, and now, it seemed to be growing day by day. Would her new sister-in-law reject her as her father had? Or would she look at her with the same kindness as her mother? Charlotte couldn't deny that she was curious to meet the young woman she'd heard so much about. The young woman who'd suffered an awfully familiar fate.

And yet, deep down, a nagging voice whispered that Charlotte had no rightful claim on the family she was starting to see as her own. If they knew who she truly was and what she'd done, they would turn from her in an instant. And she could not fault them for it.

After all, she had taken someone's life.

Walking down the corridor on her mother-in-law's arm, Charlotte drew a deep breath into her lungs, forcing the tremble the voice had conjured to still. After all, the countess had been right. There was nothing she could do about her past. But maybe, just maybe, she could help shape a future in which her husband's family would be united once again.

As they walked down the long corridor and the front hall came into view, Charlotte squinted her eyes as she saw two figures standing there, holding hands, their heads bent toward the other in confidence.

"I see my son has already found her," the countess mumbled beside Charlotte. "Somehow, he's always known where to find her. It's a special connection they have."

Stopping in the arched door frame, the two women watched as brother and sister spoke to each other, their quiet voices reaching their ears like a gentle echo in the vaulted room. "Please, Sebastian," his sister implored, her deep blue eyes holding his, "you know as well as I do that a marriage of convenience is the normal way to go about conducting these affairs."

Inwardly, Charlotte cringed. Despite everything that had happened to her, she had been spared the fate of marrying a man she didn't want. Victoria, however, had not been so lucky, and although she did her utmost to convince her brother of the opposite, Charlotte could see the tell-tale signs of a broken heart and a dying soul.

"Before Victoria came into our lives," the countess whispered beside her, her eyes fixed on the two siblings, "Sebastian was all alone in this family." She sighed. "But then, when Victoria was born, Sebastian took one look at his little sister and lost his heart to her, suffering with every scrape and cut, every heartbreak and sorrow."

For the second time that day, tears brimmed in Charlotte's eyes as she found herself reminded of Kenneth yet again. He had always been near, always watching, always protecting, always taking care of her. Somehow, he had always seen inside her heart with a single look.

Watching her husband with his sister, their eyes saying more than their lips dared, Charlotte recognised the depth of their connection and her heart ached for them.

"I *need* you to be happy, do you hear me?" Victoria implored her brother. "I need you to smile and laugh and find love. I need you to find a woman who is your match. I need at least one of us to be truly happy."

Charlotte froze the very moment her mother-in-law squeezed her hand and cast her a delighted smile. *A woman who is your match? A woman to love?*

Closing her eyes, Charlotte sighed as guilt washed over her. By accepting her husband's proposal, she had robbed him of every chance for happiness. Although it had been him who had proposed a *marriage of convenience*, she should have known better. Anger had fuelled his decision that day, not reason. He had been angry at his father and sought revenge. She ought to have stopped him, but instead, she had given in, afraid of what might become of her. How could he ever forgive her for this?

"I'm married, dear Sister."

As her husband's words echoed through the vaulted room, the

countess strode forward, pulling Charlotte along. "Victoria," she exclaimed, releasing Charlotte's arm and rushing toward her daughter, "I'm so glad you've arrived. Are you all right?"

While mother and daughter embraced, Charlotte glanced at her husband, his face aglow with delight as he watched them. Then his gaze drifted to Charlotte, and he stepped toward her. For a moment, his eyes held hers and a hesitant expression rested in them before he held out his hand to her.

Taking a deep breath, Charlotte took it, strangely comforted by the gentle warmth of his hand closing around hers.

"Victoria," her husband said, his voice ringing with pride, "allow me to introduce my wife, Lady Huntly."

Forcing her nerves back under control, Charlotte stepped forward and met Victoria's eyes as she released her mother and came toward her, a curious smile playing on her lips.

"And this is my sister," her husband continued, "Lady-"

"Let's not be so formal," his mother interrupted, surprising everyone. "After all, we're family. Victoria, this is Lotte. Lotte, this is my daughter Victoria."

"It's a pleasure to make your acquaintance," Victoria said, her watchful eyes drifting over Charlotte's face, asking, wondering, assessing. And yet, there was nothing hostile in her gaze, merely curiosity as well as a hint of sisterly protectiveness. "I must admit I'm quite surprised," she said, glancing at her brother. "I didn't even know Sebastian had been betrothed." She turned to him. "Why didn't you tell me?"

Their mother chuckled. "Because they've only known each other a fortnight."

"What?" Victoria's mouth gaped open. However, before she could say another word or rather ask another question, her mother looped her daughter's arm through her own and whisked her away. "I'll tell you everything. Come, you must be tired from your long journey."

Overwhelmed by the rather startling developments of that day, Charlotte stared after the two women. The countess was truly a different person when her husband was not around. Charlotte couldn't imagine this kind and strong-willed woman to ever have been subservient to her husband's wishes, willing to neglect her children in the process.

It happens to the best of us, does it not? Kenneth's voice echoed to her ears as he had once counselled her. No one was free of mistakes. No one was above hopes and desires, fears and despair. Everyone could fall.

Only not everyone could rise again.

Blinking, Charlotte shook her head, willing away the reminders of the past. Then she turned to find her husband standing beside her, frozen like a stone pillar, still staring at the door through which his mother and sister had vanished. While his body seemed unresponsive, his face spoke of the many emotions that had come rushing back upon his sister's return.

"You love her very much, do you not?" Charlotte whispered, reluctant to disturb the moment, and yet, unable to remain silently by his side.

His chest rose and fell as he inhaled deeply, then turned to look at her. "She's my sister." At a loss, he shook his head. "There are no words. I ..." His eyes met hers. "I wish your brother had lived so you could truly have understood what it means to have someone who walks with you every day of your life ... even when they're far away."

Seeing the raw emotions in his eyes, Charlotte found herself compelled to reciprocate. The words left her mouth before she even knew what she would say. "There was someone once," she whispered, "who was like a brother to me."

Intrigued, her husband's eyes narrowed, and he took a step closer.

"He was always there." Swallowing, Charlotte stared at her clenched hands. "He always knew where to find me, always knew what to say to ... make it better, to soothe and heal and comfort." A soft smile came to her face at the memory of Kenneth's faithful eyes. Never uncertain. Always confident as though nothing could surprise him. "I was never afraid," she continued, lifting her gaze, "because I knew no matter what would happen, he would be there right beside me, holding my hand."

A look of delighted surprise on his face, her husband nodded. "Sometimes it is as though I can feel her heart beat," he whispered, and his features darkened. "When I was on the continent, there was a day when I felt ... not like myself as though I was deathly sick. I couldn't make sense of it." He swallowed. "Later, I found that it had been my sister's wedding day."

Charlotte took a deep breath. "I'm so sorry. I ..." There was nothing she could say to ease his pain.

"As am I." Exhaling, her husband met her eyes. "Where is he? The man who was like a brother to you? What happened to him?"

Again, her hands clenched as raw pain erupted in her heart. "He died," she forced out through gritted teeth, willing the tears away that gathered in the corners of her eyes. Then she quickly stepped back and turned around, determined to hide the weakness that lived within her.

"Wait!" her husband called before she had taken more than a few steps.

As she stood in the large foyer of Hartridge Hall, tears streaming down her face, Charlotte heard her husband's soft footsteps on the marble floor as he walked up to her.

"Will you look at me?" he asked, and although Charlotte couldn't say why, she turned to face him. "I'm deeply sorry for your loss, and I know that nothing I can say will ease the pain." Holding her gaze, his piercing blue eyes shone gentle and kind. "What was his name?"

Charlotte took a deep breath, her voice shaking as she spoke. "Kenneth. His name was Kenneth." Shaking her head, she met his eyes. "It has been a while since I spoke his name. Somehow it makes the memories of his loss more acute. I ..." As her vision began to blur once again, she frantically wiped her hands over her face, trying to erase the evidence of her pain.

Charlotte barely heard his soft footsteps as he approached. Only when his hands settled on hers, stilling their movement, did she look up, blinking away her tears. The breath caught in her throat at the feel of his skin against hers, and for a moment, panic seized her.

It was like an instinct, a reflex.

Not a conscious thought or a decision she had control over.

As her body froze in shock, her eyes found his, and the compassion she saw there, the kindness and respect, slowly freed her from the iron shackles fear had forced on her a long time ago. Her heart continued to beat in a steady rhythm, and her breathing evened.

"I'm deeply sorry," her husband whispered, his hands still holding hers, tightly, protectively but not demanding anything. "I know that it might be little comfort to you now for we are all but strangers, but," he nodded, his eyes gazing into hers, "I want you to know that you're not alone. You have a family now, and over time, I can only hope that you'll deem it safe to open your heart to us and allow us to love you the way you deserve."

Touched beyond words, Charlotte stared up at him, wondering what had happened that had suddenly brought them so close. How was it that he always knew what to say?

After all, he was right, they were nothing but strangers. And yet, they were husband and wife as well, and the promise he'd just made her warmed her heart in such an unexpected way that Charlotte found herself stepping forward, closing the distance between them, and placing her head against his shoulder. Leaning into him, she sighed and allowed her eyes a moment of rest.

At first, her husband remained still, probably taken aback by her sudden forwardness. Then he sighed, and his arms came around her slowly, carefully, asking permission.

When she didn't step away, he wrapped her in a warm embrace, resting his chin on the top of her head.

They stood like this for a long moment, and Charlotte felt a soft smile tug at the corners of her mouth. Breathing in his scent, clean and honest, she suddenly realised that she trusted him. Stranger or not, she trusted him.

That realisation hit her so suddenly that her head jerked back. What was she doing? She couldn't trust him! He was-

"Are you all right?" he asked, concern in his blue eyes, as he looked down at her. "Was this ...? I mean, ... I'm sorry. Shouldn't I have-?"

As she stepped back, he immediately dropped his arms, and yet, a pained look came to his eyes that twisted Charlotte's heart. Did he truly care for her? Was she right to trust him?

Taking another step backward, Charlotte was about to turn around when he came toward her, hands raised, signalling that he wasn't a threat. "Listen. Please. Before you go," he began, his eyes imploring, "you need to know that I would never hurt you. I know you have a reason to distrust men, but we're not all the same. Ask anything of me to prove myself to you, and I shall do it."

Holding his gaze, Charlotte frowned. How did he know that she had a reason to distrust men? Had she told him anything? Trying to recall their conversations, Charlotte shook her head. Although he had a way to make her talk and say more than she intended, she was certain that she'd never mentioned ... that night. How could he possibly know?

"If you do not feel comfortable to speak to me," her husband continued, watching her as closely as she watched him, "then speak to my mother or my sister. They are your family now, too." He nodded to her. "Please."

Charlotte swallowed. "I'll think about it."

"Good." A hint of relief played over his features at her answer.

Taking a deep breath, Charlotte took a step back, then turned and walked away, wondering who this man was she called her husband and what he knew about her.

And how?

Chapter Nineteen

HUSBANDS & WIVES

Charlotte spent the day of Victoria's arrival at Hartridge Hall alone.

While the rest of her new family sat together in the parlour, talking and laughing, Charlotte wandered from room to room, gazing out the windows, forcing herself to stay away.

After all, she didn't belong.

Not really.

However, when she happened to venture close and the echo of their shared enjoyment reached her ears, she longed to join them. Finally, life had returned to Hartridge Hall, and the desire Charlotte hadn't been quite able to quench, the desire for a family of her own, grew until it echoed within her chest, reminding her at every turn what awaited her around the corner.

And yet, she feared what they would see if she joined them. For what reason, she could not say, but her new husband had the unsettling ability to peer into her soul and know exactly how she felt and what she thought. Her mother-in-law, too, had proved quite intuitive. What would they see if she spent too much time with them?

And so, fear kept her away.

During supper, she once more observed the strange effect the earl's presence had on his family. Seated around the large table, they mostly kept their heads lowered, merely offering a word of observation here and there, about the food, the cold weather or the coming holidays. Their faces remained almost impassive, reminding Charlotte of her own, of the time she had viewed the world around her through a thick fog.

However, once the earl retired to his study, smiles came to his family's faces. They turned to each other with open eyes and shared more intimate and personal thoughts of themselves.

Fascinated, Charlotte watched their exchange, noting the relief and joy on her husband's as well as her mother-in-law's face when Victoria confirmed that she would stay until the beginning of the new Season and then accompany them to London.

The following days passed in a similar fashion. Torn between her desire for company and her fear of being discovered, Charlotte kept to herself.

When it began to snow two days before Christmas, Charlotte headed toward the back parlour, which offered a magnificent view of the gardens. A jolt of excitement, an echo of her childhood, coursed through her at the thought of a snow-covered world. With a quick step, she pushed open the door...and stopped.

Standing in front of the windows, her back toward her, was Victoria.

"Oh, I'm sorry," Charlotte mumbled. "I didn't mean to intrude." She was about to leave when a suppressed sob from the other woman drew her back. Eyeing Victoria's hunched back and tense shoulders with unease, Charlotte approached. "Are you all right?" she asked, closing the door behind her. Somehow, she knew that Victoria had retreated to the back parlour, hoping that her family would not come upon her there.

Dabbing a handkerchief to her eyes, Victoria took a deep breath, then slowly turned around. "I'm glad it's you," she whispered, her voice heavy with sadness and despair-two emotions Charlotte knew only too well. Her eyes were red-rimmed and swollen, and when Victoria tried to blink back tears, more rolled down her cheeks.

BREE WOLF

"Is there anything I can do for you?" Charlotte asked, slowly stepping around the settee. "Should I fetch your mother or-"

"No!" Victoria shook her head, wiping tears off her cheeks. A hint of anger came to her eyes when still more spilt forth. "This is ridiculous."

"What is?" Charlotte asked, unable to walk away. It was clear that Victoria had retreated here to be alone, and yet, she hadn't gone to her bedchamber. Maybe a part of her knew that she needed something else more than solitude. "Is something wrong?"

Meeting Charlotte's eyes, Victoria drew in a shaky breath, her lip quivering. "I wouldn't ... I ... I can't ... There ..." Then she took another deep breath and shook her head, forcing a smile on her face. "It's nothing. I'm fine."

How often had she said that herself? Charlotte wondered. When people had asked? Even when Kenneth had asked? And how many had believed her? All of them? Except for Kenneth, of course. Had people truly believed her to be all right? Or had they merely thought it none of their business? Or worse, had they simply not cared?

Stepping up to her sister-in-law, Charlotte raised her chin, her eyes soft as they sought the other woman's gaze. "I know what it is like," she whispered, curling her fingers into the fabric of her dress as they began to tremble, "to feel as though one is drowning. Right there, in front of everyone, for all the world to see, and to not have anyone notice."

At her words, Victoria slowly lifted her head, and her eyes narrowed as she gazed at Charlotte, surprise and confusion evident on her face.

Charlotte could not say what exactly convinced her sister-in-law that she was trustworthy. Her words alone? The tone in her voice? The look in her eyes? The mere fact that she had not walked away? It didn't matter.

Hands clasped together, Victoria nodded, a hint of relief in her eyes. "I don't know where to begin," she mumbled, glancing out the window and around the room, anywhere but at Charlotte.

"Anywhere." Walking up to the window, Charlotte gazed at the beautiful garden as powdery snowflakes danced through the air and landed on the lawn, the hedges, bare tree branches as well as ever-greens. It was a stunning sight, and yet, completely at odds with the heavy emotions that hung in the air.

Keeping her gaze focused outside, Charlotte hoped that Victoria would feel comfortable enough to share her pain if she didn't think herself the object of scrutiny.

A desperate chuckle escaped her sister-in-law as she began to pace. "When you hear what it is, you'll think me a fool for being so upset." Her skirts rustled as she marched up and down the Persian rug. "After all, it's nothing. Nothing that thousands of women do not handle every day without breaking down."

"How do you know?" Charlotte asked, keeping her back turned. "Do you not also hide your pain when you go outside? Do you not think it possible that other women would consider you to be one to handle *it* well?"

Stopping in the middle of the room, Victoria drew in a deep breath. "I hadn't thought of it like that. Do you truly believe that to be possible?"

"I do, yes."

Returning to her pacing, Victoria cleared her throat. "I suppose you could be right. However, it is a terrifying thought indeed. All those women, all those lives, it's just ..." Again, she drew in a deep breath as though gathering courage to speak of something she had barely admitted to herself.

Then she stopped in her tracks. "I ... I ... do not care for my husband," she whispered as though the thought alone would bring about his wrath. "I know it is awful to speak like that. He is, after all, my husband, and I owe him respect and loyalty, but I ... I wish I didn't have to return to his house." Instantly, she clasped her hands over her mouth, shocked at the words she had spoken, torn between confiding in another soul and the notion that it would be a betrayal of her vows.

"Your brother told me that your father ... insisted on the marriage," Charlotte said, hoping to ease Victoria into confiding in her. Oh, how much she would love to be able to do the same!

"He did," Victoria said, pacing up and down the room once more. "He is from a suitable family of great fortune. My father ... he ... It was simply a marriage of convenience. Nothing out of the ordinary. Not for any of them. Especially not my father."

"But for you."

"Yes."

"And for your brother," Charlotte added, "because he loves you and places your happiness above worldly gains."

Victoria sighed, and Charlotte knew that she was smiling. "He does. He truly does," she whispered, a hint of awe in her voice. "All my life, he's been true and honest, taking care of me at the expense of his own wishes." She took a deep breath and stepped up to the window, coming to stand next to Charlotte. "And when Father suggested he travel the continent, I could see that he wished to go. I told him I would be fine and I would love nothing more but to hear of his adventures."

"You couldn't have known what your father had in mind," Charlotte counselled, knowing that rational thought had very little effect on guilt and regret.

"I know that. I've told myself so countless times," she confirmed, shaking her head, "but it doesn't help. And neither does it help Sebastian. He blames himself for what happened ... because he wasn't there. Seeing him so tortured, it ... it breaks my heart. I weep for him as much as I weep for myself." Silent tears spilt over and ran down her cheeks. "I don't know what to do. For a little while, I thought that soon I would simply wake up and feel like a wife, that it would take time to settle into a new life, a new position." She shook her head. "I don't believe so any longer. I don't think I'll ever feel as though I belong." A sob suddenly tore from her throat, "There are days that I feel as though I cannot go on like this for it is too painful. I don't know what to do." Burying her face in her hands, Victoria wept.

As the young woman's pain echoed within her own heart, Charlotte drew her into her arms and let her cry, reminded of the simple kindness her own mother-in-law had bestowed on her a few days ago.

When Victoria's sobs quietened, Charlotte drew her to the settee and had her sit down. "Will you tell me of your husband?"

Instantly, Victoria's head snapped up, eyes wide.

"Your mother as well as your brother simply refer to him as *that man*," Charlotte explained. "They call him the devil and a man without honour. What do *you* call him?"

Victoria swallowed, eyes resting on her hands curled up in her lap. "I call him my husband for that is what he is. However, he often reminds me of my father just as I find myself reminded of my mother in the ways I handle being his wife." Sniffling, Victoria dabbed a handkerchief to her eyes and then to her nose. "He does not care for me, nor does he pretend he does." Taking a deep breath, Victoria lifted her eyes and met Charlotte's. "He is only interested in increasing his fortune and lifting his social standing. I suppose that is why he chose to wed the daughter of an earl with a large dowry. To him, I'm an accessory, a trophy, something to be paraded around the room."

Watching her sister-in-law, Charlotte noticed with pleasure that her voice had grown stronger with each word leaving her lips. In the beginning, she'd seemed defeated, but now, it was clear that there was still some fight left in her. If only, she had something to fight for. Short of her husband's death, there was no legal way for her to be free of him.

"What frightens me most is the thought that one day I'll be like my mother," Victoria continued, lips pressed together defiantly as she shook her head. "I assure you I do not mean to belittle her. I know that life has dealt her as harshly as it has dealt me." She took a deep breath. "These past ten years we've been very close, and she's been a real mother to me. However, I also remember the days when she barely saw me, when she walked the halls like a ghost, withdrawn from the world, only living inside her own head, locked in her own misery. The days when I only had my brother. What if I become like her? What if I cannot love my own children?" Her voice broke as new tears streamed down her cheeks.

Covering Victoria's clenched hands with her own, Charlotte sighed. "It is a dark fear indeed. But maybe your mother's example can be your warning, your reminder to help you avoid the same fate."

"I'm not certain I'll be strong enough," Victoria confided, her teeth chattering as fear ran rampant in her body. "Without Sebastian, I would never even have known what it was to love someone and be loved in return. I don't know how he did it. After all, he had no one growing up."

"I think you taught him," Charlotte whispered, remembering her mother-in-law's words.

"Me? But how? I-"

"He took one look at you," Charlotte said, "and he loved you. The same way parents fall in love with their children ... if they haven't closed off their hearts. You saved him the same way that he saved you. You simply loved each other."

A soft smile came to Victoria's face. "I miss him," she whispered, longing ringing in her voice. "He always says that I'm his sunshine, but he is mine as well. In a strange way, his love makes me suffer even more now because I know that it can be different. Because of him, I expect more of the world. I wish for more, and I don't know if I'll ever be able to accept my fate." Lifting her head, Victoria met Charlotte's eyes. "Will my life be a constant struggle?"

Charlotte sighed. "Dreams are beautiful, and sometimes they even come true. At least, for a few people. I suppose that most find themselves thrust into a harsher reality than they ever expected."

Holding her gaze, Victoria nodded, her eyes thoughtful. "You truly understand, do you not?" she whispered as though to herself. "What I speak of is something you've felt yourself. I do not need to explain how I feel for you already know."

Charlotte took a deep breath. "Once I had dreams as well," she admitted, once again feeling compelled to speak truthfully considering the trust Victoria had bestowed on her, "but they were shattered. I lost everything: my family, my ... reputation, my ... my dearest friend ... as well as my life. But none of that even compares to losing oneself. If you cannot be who you are, then all is truly lost."

"You lost yourself?" Victoria asked, her watchful eyes taking in every little detail of Charlotte's face as she spoke of the darkest moments of her life. "Like my mother?"

"Worse," Charlotte admitted, feeling her hands begin to tremble. "I became someone I ... I did things that ..." Inhaling deeply through her nose, Charlotte gritted her teeth together as her emotions threatened to overpower her.

"It's all right," Victoria whispered, gently laying a hand on Charlotte's. "You don't need to tell me. I'm simply grateful that you're here." A sad smile came to her lips. "It feels good to speak to someone who can understand."

"It does," Charlotte agreed, feeling a sudden kinship to her new sister-in-law. Never would she have thought to find herself wanting to love again. And here she was surrounded by a new family she didn't deserve.

"And then you met my brother?" Victoria inquired, her eyes lingering on Charlotte's face.

"I did."

"It wasn't a love match as my mother believes, was it?"

With an apologetic look in her eyes, Charlotte shook her head. "I'm afraid it was not." She could only hope that Victoria would not hold it against her considering that she had begged her brother to find a woman he could love.

"But he cares for you."

Charlotte's eyes narrowed as she met Victoria's knowing gaze.

"He does. I can see it. And you like him as well."

Dropping her gaze, Charlotte took a deep breath.

"But you're afraid," Victoria whispered, obviously sharing her brother's ability to read Charlotte like an open book. "Afraid of what happened and what might happen again."

Closing her eyes, Charlotte nodded. She did like him, didn't she? She'd tried not to, but ... she did. If everyone could see it, it had to be true, didn't it?

"Is it wrong of me to still dream of a man who loves me?" Victoria whispered. When Charlotte opened her eyes, she found her sister-in-law reduced to tears once again. "I know I shouldn't. It isn't right, but ... I cannot help it." She shook her head. "I must be a truly awful person to speak so."

"Not at all. We all deserve love, do we not?" Nodding to Victoria, she wondered if that was even true. Did she, Charlotte, deserve to be loved after all she had done? "Maybe one day your fate will take you somewhere else, to a new life, with a man who loves you."

Did Sebastian love her? Charlotte wondered. Certainly not. But he cared about her. Had Victoria's dream already come true for her?

Chapter Twenty

SET ON THE SAME PATH

After searching half the house and finding neither his wife nor his sister, Sebastian headed down the large staircase in the front hall and caught sight of his father as he headed toward his study. However, as the earl turned into the corridor, he stopped, then stumbled a few steps forward before leaning heavily against the wall.

"It would seem your evil deeds are finally catching up with you," Sebastian said, a large smile on his face, as he walked up to his father.

Spinning around-at least as fast as he could considering his condition-his father glared at him, his breath coming in ragged gasps. "Say what you will, but one day you will be grateful for what I've done for you."

Shaking his head, Sebastian laughed without humour. "*For* me? You must be deluded, dear Father."

"Without my foresight and diligence regarding furthering our family's standing," his father wheezed, right hand clutched to his chest as though that would ease his breathing, "the estate and title would not have the reputation and fortune attached to it that they do now." A coughing fit shook his massive frame, and his head turned dark red.

"Even next generations will profit greatly from this. Whether you like it or not, you will inherit my title as will your son after you."

Savouring the moment, Sebastian took a step closer, eyes trained on his father, a malicious smirk on his face.

In answer, his father's eyes narrowed and the wheezing sound of his laboured breathing increased as he regarded his son with suspicion ... as well as a hint of fear.

Surprised, and yet, delighted, Sebastian leant forward and whispered, "There will be no son, at least not a legitimate one."

"Nonsense!" his father snapped, his fingers curling into the front of his shirt. "Whether your wife is from a suitable family or not does not matter. You're married, and any child born to her will be yours and, therefore, legitimate."

"You're not listening, Father," Sebastian said in a honey-sweet voice that barely managed to veil the underlying malice. "My wife and I agree not to have children." His father's eyes widened, and his face turned ash white. "So, you see. There will be no son, no one to inherit the title. With my death, the title will pass outside the immediate family to some distant relative, and then, dear Father, everything you've done will have been for nothing."

For a long moment, his father simply stood before him, staring at him as though he was a ghost, a spectre, something incorporeal and from a different realm. Then instead of raging and voicing his anger, his father simply turned around and stumbled down the corridor.

Watching his father's receding form, Sebastian smiled when the door closed behind the man, who had never in all honesty cared for him, knowing the turmoil currently raging within his father's heart-if indeed he possessed one.

The smile still playing on his lips, Sebastian turned to walk away, but stopped in his tracks before he had taken more than a single step.

For right there, in front of him, a disappointed look in her luminous eyes, stood his sister. "How could you?" she asked, and the smile slid off Sebastian's face. "How could you intentionally hurt him like this?"

Confused, he stepped forward, meeting his sister's eyes, trying to understand what had upset her. "Why would you ask me this? After everything he's done to you, do you truly feel compassion for him?"

Shaking her head, Victoria lifted her hands and gently placed them on his chest, her clear blue eyes looking up into his. "This is not about Father. It never was." She swallowed, then took a deep breath before continuing. "Sebastian, you know that I love you dearly. You're kind and caring and compassionate, and you know how to love." The blue in her eyes darkened. "But just now, I couldn't see the brother I've always known. What I saw frightened me."

Shocked by her words, and yet, confused about their meaning, Sebastian frowned at her. "I don't understand. I could never forgive him for what he did to you, and I thought that neither could you. Why-?"

"Because this is not about Father," she reminded him. "What I just saw was not the man who cared for me all my life, but a stranger set on the same path as Father."

Sebastian swallowed as the blood in his veins turned to ice.

"All I saw was a man consumed by revenge," she whispered, pain in her voice, "but that is not who you are. You may be his son, but never have I seen even a single spark of his character in you. Never. Why now? Why would you allow Father to alter who you are? Do not give him that power over you, for he does not deserve it." She took a deep breath, and a single tear ran down her cheeks. "Unlike myself, you are married to a kind woman, a woman capable of love. She, too, has suffered hardship, and if you would only look at her more closely instead of setting your sights on destroying our father, then you would see that her heart aches for someone like you." Her hands slid off his chest and grasped his, squeezing them gently. "Don't waste your life, Sebastian. For if you continue down this path, you'll end up like Father, a gentleman of good standing and fortune, but ultimately alone and unloved. Do you truly want this? Is this the future you desire?" As she shook her head, her auburn curls danced on her shoulders. "I do not believe it is, and, therefore, I implore you to think about what you're doing. Not everyone is fortunate enough to have a choice. Do not throw yours away so lightly for I promise the day will come that you'll regret what you've done." After giving his hands another gentle squeeze, Victoria released them, then took a step back. "Think about it, dear Brother, for I love you too much to watch you continue down this path." Then she turned away and left him standing in the hall.

Watching her walk away, Sebastian felt his heart ache as it had the day of his sister's wedding, and he cringed inwardly. For a moment, he closed his eyes, waiting for the pain to subside before he took a deep breath. How could he not have seen it? Was he truly becoming like his father? A man incapable of love? A man who did whatever he wanted with no regard for others?

Lotte.

Conjured by his sister's words, his wife's sad image drifted before his eyes. Yes, she had indeed suffered hardship, and he had used her hopeless position to force her into this marriage. His actions toward her had truly been despicable. How could she ever forgive him?

Gritting his teeth, Sebastian shook his head. No, he would not give up. Victoria was right. Punishing his father would not accomplish anything. And although he could not set his wife free of the vows they had taken, he could be the kind of husband she deserved.

A genuine smile on his face, Sebastian turned his thoughts away from his father and toward his wife.

Chapter Twenty-One

TO PUNISH OR PROTECT

Walking up and down the window front in the drawing room, Sebastian sighed, glancing out at the darkening sky. While the day had started out promising, it now ended with the doctor called to the manor on Christmas Eve.

After a coughing fit, the earl had collapsed and lost consciousness. Taken to his bedchamber, he had been made comfortable, and the doctor had been sent for.

Awaiting the man's verdict, Sebastian strode up and down the large Persian rug, arms linked behind his back, shoulders tense. He did not know what to think or whether the thoughts that occasionally surged to the front of his mind were a bad omen for they all circled around his father's death ... a joyous occasion.

When the door opened, Sebastian spun around, eyes searching for the balding doctor, wondering if he would be able to read the news on the man's face. However, it was not the doctor who entered, but his wife instead.

"Are you all right?" she asked, her hazel eyes searching his face.

Sebastian shrugged, averting his gaze. "I hardly know for I've not yet received any news."

In answer, his wife's eyes narrowed as she approached and studied him with frank curiosity. "What will you do when your father dies?"

"Rejoice." The word slipped out before Sebastian had even contemplated what to say, revealing only too plainly how bitter he was and how much he had allowed his father's behaviour to change his own. Was it too late for him to return to his old self? Was he now doomed to replace the man he so despised?

A hint of disappointment in her beautiful eyes, his wife took a deep breath. "I understand your anger and frustration," she said, "after all, you've got reasons to think of your father as you do. I felt the same way when I-" She broke off and lowered her gaze to the ground as her hands clenched around the handkerchief she was holding. Then she took a deep breath and forced her eyes upward again. "Truly, I do understand, and I know that it is far from easy to step back and allow such an atrocity to go unpunished. However, the man you would have to become to do so would not be you any longer."

His sister's words echoed in his mind, and Sebastian wondered if the two of them had spoken about him.

"It will only lead you to a place that will ultimately destroy you," his wife continued, her gaze holding his as she spoke from the heart, forcing herself to relive memories that quite obviously tortured her to this day. "Instead of punishing your father, you ought to focus your energy on protecting your sister."

Sebastian sighed. "Don't you think I've tried," he snapped, immediately regretting the sharp tone to his voice. "I'm sorry. I know you mean well, but she's married. There's no way of changing that. My father knew what he did when he sent me away. He knew that the only thing I could have done to protect her would have been to prevent the wedding from ever taking place." Gritting his teeth, he drew in a deep breath. "Now, it's too late."

"So, you'll just turn away from her?" his wife asked, her open eyes gazing at him curiously. "You simply give up?"

Staring at her, he swallowed. "What else is there for me to do?"

Holding his gaze, she took a step closer. "Sometimes the hero cannot save the damsel in distress from the dragon," she whispered. "Sometimes the only thing he can do is to be there, to listen and to comfort." She took a deep breath, and he could see that her own heart bled with the emotions she spoke of. "Your sister feels alone in the world, suffering her fate without anyone by her side. No one to confide in. No one to hold her and comfort her. Even knowing that there is someone out there who cares, who will always be there for her, can help."

"But I am," Sebastian objected, knowing in the moment he said it that it wasn't the truth.

"Your energy is focused on destroying your father," his wife reminded him. "You married me to spite him. Do you remember how I thought you wanted me to be your sister's companion?"

Sebastian nodded.

"Maybe that would have been a better idea. I'm sorry I did not insist you reconsider. She's a wonderful woman, and I feel a connection to her. Maybe it would have been good for the both of us."

Sebastian cringed, remembering why he had not even considered that option. It had been for a very selfish reason that now continued to haunt him. He had wanted Lotte for himself. He had acted like his father.

Raking his hands through his hair, Sebastian turned away. He could not look at her face any longer, holding equal part disappointment as well as hope for she had expected more of him and still did, more than he ever had of himself.

"Maybe you could speak to her husband," she suggested, a hint of doubt in her voice nonetheless.

Shaking his head, Sebastian remembered the man's disdainful look in his eyes upon his last visit. He did not care for his sister and never would. Nothing Sebastian could say would ever change that. There was no hope for them. "That man has neither heart nor conscience. It would be a futile attempt." Turning around, he met his wife's eyes. "Please do not believe I wouldn't do anything to help my sister. I simply think ... no, I know that it would do no good."

After holding his gaze for a moment, she nodded. "I never meant to imply that you don't care for your sister for you so obviously do. I simply thought to suggest a different approach. Not all goals can be reached or all problems solved, but generally I find that there is something that can be done."

A wondrous smile came to Sebastian's face as he held her gaze, determination shining in them. "You do not give up, do you?" he whispered, a touch of awe to his voice. "Ever."

Instantly, her gaze dropped from his, and a hint of red crept up her cheeks as she seemed to study the pattern on her handkerchief with rapt attention. "This has nothing to do with me," she whispered, embarrassment in her voice as though she thought his compliment undeserved ... or rather knew it to be. "I simply meant to suggest that you think of another way." Slowly, she lifted her chin, and yet, her eyes didn't quite meet his. "As they say, where there's a will, there's a way. After all, she's your sister. Is there a greater motivation?"

Sebastian took a deep breath as his eyes sought to meet hers, hoping to understand or at least glimpse a hint of the pain that constantly accompanied her words. However, the moment she sensed his inquisitive gaze travelling over her face, she turned away and stepped toward the door.

Unable to let her leave, Sebastian straightened his shoulders and hoped with all his heart that he wasn't about to make an enormous mistake. Then he asked, "What happened to you?"

Instantly, she stopped in her tracks, and her body stilled as though she was frozen in place. Then after a small eternity, she inhaled deeply and turned to face him.

Her warm, hazel eyes shone dark in the dimming light as she met his gaze. He thought to see a deep sense of shame and regret rest in them before she closed them for the barest of moments as though unable to face the world a moment longer. Then she spoke, and her voice sounded weary and defeated ... and it chilled him to the bones. "I died," she whispered, "only my body refuses to let go."

Stunned into speechlessness by her words as well as the utter hopelessness in her eyes, Sebastian stared after his wife as she turned once more and left the room.

Who was this woman he'd married? He wondered yet again, feeling more and more determined to uncover the secret that haunted her to this very day.

A part of him felt guilty for the desire to uncover a secret she clearly wished to keep hidden. And yet, Sebastian felt certain that if he did not, then they would continue to live side by side without ever connecting on a deeper level. Never would she allow him near her or share the pain that lived in her heart, and ultimately, his own would grow tired and abandon all hope.

"Are you all right?"

Sebastian blinked, then shook his head and for a moment simply stared at his sister, who eyed him with a hint of concern in her eyes.

"Are you all right?" she repeated, stepping closer, her watchful eyes gliding over his face.

Sebastian cleared his throat. "Yes, I'm fine. I was simply ..." He shrugged. "How is Father?" he asked, unable to ignore the cold that once more seeped into his heart. How was it that his heart could be filled with compassion and devotion one second and then only experience indifference and apathy the next?

"He is fine," Victoria replied, her eyes betraying her true interest as they held his, a question resting in them. "At least for now. Dr. Waldon said it was imperative that he remain abed and rest. However, he did suggest that ... it might not be enough."

Sebastian nodded, wishing he could make himself care ... if only for his sister's sake for the thought of disappointing her pained him more than the notion of his father's impending death.

"Tell me what's going on." Stepping closer, Victoria reached out for his hand, gently holding it in hers. "I know it's not Father who is on your mind." Again, she eyed him closely. "Is it your wife?"

A soft smile came to Sebastian's lips. "You know me too well, dear sis."

"As well as you know me," Victoria replied, nodding at him in encouragement. "Tell me."

Sebastian sighed. "There isn't much to tell. Every day, I realise more and more that I know very little about the woman I married."

"But that is not what's bothering you, is it?"

"Should it not?"

An indulgent smile on her face, Victoria shook her head. "That's not what I said. I was simply wondering why it should bother you now and did not before."

Sebastian shrugged, "I suppose I didn't think about it before."

His sister chuckled, shaking her head at him as though he was the immature younger brother and she the wiser older sister. "You know as well as I do that it didn't bother you before because you were too busy falling in love with her to ask questions."

Sebastian's mouth opened in protest, but Victoria stepped toward him, shaking her head and silencing any objections he might have conjured. "You know as well as I do that I'm right, dear Brother."

Averting his gaze, Sebastian swallowed. "Maybe," he mumbled, trying to ignore the knowing smile on his sister's face. "But what does ... that ... have to do with her past and what little I know about it?"

Victoria sighed, "You can be quite daft sometimes, Sebastian." Rolling her eyes, she looked at him indulgently. "A first infatuation does not require the kind of closeness that stems from shared memories. But now that you've walked one step farther, you realise that without knowing more about her, there will always be something standing between you, something keeping you apart, and that's what's bothering you."

"How do you know so much about these things, little Sis?" Sebastian couldn't help but wonder before the hopelessness of Victoria's own situation came rushing back.

"It is not from personal experience I assure you," she said, her eyes suddenly clouded as her own thoughts strayed to the man she had been forced to marry. "I may not ever have loved like this myself, but sometimes I see it in others, as I see it in you and your wife. It gives me hope. Not for myself, but it is good to know that such feelings actually do exist even if I don't get to feel them myself." A single tear ran down her cheek, and she quickly brushed it away, clearing her throat. "Be that as it may," she continued, determination in her voice. "This is not about me, dear Brother. So, do not attempt to change the subject." A mischievous smile came to her voice. "Tell me."

"Tell you what?"

Again, she rolled her eyes at him. "I saw her leave, and then I found you ... well ... changed. There is something in your eyes that is different. So, what happened?"

Sebastian shrugged, "I couldn't tell you even ..." He took a deep breath, trying to understand the need he suddenly felt to know his wife. "She said something that ... scared me."

Victoria's eyes widened. "What do you mean?"

Meeting his sister's gaze, Sebastian hesitated. "I'm not certain it is my place to repeat what she said. After all, she rarely speaks about herself and when she does, it's usually in vague terms."

Victoria nodded. "Yes, I've noticed that myself."

"So, you spoke to her?"

For a moment, Victoria dropped her gaze, and Sebastian could see that there was something she didn't want him to know. "A few days ago, she found me in the back parlour, and we ... talked." Lifting her gaze, she met his eyes. "I know what you mean. I don't feel comfortable repeating what she told me either."

"I understand," Sebastian said as the need to know burned in his veins. "But ... did she ...? I mean, can you tell me if ...?"

"She didn't tell me anything specific," Victoria said, compassion ringing in her voice. "Nothing about what happened to her. I wouldn't be surprised if no one knew."

Sebastian nodded, wondering if his wife was truly all alone in the world. Was her family truly gone? Or had she simply left them behind? Or had they abandoned her?

"I wish I knew."

Victoria nodded. "I understand. Maybe one day you will. Maybe one day she will tell you."

Sebastian took a deep breath, wondering if he could wait that long.

Chapter Twenty-Two

MEMORIES

With the earl tied to his bed, Christmas Day was a rather lively occasion, and despite a sense of guilt for thinking so, Charlotte was grateful for the earl's absence and the family's joyous mood.

Laughter echoed through the house as the smell of burning wood mingled with the delicious aromas of a hearty Christmas supper. Fresh greens hung everywhere, in doorways and over windows, and added their own fragrance to the comfortable warmth that hung over the house. Candles glowed brightly, offsetting the warm flames dancing in the hearth, and Charlotte felt herself reminded of home.

Gazing out the window at the rigid landscape trapped in the throes of cold winds and icy rain, a part of Charlotte hoped and feared that if she were to turn around, she would find herself back home, her mother and father sitting by the fire. How often had she played a game of chess with her mother while her father had read to them? It had become a Christmas tradition sometime in the early years of her childhood, and Charlotte had cherished it as one of the few perfect moments of her life.

Now, it brought tears to her eyes.

As soft footsteps echoed to her ears, Charlotte blinked her eyes frantically, dreading the questions a tear-streaked face would inevitably bring forth. However, no one approached her, and she breathed a sigh of relief.

"That was a truly wonderful meal, was it not?" Victoria mused, her voice heavy with contentment. Crossing the room, she sat down at the pianoforte in the corner while her mother took her usual seat by the fire, yet another needlework in her hands.

A soft melody filled the room-one often heard during the holidays-and Charlotte found herself gritting her teeth against the memories it conjured. New tears threatened as her heart twisted in agony, torn apart by longing one moment and ripped to pieces by hopelessness the next.

Holding herself rigid, she willed her shoulders not to tremble with the sobs that threatened to burst from her throat. With her back turned, Charlotte stood before the window, forcing the pain back down and locking it away where no one could find it. Then she wiped away the evidence of its presence and breathed in and out deeply, hoping that her eyes were not red-rimmed and swollen.

When she felt herself sufficiently recovered, Charlotte turned around, a plastered smile on her face. With Victoria's as well as her mother-in-law's attention directed elsewhere, she thought her chances of slipping from the room undiscovered were favourable.

Taking a deep breath, Charlotte stepped forward. "It's been a wonderful day," she said, willing her voice not to shake. "However, I must admit that I'm quite exhausted."

"You're going to bed?" Victoria asked, displeasure ringing in her voice, and her fingers immediately stilled.

Without the music to cover her shaking voice, Charlotte did her best to smile. "I'm afraid I must," she said, stepping toward the door, hoping that the soft echo of her footsteps would drown out the sadness hanging on her words. "I bid you a good night."

Eyes fixed on the arched door frame as though it represented a haven, Charlotte did not hear the footsteps that approached from the other direction. Only when her way was suddenly barred by her husband's tall frame did she look up.

"Retiring already?" he asked, dimples forming on the sides of his mouth as he smiled at her in such a way that the breath caught in her throat.

Taken aback, Charlotte swayed on her feet, her eyes fixed on his, before she took a step backward to maintain her balance. For a split second, she thought that his arms had moved forward, prepared to steady her, before he had thought better of it and they had dropped to his sides once more.

"I'm quite tired," she mumbled, averting her gaze and dabbing a handkerchief at her burning eyes.

Instantly, the smile vanished from her husband's face, and his eyes narrowed. Again, he lifted his hand as though wanting to raise her chin so as better to inspect her face. However, he thought better of it yet again. "Is something wrong?" he whispered instead.

Unable to meet his eyes, Charlotte could still feel them touch her face, following the line of her brows and the soft dip of her nose. They traced the tear that she hadn't even been aware of before it spilt over and ran down her cheek, touching the corner of her mouth.

Swallowing, Charlotte lifted her head and met the deep, penetrating blue of his eyes. "I'm fine," she said, feeling herself tremble as her body suddenly became aware of the minimal distance between them. She could feel his breath on her skin, and the warmth of his body warmed her chilled bones.

"I believe a kiss is in order," Victoria's delighted voice cut through the silence.

Confused, Charlotte turned to look at her and found her sister-in-law pointing at something above their heads.

Mistletoe!

The sudden realisation hit Charlotte before she had even lifted her head, and panic welled in her heart. Meeting her husband's eyes, she felt her own breath quicken as she recognised the desire she saw there.

For a long moment, his gaze held hers before it travelled down to her lips and he drew in a deep breath.

Was this it? Charlotte wondered. Would he break his promise, ultimately blaming a silly tradition for his own lack of virtue?

Could she stop him? She wondered, remembering her sheer helplessness when Lord Northfield had cornered her in the library. Nothing she had done then had made a difference.

But it would now, wouldn't it?

Indeed, it would. Whether her husband liked it or not, she could simply walk away or refuse his kiss, could she not?

As her insecurities bubbled under her skin, stealing her breath and clouding her mind, Charlotte found herself quite unexpectedly wondering what her husband's kiss would feel like. Would it be hard and demanding? Forceful? With no regard for her?

Worrying her lower lip, Charlotte glanced up yet again, her hands clasped together to still their trembling.

With his head slightly bent toward hers, her husband looked down at her, his eyes studying her face. They slid over her quivering lips, down to the tense rigidness of her shoulders and farther on to the strained sinews standing out white in her clasped hands.

"What are you waiting for?" Victoria called, a touch of excitement in her voice.

Chapter Twenty-Three

MOMENT OF TRUTH

At his sister's question, Sebastian swallowed.

Indeed, what *was* he waiting for? If he was honest with himself-and he at least ought to be honest with himself-he had to admit that the thought of kissing his wife appealed to him greatly. Not until this moment when they stood before one another and the possibility of a kiss hung in the air had he realised how much he longed to have a physical relationship with his wife.

And yet, one look into her warm, hazel eyes told him that this was neither the time nor the place.

After all, even a blind man would have noticed the terror that held her rigid. Tense to the point of breaking, she stood before him, eyes slightly widened, unable to meet his, and yet, unable to look away as though he would pounce the second she averted her gaze.

Seeing her fear and understanding her need for reassurance, Sebastian sought her eyes and a gentle smile lifted the corners of his mouth.

For a moment, she seemed to freeze before she exhaled slowly, relief shining in her beautiful eyes.

Then he lifted his head and met his mother's and sister's expectant gazes. "I'm afraid I cannot," he said, and his wife beside him tensed even more. Did she truly fear he would reveal the nature of their agreement to his family?

"Why ever not?" his mother asked, her eyes slightly narrowed as she glanced from him to his wife. "Is something wrong?"

Wishing to put his wife at ease as well as resolve all doubt that something was indeed wrong, Sebastian chuckled, his chest swelling with unexpected pride as he finally found himself able to protect someone he cared for deeply. Even if this was merely a small matter. "Well, if you insist on knowing," he laughed, a touch of mischief in his voice, "the lady and I made a wager."

While his wife looked up at him with a frown on her face, his family seemed eager to demand details. Sebastian, however, quickly interfered, hoping to silence them. "I can see that you're most impatient to know more. However, all I am at liberty to reveal at present is that I lost and am, therefore, in no position to steal a kiss." He glanced at his wife, a confidential smile on his face. "It is the lady's prerogative, and as far as I can tell she is determined to see me suffer."

His heart skipped a beat as a soft smile flashed over his wife's face and she dropped her gaze, a touch of red stealing into her cheeks. Never had they shared such an intimate moment, conversing without words, understanding the other's thoughts without the need to express them.

For all the times when Sebastian had felt at a loss, knowing that there was something hiding in her past that stood between them like a gigantic wall, keeping them apart, he now cherished this moment even more as they stood side by side, and he realised that he wanted more.

He wanted to be her confidant. He wanted her trust. He wanted her to confide in him. He wanted to know, and he wanted her to want him to know.

How he would go about to make this happen Sebastian didn't know. However, this small moment allowed him to believe that it was possible ... if he were patient, if he were considerate above all else.

And he fully intended to be, no matter what it would cost him.

Although disappointed, his mother and sister ultimately gave up when he continued to refuse them the answers they sought.

Seeing the strain on his wife's face, he offered her his arm. "Allow me to escort you upstairs?"

Again, she hesitated as though first needing to gather her courage before she could bear his touch. The thought pained him greatly, and yet, he thought he could understand. For all he didn't know about her, her behaviour spoke volumes about the atrocities of her past.

"Thank you," she finally whispered, hesitantly sliding her hand through the crook of his arm.

Silence fell over them as they slowly made their way up the large staircase and then turned down the corridor toward their bedchambers. Acutely aware of the slight tremble that ran through her body, Sebastian did his best to maintain his distance. However, when he leant forward to open the door to her room, his body touched hers in a more intimate way, and she immediately shrank back, eyes wide.

"I'm sorry," he quickly assured her, cursing himself for his thoughtlessness. "I didn't mean to ... I merely meant to open the door for you." Gesturing to the door at her back, he smiled at her apologetically.

Understanding as well as a touch of embarrassment came to her face, and she nodded. "I'm sorry as well." She swallowed, then met his eyes. "Thank you for what you did, for keeping your word."

"Did you doubt that I would?" he couldn't help but ask, wondering if he truly wanted to know.

Again, she took a deep breath, and for a moment, her eyes became distant. "No, I did not," she mumbled as though realising it just then. "However, there's a part of me that ... lives in constant fear. It's like a reflex. I cannot help it. It always resurfaces at its own will, overpowering everything I think I know."

Surprised at her willingness to share such personal thoughts with him, Sebastian swallowed. "Who hurt you?" The moment the question left his lips, Sebastian knew it to be a mistake, and yet, he had been unable to control himself.

For a moment, her eyes widened in shock before she stepped back and shook her head, a new tremble seizing her body as she sought to retreat from the memories his question had undoubtedly conjured. "This is ... It doesn't matter." Gritting her teeth, she raised her chin and met his eyes. "I'm not yours to protect, remember?" She swallowed, and he thought to see a hint of regret on her face. "Ours is a marriage of convenience. Take care of Victoria."

Swallowing, Sebastian nodded, knowing that he could not force the matter. One day, she would tell him, but he had to be patient. Very patient. And yet, he needed her to know that he would not walk away.

Holding her gaze, he took a careful step toward her, doing his utmost not to appear threatening in any way. "Can I not protect you both?" he asked, savouring the moment as her eyes looked deep into his and her breathing hitched ever so slightly as though temptation had just seized her unexpectedly.

Maybe all was not lost after all.

"Good night," she whispered, then forced her eyes away and retreated to her chamber, closing the door behind her.

"Good night," Sebastian said to the empty corridor, vowing to find a way to protect them both.

Chapter Twenty-Four

A HEART'S DESIRE

Despite a certain awkwardness whenever she would come across her husband, Charlotte had to admit that she enjoyed the following few weeks they spent at Hartridge Hall. While the earl had to keep to his bed, the rest of his family rejoiced in being together under the same roof once more. Although Charlotte could not be certain, she suspected that, at least for the moment, they had all wordlessly agreed to pretend that things had never changed, that Victoria had never gotten married and moved away.

The days were filled with laughter and music, with excursions into the gardens despite the icy weather with games of chess and good books read in front of the fire. Occasionally, one of them would be touched by a bit of melancholy, but usually it was quickly chased away by a firm determination to enjoy what little time they had together.

Then the new Season came, and with it a return to London ... and reality.

Since the earl was still too sick to be moved and cared very little for the company of his kin, the remainder of his family soon found itself bundled-up warmly in a carriage on their way back to Town.

"I'm certain this Season will be just lovely," the countess exclaimed with forced joviality, eyes gazing out the window as London came in sight. "Just lovely."

Glancing around the carriage, Charlotte noticed that comparatively few words were spoken as each sat lost in their own thoughts. As much as they had tried to will away reality, it had finally caught up with them. Charlotte couldn't help but wonder what waited her in Town.

Terrified by the thought of destitution, Charlotte had never once stopped to contemplate what it would mean for her to marry a man of the ton. Naturally, such a decision led her back to the upper society who believed her dead. The thought of stumbling upon her parents in some ballroom choked the air from her lungs, and her eyes misted with unshed tears.

"I always loved the beginning of the Season," Victoria mumbled, eyes fixed on her hands folded in her lap. "Now, it is very different." She sighed and glanced at her family. "Choosing new gowns and accessories for ball after ball as the excitement built with each dance, it was a truly wonderful time. Carefree and full of promise." A single tear ran down her cheek. "I had such hopes. Now, that is all gone."

"Oh, my dear," her mother exclaimed, pulling her into her arms. "You can still dance and mingle and enjoy yourself. Nothing can ever take that away. We are a family, and we will always be here for you, for the laughter as well as the tears."

As mother and daughter clung to each other, Charlotte glanced at her husband, who sat beside her with a stony face, guilt edged into the strong line of his jaw. "Victoria will stay with us, won't she?" Charlotte asked, knowing the answer full well but feeling the need to speak.

Her husband drew in a long breath. "I'm afraid not."

"Do you have fond memories of London?"

Again, he sighed before he glanced at her, the ghost of a smile on his face. "Like Victoria said, London used to be a wonderful place. Only now, all that is in the past, and everything that once held a joyous memory now only serves to remind us of what will never be again, of what we lost." He cleared his throat, his brows drawn down in anger. "Of what my father stole from us."

For a long moment, silence returned to the carriage before her husband once more cleared his throat, the look on his face apologetic.

"I'm sorry to have spoken so," he said, casting a gentle smile in her direction. "I cannot deny that this is a hard time for all of us, but maybe it is unwise to dwell only on the darker side of life." He took a deep breath, willing the clouds away. "What about you? Do you have any fond memories of London?"

Understanding exactly how the family felt, Charlotte, too, felt drawn to the pain and misery she now associated with this city. However, as their overwhelming weight began to settle on her shoulders once again, she lifted her head and took a deep breath, forcing her thoughts in a different direction. "We would always cross Westminster Bridge on our way into London," she began. "When I was little, my mother would hand me a coin, and I would hurl it as far as I could toward the Thames." To her surprise, a slight chuckle rose from her throat at the memory. "If it hit the water, my mother would encourage me to make a wish, urging me not to reveal my heart's desire to anyone for then it couldn't come true."

A smile on his face, her husband gazed at her. "And did it come true?"

"Sometimes. Depending on the wish I'd made."

"And what did you wish for?"

Meeting his eyes, Charlotte smiled. "But my lord, were you not listening? If I were to reveal my heart's desire to you, it couldn't possibly come true."

"Your heart's desire," he repeated in hush tones, gazing down into her eyes. As he shifted in his seat, his shoulder brushed against hers for the barest of moments.

A jolt went through Charlotte, and yet, the panic that usually seized her in such situations failed to appear. Had it been too innocent a touch for it to serve as a reminder of what she had suffered? Or could it possibly be an indication that her soul was beginning to heal?

Whatever the answer, Charlotte couldn't help but smile, seeing an equally delighted expression on her husband's face when she didn't shrink back from him.

After delivering Victoria to her husband's townhouse, they continued, their spirits even more subdued than before. The remainder of the day was spent in a quiet fashion, each one of them tending to their own thoughts as the servants carried trunk after trunk into the house, readying everything for the season ahead.

Standing by the window of her bedchamber, Charlotte gazed down at the busy street, its sounds and smells more familiar than anything she'd experienced in the last year. Again, she felt certain that if she were to turn around, she would find herself back home in her old room in her parents' townhouse.

When a knock sounded on the door, Charlotte took a deep breath and turned around. "Enter."

Surprised to see her husband walk toward her, Charlotte swallowed, then lifted her chin.

"Do you have everything that you need?" he asked, his eyes searching her face as though trying to reclaim the moment of intimacy they'd shared in the carriage.

"I do. Yes. Thank you."

Standing before her, he simply looked down into her eyes, seemingly at a loss for words, and although Charlotte could not bring herself to object to his presence in her chamber, the silence that stretched between them began to grow heavy. "If you don't mind my saying, my lord," she began, turning away and reclaiming her spot by the window, "I believe it would not be such a good idea for me to attend social events."

"It would not?" he asked, a touch of humour in his voice.

Charlotte drew in a deep breath as her fears hammered in her chest. "If I did, people would immediately know that I'm not one of them and treat me accordingly. I admit I'd rather not see their pity and disapproval." Glancing over her shoulder, Charlotte wondered if he believed her. "Do you not think you punished your father sufficiently simply by marrying me? Or do you truly intend to ruin his reputation-as well as your own-further by parading me around upper society?" Once more turning her back to him, Charlotte held her breath, hoping that he would release her from the agreement they'd made.

For a moment, he remained quiet, and she almost thought he'd slipped from the room unnoticed. Then, however, the soft footfall of his steps carried him closer until he came to stand behind her.

Goose bumps rose on Charlotte's skin, and her breath caught in her throat as she felt his presence with every fibre of her body. As the silence stretched on, Charlotte could barely keep herself from turning around. Yet, she feared to meet his eyes and see his heart's desire plainly and unveiled.

"For as long as I've known you," he spoke into her ear, his breath tickling her skin, "I've never seen you behave any differently than the well-brought up lady that you are."

At his words, the blood froze in Charlotte's veins, and before she could stop herself, her head snapped up and she spun around, her eyes searching his. "What did you say?"

As his penetrating gaze held hers, a gentle smile curved up his lips. "You have the manners and graces of someone belonging to upper society. I suppose I would have realised it sooner," he explained, "had I not been so determined to marry a woman of inferior standing in to spite my father. It was a foolish plan. I realise that now; yet, I cannot regret what happened."

Charlotte swallowed. He knew! Her mind screamed. How much did he know? Did he know who she was? But how would he have-?

"How did you come to be in the woods near Farnworth Manor?" he asked, all humour gone from his voice.

Inhaling deeply, Charlotte felt her tense muscles begin to tremble with the sudden desire to share her story. Her whole story. A part of her felt as though she would burst if she remained silent even a moment longer. And yet, her fears stole her voice, and so she merely shook her head, taking a step back until her back came to rest against the cool pane of the window.

Disappointment darkened his eyes, and he sighed. "Do you fear me?" he suddenly asked, his eyes narrowing slightly as though the thought had taken him off guard.

"I fear your questions," Charlotte heard herself say, feeling a small weight lifted off her shoulders at the truthfulness of her answer.

"I see." Nodding, he took a step closer, and Charlotte's eyes widened. "Do not fear, my lady," he assured her, the tone in his voice sincere as he held her gaze. "I shall not betray your secret for it will only betray my own."

Charlotte frowned. "Yours, my lord?"

A soft smile came to his face, and his gaze travelled over her lips before meeting her eyes once more. "I shall always honour my promise," he whispered, leaning closer. "However, this is no longer a marriage of convenience for me."

Feeling the intensity of his gaze, Charlotte felt a jolt go through her, sending shivers up and down her body.

Her husband had to have noticed the effect his words had on her for a gentle smile curled up the corners of his mouth and he lifted his hand to her face. "May I?"

With her hands clasped together so tightly that her fingernails dug painfully into her skin, Charlotte stared at him as the desire she saw in his eyes took her back to a time she'd rather forget. Panic seized her, and yet, there was a quiet, little voice somewhere in the back of her mind that reminded her that she could trust him.

Torn, Charlotte was momentarily tempted to grant her permission and find out what the touch of his hand would feel like on her skin. However, the quiet, little voice was instantly drowned out by the overpowering volume of her conditioned fears screaming in her ears.

Feeling the need to step back, but unable to do so, Charlotte pressed her back even tighter against the window behind her. Then she swallowed, praying that he would not prove false, and shook her head. "You may not."

At her words, his hand slowly fell back to his side, and an understanding smile came to his lips. "Did I pass your test?" he asked, gentle humour in his voice.

"My test?" Charlotte mumbled to herself, realising for the first time that he might understand her better than she had thought.

"Test me as much as you like, my lady," he whispered confidently, "but do not forget to test your own heart as well, or one day you might refuse me out of habit alone." Then he nodded his head at her, turned on his heel and quit the room.

Staring at the closed door, Charlotte felt her knees grow weak as his words echoed within her mind. With her breath coming in gasps, she sank into the armchair to her side, hoping that he was truly a man of his word for their heart's desires seemed to be guiding them into very dangerous terrain.

Chapter Twenty-Five

LORD TINSWELL'S BALL

As he waited in the front parlour while his wife was upstairs putting the finishing touches on her appearance, Sebastian began to pace the length of the room, wondering if he was making a mistake.

Constantly torn between allowing his wife to set the pace in their relationship to put her at ease and the fear that she would retreat from him altogether should he give her the opportunity to do so, Sebastian had insisted that she accompany him to a ball.

Any ball.

At least once.

From her reaction, he felt certain that she feared to be discovered. By now, he had no doubt that she'd once belonged to upper society and suspected that her refusal to mingle with the ton stemmed from the dreaded notion of having her identity revealed.

What he wasn't so clear on-besides the question why she would need to hide her identity in the first place-was whether she feared *him* to find out or society in general.

Maybe both.

Although his wife had tried her best to dissuade him from this idea, she had ultimately relented, choosing Lord Tinswell's ball for them to attend that weekend.

Judging from the past few years, it would be a large ball with at least half of society in attendance since Lord Tinswell's opulent town-house allowed for a vast crowd. Four years ago, Sebastian had not even glimpsed his childhood friend Leopold Lancaster, Marquess of Elmridge, at said event, only to find out days later that they had indeed both been there.

Was that why she had chosen Lord Tinswell's ball? To hide in the crowd?

As soft footsteps echoed to his ears, Sebastian stepped out into the entrance hall. The moment his eyes fell on his wife as she elegantly descended the large staircase, his heart skipped a beat and he was certain that his mouth stood open for more than a second.

However, his reaction had nothing to do with the gown she had chosen and everything with the woman who wore it.

Dressed in a simple colour, plain and inconspicuous, his wife did seem to blend into her surroundings. The way her hair curled around her head, here and there partially hiding her face, seemed to prove his suspicions right. On closer look, Sebastian even noticed that her hair seemed to be of a slightly darker shade than before.

His wife had truly done everything within her power to alter her appearance.

And yet, the look in her eyes was one of impending doom, and Sebastian cringed as guilt seeped into his heart.

Was he making a mistake? He asked himself for the millionth time that night.

Ignoring his doubts, Sebastian straightened and smiled at his wife. "You look radiant, my lady," he said, holding out his hand to her.

"Thank you," she whispered as her eyes shifted to his offered hand. Then she took a deep breath and slid her own into his.

Escorting her into the carriage, Sebastian did his best to assure her of a wonderful evening ahead. However, the expression on his wife's face proved that he was less than successful. If only he knew why she feared discovery! However, without knowing her real identity, his hands were tied.

When the carriage finally reached Lord Tinswell's townhouse and they climbed the stairs to the front doors, Sebastian noticed her hand tightening on his arm.

Again, he was torn. Did her reaction speak rather of fear or trust?

Shaking his head, Sebastian didn't dare contemplate an answer as he led his wife through the throng of people, some of which looked at them-particularly his wife-with a curious eye. From his mother, Sebastian knew that his wife was one of the major topics of gossip these days. Apparently, his initial plan of ruining his father was working quite well.

Too well. Seeing the tortured expression on his wife's face as she kept her head slightly lowered and turned toward him, away from the people gawking at her, Sebastian had to admit yes, this had indeed been a mistake!

After escorting his wife toward the large window front, which opened the ballroom to the starry night, Sebastian strode toward the refreshment table. Across the room, he glimpsed the new Lord Elmridge, Leopold's younger brother, who had inherited the title after Sebastian's childhood friend had died not two years ago-presumably poisoned. However, nothing had ever been proved.

"I see you've finally brought your wife," Lord Tinswell slurred from behind him.

Reluctantly, Sebastian turned around. "Tinswell," he greeted the man, annoyance clear in his voice. "Already too deep in the cups, I see."

Lord Tinswell laughed as though Sebastian had just told the most marvellous joke. "Why would you hide her from society?" he sneered as his eyes travelled across the room and locked onto Sebastian's wife. "Despite her reputation, she clearly possesses pleasing qualities."

As the earl started to laugh, Sebastian felt the desperate desire to punch him in the face. However, that, too, would have drawn unwanted attention, and so he swallowed his pride, ignored Tinswell and strode across the room to save his wife from the gossiping ladies slowly pooling around her.

With her back almost pressed to the window, his wife stood, head lowered, trying her best to evade the growing circle of ladies asking her all sorts of inappropriate questions.

When she caught his eye for a split second, Sebastian thought to see immense relief, and he immediately quickened his steps. "Excuse me, my ladies," he said, breaking through the circle. "I understand your desire to become more acquainted with my lovely wife; however, at present, I am most unwilling to share her."

Under a mumble of objections, Sebastian guided his wife to the other side of the ballroom, revelling in the feeling of her holding him close-even if it were for the wrong reasons. "Maybe this wasn't the best idea," he admitted, handing her a glass, then taking a sip from his own. "I apologise for allowing my desire to dance with you to interfere with my better judgement."

As she swallowed the sip she had taken, her eyes snapped up to look at his face. "Dance?" she croaked, then cleared her throat.

"Dance," he confirmed, smiling at her. "Has it never occurred to you that my insistence on attending a ball merely stemmed from the desire to hold you in my arms?"

Yet again, a sense of panic filled her lovely eyes, and she took a deep breath. "I admit it did not," she whispered, not quite meeting his gaze. However, for a fleeting moment, the ghost of a smile danced across her face, and Sebastian felt his heart dance in his chest.

Clearing his throat, he set down his glass and held out his hand to her. "May I have this dance, my lady?" he asked, finding himself beyond nervous as he waited for her answer.

Lifting her eyes, she studied his face, contradicting emotions playing over her own.

"Of course, you are free to refuse," he assured her, sensing her doubts. "After all, you have no reason to believe me an accomplished dancer," he said, humour in his voice. "Maybe it would be wise to refuse me."

Again, the ghost of a smile came to her lips, and a moment later she set down her glass and met his eyes. Then she took a deep breath and accepted his arm. "We shall see," she replied, then glanced at him, a touch of mischief in her eyes. "At least this way I am safe from those circling vultures."

Noticing the hint of humour to her words, Sebastian turned to her, feigned shock widening his eyes. "My lady, are you in all honesty saying that it is not your heart's desire to stand up with me? Am I merely a means to an end?"

The smile that came to her lips lingered for a moment longer than the one before, and Sebastian felt a shiver run over him at the fragile connection quietly growing between them. "One does not exclude the other, or does it, my lord?" she replied, and her gaze held his with such unexpected boldness that it knocked the air from Sebastian's lungs.

Almost gasping for breath, he forced his shoulders back and took his place across from her as they stood up for a country dance. Then the music began to play, and they glided around the room as though a puppeteer was guiding their movements.

With very little attention for his surroundings, Sebastian noticed all the small changes in his wife's posture and expression. When the dance led them apart, their eyes held the connection as though they formed an invisible lifeline without which they would drift apart, never to return. As the steps brought them back together and his hand touched hers, he could feel a slight shiver run down her arm, and she immediately averted her eyes. Never had he noticed his wife react to his presence, his touch with such open and utterly direct pleasure.

If his eyes weren't deceiving him, then she was as affected by him as he was by her.

Maybe attending Lord Tinswell's ball hadn't been such an enormous mistake after all!

Maybe it was merely the beginning of something he had been dreaming about for the past few weeks.

When the dance ended, Sebastian offered her his arm and then proceeded to lead her off the dance floor. However, as he managed to wrench his eyes from her for a split second, he spotted the circling vultures over her shoulder, already drawing near once more.

Hesitating for only a moment, Sebastian drew her back onto the dance floor as the first notes of a waltz began to play.

For a moment, she looked confused, a touch of doubt and apprehension in her eyes that send an icy chill down Sebastian's back.

"The vultures have returned," he whispered, once more offering her his hand, knowing only too well that he welcomed every excuse to touch her. "The choice is yours, my lady, as always."

Her eyes shifted from his hand to his face, a quizzical expression on her own, before she glanced over his shoulder and understanding came to her eyes. Taking a deep breath, she turned to him and hesitantly took his offered hand.

With his pulse hammering in his veins, Sebastian pulled her closer. Gazing down into her face, he found her head lowered once more and cursed the change in situation that had ruined the magical moment they had shared before.

Sliding his hand to the small of her back, he felt her draw in a sharp breath as her body tensed.

This was too much too soon, and Sebastian knew it, knew how devastating such forced contact could be for the fragile connection that was only just beginning to bloom.

Determined, he stepped back. "Maybe you'd rather go for a walk," he suggested, unable to keep the disappointment he felt from showing in his voice.

Lifting her head, his wife looked up at him, eyes slightly narrowed, and studied his face.

For the life of him, Sebastian couldn't have explained what happened in that moment. However, something she glimpsed in his eyes must have reassured her because a soft smile came to her face, and she took a step toward him. "No, I'd rather dance," she whispered. "If you don't mind."

Unable to hide the delighted grin that came to his face, Sebastian nodded. "Not at all. Quite on the contrary." Then he gently pulled her into his arms once more, and although he felt her tense, her eyes held his, and the smile on her face only grew deeper.

As they began to sweep around the large room, he felt his wife relax. Her strained muscles grew slack, and her breathing evened. "You're an accomplished dancer."

"As are you, my lord," she replied, a curl to her lips. "After your comment, I half-expected you to step on my feet."

Sebastian chuckled, "I promise I shall do my utmost not to injure you." As she laughed, Sebastian took a deep breath, and the humour in his voice was replaced by sincerity. "I apologise for being so blunt, but I feel compelled to tell you that ... that I very much enjoy dancing with you." He swallowed as her face sobered. "I enjoy holding you in my arms, feeling your body against mine."

Although he had expected it, the fear that suddenly returned to her eyes felt like a punch to his stomach. "It frightens you, does it not?"

Taking a deep breath, his wife nodded, her head lowered slightly, her eyes no longer meeting his.

"Why?"

Closing her eyes, she shook her head, then unexpectedly looked up. "It has nothing to do with you, my lord," she whispered, her eyes pleading with him to believe her. "You've proved yourself a gentleman time and time again."

Sebastian swallowed, arguing with himself whether to ask the next question. "I gather you once knew a man who did not prove himself a gentleman, did you not?"

From one second to the next, her body tensed and grew rigid. Her jaw clenched, and she once more closed her eyes as a shiver ran over her.

Gritting his teeth at the sight of her misery, Sebastian lowered his head to her ear and whispered, "Tell me his name, and I shall call him out."

At his words, her head snapped up, and she stared at him as though he'd just slapped her. Then she swallowed, and her eyes drifted from his to something past his shoulder.

Sebastian was just about to say something, press her for details, when she froze.

As though rooted to the spot, she stood in the middle of the dance floor, staring over his shoulder. Her face had grown pale, and a cold spread through her body that he felt even through the layers of fabric separating them.

"Are you all right?" he asked, eyes searching her face. As his heart hammered in his chest, he tightened his hold on her, trying to force her out of the paralysis that had befallen her, until an awful thought found its way to the front of his mind. "Is he here?"

Chapter Twenty-Six
A VICTIM NO LONGER

The moment she saw him, time stopped.

Staring over her husband's shoulder, his hands holding her so tightly that a little voice in the back of her mind urged her to object, Charlotte once more found herself drawn back to the past.

There had been a ball, too, that night.

And he had been there, just returned from the war, downing one drink after the other to escape the memories that haunted him.

The memory of Kenneth's death.

Then, she hadn't been able to feel compassion, to pity him for the turmoil he'd lived through. Then, her heart had been numb, unfeeling, unable to see that his pain had been as real as her own.

Seeking him out, she had spoken to him that night, unwilling to end her misery without knowing how Kenneth had died, without knowing his final moments.

Only then something had changed.

Seeing the guilt on his face, a new thought had claimed her heart, filling the wasteland it had become with a new purpose.

A life for a life.

That thought had echoed in her mind, urging her on, preventing her from seeing the truth.

The poison she'd managed to procure for herself, the poison she'd intended to use on herself that night, had somehow found its way into *his* glass.

To this day, Charlotte couldn't quite remember how it had happened. She couldn't remember her hand slipping into her reticule to retrieve it. She couldn't remember pouring it into a glass and ordering a waiter to offer it to him. She couldn't remember any of it, and yet, she knew it to be true.

And then something had gone horribly wrong.

For it hadn't been Frederick who'd downed the glass with the poison, but his brother Leopold instead. A man who'd had a wife and a little daughter.

He had died that night in his wife's arms.

And Charlotte had lost all hold on reality.

Driven by vengeance, she had gone after Frederick again and again, almost killing his new wife and unborn child in the process. Until he had stopped her and sent her to Winham Institute.

And now, he was here.

And so was his wife.

With her arm linked through his, the marchioness stood by her husband's side, a gentle smile on her scarred face as she gazed up at him. In answer, his lips curled up as well, and he leant over to whisper something in her ear.

Lost in each other, they didn't notice her, didn't see the enemy that had once sought to destroy them.

Frederick.

His name echoed in Charlotte's mind, and her heart twisted and turned in agony as the memories of her atrocities returned.

He had committed her to Winham Institute-in agreement with her family-because he believed her to be a danger to him, to his family, to society in general.

He hadn't been wrong.

And yet, Charlotte knew that she would have deserved far worse, and a part of her had hoped that she would be allowed to pay the ultimate price. For only then, could she ever have considered her debt repaid.

Instead, she was now married to a man whom her heart was starting to care for ... deeply, welcomed into a new family and currently enjoying a night dancing with her husband.

None of this was right.

None of this was what she deserved.

"Are you all right?"

Startled, Charlotte blinked, and a single tear ran down her cheek.

Stepping back, her husband lowered his head, looking into her eyes, his own narrowed in concern. "Are you all right?" he repeated. "Who did you see? Was it-?"

"No one." Shaking her head, Charlotte once more glanced over his shoulder at the happy couple whose life she'd almost destroyed. "No one."

Her husband took a deep breath. "Please be honest with me. I promise there is nothing to fear. I will protect you."

Slowly, her eyes shifted back to his, and she saw the sincerity of his words plainly visible on his face. He truly cared for her, did he not?

Yes. She was certain of it now. He would stand by her and see her safe, and all he asked for in return was honesty.

Honesty.

Charlotte's head swam as the reality of her situation suddenly stood before her, plain and simple: he knew nothing about her, nothing of whom she truly was, and if he did, he would turn from her without a look back.

And she deserved nothing less.

"Would you mind if we returned home?" she asked, trying to find a way through the chaos in her head. "I'm not feeling too well." Keeping her head down, she avoided his questioning eyes.

After a while, he nodded. "All right." Then he escorted her out of the ballroom, down the steps and into their carriage.

The entire drive home, Charlotte sat in her seat, eyes fixed on something she couldn't name while her mind replayed the moment she had caught sight of Frederick and his wife.

Frederick, her old friend. How had it come to this?

Back at their townhouse, Charlotte allowed her husband to guide her up the stairs as her mind was still elsewhere. She barely noticed the touch of his hand or the frown that drew down his brows as he watched her carefully, waiting for an explanation or possibly a breakdown. Who knew what he thought of her in that moment?

Outside the door to her bedchamber, Charlotte turned to him, forcing her attention to remain in the here and now...at least for a moment. "I'm sorry we had to leave early. I truly did enjoy myself. Thank you." She smiled at him then, realising quite unexpectedly that for once she was not lying. "Good night." Then she turned around and stepped over the threshold into her room, closing the door behind her.

Instantly, the here and now vanished, and her mind was once more drawn to a time and place that meant nothing but shame and regret, pain and torture. Yet, she couldn't stay away because deep down she knew she deserved it. No one could escape her past, especially a past like hers. She understood that now, finally accepting that the life she had falsely acquired was nothing but a dream. After all, she had no right to be happy. She had lost that right a long time ago.

Her head began to pound. However, before she realised that it hadn't been her head after all, but a rather insistent knock on the door, said door flew open and her husband strode in, his face tense and rather determined as he came toward her. "I apologise for invading your privacy," he said, regret in his voice as well as an urgency that betrayed his unrest better than the slight tremble in his hands, "however, I insist that you tell me what happened tonight. Whom did you see?"

As her heart hammered in her chest for more than a single reason alone, Charlotte stared at him, understanding his desire to know the truth, and yet, knowing with absolute certainty that the truth he thought he wanted to know was not the one she could give. "I saw no one," she replied, forcing herself to hold his gaze. "I was merely overwhelmed by such a large crowd. Never in my life have I-"

"Nonsense!" her husband snapped. "You were not overwhelmed. You were terrified. For a moment, I feared you would drop dead on me." Gritting his teeth, he stepped toward her, the pulse in his neck beating at an erratic pace. "Tell me what happened. I think I deserve to know."

Taking a deep breath, Charlotte nodded. "You're right. You do deserve to know; yet, you do not deserve the burden of knowing. I'm sorry for everything I've done to your life. I should never have agreed to marry you. I should have known better, and yet, a part of me truly wanted to." A soft smile came to her lips as she looked at him, his face aghast with surprise. "I didn't realise it then, but from the moment we met, I recognised you as a good man, a man I could trust, a man I could even come to ..." Swallowing, she bit her lower lip, knowing that revealing how she felt would only make matters worse. "None of this matters right now. What I did was wrong, and I promise I shall do whatever I can to give you back your life without further harm coming to your family."

His eyes narrowed as he studied her face, trying to understand. "What are you saying?"

"I am not who I claimed to be," she said, feeling a heavy weight lifted off her shoulders for the small truth she allowed herself to reveal. "I think you already know that; do you not?"

Inhaling deeply, he nodded. "I suspected, yes. Then who are you?"

Charlotte shook her head. "That is for me alone to know."

Again, his eyes narrowed and his jaw tensed. "I think I deserve to know who my wife is," he growled out, his arms trembling with the effort it took him to remain calm.

"I am not your wife."

"What?" His eyes widened as he stared at her.

"Since the name I gave you is not mine," she began, her heart twisting in agony at the pain that slowly took over his face, "we are not truly married." She took a deep breath. "When you first came to me with your proposal, I spent all night lying awake, thinking about what to do. I was torn for I knew I could never truly be your wife."

"The condition?"

Charlotte nodded. "I wanted you to understand that we would never truly be husband and wife, that I would never give you a child, an heir. I needed you to understand." For a moment, she held his gaze as the memory of their conversation returned to him. "You agreed, and so I didn't think it important that we would not be truly married. If you knew who I was, you'd understand why I care very little for my reputation. And since there would be no children who might eventually be found out to be bastards, I didn't care."

His eyes returned from the past and focused on her. "Then tell me who you are."

"I can't." Shaking her head, she took a step back. "What matters is that you're free. If you want me to leave tonight, I will."

"Leave?" His eyes widened.

"Otherwise, I'll do my best to make arrangements quickly and leave within a week or two. Explain my disappearance any way you like. Have me declared dead," an image of her parents flitted before her eyes, "or reveal me to be an impostor and our marriage void. Do as you wish. I would never hold it against you." Turning to step around him, Charlotte suddenly found her way blocked as he came toward her, forcing her back until she stood pressed against the wall.

As her heart hammered in her chest, old fears returned. "What are you doing?" she gasped as he leant forward trapping her between his body and the wall, his hands resting beside her head, keeping her from slipping away.

Although his eyes burned with anger, his voice was gentle as he spoke. "You have nothing to fear. I gave you my word, and I shall never break it." He swallowed, his eyes holding hers, and she could see the deep emotions that rested within him. "But I won't let you leave."

"But-"

"Never!" His voice sounded like a growl. Then he leant closer until his cheek was almost pressed to hers, but not quite, and whispered in her ear, "Tell me your name."

"No."

"Tell me!"

"Why?" Confused, Charlotte wished she could see his eyes. However, she didn't dare move, afraid of what would happen should she touch him.

"So that I can marry you again," he whispered, his breath tickling her ear. "For real this time and forever."

Stunned, Charlotte lifted her hands and hesitantly placed them on his chest, pushing him back. She needed to see his eyes! "Why? This is madness! Even if, the condition I presented you with that day would always stand between us. You cannot want this!"

"I want you," he whispered, his eyes travelling over her face, and a soft smile came to his lips. "I thought you knew."

"But why?" Charlotte demanded, terrified as the words he whispered echoed within her own heart. "You know nothing about me."

A slow smile curled up his mouth. "I may not know your true name, but I know more about you than you think." He took a deep breath and met her eyes. "Despite all the secrets you keep-for whatever reason-you're an honest person. You despise lying. Every time you open your mouth, knowing that you cannot speak the truth, you cringe. I've watched you. I know it to be true."

Staring at him, Charlotte felt herself tremble as he dragged her actions before her eyes.

"You are gentle and caring, sweet and compassionate. Although she barely knows you, my sister confided in you, did she not?"

Swallowing, Charlotte nodded. "But that is of no importance. It is always easier to confide in someone whom you cannot hurt with the words you speak."

"That may be true," he agreed, "but it doesn't change the fact that she chose you. Only you." He inhaled deeply, and the expression in his eyes grew serious. "There is something in your past that brought you to your knees."

At his words, Charlotte flinched, and she saw her own pain reflected in his eyes.

"Something that stole every bit of self-esteem that you had," he continued, the pain he felt over her suffering clear in his voice. "Something that crippled you; yet, you found the strength to rise again."

As tears streamed down her face, blurring her vision, Charlotte wanted nothing more but to lean against him and let go of all the pain and be free of it. But she knew it to be wrong for he thought her a victim.

She had been. Once.

But she wasn't any longer.

Her hands balled into fists, and she raised her chin, willing her lips to stop quivering. "You know nothing of what you speak!" she cried. "You don't know what I did!"

"Then tell me," he urged. "Tell me and free yourself of this burden."

Though tempted, Charlotte shook her head. "I crossed a line," she whispered, understanding only too well the pain she'd caused others for it had been hers as well, "and there's no going back."

As he looked down at her, tears misted in his eyes and he swallowed. "So, you'll simply walk away."

"I have to."

His lips pressed into a thin line. "I will not let you."

"It's not your choice."

Swallowing, he nodded, then hung his head as though the burden had suddenly become too much to bear. "All right, I'll make a deal with you." Lifting his head, he met her eyes. "I will let you leave," he took a deep breath and exhaled slowly, "if you tell me the truth. Everything."

Charlotte's eyes opened wide. "I can't. I ..."

"This is it," he pressed before she could say anything more. "My only offer. Think it through, but don't for a second believe that I'll let you slip away unnoticed." Gritting his teeth, he stepped back. "I vowed to protect you, and whether it is legally binding is of no importance to me. I cannot simply let you walk out of my life."

As he shook his head, determination shone in his eyes, and Charlotte knew that there was nothing she could do to dissuade him from the decision he'd made. In that moment, he reminded her of Kenneth. She would have to find another way.

For in her heart, she'd vowed to protect him as well.

And the only way to do so would be to leave.

Chapter Twenty-Seven

A NEW SECRET

T he next few days passed in awkward silence. Although Charlotte could plainly see her husband's desire to speak to her, he kept his distance, giving her time to think about his offer.

And yet, there was nothing to think about.

She couldn't tell him.

And he couldn't know.

There had to be another way.

After three days without a brilliant thought of how to solve her dilemma, Charlotte felt the almost desperate need to escape her husband's watchful eyes for at least a few hours. Knowing that he would never allow her out of the house alone for fear she would not return, there was only one choice.

Dressed in a warm coat, Charlotte headed toward the front doors just as the carriage she had ordered arrived outside.

However, even before the footmen could allow her through, her husband appeared as though he had been hiding behind the large curtains. "Where are you going?" he demanded, his voice vibrating with fear and longing as his eyes studied her face almost lovingly.

"To see Victoria." Meeting his gaze, Charlotte couldn't help but cherish the moment he looked at her with such intensity that she would have preferred to stay with him instead of stepping out into the cold. "Am I permitted to go?" she asked, a touch of humour in her voice.

In answer, his lips curled up into a smile. "Of course." As she stepped back and turned to the door, he added, "Hurry back."

Ignoring the tantalising shiver that ran down her back, Charlotte fled the house ... or rather her husband's presence. Although she was not yet ready to admit to herself how much she longed to be near him, she could not hide from the fact that the mere sight of him warmed her body inside and out.

Something truly strange was happening to her.

Maybe she had caught the flu.

Arriving at Victoria's townhouse, Charlotte was still deep in thought and barely heard the butler's mumbled words as he led her into the front drawing room. As he stepped out to alert the lady of the house to her guest's presence, Charlotte sat down on the settee ...

... only to rise again a moment later.

Despite all the sleepless nights of the past few days, energy coursed through her body, making it almost impossible for her to sit still. Unable to direct her own fate, Charlotte sighed in frustration as all her thoughts continued to reveal that there was very little she could do.

The only option was for her to leave. Her husband, however, continued to interfere with her plans. His determination to keep her by his side brought a smile to her face instead of a scowl.

"Oh, it is so wonderful to see you," Victoria exclaimed as she strode into the room, her large steps carrying her across the Persian rug in no time before she threw her arms around her guest with a desperate fierceness that surprised Charlotte. "I know we haven't known each other for long," she mumbled, still holding on, "but I must admit I missed you terribly."

Confused, Charlotte closed her arms around her sister-in-law, then gently stroked her back as Victoria continued to hug her with such desperate need as though she were drowning and Charlotte the only lifeline in sight. "Are you all right?" Charlotte mumbled into her hair. "Has something happened?"

After taking a deep breath, Victoria reluctantly drew back her arms and straightened, the expression on her face tense as the corners of her mouth curved up into a grotesque impression of a smile. "Of course, I am. I simply missed you." Turning away, she kept her back to Charlotte for a long moment before settling on the settee. "Please, take a seat."

Sitting down across from her sister-in-law, Charlotte watched her closely, knowing in her heart that something was terribly wrong. "I was surprised not to see you at Lord Tinswell's ball," she said, hoping her words would elicit a reaction. "Your mother said you weren't feeling well. I hope it was nothing serious."

Eyes fixed on the folded hands in her lap, Victoria took a deep breath. Then her lower lip began to quiver before she gritted her teeth together, momentarily closing her eyes, forcing back the emotions that were so evident on her face.

A moment later, she met Charlotte's gaze, and the forced smile returned to her face. "It was nothing. Merely a headache. I suppose being back in Town is more stressful than I thought."

"I, too, find it overwhelming," Charlotte said, hoping the ring of truth in her words would encourage Victoria to confide in her. "I know very few people here, and even the ones I do know, I am not on speaking terms with. I feel very alone in this big city."

"I know what you mean," Victoria mumbled, and the mask on her face slowly evaporated, revealing the misery she felt in her heart.

Sighing deeply, she opened her mouth, only to close it again, uncertain of what to say or where to begin. Tears came to her eyes, but she blinked them away, her mind and heart still at war about how to proceed and whether to trust in another person.

For a long moment, they sat in silence. While Victoria averted her eyes, Charlotte's were almost forcefully drawn to the young woman's face. However, when her sister-in-law shifted on the settee, Charlotte's gaze dipped lower and came to rest on Victoria's right hand as it lay carefully, even protectively, draped over her belly.

It was such a small, ordinary gesture that it took Charlotte a moment to realise its significance.

Taking a deep breath, Charlotte willed her own hammering heart to calm down. "You're with child; are you not?" she whispered as tears rose to her eyes.

Instantly, Victoria's head snapped up, eyes wide with shock, and yet, it was quickly replaced by a deep sense of relief. Her breath came quickly as though she had been denied oxygen for too long and now relished in its life-sustaining presence. "How do you know?" she whispered. "Not even Mother saw it." Glancing around, she leant forward. "No one knows."

"Not even your husband?" Charlotte asked, forcing herself to focus on Victoria as an old pain returned with such force that she never would have expected it.

Victoria shook her head vehemently. "I can't. I ... I ..." She swallowed, arms wrapped around herself as though cold. "I don't want him to know, not yet. I can't ... I ... I hope he won't read it on my face."

"I doubt it," Charlotte said as her eyes became distant, and her own hand involuntarily travelled to her empty belly. "Few people see the truth that is right in front of them. Only those who can relate know what to look for, know the signs."

Taking a deep breath, she raised her eyes and found Victoria looking at her, a quizzical expression on her face. "Do you have a child?" her sister-in-law whispered, shock evident in her voice.

Swallowing, Charlotte shook her head. "No, but I was with child once," she admitted as another burden left her shoulders with the small truth that spilt forth. "A child that I loved and hated at the same time."

Tears filled Victoria's eyes as she held her gaze, then nodded, a new sense of desperation coming to her beautiful eyes. "I don't know what to do. I think I'm a horrible person for feeling so; yet, I cannot help it."

"You're not a horrible person," Charlotte assured her as tears of her own spilt over and ran down her cheeks. "Life is not always black and white. Yes, a mother is supposed to love her child, but sometimes it isn't that simple."

"But how can I not?" Victoria sobbed. "I've always wanted children. I just ..."

"You don't want his."

Meeting her eyes, Victoria nodded her head. "He's my husband, and yet, the thought of baring his child ... it terrifies me."

"It terrified me, too," Charlotte whispered, remembering how love and hate had warred over her heart whenever she had thought of her child.

Shortly after Kenneth had persuaded her to agree to his proposal, she had discovered that she was with child. Northfield's child. A man who continued to haunt her dreams. A man whose mere presence made her feel sick to her stomach. A man whose face she would one day see in the child in her arms.

Children reflected their parents; did they not? How often had she heard proud mothers exclaim, 'He looks just like his father'? Or 'He gets his tenacity from his father'?

Could one despise a man but love his child? Could one ever truly forget how that child had come to be? Was there ever a moment when that knowledge would cease to matter?

Despite Charlotte's best efforts, Northfield's face rose before her inner eye in that moment. She saw the sneer that curled up his lips, the disdain in his eyes as he'd looked at her, and a cold shiver ran down her back as though he was right there in the room with them.

"What happened?" Victoria asked, compassion in her eyes as she looked at Charlotte. "What happened with your child?"

"One morning, I woke up and it was gone," she whispered, wondering if it had all truly happened or had merely been a dream. A nightmare.

Victoria sighed, hands clasped together. Then she glanced at her belly. "How did you feel then?"

Charlotte swallowed, then met her eyes. "It didn't help. I was as torn then as I was before. I felt incredible sadness as well as unadulterated relief." She took a deep breath. "But more than anything, I felt guilty for feeling either."

Nodding, Victoria closed her eyes. "I'm sorry," she whispered, then met Charlotte's gaze. "I'm truly sorry."

"Me, too."

Nothing they'd said would change what was. Facts were facts. And the fact was that Victoria was expecting her husband's child. A man she despised. And yet, facts weren't all there was to life.

Knowing that she wasn't alone in her feelings, knowing that others experienced the same regret and shame, the same confusion and uncertainty was utterly liberating. Charlotte could see it on Victoria's face and feel it in her own heart, and she couldn't help but wonder what would have happened if she'd been able to share her own feelings back then with someone who would have understood.

She could not change what was, but she could help Victoria not to lose herself in this turmoil of right and wrong, of knowing and feeling. Maybe, just maybe, Victoria could come to love her child and see him as a separate person from the man who had fathered him.

Rising from their seats, the two women took a step toward each other, forever connected through their shared experience, when the door opened and footsteps echoed on the parquet.

As Victoria quickly wiped the tears off her face, Charlotte turned to the door, disappointment filling her heart at having this intimate moment interrupted.

A man strode in. A man who failed to greet them. A man who crossed the room in long strides and poured himself a drink, his back turned to them. "I insist that you accompany me to the theatre tonight," he ordered, his voice hard. "After all, you're my wife, and we have certain societal obligations. What you choose to do with the rest of your time is of no interest to me, but I will not have you sully my good name." He turned on his heel and met his wife's eyes, his own hard as steel. "Am I understood?"

In that moment Victoria's husband noticed they weren't alone in the room, Charlotte felt as though she would faint.

For right there, only a few steps away, stood the man who had ruined her life.

Lord Northfield.

Victoria's husband.

Chapter Twenty-Eight
A NIGHT AT THE THEATRE

Like a ghost who had risen from the earth below, Baron Northfield stood before her, shock evident in his eyes as they stared into hers. "You're dead," he mumbled, and the drink slid from his hand, the glass bursting into a million pieces, its explosion almost deafening in the life-shattering silence that had hung over the room a moment earlier.

As though nothing had happened, as though no time had passed, Charlotte felt herself respond to his presence with the same repulsion and disgust as the last time she had laid eyes on him.

Instantly, the memories of that night returned with such force that her knees began to tremble and the breath caught in her throat. Terror seized her, and her stomach threatened to expel its contents.

"How is this possible?" he mumbled, eyes fixed on her face, completely unaware of the confusion resting in his wife's eyes as she glanced back and forth between them. "You're dead. They said you were dead. Thrown off a horse." Taking a step toward her, his boots scrunched on the glass shards littering the floor.

The sound pierced Charlotte's ears, shaking her awake. Seeing him advance on her once again, instinct took over, sending her from the room as fast as her feet would take her.

Blindly, Charlotte fled down the corridor and crossed the front hall, eyes fixed on the door that was her means of escape. As the footmen saw her coming, their eyes widened in surprise, they could barely pull open the doors in time to let her pass.

Almost tripping on the hem of her dress, Charlotte sailed down the few steps to the pavement, her legs unwilling to slow down, and continued down the street. Dimly, she heard someone call her name.

The coachman, yes.

Deep down, Charlotte knew she ought to return home. After all, she had nothing with her but the clothes on her back and nowhere to go. And yet, she could not bring herself to stop.

For if she stopped, the reality of the situation would bring her to her knees.

No, she couldn't stop. She needed to keep going.

Climbing the large staircase to the upper floor of Covent Garden, Sebastian glanced around at the crowd pouring in through the doors, and he couldn't help but wish that his wife was among them. A night at the theatre might just be what they needed!

As his eyes swept over people he'd known most of his life as well as those he'd rather not meet again, let alone speak to, Sebastian reminded himself that it was probably for the best that his wife had gone to call upon his sister that afternoon.

Her insistence on leaving his life, on leaving him, had shaken him to his core, and in that very moment, he had realised that he loved her.

It was as simple as that.

He loved her.

Finally realising that, he felt liberated; yet, the threat that loomed over his happiness occasionally choked the air from his lungs.

Now, she was with Victoria, he reminded himself, and maybe, just maybe, his sister would find the right words to convince his wife to stay. Not that she knew of the looming threat on the horizon, but ...

Shaking his head, Sebastian sighed. Had life always been this complicated? While he knew that his wife was not who she claimed to be, the rest of his family did not. And yet, his wife and sister had shared ... something with each other. Almost from the beginning, there had been a silent understanding between them as though they'd recognised one another as kindred souls. Therefore, it wasn't all that far-fetched to assume that his sister knew more than he thought. Maybe she knew more than even he did.

He had to speak to her!

Turning on his heel, Sebastian hurried back toward the large staircase, knowing that even the most engaging play would not be able to distract him sufficiently as he'd hoped to achieve in coming here.

"Huntly!" a voice called over the buzzing excitement of the crowd moving toward their seats, and Sebastian stopped in his tracks.

Craning his neck, he felt a small stab of pain pierce his heart as he glimpsed the Marquess of Elmridge and his wife moving toward him. Would he ever be able to look at his friend's younger brother and not feel Leopold's loss as acutely as the day he'd learnt of his death?

"It is good to see you," Frederick Lancaster greeted him, one hand gently clasped over his wife's as it rested on his arm. She had been a beautiful woman once until a fire had tainted her beauty with ugly scars, and yet, the happiness and love that radiated from her eyes whenever she smiled up at her husband made her shine. "I heard you'd travelled to the continent."

Sebastian sighed, knowing only too well that the mention of the continent meant nothing more but the memory of war to Frederick. "I did," he admitted, trying to think of something to say that would steer their conversation into a different direction. "And I've heard that you have a son now."

A beaming smile came to Frederick's face. "Yes, he's almost one year old now and the most wonderful little boy you can imagine."

Chuckling slightly, the marchioness looked at her husband, then turned to Sebastian. "Well, Leo *will* be one year old ... in a few months."

"Leo?" Sebastian asked as his heart twisted with the memory of his friend.

His face sober again, Frederick nodded. "Yes, we named him after my brother." He took a deep breath then, his own sadness just as evident as Sebastian's.

Gently squeezing her husband's arm, the marchioness looked up at him, and a soft smile came to her face.

Watching them, Sebastian could see the comfort Frederick drew from his wife and the closeness that existed between them. Words were unnecessary. A single look was enough for her to know exactly how he felt just as he understood without a doubt that he wasn't alone, that there was someone right beside him ... and always would be.

Sebastian could only hope that he and his wife would one day be that close.

Swallowing, he decided to acknowledge rather than ignore the loss of Leopold Lancaster, his childhood friend. "Allow me to renew my condolences," he said, his voice barely a whisper. "Sometimes I still cannot believe that he is gone."

Frederick nodded. "I know how you feel. Some days, I still expect him to walk through the door or rescue Mathilda from the crown of yet another tall-standing tree." A wistful smile curled up the corners of his mouth, and yet, his eyes held utter sadness.

"How are Maryann and Mathilda?" Sebastian asked, remembering that both Lancaster brothers had found true love in life.

"It was hard for them for a long time," Frederick said, "and sometimes it still is. But I think they're beginning to do better. In fact, Maryann and my mother are here with us today. However, they wished to avoid lingering out here in the crowd and proceeded to our box."

"I'm glad to hear it. I-"

"Sebastian!"

Frowning, Sebastian turned toward his sister's voice, her face tense and rather pale, as she came toward him on her husband's arm.

Something was very wrong. He was certain of it.

"Please excuse me," he apologised to Frederick and his wife, who graciously nodded their heads and then proceeded to join Maryann and the dowager marchioness in their box.

"Victoria, what are you doing here? I thought ..." Stopping in his tracks, Sebastian finally noticed the strange sneer plastered on Northfield's face as the baron studied Sebastian with rather unexpected curiosity. Turning to the man, he drew himself up tall. "Is something wrong?"

Northfield laughed, an evil tone to his voice. "Nothing at all," he replied, his eyes still regarding Sebastian as though he were an oddity sprung from the earth. "I merely wish to congratulate you on acquiring a *wife*. To my great regret, I didn't have the opportunity of *making her acquaintance* until today." Again, his lips curled up into a sneer. "I must say she is quite a surprise. Do tell, where did you meet?"

Eyeing his brother-in-law with apprehension and no small amount of suspicion, Sebastian could tell that Northfield was fishing for information. Who was this man? And how did he know his wife? From what he said, it was utterly clear that he did. "Through a mutual acquaintance," Sebastian said, doing his utmost to remain vague. "If you would excuse us, I need to speak with my sister in private."

Taken aback, Northfield's eyes narrowed. "She's my wife," he declared, a rather possessive tone to his voice.

"And my sister," Sebastian insisted, holding the baron's challenging gaze.

"Fine," Northfield relented after a while. "I shall be in our box."

As he disappeared in the crowd, Victoria breathed a sigh of relief. "I'm so glad to see you here. Something utterly strange happened today, and I'm truly worried about Lotte."

At his sister's words, Sebastian's breath caught in his throat, and it took him a moment to speak. "What are you talking about? She told me she intended to call on you. Did you not see her?"

Victoria nodded, wringing her hands nervously as the pulse in her throat hammered the way he'd never seen it. "She did come, and we … talked." Her eyes dropped to the ground for a second, and Sebastian knew that they'd shared something with each other he wasn't privy to. "But then …" She shook her head, at a loss for words.

"What happened?" Sebastian pressed, regretting the harshness of his tone. "Where is she?"

"I don't know," his sister replied, and the blood froze in his veins. "She didn't come home?"

Sebastian shook his head. "When did she leave?"

"About three hours ago," Victoria said, her eyes round with fear. "She stormed out when ..."

"When what?" Sebastian snapped, grabbing her by the arms. "When what?"

Victoria swallowed, then met his eyes. "When my husband walked in," she whispered, tears coming to her eyes. "I don't know what happened, but when they saw each other, it was as though they were both seeing a ghost. I heard him mumble 'You're dead.' as he stared at her the same way she stared at him." She swallowed, wiping away her tears. "They knew each other. Somehow, they knew each other, and now she's gone and ... Oh, Sebastian, how do you think they know each other? Where could she be? She looked so terrified. For as long as I live, I shall never forget the look in her eyes."

As stars began to dance before his eyes, Sebastian forced himself not to submit to the blinding panic that seized him, squeezing the air from his lungs. "I don't know," he whispered, trying to remain calm ... if only for his sister's sake. "Go to your husband before he ..."

Gritting his teeth, Sebastian met his sister's eyes and realised that she, too, was in desperate need of rescuing. He would have to find a way to free her from this marriage, and he would. However, tonight, he needed to go before his wife vanished from his life for good. "I'll find her," he whispered, planting a gentle kiss on his sister's forehead. "And then I'll come for you."

A soft smile came to Victoria's lips as she nodded, tears standing in her eyes. "I'm not yours to protect, but she is."

A memory echoed in his mind, and Sebastian leant forward, eyes determined as he nodded. "I shall protect you both."

Chapter Twenty-Nine

IN ANOTHER REALM

After returning to his townhouse and assuring himself that his wife had not returned in his absence, Sebastian was at a loss. Where was he to look for her in a city as large as London? Was she even still in the city, or had she already made it out?

That thought scared him more than anything he'd ever known.

"Did she ever mention anything to you about her family?" Sebastian asked his mother as he paced up and down the length of her bedchamber. Lying in bed with a cold, the countess shook her head. "A name? A place? Anything?"

"I'm sorry, Dear," his mother said, her eyes darting from side to side as she tried to remember something that might aid him in his search. "We spoke of them once, but she never mentioned anything about where she was from or where she'd lived before you met her at Farnworth Manor. Apparently, she and her mother had a falling-out, and she wouldn't even write to her about her marriage."

Her mother? Sebastian stopped in his tracks as his wife's voice echoed in his mind.

We would always cross Westminster Bridge on our way into London. When I was little, my mother would hand me a coin, and I would hurl it as far as I could toward the Thames. If it hit the water, my mother would encourage me to make a wish, urging me not to reveal my heart's desire to anyone for then it couldn't come true.

"She grew up here in London," Sebastian whispered to himself, trying to straighten his thoughts. "At least during the Season."

"How do you know?" his mother asked.

However, Sebastian barely heard her. "Westminster Bridge," he mumbled before his head snapped up, and he strode to the door.

"Where are you going?" his mother called after him before a coughing fit silenced her.

Rushing down the stairs, Sebastian went out back through the servant's entrance and headed to the stables, not bothering to call for a stable boy. After all, time was more of the essence than it ever had been!

In the dim light, Sebastian raced through the streets of London as fast as he dared, afraid that he would be too late, that she'd already left or … worse.

When Westminster Bridge finally came in sight, his heart stopped as his eyes searched the stony arch across the Thames, which glistened in the moonlight overhead. Dark shadows loomed everywhere, and he found himself reminded of the River Styx where departed souls were ferried into the land of the dead.

Glancing down into the dark water, he truly felt as though he were standing on the threshold to another realm. Had his wife been here? The thought of her body being dragged down into that cold, dark abyss chilled his bones and froze his heart.

Like a madman, he raced down the side of the bridge, eyes glancing left and right, hoping against hope that she was still here, standing at the railing, looking down into the water, instead of …

When he finally caught sight of her, Sebastian stumbled onward, believing himself deceived.

He blinked again and again until he could be certain of what he was seeing.

Without a coat to shield her from the cold night air, his wife stood by the railing, her hands gently draped on the rough stone. The wind tore at her hair, swirling it around her head, and her skirts billowed around her legs. Her shoulders were tense as she fought the shivers that shook her, and her eyes were wide, staring, unblinking as she gazed down into the water.

Afraid that he would scare her, that she would feel threatened and jump, Sebastian approached slowly, setting one foot before the other quietly, forcing himself not to rush her. His muscles trembled with the tension he forced on them, and it seemed like a small eternity passed before he reached her side.

As though frozen in place, she remained where she was, not acknowledging his presence in any way.

Sebastian swallowed, uncertain how to proceed, and so for a moment, he simply remained beside her as she continued to tremble, her breathing fast and unrelenting.

"How did you find me?"

Blinking, Sebastian stared at her as though she had just risen from the earth. Then he swallowed, relieved that she recognised him. "I remembered what you told me about your mother," he said, taking a careful step closer, "about throwing a coin in the water and making a wish."

A fleeting smile came to her lips at the pleasant memory of times long gone. "I don't even know how I got here," she said, her eyes still staring down into the cold wet. "What am I doing here?"

"I don't know," Sebastian whispered, shrugging off his coat. "But I can see that you're cold; please take my coat." When she didn't reply, he stepped closer, careful not to touch her, and placed his coat over her shoulders.

"Thank you," she whispered, her voice distant as though her mind was elsewhere.

Watching her, Sebastian was at a loss. Somehow, she seemed different from the woman he knew.

Although she had never hidden her fears and insecurities, she had always seemed so incredibly strong to him as though nothing could harm her. And yet, he knew that someone had. Who was Northfield? And how did he know her? How did she know him? Was he the man who ...?

Sebastian took a deep breath, uncertain how to address the woman before him. A woman who seemed to have lost touch with the here and now. For although she stood before him, even spoke to him, there was something in her eyes that made him think that only a small part of her was even aware of his presence.

"What happened tonight?" he asked. Although his wife had always refused to share details of her past with him, maybe the woman before him would be less adamant. Maybe she would tell him. "What happened at my sister's house?"

"She was so sad," his wife whispered, "like I once was."

Again, his heart twisted at the thought of his sister's misery. "Sad about what?"

"About the baby."

"The-? What?" Staring at her, Sebastian felt the world around him begin to spin. "My sister doesn't ... have ... a ... baby," he mumbled as his thoughts raced and finally, finally understood what his wife was saying. "She's with child? Victoria is with child? Are you certain? Why would she be sad about being with child? My sister loves children."

His wife sighed. "Because it's also his child."

As understanding dawned, Sebastian took a deep breath. Then he stepped forward and carefully placed his hand on her arm. To his surprise, she didn't shrink back. She didn't even flinch. It was almost as though she couldn't feel him. "Allow me to take you home."

Again, she didn't reply, but when he gently urged her away from the railing, she began to walk without resistance.

Sebastian retrieved his gelding, which luckily hadn't run off, and after lifting her into the saddle, he walked the horse through the deserted streets of London. Although he longed to hold her in his arms, he didn't dare ride behind her for fear his touch would send her into a panic. At least for now, until he had her back home, the current state she was in was preferable.

Leaving the horse with a stable boy, Sebastian escorted his wife upstairs into her bedchamber.

Since she did not move of her own volition, he stepped into the room behind her, expecting her to object.

Only she didn't, and his concern for her grew.

Something was terribly wrong. What would he do if she didn't return to him? If she chose to stay in the place her mind had retreated to to feel safe? To shut out the pain and fear?

Helping her out of her shoes and his coat, he urged her to lie down and wrapped the thick blanket tightly around her. Then he drew up a chair and sat down beside her, unsure what else to do.

For a long time, they sat in silence as his wife stared into the darkened room, and he stared at her.

Torn between wanting to stay and the nagging suspicion that it was his presence that kept her awake, Sebastian rose from the chair.

However, the second he stood, her arm shot out from under the covers, and her cold hand grabbed his wrist. "Don't leave me," she whispered, her eyes still as distant as before.

Momentarily shocked, Sebastian froze before an unexpected warmth flooded his heart and a soft smile came to his lips. "If you want me to, I'll stay." Sitting back down, he rearranged the blanket that had slipped from her shoulders.

As he moved, her hand tightened around his wrist as though she feared he would disappear into thin air.

"Sleep," he whispered, and his hand gently closed over hers. "I promise I'll stay. I won't go."

After a moment, she took a deep breath before her eyes finally closed, and she fell asleep.

Chapter Thirty

REVELATIONS

Charlotte spent the night wrapped in a warm cocoon. Only when her mind slowly retreated from deep slumber did the events of the previous night slink back into her consciousness. Slowly, ever so slowly, she remembered the moment she had found herself face to face with the ghost of her past. She remembered the shock in his eyes. She remembered the sound of his glass shattering on the floor, the sound of his boots as he had started toward her. And she remembered the moment instinct had taken over, sending her out the door and urging her legs onward until exhaustion had finally slowed them down.

At first, fear had gripped her heart, bringing with it its companions of the past. Her body had ached with the onslaught of these emotions, and more than once she'd thought they'd bring her to her knees.

But somehow, she had kept going, and eventually, step by step, everything had fallen away until there had been no more fear, or pain, or terror, no more shame or revulsion.

A familiar, old nothing had claimed her, dulling her senses and shielding her heart from the harsh world around her, keeping her safe in a place she had visited before.

Months ago, only the imminent threat to her life had brought her back.

The fire at Winham Institute.

The fire that had ultimately led her here. To Westminster Bridge.

And then Sebastian had found her.

Through the dense fog, his presence had reached her mind, and she had heard him. She had heard his voice and sensed his concern even though her own emotions had still been muted.

And she had allowed him to take her home.

Had it been a mistake? She wondered as she carefully cracked open an eye and found him sleeping in a chair beside her bed, his head resting on his crossed arms, his hand still holding hers.

Her fingers began to tingle as she felt the warmth of his skin against hers.

Somewhere in the back of her mind, Charlotte remembered that she had been cold-so very cold-until a small fire had been lit near her. A fire that had warmed her limbs and chased away the darkness clawing at her heart.

Sebastian.

Lost in her thoughts, Charlotte almost flinched when a soft knock sounded on the door to her room. Holding her breath, she waited and then quickly closed her eyes when her husband began to stir.

Robbed of her sight, Charlotte heard his breathing grow deeper before he pushed himself up and yawned.

Again, a soft knock sounded on the door.

Clearing his throat, her husband called, "Enter."

Charlotte heard the door slide open.

"Victoria," her husband exclaimed, surprise in his voice, before he stood, his hand still holding hers. Then he shifted and carefully laid her hand back down on the mattress, squeezing it gently before letting go.

Regret filled Charlotte at the sudden loss of his warmth, and in that small, rather insignificant moment, she realised that she loved him.

"How is she?" Victoria whispered, her soft footsteps barely audible on the carpet.

"I don't know," her husband said, tension in his voice. "She hasn't woken up yet."

"Where did you find her?"

He sighed, "On Westminster Bridge."

Victoria drew in a sharp breath. "Are you saying she wanted to … to jump?"

"I don't know. I hope not. I don't think so. I …" Taking a deep breath, her husband began to pace the floor. "I found her standing there, staring down into the water, but I'm not entirely certain she even saw it."

"What do you mean?"

"When I spoke to her, she barely realised I was there," he said, frustration in his voice. "I think whatever happened shocked her out of the here and now. She seemed so distant, so unfeeling as though the pain had become too much and her heart had simply blocked it out for fear it would not be able to bear the burden and break."

"Did she say anything?" Victoria asked. "Do you know what happened that scared her so?"

"No, nothing." Again, her husband sighed deeply, then took a few steps. "Did your husband say anything to you?"

Carefully opening her eyes a little bit, Charlotte saw Victoria shake her head, her eyes full of sadness. "He did not. Only he kept looking at me as though all this was truly amusing to him. He asked me about Lotte, where she was from, how you met." Lips pressed into a tight line, Victoria looked at her brother. "It was as though he enjoyed her misery."

As the muscles in his jaw convulsed, a dark growl rose from her husband's throat.

"Do you know how they know each other?" Victoria asked. "You never told us much about her. Do you know anything about her family, about where she is from?"

Sebastian shook his head. "Very little. I have a few suspicions, but so far that's all there is." He took a deep breath. "What happened yesterday when she came to you?"

Averting her eyes, Victoria took a deep breath. "We … talked and-"

"About what?"

Swallowing, Victoria opened her mouth. "Well, we ..."

"About the baby?" A soft smile on his face, Sebastian looked at his sister, whose eyes had gone wide. "Please, don't feel as though you cannot talk to me."

"She told you about the baby?" Victoria stammered as a slight blush came to her cheeks.

"I don't think she meant to," her husband assured her. "When I found her on the bridge, she was ... not herself."

Unable to look at her brother, Victoria averted her eyes and gazed down at her folded hands resting gently on her belly.

"Please, don't hide from me," Sebastian pleaded, gently lifting her chin. "I'm glad you spoke to Lotte. You should not go through this alone."

"I didn't tell her," Victoria whispered. "She knew. She simply knew."

A frown drew down Sebastian's brows. "She did? How?" He glanced at his sister's flat belly.

Victoria shook her head. "No, it's too early for that." She took a deep breath, and a hint of relief shone in her eyes. "She said she knew because she knew what to look for. She knew the signs as only someone can who's been through the same experience."

"The same experience?" her husband mumbled, staring at his sister before his gaze shifted to the bed.

Quickly, Charlotte closed her eyes as her heart hammered in her chest. She had revealed Victoria's secret, and now, Victoria was revealing hers.

"What are you talking about?" her husband demanded.

"Oh!" Victoria exclaimed, shock in her voice. "You mean, she didn't ... You don't know?"

"Don't know what?" His breathing quickened as he spoke. "Are you saying she has a child?"

"No! She-" Breaking off, Victoria brushed past her brother. "I'm sorry. I shouldn't have said anything. It is not my place. Please don't ask me anything."

Walking up to his sister, Sebastian took a deep breath. "How can I not? I'm married to a woman I know nothing about. Yes, I know that I knew this from the very beginning, but I didn't expect to fall-"

"In love with her?" Victoria asked, a smile in her voice as she spoke. "I don't think she did, either; I don't think she is keeping this from you to hurt you. I don't know what happened in her past, but I believe it must be truly awful. She understands exactly how I feel, and she couldn't if she'd never ..."

Sebastian took a deep breath, and although Charlotte couldn't see his face, she understood the pain he felt as well as the confusion. Did he truly love her? The thought made her heart skip a beat, and yet, it also conjured moments of pain and degradation. Would she ever be free to love without fear? Did she deserve to?

Occasionally, Charlotte would find herself almost forgetting the atrocities she had committed. After all, she had found a new life, and the previous day notwithstanding, she had come to love it, love the people in it, secretly harbouring hopes for a future she remembered from a long time ago ... when she had been young and had still dared to dream.

And then she would remember.

She would remember that she wasn't simply a victim, that she hadn't been for a long time. And she would remind herself that although she had gone unpunished by society's laws, this just might be the punishment she deserved.

To have love and happiness within her grasp, and yet, so far away that no matter how many miles she travelled she would never be able to reach them.

And still it was there, right before her eyes, reminding her of what she had done.

Every day.

For the rest of her life.

Chapter Thirty-One

OUT OF CONVENIENCE

After Victoria had left, Sebastian returned to his wife's side. Watching her, he couldn't help but picture her with a baby in her arms and wondered for the thousandth time what had happened to her. From Victoria's reaction, he felt certain that she didn't have a child at present. But had she had one once? Had it died? Had she miscarried?

Who had been the child's father?

Only someone who's been through the same experience, his sister had said. What did that mean?

After all, his sister was married, and to the best of his knowledge-although admittedly it wasn't extensive his wife had never been married ... but betrothed.

Had she despised her betrothed like Victoria despised her husband? Had she, too, been sad to find herself with child because of who the child's father was? Because of the memories that would forever be attached to that young life?

Carefully, Sebastian reached out, his hand reaching for hers, still lying on the mattress where he had set it down when Victoria had come in. The warmth of her skin had kept him awake for the greater part of the night as he had cherished the feel of her, so unexpected, so rare. He had watched her sleep: her chest rise and fall with each calm breath. Every now and then, he had gently squeezed her hand, wanting ... needing to make his presence known to her, and to his utter delight, the ghost of a smile had flashed over her face.

At first, he hadn't been certain that his eyes had not deceived him ... until he had tried again, craving her first, honest response to his touch.

As his fingers brushed against her skin, he felt a jolt go through her, and her eyelids twitched.

Shocked-and rather ashamed-at first, Sebastian stopped, his eyes narrowing as he watched her face. Then he took a deep breath. "How long have you been awake?"

In answer, her eyes squeezed shut more tightly.

"Do you want me to go?" he asked, hoping that she wasn't pretending to be asleep merely to escape his attention.

After a while, she took a deep breath before her eyes slowly fluttered open. Then she met his gaze, and for an instant, his heart stopped.

"I'm sorry," he said, head slightly bowed. "I promised I wouldn't touch you without your permission."

"You didn't," she whispered, and he lifted his head to look at her. "I took your hand, remember?"

Sebastian nodded, and a soft smile came to his lips. "I do, yes." He took a deep breath. "I liked that very much."

For a second, her teeth seemed to be chattering as though she were cold ... or scared ... before she dropped her gaze, a touch of red coming to her cheeks.

Patience, Sebastian counselled himself. "Do you remember what happened last night?" he asked, partly because he was dying to understand but also because he thought it best to change the subject from the gentle bond that was slowly forming between them, the bond that seemed to terrify her to her very core.

"I do." Although reluctant, she met his eyes. "How did you find me?"

"I remembered what you told me," Sebastian told her once more, "about your mother and tossing a coin into the water in order for your heart's desire to come true."

A wistful smile came to his wife's lips. "That was a long time ago."

Sebastian nodded. "Sometimes our childhood seems like it was an eternity ago, like a different lifetime. Things change in such a way that it is difficult to believe that we were them once, those innocent creatures ready to believe in wishes and dreams."

"I often wish I could return to that time," his wife whispered, her eyes distant. "Life was easier then. Happier, too."

Sebastian nodded. "Why did you leave Victoria's house in such a rush?" he blurted out before his courage could fail him. "What scared you so? Was it her husband?"

Instantly, her muscles tensed, and she drew her hand closer to her body ... and away from him.

"I don't understand what happened," Sebastian said, hoping that honesty would serve him, "but I would like to. From what my sister said, I believe that it was her husband who sent you into such a panic. Do you know him? Have you met him before?"

For a long moment, his wife remained quiet. Then she looked up. "You yourself proposed a marriage of convenience," she said, her voice almost cold as she spoke, and his hopes fell, "and that is all I can give you."

"What are you so afraid of?" Sebastian demanded, annoyance over her stubborn insistence running through his veins. "Why won't you allow me to help? Even if you truly see ours as a marriage of convenience, I do not."

Again, her eyes met his, and he could see that his words unsettled her, and yet, he thought to glimpse a spark of temptation before she averted her gaze.

"Whether you like it or not, you are my wife," Sebastian declared as his heart thudded wildly in his chest, "and it is not only my duty but also my desire to protect you. Why do you think I spent the past night sitting by your bed? Out of convenience?" He took a deep breath. "Was it out of convenience that you wanted me to stay? Was it out of convenience that you took my hand? Tell me!"

Meeting his gaze once more, she took a shaky breath. Her eyes were far from hard, and the cold had vanished from her voice as she spoke. "Because I trust you," she whispered as though the words surprised even here. "Because I feel safe with you. I haven't felt safe in a long time, and I almost forgot what it was like to have someone to lean on."

Not expecting such a heartfelt declaration, Sebastian stared at her, and warmth filled his chest. "Then tell me what is going on, and I promise I shall keep you safe for the rest of my days."

"You don't know how much I wish I could," she said, tears misting her eyes. "It truly is my heart's desire." She took a deep breath, and her lower lip began to tremble as she forced back the tears that threatened. "What hides in my past is much more than just the reason for my reaction yesterday. How I know your sister's husband is but a small part of it. If I told you all there is to know, you wouldn't look at me the way you do any longer." Her fingers curled into the pillow under her head. "And I admit I couldn't bear that. I'm being selfish, I know, but I'm not ready to let go yet. I might never be."

As his heart ached in his chest, Sebastian asked, "How do I look at you?"

Pressing her lips together, she smiled shyly. "As though I'm someone who deserves to be loved and cherished. Someone who is good and pure. Someone who matters. Someone who is not alone in the world." For a moment, she closed her eyes, and the tears she'd held back spilt over and ran down her cheeks, wetting her pillow. "I know it's not true, but it's a wonderful dream. It's all I have left, and I'm not ready to lose that."

Not knowing what lay in her past, Sebastian could only hope that he would find the right words as he leant forward, his arms coming to rest on the mattress beside her. "It is true," he whispered, holding her gaze, not allowing her to ignore the truth of his words. "It is. I may not know what happened to you or what you did or even the person you once were, but I know the person you are today. And I can tell you that the way you see yourself is wrong. You are everything and more you dream to be, and nothing—nothing-will ever sway me from your side."

She smiled at him then. However, it was a wistful smile, and he could see that she did not believe him. "I wish you were right. Truly. But you don't know ..., and you can never know."

Feeling her slip away, Sebastian felt a wave of panic rise. "Please tell me, and you will see that nothing will change."

"I can't."

Closing his eyes, Sebastian took a deep breath. "Then where do we go from here?"

"Nowhere," his wife said, her voice choked as more tears spilt down her face. "We go nowhere. This is all we have."

Chapter Thirty-Two

A PROPOSAL

In the days that passed, her husband kept trying to talk to her, trying to persuade her to place her trust in him. But Charlotte couldn't. After all, she had taken someone's life. No one could forgive that. No one ought to.

Her husband, however, did not know what he was asking of her. He did not know of her crime, and, of course, he couldn't fathom her committing a crime like that. Who could? If one cared for another, even loved another, one walked the world blinded by the truths surrounding that person.

Charlotte had seen it many times. How many of her friends had fancied themselves in love, only to wake up one morning married to a man who was so very different from the person they'd thought him to be? Could love and truth ever walk hand in hand? Or did one exclude the other?

After everything that had happened, Charlotte knew that she had to leave. And her husband knew it, too, for he refused to let her out of his sight.

While he kept his distance, was respectful and considerate, he thwarted every opportunity she might have had of leaving the house undetected.

A week passed, and Charlotte still didn't know what to do.

Of course, she couldn't stay. Not after what had happened.

After all, Lord Northfield knew that she was alive. He knew where she lived. He knew that the identity she had given her new husband was false. Any moment now, he could reveal her lies to the world at large. To anyone he chose.

And yet, he didn't. That scared Charlotte even more for she couldn't understand why.

A fortnight passed, and Charlotte was no closer to figuring out what to do when the butler informed them of a surprise supper guest that night.

Bowing to the countess as well as her son and daughter-in-law as they stood in the parlour, he announced, "Lord and Lady Northfield."

For a moment, Charlotte thought she would faint on the spot. The world around her began to spin; her knees felt weak, ready to give up their post. Out of the corner of her eye, she saw her husband's shocked, and yet, concerned face as he came toward her, his hands reaching for her as she began to sway on her feet.

"Are you all right?" he asked, his blue eyes searching hers, his hands a hair's breadth from her arms, ready to catch her should she need him to. "Shall I escort you upstairs?"

"Is something wrong?" the countess enquired, the look in her eyes almost identical to her son's. Only hers held confusion instead of apprehension for she did not understand the meaning of her son-in-law's visit. How could she?

Before Charlotte had a chance to make up her mind, much less reply, the butler stepped aside and Lord and Lady Northfield walked in.

While Victoria's face held regret, her eyes begged Charlotte to forgive her; her husband's sparkled with excitement. A smug smile drew up the corners of his lips as his gaze fell on Charlotte. "Good evening," he said, his voice strong and seemingly polite. However, Charlotte recognised the thinly veiled condescension and disregard he generally bestowed on people he deemed inferior to him ... which included anyone he had ever met.

"How kind of you to accompany Victoria tonight, my lord," the countess greeted her son-in-law. Though her voice sounded as polite as his, the insincerity with which she spoke was not lost on the baron for he looked at her with a hint of disgust before his attention returned to Charlotte.

The countess, too, noticed his fixation on the newest member of their family, and her eyes narrowed as they shifted from her most unwelcome guest to her daughter-in-law. "Dear, are you unwell?" she asked, stepping forward, and her gaze travelled to her son. "You look pale."

"Oh, but she looks radiant, does she not?" Lord Northfield beamed, a big grin on his face as he stepped forward. "Like life itself." His brows rose as he spoke, and Charlotte clearly understood the mockery in his words.

As her heart hammered in her chest and the blood rushed in her ears, Charlotte heard everything around her as though spoken in muffled tones.

Lost, all she could do was to keep a tight grip on her nerves, lest she lose all hold on reality and do something unwise. Her mind raced as she tried to make sense of what was happening.

Trapped in the same room with her new family as well as the nightmare of her past, Charlotte was at a loss. Had he come to reveal who she truly was? Was he intent on ruining her ... again? Why had he waited this long? Why was he not telling them this very instant? And why was he looking at her with such sickening delight?

"Shall I escort you upstairs?" her husband whispered, and Charlotte turned her head, meeting his eyes. Almost dark blue in their intensity, they held such concern that Charlotte felt the impulse to wrap her arms around him and bury her head in his neck.

Instead, she took a deep breath, then shook her head. "No, I'm fine. I merely felt light-headed for a moment, but it has passed."

Her husband nodded. However, Charlotte could see that he did not believe her. But what was she to tell him? She could not leave this room, not knowing what Lord Northfield would tell her family in her absence. She had to discover what his agenda was for there was not a single fibre in her body that believed that he had come here that night without a plan to hurt her once again. Maybe if she knew what it was, she would be prepared.

Hope.

Her heart still held hope, for despite her intentions to leave, she had never truly wanted to. After all, this was her home now, her family, and she wished for nothing more but to be able to stay with them.

However, seeing the baron here, now, Charlotte knew that there was no sliver of hope left. Now, it lay dead at her feet, and she had to face the hard truth. She had to leave. That was final now; yet, she couldn't without knowing that her family would be safe.

By the time, they were all seated around the large dining room table, the silence that hung over that evening had stretched to an almost unbearable length. Besides Charlotte herself, Victoria was the one who looked most uncomfortable as she kept her eyes fixed on her plate, barely lifting her head and not uttering a single word. The countess as well as her son observed the proceedings, their guest through narrowed eyes, no doubt attempting to assess the situation that had so unexpectedly found its way into their midst.

More than once, Charlotte felt her husband's as well as her mother-in-law's concerned eyes on her, only to find their gazes shift to their supper guest a moment later, an almost scowl-like expression on their faces.

Deep down, a part of Charlotte recognised that they were trying to protect her, and it warmed her heart like nothing had in a long time.

Her new family knew something was wrong. They knew that a threat had entered their house in the form of Victoria's husband, and they knew from Charlotte's reaction that she was terrified.

Only, they didn't know why.

And they could never find out.

As Lord Northfield proceeded to make pleasant conversation, not in the least disturbed by the flat and downright rude replies from his hosts, Charlotte was almost frozen in her seat. As much as she wished she could engage him in conversation and find out why he had come here that night, his mere presence robbed her of every bit of self-esteem she had left. Her stomach twisted and turned, and not a morsel of food could be forced down her throat.

"I admit I was rather surprised to hear of your wedding, dear Brother," Northfield exclaimed, grinning at Charlotte's husband with a hint of speculation in his eyes. "And even more so when I heard your wife was not of our standing. To be frank, I believed you to have made a monumental mistake," his gaze travelled to Charlotte, and instantly, the bile rose in her throat as his eyes lingered on her face. "However, now that I've seen what a charming and *innocent*, young lady you've *claimed as yours*, I find myself most willing to express my congratulations. She truly is one of a kind."

His taunting words echoed in Charlotte's ears as he unscrupulously reminded her of the night in the library.

Averting her eyes, she found a scowl on her husband's face as he stared across the table. Although he could not possibly understand the hidden meaning of the baron's words, he understood the insult as well as the injury they were meant to convey and inflict.

"I assure you," he replied, his jaw clenched, "that I could not have found a more suitable wife had I searched the whole face of the earth. She is my match in every way and a wonderful addition to this family."

"I am certain she is," the baron agreed, a sneer on his face as he continued to look at her. "I can only hope I will have the opportunity to get better *acquainted* with her in the future."

Instantly, her husband's hand balled into a fist as he was all but ready to jump to his feet and attack their guest.

"Shall we return to the drawing room," the countess suggested, a warning in her eyes as she looked at her son. "After this lovely dinner, I believe a little music would be ... beneficial. Victoria, if you would be so kind."

"Of course, Mother." Rising from her chair, Victoria looked at Charlotte. Although her cheeks looked rather pale and her hands were far from steady, a touch of urgency rested in her gaze. "Dear Lotte, would you be so kind as to show me the new sheet music you spoke about during your last visit?"

"Sheet music?" Charlotte mumbled, momentarily confused.

"Yes, don't you remember?" Victoria insisted, her gaze almost drilling into Charlotte's.

Understanding dawned, and Charlotte nodded. "Of course." Then she turned to the others. "If you'll excuse us for a moment."

Ignoring the displeased frown on Northfield's face, Charlotte followed Victoria out into the hall as the rest of their party headed to the drawing room. "Thank you," she whispered as the two women climbed the stairs.

"I'm so sorry," Victoria exclaimed in hushed tones, casting a careful look over her shoulder. "I should have sent word, but he only made his intentions known once I was almost out the door."

"It's all right. You couldn't have known." Opening the door to her bedchamber, Charlotte wondered how much Victoria knew or at the very least guessed at. "Did he tell you anything?"

Closing the door behind her, Victoria shook her head, a sour and rather exhausted looking smile on her lips. "Although we are husband and wife, we do not speak to each other more than need be. I know nothing about what he thinks." She swallowed, then stepped closer and took Charlotte's hands. "But I saw the way you looked at him then, and I saw the look on your face tonight, and as you said, those who experienced the same recognise the signs."

Considering Victoria's compassionate face, her own pain so evident in her large eyes, Charlotte felt her heart open and tears stream down her cheeks.

"Does my brother know?" Victoria asked, squeezing Charlotte's hands.

Tensing at the mere suggestion, Charlotte shook her head. "I don't want him to know."

"Do you believe he would hold it against you?"

"I know he wouldn't," Charlotte admitted, an affectionate smile drawing up the corners of her mouth. "He's a truly good man, and I believe on some level he suspects."

"Then why don't you tell him? Maybe he could help you." Nodding encouragingly, Victoria held her gaze. "He loves you, you know?"

"I know, and I love him, too," Charlotte whispered, shocked at the words that left her mouth, and yet, feeling strangely euphoric. At least for a moment, before the dark cloud of her past reclaimed its place over her head. "Only there is more," she admitted, averting her gaze. "Things I could never tell him. Things that would make him hate me."

"He would never!" Victoria exclaimed.

"If you knew what is in my past, you wouldn't say that." Charlotte sighed, blinking back the tears that clung to her eyelashes. "There's no happily-ever-after for us."

"Nor for me," Victoria replied, sadness hanging on her face like early morning dew. "I suppose sometimes Cinderella does not get her prince, does she?"

Charlotte shook her head. "I guess not."

Victoria sighed, then let go of Charlotte's hands and turned to the door. "Will you come down again?"

"I will," Charlotte said. "In a moment."

As the door closed behind Victoria, Charlotte almost crumpled into a heap of misery onto the floor. Her knees felt like pudding, completely inadequate to support her weight, and she staggered toward the bed collapsing onto the mattress. Fresh tears spilt down her cheeks, and heart-breaking sobs tore from her throat. Her heart ached with such painful intensity that she felt as though it would surely break in half any second now.

And yet, it didn't.

The pain remained, torturing her in a most acute way as it had then ... a long time ago.

The wound had not healed. The pain had merely been dulled, hidden away until she would be made to feel it again. Would it ever cease?

Knowing that she couldn't hide in her room forever, Charlotte pushed herself into a sitting position, then quickly dried her tears. After glancing into the mirror on her vanity, she closed her eyes, then rose and proceeded to hide the remnants of her breakdown. Fortunately, her eyes were not swollen, merely a little red, so she splashed some cold water on her face, savouring its freshness. Then she stepped toward the door, took a deep breath and opened it.

Silence met her, and she slowly placed one foot in front of the other, hoping to regain her composure before she reached the drawing room. Somehow the staircase didn't seem to end, and yet, the steps she took only increased the thudding of her heart.

Upon reaching the ground floor, Charlotte stood up straight, pushed back her shoulders and took another deep breath. Still, she didn't feel any more prepared than she had upstairs in her room.

"You look beautiful," a voice spoke out from behind her, "especially for someone who has been dead these past two years."

At the sound of his voice, terror filled Charlotte, and she spun around. "What are you doing here?" she gasped, as her mind took in the empty hall as well as the pleased smile on the baron's face as he came toward her.

"Fortunately, my wife experienced a moment of dizziness," he explained, still advancing on her. "Thereby, giving us the opportunity to renew our acquaintance while your dear *husband* as well as his mother tend to her."

At first, Charlotte had been determined to stand her ground, no matter how loudly her instincts screamed at her to turn and run. However, when the living embodiment of her nightmares stood no more than an arm's length away from her, her feet retreated as though of their own accord.

At her sign of fear, a pleased smile curled up his lips. "I see you haven't forgotten me," the baron sneered, his eyes travelling over her body, "and I do admit that I often relive our encounter in the library. Few women have ever held such an allure. I admit I was quite surprised when you did not accept my marriage proposal."

Farther and farther, Charlotte retreated, eyes wide with horror, until her back came to rest against the wall ... and there was nowhere else to go.

A slow smile spread over the baron's face, and his hard eyes drilled into hers. "However, your father assured me that it was simply female modesty on your part and that you would realise your good fortune before long."

Charlotte swallowed, but her mouth felt dry as though she was dying of thirst. She knew she ought to step away, call someone, or ... do something. Her legs though were as heavy as lead, and her voice died in her throat. Paralysed, she stood, staring at the monster before her, a part of her unable to believe that this was truly happening.

Maybe this was another nightmare.

Maybe all she had to do was wake up.

"And then you died," the baron growled, his voice accusing as though she had intentionally thwarted his plans, "and all I had worked for went up in flames." With anger marking his face, the baron inhaled deeply, then lifted his hand toward her.

Shocked, Charlotte sucked in a breath.

A slow smile curled up Northfield's lips, and enjoyment danced in his eyes as his fingers gently touched a curled strand dangling from her forehead. "I'd set my sights on you," he whispered, "and it took me quite some time to find a woman equal to you. However, seeing you now, I admit I am very tempted." He leant closer. "Do you ever think of me?"

Gritting her teeth to keep them from chattering, Charlotte stared over his shoulder, keeping her eyes fixed on a point at the wall, waiting, hoping that he would simply grow tired of this game and leave.

But he didn't.

"The time we spent together was special," he whispered into her ear, his warm breath brushing over her skin, bringing back details of that night she had thought forgotten, "it would be a shame not to experience it again."

At his implication, her heart stopped, and Charlotte's head snapped back, her eyes meeting his. "What?" she croaked, her voice raw and yet strangely calm.

Again, a sickening smile drew up the corners of his mouth and his hand fell from her hair and settled on her waist, sliding to her back until she stood pressed against him. "Your husband does not know who you are, does he? Nor does the rest of his family I assume."

Trembling, Charlotte could barely form a conscious thought as his touch burned itself into her skin, so familiar, so sickening. More than anything, she wanted to free herself of him, but her arms wouldn't move. It was as though her body was no longer hers to command.

This was worse than the night in the library.

Then she had fought him. She had made her position unmistakably clear although it had done her little good.

But now, she wouldn't even have the knowledge that she had fought and lost, that she had done everything within her power to protect herself.

Was this the final act that would destroy her soul? That would rip everything human from her heart and leave her an empty shell? Never to return to the woman she had once been?

If she didn't fight him now, Charlotte knew she would be lost for good. There would be no coming back.

"Although I admit I was quite displeased with your reaction to my honourable intentions," the baron continued, "I must say that I consider myself quite fortunate to have found you once again. I suppose some people would call that fate." Stepping back, he met her eyes, his hand still resting at her side. "I'll be frank, my dear. I have a wife now. A suitable wife with a large dowry and a social standing that benefits me greatly. A wife who will no doubt give me the heir I want before this year is out." His eyes dropped from hers and touched her lips. "What I need now is a mistress."

His words were like a slap in the face, and Charlotte blinked.

Did he truly think she would agree to become his mistress? Could he not see how much his presence repulsed her? Or did he simply not care? Was this truly about desire? Or rather about power? Power over another? To have her submit to him and see how it tortured her?

"No." It was one word. One short word spoken in a clear, steady voice that Charlotte didn't recognise as her own.

"No?" he asked, incredulity evident in his eyes. For a moment, he stared at her. Then his eyes narrowed, and he glared down into her face. "I will destroy you," he hissed. "I don't know what game you're playing, but do not for a second doubt that I'd hesitate to reveal you as the conniving woman you are."

Anger tightened his grip on her, and Charlotte drew in a sharp breath before her teeth ground together in defiance and she met his gaze without flinching. "Do what you must," she declared, "as will I." Then she lifted her arms and pushed his off her waist.

Aghast, he stared at her, a kink in his armour of self-confidence.

Then he drew in a deep breath, raised his head and was back in control. "I'll give you a fortnight to think about my proposal. Then I shall speak to your husband."

"What proposal?" came her husband's carefully controlled voice from her right as he stood in the half-open door to the drawing room. "What is going on here?"

While the baron quickly regained his composure, Charlotte could barely meet her husband's eyes as they searched hers, asking for an explanation.

"Are you all right?" he demanded, coming to stand before her. "What did he say?"

"I merely expressed my-" the baron began, but was immediately interrupted.

"I'm speaking to my wife!" her husband snapped, glaring at their guest. "Go and see to your own," he growled, and Charlotte could see how deeply it pained him to entrust his beloved sister to such a monster.

As the baron vanished through the door, Charlotte swallowed, then looked up. "How is Victoria?"

Her husband sighed. "Fine. I suppose considering her condition, light-headedness is nothing unusual, is it?" It was a simple question, and yet, the way his eyes bore into hers, Charlotte knew that he was asking for more than her opinion. He was asking if she knew it to be true from personal experience.

Taking a deep breath, she held his gaze. "It is."

For a moment, his eyes closed, and then he nodded, understanding written over his face. "What did he want?" he demanded, tension marking his features as he stared at the door through which the baron had left. "What did he say to you?"

Charlotte swallowed. What was she to say? Even if she were to tell him the truth, it would take more than a few words to explain what had happened there.

As she hesitated, her husband drew in a deep breath. "Did you tell him to go to hell?" he asked, a touch of grim humour in his voice.

Taken aback, Charlotte stared at him before a fleeting smile drew up the corners of her mouth. "I did."

"Good," her husband said, his eyes glowing brightly as he looked at her. "I'm proud of you."

For a long moment, they looked at each other, and Charlotte couldn't help but feel as though he knew exactly what was going on. He knew what had happened, how she felt and what she needed to hear. And he was here, by her side, holding her hand ... even though he still hadn't touched her.

And he wouldn't. Not without her permission.

As terrified as Charlotte had been moments earlier, right then and there, she couldn't remember ever having felt this safe. Somehow, without her noticing, her husband had found a way to her heart, and once the time came to leave, it would-as sure as the sun rises in the east-break beyond repair.

Quite a fitting punishment.

"Go upstairs and rest," her husband said, glancing at the door once again. "I shall see our guests to the door." Again, he met her eyes. "We'll speak tomorrow."

Charlotte nodded, not trusting her voice as she whispered a silent goodbye.

If she wanted to leave-and she needed to, now more than ever-then it had to be tonight.

It was her last chance.

Chapter Thirty-Three
A SECRET REVEALED

His mind buzzing with the events of that night, Sebastian was still downstairs, pacing the length of the drawing room when the clock struck midnight. His eyes again travelled to the settee where Victoria had lain not too long ago, her cheeks pale and limbs tired.

One moment she had been fine, and the next she had started to sway on her feet, her hands reaching out blindly for anything to hold on to.

Sebastian had caught her then, had gently picked her up and carried her to the settee.

Always had he caught her no matter how often she had fallen.

Except for once.

The one time when it had truly mattered, he had let her fall.

He would never forgive himself for that, remembering the dull pain that rested in her eyes these days.

And then there was his wife and the terror he had seen in hers.

Even if Sebastian hadn't already had his suspicions after the night he had found her on Westminster Bridge, he could now be certain that the nightmare of her past was none other than Baron Northfield, his sister's husband.

Two women. Two lives ruined by one man.

What was he to do?

Quiet footsteps drifted to his ears from the hall interrupting his moment of self-torture. Who would be up this late? Sebastian wondered, silently approaching the door.

As he peeked through the small gap, he was surprised-although he shouldn't have been-to see his wife, dressed in a warm winter coat with rather a large bag slung over her shoulder, descend the stairs. With her eyes scanning her surroundings, she crossed the front hall and proceeded to the back of the house toward the servants' entrance, her left hand reaching up to pull the hood of her coat deeper into her face.

Taking a deep breath, Sebastian followed as quietly as he could.

So, this was it, he thought. If he hadn't been up this late, if he had gone to bed, she would have slipped out of his life without a look back.

Never had Sebastian felt so grateful for a sleepless night!

As the cold night air hit him, Sebastian wrapped his arms tightly around himself as he followed his wife across the courtyard to the stables. He should have taken the time to bring a coat as well, he thought to himself, shivering as the cold rose goose bumps on his arms and legs.

When his wife slipped into the stables and was lost from his view for a moment, Sebastian's heart skipped a beat and fear clawed at his soul.

He could not lose her! It was a truth he knew like no other. Just the thought of her gone drove him mad.

Quickening his steps, he reached the stables a mere minute after she had and quietly opened the large door, welcoming the warm air that engulfed him as he stepped inside.

In the dim light, the stable lay in near silence. The only sounds came from the horses that turned their heads with interest as they examined the nightly intruder in their midst. Watching his steps, Sebastian proceeded down the long corridor at the back of the stable, eyes scanning the shadowy world around him for signs of his wife. Had she already slipped out again?

She couldn't have! He reasoned. No one could saddle a horse that fast, and the only reason for her to stop at the stables was to procure herself a faster method of transportation.

Sebastian frowned. Where did she intend to go?

"Quiet," his wife's whispers reached his ears, and Sebastian stopped, searching. "We shall be off in a moment."

No, you shall not! Sebastian thought with vehemence as he came around the stable master's small office and found his wife standing with her back to him, gently sliding a saddle onto a chestnut brown mare.

Taking a deep breath, Sebastian stepped forward. "Were you not even going to say goodbye?"

At the sound of his voice, his wife flinched, then spun around, eyes wide, staring at him as though he was a ghost risen from the ground. "What are you doing here?" she stammered as her gaze wandered around her surroundings.

Did she think he'd brought reinforcements? Sebastian thought, wondering about all the many things he didn't know about her ... but would love to nonetheless.

"Were you not even going to say goodbye?" he repeated, aware that his voice held a clear accusation. He could see the pained look in her eyes, and yet, he could not hide his own at the thought of her leaving.

Taking a deep breath, she met his gaze. "If I had told you, you wouldn't have let me go."

"Of course, I wouldn't have."

A quick smile drew up the corners of her mouth before they dropped down once more. "Then I made the right choice." She sighed, "If only you had slept more soundly."

"I never even went to bed," Sebastian said, stepping closer, his eyes holding hers. "After what I witnessed tonight, how can you expect me to sleep?"

Her eyes dropped from his as his words conjured the memory of earlier that night, and once more he could see the terror that had seized her clearly edged into her face as though it was a part of her, never to leave.

Again, she drew in a deep breath before looking up. "There's nothing left to say, and I need to go."

As she turned to fasten the saddle, Sebastian felt red hot anger surge through him.

In two strides, he was beside her and all but ripped the saddle out of her hands, throwing it onto the floor with a loud *thud*.

Aghast, his wife stared at him: her eyes wide, her face pale as she stepped back, her back resting against the mare's soft coat.

Despite the blood pulsing in his veins, Sebastian could see the touch of fear that rested in her eyes, and it ate at him like nothing ever had. Gritting his teeth, he took a step back. "I have a right to be angry," he forced out as calmly as he could, "but that does not mean that I will hurt you." He held her gaze for a long time. "I would never, and I can only hope that at least a part of you can believe that."

Her eyes lingered on his face as though reading his expression, trying to gauge the meaning behind his words, his actions, before the tension slowly left her face. She swallowed then and took a step toward him. "The part of me that is truly me," she whispered, utter honesty ringing in her voice, "trusts you. Truly, it does." A soft smile touched her lips, and she nodded her head in emphasis. "However, there is this other part of me," for a moment, her eyes dropped to the ground, "that only knows fear and distrust." A hint of embarrassment came to her face as she shook her head, helpless. "I have no control over it. It's like an open wound. It bleeds, and as much as I will it to stop, it simply doesn't."

Touched that she would allow him to see such a vulnerable side of her, Sebastian nodded, his anger vanished into thin air. "I understand," he replied just as honestly as she had spoken, "and I do not hold it against you. How could I? All I meant to say is that we are bound to disagree every occasionally, we're bound to argue, even yell and snap at each other." He looked deep into her eyes, hoping that at least part of her would believe him. "However, I would never lay a hand on you. Only someone who is in the wrong would use violence to make his point for it is a weak argument of no substance, and quite frankly, it is beneath me. Respect is earned, not stolen." He sighed, "It's one of only a few lessons I learnt from my father."

For a moment, she remained still, lost in thought, before her gaze met his once more. "It helps to speak about it," she admitted. "When someone scares me, I lose all rational thought, and then I cannot judge someone's actions with a clear head."

Sebastian nodded. "Then let's speak about it," he agreed, hoping she would not regret her words. "How do you know my sister's husband?"

Instantly, his wife froze, terror back in her eyes, and it was as though a wall went up, trying to shield her from the pain she knew would come ... but failing to do so. "Don't ask me that," she whispered, then shook her head and walked away.

Hurrying after her, Sebastian stepped in her path. "Is he the one who hurt you?" This was it! Now or never! And never was not an option!

Unable to flee, his wife stared at him. "Who told-? How do you know?"

"You did," he said. "You told me." He took a deep breath, remembering the night at the inn in Gretna Green. "The way you spoke of marriage, or marital rights and duties, the way you looked at me ..., I suspected even then. A part of me knew that someone had hurt you. Only I didn't know who. At first, I thought it might have been your betrothed."

Her eyes widened in shock. "Kenneth?"

Sebastian shrugged. "It was just a thought. After all, I never met him."

A wistful smile came to her lips as a memory claimed her attention, and Sebastian felt a stab of jealousy for a man he had never known, a man who-as far as he knew-had died at least a year ago.

"He would never have hurt me," his wife whispered, her eyes distant. "Kenneth was my best friend, my saviour, my protector." Smiling, she looked up at him. "Only after seeing you with Victoria did I realise that he was the brother I never had."

At her words, Sebastian exhaled, relief filling him, and yet, a sense of dread remained at the thought of a sister being without her brother.

"Whenever I needed him, he was there," she continued, her voice growing stronger as she shared a memory dear to her. "He knew me like no one else ever had." Then her face darkened, and for a moment, Sebastian thought she would refuse to go on. "When ... Northfield ...

when he ..., Kenneth knew that something was wrong. He could see it on my face, and ... he made me tell him." Closing her eyes, she shook her head. "And then he sacrificed his happiness for mine, and I let him because I was scared."

"He asked for your hand?" Sebastian asked, suddenly wishing he had known the man who had done his utmost to protect the woman he thought of as a sister.

His wife nodded.

"To save your reputation? Or did he not think of you as a brother would?"

"He never loved me the way you ..." As she dropped her gaze, a tinge of red came to her cheeks, even visible in the dim light in the stable. "He offered himself as a husband so that I wouldn't have to accept Northfield's proposal."

Her words felt like a stab into his middle, and Sebastian almost toppled over with shock. "Northfield's proposal?"

Gritting her teeth, his wife swallowed. "Apparently, he had set his sights on me because I was the only heir to my father's fortune, an earl's daughter, a perfect match." Then she looked up and met his gaze, and her eyes suddenly went wide. Clasping a hand over her mouth, she stared at him.

Smiling at her, Sebastian stepped forward. "An earl's daughter?"

"I never should have ..."

"I knew," Sebastian interrupted as the colour drained from her face. "Not that you were an earl's daughter precisely, but I told you before that you struck me as someone of the upper society. Honestly, this does not come as a surprise to me."

Taking a deep breath, his wife began pacing in front of the boxes, their inhabitants watching her curiously, reaching out their necks in hopes of a treat.

For a long while, Sebastian watched her as she worked through all the new revelations in her head. Then he asked, "You told me before that the name you gave me was not yours."

Meeting his gaze, she nodded, reading his question in his eyes. "I am ... or at least I was until my parents had me declared dead ... Lady Charlotte Frampton."

Declared dead? Sebastian wondered, but then pushed away that thought, deciding to focus on the more important issue. "Charlotte?" he whispered, intrigued. "Lotte? I see." Holding out his hand, he said, "It's a pleasure to make your acquaintance, my lady."

Smiling, his wife–Charlotte-carefully placed her hand in his, humour in her eyes before they grew serious once again. "I do apologise for the deception. I never meant to hurt you."

"I do believe you." Then his eyes dropped to her hand still resting in his. "May I?"

For a moment, her brows drew down in puzzlement before understanding dawned. Hesitating, she held his gaze before she finally nodded, her hand trembling slightly.

Smiling at her reassuringly, Sebastian stepped closer, then bent forward in a bow and gently pressed his lips to the knuckles of her fingers.

His wife drew in a sharp breath. However, she did not try to extract her hand.

When he met her eyes again, Sebastian thought to see a touch of excitement in them. "Lady Charlotte Frampton," he mumbled, then stopped. "I feel as though I've heard that name before."

Instantly, her body froze as though time had stopped. Then she pulled back her hand, barely meeting his eyes, remembering why she had come there that night. "I need to go," she whispered. "Goodbye."

With his heart hammering in his chest, Sebastian once more stepped into her path. "Why? Why now? What happened with Northfield that you feel you cannot stay another night?"

With her hands clenched painfully, she stared up at him. "I told you before I needed to leave."

"But so far, you've been rather patient," he reminded her, desperate to make her see that running away would not serve her for eventually her past would catch up with her. "You could've slipped out into the night before. Why now? What happened? What did he say?"

With lips pressed into a thin line, she looked up at him rather defiantly, and he finally realised the depth of her fear. However, he could not allow her to leave. What if Northfield found her again? "If you won't tell me," he threatened and hating himself for it, "I will speak to ... my brother-in-law."

"What?" his wife gasped. "You wouldn't!"

"If there's no other way. After all, he is my sister's husband," he reminded her. "I need to know."

Eyes darting every which way as though hoping to find a solution, his wife looked like misery itself. Her teeth chattered, and she bit her lower lip to keep it from quivering as tears came to her eyes. "He said he would tell you ... all of you ... who I truly am."

Trying to ignore her pain, Sebastian pressed on. He needed to know. "Why?" His eyes narrowed. "What did he want to keep quiet?"

She blinked then, and her tears spilt over and ran down her cheeks. "He demands I become his mistress. He wants my answer within a fortnight."

As though a fire had been lit, red hot anger seized Sebastian once more, burning in his veins. His hands balled into fists as his muscles tensed to the point of breaking. "I'll kill him," he growled out through clenched teeth, his jaw aching painfully. "I'll kill that bastard."

"No! You mustn't!" Fear in her eyes, his wife rushed toward him, shaking her head.

"I'll call him out. It is my right after all."

Again, she shook her head, her eyes pleading. "He doesn't fight fair. He'll find a way to make certain that he will be the one left standing." Fresh tears spilt from her eyes. "I already told Kenneth, but he didn't believe me."

"He called him out?" Sebastian asked, wondering if that was how he had died. No, he hadn't, Sebastian suddenly remembered. He'd died in the war, hadn't he?

"He didn't. I asked him not to, and so he didn't."

"Then what-?"

"It was a while after Kenneth had died that I realised it had been Northfield's doing," she sobbed. "I blamed someone else at first, and I did ... something awful. I ..." Gritting her teeth, she inhaled deeply through her nose, trying to regain her composure. "I finally read a letter Kenneth had left for me, and from what I could gather, I realised that Northfield had tricked him into ... going after his friend."

"His friend?" Sebastian asked, somewhat confused.

His wife shook her head. "It doesn't matter now, really. He died in the war by an enemy's hand, but it was Northfield who'd placed him in the face of danger." Grasping his hands, she looked up at him. "Promise me, you will not call him out! You must not speak to him. Don't let him know that you know anything. Just let me leave, and ... you will be safe."

Savouring the feeling of her slender fingers wrapped around his, her soft skin warm against his own, Sebastian looked down into her pleading eyes. "I can't," he whispered. "If I let you go, I know I will regret it for the rest of my life."

Abruptly withdrawing her hands, she stepped back, anger burning in her eyes. "You will regret it if you don't," she snapped, exhaustion clear on her face. "You have no idea who he is and what he is capable of doing."

Sebastian nodded, already missing the feel of her touch. "I think I do, and I understand why you're asking me this." For a moment, he held her gaze. "I love you, too; I couldn't live with myself if anything happened to you."

Her mouth opened in shock. Then she turned away, brushing the tears from her eyes.

Coming to stand behind her, Sebastian took care not to touch her. "Together we can find a way."

"No, we can't," she sobbed, shaking her head. "There is something else you don't know, something that ... would destroy us. I cannot stay."

As his head spun with all the new information, Sebastian held on to the one thing he could: his dream of a future with his wife. "Does Northfield know?"

Arms wrapped around herself, she shrugged. "I don't know. I don't think he does."

"All right," Sebastian said, stepping around her so that she would look at him. "Even if you're not willing to do it for yourself ... or for me, would you at least stay for Victoria's sake?"

A frown came to her face as she looked up at him. "Victoria," she mumbled, then shook her head. "Her fate truly is worse than mine.

Whatever happened to me, I never had the misfortune of becoming his wife."

Sebastian swallowed. "I failed her once, but I will not fail her again." He took a deep breath, determined to face his own demons with the same courage that his wife had shown that night. "For a while, I thought if I stayed away, I could forget her misery. But that was cowardly, and it made me a man I never wanted to be." Lips pressed together, he looked down at his wife imploringly. "I need to free her, and I need your help to do it."

For a long time, his wife remained silent, her eyes studying his face as though he were an open book. Then she nodded, determination shining in her eyes. "I'll stay," she whispered, "until Victoria is safe."

Sebastian drew in a deep breath, relief mingling with dread as he realised that only uncovering his wife's secret would free her of this self-inflicted punishment. Maybe if he found out and she could see that he didn't think less of her, maybe then, they'd have a chance at happiness.

At least, he knew her real name now.

Chapter Thirty-Four
HEART TO HEART

Visiting Victoria at her townhouse was out of the question, and so Charlotte was relieved when her sister-in-law called on her early the next morning.

The two women retreated to the drawing room, and Charlotte firmly sent her husband away, knowing that it would be far easier for her to speak to Victoria alone.

"I was so worried about you," her sister-in-law exclaimed. "I had hoped to speak to you before we left last night, but my husband said that you felt poorly and had gone to bed."

Charlotte's eyes narrowed.

"It is not true, is it?" Victoria asked as her eyes studied Charlotte's face. "When I felt dizzy last night, my brother bade me to lie down. He and Mother didn't leave my side. They were so worried. But after a while, I noticed that my husband was absent, so I sent Sebastian to look for him." She took a deep breath. "What happened?"

Charlotte swallowed. The previous night had drained her, and yet, she had never felt so liberated. Sharing the pain of her past with her husband had given her strength. "He was waiting for me when I came back downstairs."

"Why?"

"Because he recognised me," she whispered, knowing that Victoria needed to know the truth ... at least as much of it as possible.

"Recognised you? What do you mean?"

Charlotte took a deep breath. "I'm not who I said I was."

Victoria's eyes widened.

"A long time ago, I was an earl's daughter," Charlotte began, surprised that after the previous night it felt easier to talk about her past, "and one night, your husband asked for my hand. When I refused him, he thought he could gain my acceptance of his proposal ... by compromising me."

With eyes as round as plates, Victoria stared at her, her face ash-white. "You mean, he ... he ...?"

Charlotte nodded. "He thought if he ruined me, I would have no one else to turn to." Shaking her head, Charlotte scoffed. "I thought he was wrong, and so I told my parents what he had done."

Victoria cringed. "They did not believe you."

"I'm not sure," Charlotte admitted. "But it didn't matter. I was ruined, and he was proposing."

"They insisted that you marry him," Victoria whispered, her voice weak with relived memories as undoubtedly her own wedding to the man in question flashed before her eyes.

"They did," Charlotte confirmed, "but I had a knight in shining armour." A soft smile came to her face at the memory of Kenneth, and Victoria leant forward expectantly.

Charlotte once more spoke of her childhood friend, of how he had seen her misery and offered his help with no regard for his own happiness ... and of how he had died in the war before they could be married. "By then, I already knew that I was with child," Charlotte admitted, remembering the soft weight in her belly before she had even been able to truly feel it. "However, I never had the chance to tell him."

"Was it his?" Victoria asked carefully.

"No." Charlotte shook her head. "He was like a brother to me. We never ..."

For a while, they remained quiet, both lost in their own thoughts.

Then Victoria glanced up, her hand resting on her flat belly. "When did you lose your baby?"

Charlotte swallowed the sob that threatened. "The night I learnt of his death," she whispered, closing her eyes. "I suppose my body knew that the war was lost. I couldn't have the child without Kenneth, and I never would have accepted Northfield's proposal ... no matter what. Had I not lost the child, I couldn't have survived."

"It pains you, does it not?" Victoria asked, tears streaming freely down her face. "To think of your child as a burden?"

Charlotte nodded, meeting her sister-in-law's eyes openly. "Never in my life had I felt this tormented as I did then. I wanted the child, and I didn't want it. I mourned it, and yet, I rejoiced that I was free again. I thought I would lose my mind, and for a moment, I suppose I did."

"What about your parents?"

Charlotte shook her head, remembering the hopelessness of her situation. "Without Kenneth to save me, my parents once again insisted that I agree to Northfield's proposal."

"But you still refused him," Victoria said, a touch of awe in her voice. "I wish I had been that brave."

Taking a deep breath, Charlotte shook her head. "I didn't refuse him," she admitted, remembering the day her parents had taken her to Winham Institute and left her there, never to return. "Honestly, I'm not certain what I would have done, but it doesn't matter. Something ... happened."

Hands clasped together, Victoria watched her with rapt attention, and Charlotte knew that her sister-in-law burned to know what had saved her brother's wife from having to marry the man Victoria herself now called husband. However, instead of confiding in her sister-in-law, Charlotte ignored her questioning gaze. "So, I vanished," she whispered as though telling her story would conjure the ghosts of her past, "and my parents had me declared dead."

"What? Why? Did they not wish to find you?"

Charlotte shrugged. "I don't know. Maybe they did love me once-when life was good-but ultimately, they cared more for their reputation than they did for me. I never thought that possible, and it was in that very moment that I first felt the ground falling out from underneath my feet. After that, I just kept falling ... until Kenneth caught me, at least for a little while, before I fell again." Meeting Victoria's shocked gaze, Charlotte swallowed. "I cannot tell you what exactly happened. I've never spoken about it to anyone, and I'm not certain I ever will be able to."

"It's all right," Victoria whispered, her hands once more resting on her belly. "I'm grateful that you've told me as much as you have. It makes me feel trustworthy and ... in a strange way competent." She sighed, "Sebastian used to shield me from everything remotely bad in the world, and then when he was gone and Father insisted that I marry, I didn't refuse, I didn't fight because," shaking her head, she bit her lower lip, "a part of me couldn't believe that it was truly happening. Nothing truly bad had ever happened in my life, and as long as I had Sebastian, I simply ... knew that nothing ever would." For a moment, she closed her eyes. "I don't know when exactly I woke up from that dream. I think I finally understood what had happened when Sebastian came to see me after the wedding." Pressing her lips together, she blinked back tears. "He looked so forlorn, so ashamed and guilty. I think it was then in that moment that I finally realised that he wouldn't save me this time. He couldn't. Suddenly, I was on my own." She met Charlotte's gaze. "Nothing had prepared me for that."

Charlotte nodded. "I know how you felt. I felt the same way. Life had always been good, and then from one second to the next, it changed without warning. Suddenly, what I wanted, how I felt didn't matter anymore. I spoke, and yet, no one heard me. I was right there in front of them, and yet, they didn't see me. A part of me feels as though that was the cruellest part of what happened. To know what it is like to be cherished, and then to lose that and be expected to go on as though nothing had changed."

With tears streaming down her face, Victoria looked at her, understanding resting in her eyes. "I wish I could vanish, too," she whispered, brushing the tears off her cheeks. "I don't know what to do. It's not simply that I don't want this life. I cannot bear it." With pleading eyes, she looked at Charlotte. "What am I to do? I am tied to that man ... for life. A man who ..." For a moment, she averted her gaze, then met Charlotte's once more. "I'm so sorry for what he did to you. I knew he was ... unfeeling, but I never would have thought he could be so cruel."

"Do not apologise for him," Charlotte insisted, seeing her sister-in-law's misery and knowing how she would fare if she remained locked in the life that was hers. "He may be your husband, but that does not reflect on you. You're a truly good person who deserves a happy life."

Shaking her head, Victoria sighed, "That I will never have. My husband is the devil," a shudder went through her as though she feared he could hear her, "and he will make certain that I'll spend the remainder of my days living in hell. A part of me doesn't even want to know what his child will be like, especially growing up with a father like that." A soft smile came to her face. "At least, you escaped him and met my brother. Sebastian will make sure you're safe, and he loves you."

Although her heart warmed at the whispered words, Charlotte shook her head. "I did things that are unforgivable and have lost every right to happiness." Then she looked up and met Victoria's gaze. "But you have not. You are truly innocent in all of this, and I swear I will find a way to right what went wrong."

Brows drawn down, Victoria stared at her. "What do you mean?"

"I cannot say now," Charlotte replied, raking her brain for a solution that seemed non-existent, "but I will think of something. I spoke to your brother, and he and I agree." She took a deep breath as Victoria looked at her with a mixture of hope and fear in her eyes. "We cannot allow your marriage to continue much longer. I promise you we will find a way to end it. One way or another."

Chapter Thirty-Five

REASSURANCES

Taking a deep breath, Sebastian knocked on the door to the drawing room. Although he hated to have to disturb them, he knew this couldn't wait.

When his wife's voice beckoned him to enter, he opened the door and found them seated near the large window front. While his sister looked rather shaken, her eyes red-rimmed and wide as though she had seen something horrible, his wife appeared rather determined, her lips pressed together and her eyes undaunted.

"I apologise for disturbing you," he said, stepping closer, his eyes shifting from his wife to his sister. "I've just received news from Hartridge Hall."

Victoria rose to her feet. "Father?"

Sebastian nodded, and seeing the apprehension in her eyes realised that the only regret and sadness he felt were for his sister's well-being. "He passed away two days ago."

"I see." Victoria swallowed, and a single tear escaped the corner of her eye and ran down her cheek. However, Sebastian doubted that it was sadness over their father's loss that had produced it, but rather the emotional turmoil that had brought her here so early in the morning. "Does Mother know?"

"She does," Sebastian replied, relieved to see that their father's death did not impact his sister's already strained nerves in a harmful way. "She is having everything packed up for our return to Hartridge Hall."

"When?"

"Early tomorrow morning."

Victoria nodded. "I should go speak to her. Maybe she needs my help." Turning to the door, she glanced over her shoulder, a soft smile on her face as she looked at him. "As the new Earl of Weston, I can only hope that you strive for happiness, dear Brother, not greatness." Then her eyes travelled to his wife, and a silent word passed between them that Sebastian couldn't understand. "After all, you have something he didn't: a wife who loves you."

Still staring at his sister when the door had already closed behind her, Sebastian found himself shaken to his core.

This revelation-if it was indeed true-had caught him off guard and made him realise the small hope he had fostered in his heart that one day-one day-his wife would come to love him. Had she?

Slowly turning on his heel, he caught her eyes, his own burning with an all-consuming question.

In answer, she dropped her gaze and a touch of red rose to her cheeks.

Never in his life had Sebastian felt so relieved and overjoyed, and a deep smile, honest and pure, drew up the corners of his mouth. It was true, wasn't it? She loved him.

Swallowing, he watched her. He saw her lowered head, her eyes firmly fixed on the ground, her hands playing with the skirt of her dress as her feet carried her around the room without direction ... merely to escape his scrutinising gaze!

Without a doubt, Sebastian knew that she was embarrassed to have her most intimate feelings dragged out into the light of day-especially without warning-and so he decided to level the playing field. Clearing his throat, he approached her, cutting off her attempt to step past him.

Stopping short, she looked up, her teeth gnawing on her lower lip as her eyes shifted back and forth between his and something beyond his shoulder. "I should see if your mother needs my help as well. I'm certain there will be a lot of -."

"I love you, too," Sebastian whispered, interrupting her nervous chattering. He had said it before-only the night before in the stables-and yet, it felt like the first time ... in the light of day with nothing to hide behind.

Instantly, her head snapped up and her eyes sought his.

"I just thought you should know," he said, seeing the pulse in her veins hammer as fast as his own. "I'm hoping that one day there won't be any secrets left between us, and so I'm starting with this one." He swallowed, holding her gaze as she looked at him, strangely transfixed, "I love you."

Slowly, she inhaled, and for a moment, her eyes touched his lips.

Sebastian smiled. "Are you thinking about kissing me?"

Clearly taken aback, her eyes went wide, and she quickly shook her head. "Of course not." Averting her gaze, she stepped back, a slight tremble shaking her frame.

For a moment, Sebastian hesitated until he realised that nothing physical would ever happen between them unless he challenged her. "Are you not curious?" he asked lightly as he stepped toward her. "About what it feels like?"

Forcing her eyes to meet his, she stood up straight, her features hardening. "I do know what it feels like," she reminded him, a slight tremble in her voice as she forced herself to stand her ground. And yet, her shoulders tensed and her body quivered as though she wanted nothing more but to turn and run.

Understanding the precarious situation they found themselves in, Sebastian held her gaze gently ... but firmly as well. "Not all kisses are the same," he whispered, drawing confidence from the spark of curiosity in her hazel eyes. "Those that are taken without permission are rarely pleasurable. However, those given freely are quite intoxicating."

A soft smile came to her lips, and she quickly dropped her gaze, inhaling deeply before meeting his once more.

Sebastian noticed how his own breathing quickened as he stepped closer. "When I touch you," he asked, praying that she would not run from him now, "does it feel the same as it did when *he* touched you?"

As expected, the smile slid off her face, and she drew in a shaky breath. However, she remained where she was and held his gaze without flinching.

For a long excruciating moment, she simply stood there, remembering the few moments he had indeed touched her: helping her into or out of the carriage, leading her in a dance or returning her home from Westminster Bridge. Then she shook her head, and Sebastian exhaled the breath he'd been holding. "No, it does not feel the same."

"Have I ever given you any reason not to trust me?" he asked, holding his breath once again. "Are you afraid I will break my promise?"

Looking up, she searched his face, then slowly shook her head. "I do trust you," she whispered. "I have for a long time, and yet ..."

"And yet?" he pressed, taking yet another step closer, unwilling to let this opportunity slip through his fingers.

With her lips pressed into a tight line, she looked at him, her eyes apologetic. "And yet, a part of me fears you."

Taken aback, Sebastian swallowed. "What? Why?"

Shrugging her shoulders, she shook her head. "I'm not sure. It's like an instinct. I've learnt to be afraid of men who look at me the way ..."

"The way I do?"

She nodded. "I cannot unlearn what that night taught me. Believe me, I do wish I could."

"Maybe you don't need to unlearn anything," Sebastian suggested, hoping that her fears would allow her to keep an open mind. "Maybe you simply need to question what exactly you *did* learn that night."

Her eyes narrowed in confusion as she looked at him, searching his face for an answer. "What do you mean?"

"Of all the men you've met in your life," Sebastian asked, "how many have truly betrayed you? Do they all deserve to be feared? Or was not the lesson you learnt that there are some, only some, you need to be wary of?"

Her eyes became distant as she considered his words, and for a long moment, she remained quiet. Then she met his gaze once more.

"You're right. I know you're right, and yet, I do not know if it changes how I feel." She took a deep breath, and her gaze dipped to his hand. "Whenever you reach out for me, I ... I feel terrified." Her brows drew down into a frown, and she shook her head. "Strangely, it is not because I mistrust you, but ... I don't know what it is. I don't know how to explain what it feels like to have ... someone overrule your own choices, your own emotions and dictate how you feel and act."

Sebastian swallowed, trying to understand. "Maybe you simply need time ... and reassurances to help you believe that not all men who find you desirable would force themselves on you."

"Reassurances?"

As an idea struck, a deep smile came to Sebastian's face. "What if I *couldn't* reach for you? Would you still be afraid?"

Her forehead in a frown, she eyed him curiously. "What do you mean?"

Holding her gaze, Sebastian stepped closer until her eyes narrowed, and he could see that his proximity began to scare her. "If I *couldn't* reach for you, if I *couldn't* take more than you're willing to give," he asked, taking a deep breath, "would you want to kiss me?"

Drawing in a shaky breath, his wife looked up at him, her eyes travelling over his face until they reached his lips, where they lingered for a moment. Then she looked up into his eyes, and a slight shiver went over her.

"Would you be tempted?" Sebastian whispered, seeing her shiver once more as his breath brushed over her cheek. "Would you?" Feeling the gentle warmth that radiated from her body like the sun's own rays that touched his skin, Sebastian found himself tempted beyond imagining to simply reach out and pull her into his arms.

But he couldn't.

If he did, all would be ruined.

All hope lost.

A soft smile touched her lips, and a hint of embarrassment came to her eyes as she met his. Then she nodded. "I think I might be," she whispered before drawing in a deep breath. "I think I already am."

Joy filled Sebastian's body, and he could barely keep himself in check as an overwhelming desire to hold her in his arms rushed through him.

Instead, though, he drew in a shaky breath, hoping to steady his nerves, and then stepped past her toward the heavy curtains framing the windows. Turning back to look at her, he untied the rope that kept the curtain from falling closed, a smile on his face. "Then let me give you some reassurance that I won't."

With confusion in her eyes, she watched as he took the rope from the curtain, allowing it to swing forward, then walked over to the fireplace and pulled one of the armchairs into the centre of the room. A smile on his face, he sat down on it and held out the rope to her. "I assume you know how to tie a knot."

With wide eyes, she stared at the rope he was holding out to her before her gaze shifted back to him as he placed the other arm on the chair's armrest. "You cannot be serious," she gasped, shock on her face; and yet, there was a spark of temptation in her eyes. "I could never."

Sebastian grinned, feeling mischievous. "You don't know how to tie a knot? That's a pity. I'd hoped-"

"I certainly do, but-"

"Good. Then this shouldn't be a problem." Still holding out the rope to her, Sebastian rejoiced as he saw the temptation in her eyes grow. Again, she gnawed on her lower lip, her eyes shifting back and forth between the rope and his face. Then her hands twitched, and she took a step forward.

Sebastian smiled.

Suddenly, she stopped, shaking her head as she glanced over her shoulder at the door. "I can't. What if someone comes in? Your sister? Or-?"

"All right." Jumping from the chair, determined not to allow anything to interfere, Sebastian pulled open the door and gestured to one of the footmen waiting by the front door to come over.

"Yes, my lord?"

"I want you to guard this door. No one is allowed in. Understood?"

"Yes, my lord," the footman answered hesitantly, a hint of confusion on his face at such an unusual request.

However, Sebastian couldn't have cared less and closed the door without another word. Turning around, he met his wife's wide eyes. "There. That's taken care of. Any other concerns?" he asked, a challenging smile on his face as he approached her.

Shaking her head at him, she bit her lower lip, trying to suppress a grin. "You do believe this is wildly funny, do you not?" she chided.

Peering into her eyes, Sebastian shook his head, and slowly the expression on his face became serious. "Not at all. I've never been more serious about anything in my life." Taking a deep breath, he watched as the humour left her eyes, revealing the tension that held her in its grip. "If you don't want to," he whispered, "then I will respect that. I would never break the promise I've given you."

Holding his gaze, his wife nodded. "I know you wouldn't." She swallowed, then licked her lips and nodded. "I do want to."

Sebastian's eyes widened. "You do?" he asked, wondering if he'd misunderstood with all the blood rushing in his ears. "Are you certain?"

"As certain as I'll ever be." Although there was a hint of mischief in her eyes, she smiled up at him shyly, then glanced at the chair. "If you'd be so kind," she said, holding out a trembling hand for the rope.

Nodding, Sebastian complied, then sat down, his own hands shaking with anticipation.

As she began to latch his arms to the chair, she kept her eyes on the task at hand, not meeting his gaze. She worked slowly, hesitantly, and yet, there was a sense of determination to her movements.

When her skin brushed against his as she tied down his other arm, a jolt went through Sebastian, and he finally realised how excruciating it would be for him to feel her so close, but be unable to touch her.

When she was finished, she rose to her feet, surveying her handiwork, her hands clenched as she stood with her gaze lowered.

Seeing how nervous she was, Sebastian tried to lighten the mood. "Have you been a sailor in a previous life? These knots look masterfully done. I can barely move." Doing his best to wiggle his arms, he found that she had indeed done an amazing job.

For better or for worse, he was at her mercy.

A smile came to her lips as she met his eyes. "I never thought I'd ever tie anyone to a chair. The whole idea seems ludicrous," she laughed, shaking her head.

Sebastian shrugged. "Well, I suppose there's a first time for every-thing." He held her gaze. "So? Have you made up your mind? Are you going to kiss me?" he teased, grinning at her. "I wouldn't hesitate to kiss you, but," again, he tried to wiggle his arms, "currently my options are severely limited."

His wife laughed, and some of the tension left her shoulders. Then she took a careful step closer, and a bright red lit up her cheeks. "Could you ... could you maybe close your eyes?" she asked. "I feel very self-conscious with you watching me."

"As you wish," Sebastian said and complied, finding it strangely exciting that he couldn't see her, couldn't see the way she looked at him, couldn't see how she felt or what she did or thought to do.

For a long time, he merely heard the soft rustling of her skirts as his patience and self-control slowly wore down. Eager to feel her touch, he was relieved that his hands were quite literally bound, and he was thus unable to do anything unwise.

When she finally touched him, he nearly jumped out of his skin.

Gently, her fingertips brushed over his cheek, then travelled down and felt his chin.

Angling his face slightly upward and to the right, Sebastian felt his body strain toward her, seeking her touch, craving it like a man dying of thirst would be drawn to an oasis.

Growing bolder, she cupped the side of his face with her hand, slowly sliding it down the line of his jaw. When she reached his mouth, she hesitated before her thumb gently brushed over his lower lip.

Sebastian sucked in a sharp breath, the fine nerve endings in his lips tingling with anticipation.

Then he felt her breath on his skin and sensed the warmth of her body as she slowly leant closer. When her lips finally touched his, he moaned.

At first, her kiss was like the touch of a feather, soft and fleeting, before it began to linger, and the pressure increased. Her hands brushed down the side of his face, along his neck and then slid back into his hair.

Fighting for control, Sebastian held himself back when all his senses urged him to deepen the kiss.

And yet, despite his own confinement, he found himself savouring every little touch and caress she bestowed on him. Her movements were tentative and inexperienced, yet curious and unexpectedly inquisitive, and before long, she was the one who deepened the kiss.

Pulling herself closer to him, she wrapped her arms around his shoulders and then slid onto his lap. With her chest pressed to his, she clung to him, and her lips explored the finer nuances of a kiss given freely and accepted just the same.

After a while, her explorations slowed, became gentler and softer until she sat back and he opened his eyes.

"Again, masterfully done," he teased, smiling up at her.

For a second, her eyes narrowed, and she shook her head. Then her mouth split into a grin, and she reached out a hand and pinched him in the arm.

"Ouch!" Sebastian exclaimed. "You didn't just-?"

"You deserved it," she chided him, a twinkle of amusement in her glowing eyes. "It is not proper to laugh at a lady."

"My apologies, my lady," Sebastian whispered, his voice teasing. "I cannot explain what came over me. For some odd reason, my mental faculties seem to be compromised now."

His wife laughed in such an honest, unrestrained way, free of doubt and regret, that Sebastian couldn't help but stare at her in awe. Never had he seen her so relaxed and untroubled. "Feel free to tie me up any time you choose," he continued to tease her, wishing more than anything that he could touch her glowing face. "Early in the morning. Late at night. You don't even have to ask."

A deep smile came to her face as she rolled her eyes at him. "As long as I compensate you with a kiss?"

"Well, yes, that goes without saying."

For a long moment, they simply looked at each other, comfortable with the new intimacy that had grown between them. Sebastian knew that they had taken an important first step toward a shared future, and although he loathed the thought of losing the lightness of her touch, he knew nothing more could happen between them that day. If he rushed her, she would retreat from him, and that was the last thing he wanted. "Maybe we should see to my mother and Victoria," he suggested rather reluctantly.

His wife blinked as though just waking from a spell. "Yes, of course. You're right." Somewhat distracted, she slid off his lap, her eyes once again darting around the room, unable to meet his. "Do you think they're in the back parlour?" she asked, heading toward the door. "Or upstairs?"

"I wouldn't know," Sebastian said, trying to suppress the laughter that bubbled up as he watched her. "However, I'd truly love to help you locate them if you would first help me."

"Help you?" she asked, turning around. "With what?"

Still sitting tied to the armchair, Sebastian grinned at her, which turned into a deep laugh the moment her eyes widened, and she clasped a hand over her mouth. "Since I'm neither a magician nor a con-artist, I fear I'm at your mercy."

Grinning, she bit her lower lip and hastened over, all nervousness vanished as she knelt beside him and began to work on the first knot. "I'm sorry. I suppose it slipped my mind."

"That's understandable," Sebastian mocked. "After all, my kisses are legendary. A certain sense of disorientation was to be expected."

Laughing, his wife shook her head. "Do you truly believe it wise to mock someone who can very easily leave you here for the rest of the day?"

Grinning, he stared at her. "You wouldn't?"

"Are you absolutely certain?"

"I'd scream for help," he threatened, enjoying himself immensely. "After all, I'm the new Earl of Weston."

His wife shrugged, clearly unimpressed. "I tied you to a chair what is supposed to keep me from gagging you?"

Staring at her, Sebastian soon broke down laughing, feeling even more euphoric when his wife joined in. This was truly one of the best days of his life!

"Now, hold still," she ordered, turning her attention back to the knot, "or I might be tempted to carry out my threat."

Sitting quietly in his chair, Sebastian watched her as she untied his arms, then quickly stood and returned the rope to the curtain, carefully fixing it back in place.

Regret filled him at the distance that so suddenly sprung up between them, and without another thought, he crossed the room. "Do you need any help?" he asked, experiencing a moment of nervousness as he grasped for something to say that would allow them to hold on to the intimacy they'd shared.

"Not necessary," she said, turning around to look at him. "Remember? I'm good at tying knots."

Sebastian smiled, holding her gaze as she smiled up at him. "I haven't forgotten," he whispered as the world around them fell away once more.

Again, she bit her lip and studied his face as though contemplating something that hadn't occurred to her before. Then she took a deep breath and took a step toward him. "Can I ask you to ... simply stand still? And not move? At all?"

Holding her gaze and seeing the same nervousness there that he felt course through his own veins, Sebastian nodded. "I'll do my best."

"All right," she whispered as though to herself. Then her gaze dropped from his, and she reached out her hands and slipped them into his, gently squeezing his fingers.

Sebastian inhaled deeply, savouring the soft touch of her skin against his.

When she pulled his arms forward and then stepped into his embrace, he thought he was dreaming. Carefully, she placed his hands on her waist, then slowly pushed them farther onto her back as she pressed closer against him. Her hands slid up his arms until they locked behind his neck, and she looked up at him, a soft, rather daring smile curling up her lips. "Don't move," she whispered as she pushed herself up onto her toes, her lips inching closer toward his.

"I couldn't if I wanted to," Sebastian breathed, closing his eyes as her warm breath swept over the curve of his mouth.

"Let me try this," she whispered against his lips before her mouth closed over his and Sebastian's heart skipped a beat ... or two.

From one second to the next, all his senses zeroed in on that one touch that connected them, and his nerve endings went into overload.

Recognising the trust she placed in him, Sebastian began to feel lightheaded.

Before, it had been safe ... for the both of them. She had been the one in control. Even if he had wanted to-and quite frankly, he had-he couldn't have touched her.

Now, though, everything was different.

There was nothing to hold him back. No sailor's knot to keep him restrained. Nothing but the trust she placed in him, and he wondered if she was even aware of the precarious situation they suddenly found themselves in.

Willing his hands to remain where they were and not explore her body further, Sebastian concentrated on the kiss, savouring each soft touch, each shared breath as she pressed herself against him. And yet, he found himself unable not to respond to the passion that burnt between them.

As he deepened the kiss, the muscles in his arms tightened, holding her closer, and it was all he could do not to crush her in his arms.

Before long, her own explorations waned, and a nervous tension came to her body.

Cursing himself, Sebastian instantly released her, forcing himself to step back. "I'm sorry," he said, swallowing before he dared meet her eyes, afraid what he might see there. "I suppose I got carried away."

"I noticed," she said, breathing heavily as she held on to his hands.

Relieved beyond imagining that her eyes held neither fear nor regret, Sebastian smiled at her. "Maybe it would be safer for the both of us if we had some reassurances. At least for now."

Smiling, his wife closed her eyes for a moment. "Maybe you're right." She took a deep breath and held his gaze. "But it did feel ... intoxicating."

"I'm glad it did," he whispered, gently squeezing her hands, reluctant to let go.

Then a knock sounded on the door.

Chapter Thirty-Six

THE ENEMY

She had *kissed* him.

Was she mad?

Rolling around in her bed unable to keep still, Charlotte spent the night before their departure to Hartridge Hall alternately staring up at the ceiling and burying her face in her pillows.

She hadn't planned on kissing him. Quite frankly, she had been certain she would never again kiss anyone ... ever again.

Naturally, once upon a time, she, too, had dreamed of love and marriage and a family of her own. But then one night had shattered it all, and from then on, the present as well as the future had merely been about surviving.

Not about finding love.

Not about finding happiness.

Out of the shadows, it had sneaked up on her, seizing her when she'd least expected it.

After Lord Northfield had re-entered her life, Charlotte had been certain that all was lost. She had resigned herself to giving up the family she had found so unexpectedly and returning to the shadows.

Only now, everything was different.

Or was it?

While her mind argued that nothing had changed, that Northfield *could* and *would* still reveal her past to her new family, to her husband, her heart simply didn't care.

All it cared about was the feeling of peace, of belonging, of being whole again that her husband's kiss-*her kiss*-had stirred within her.

Even now, hours later, her body hummed with the memory of his touch. Never had she thought it possible that a man's touch could feel … pleasant. More than pleasant. It truly had been intoxicating, and a part of her hadn't wanted to stop.

And she hadn't, had she?

He had stopped.

Somehow, he had known that she hadn't been ready, that they needed to take things slow, and despite the lack of *reassurance*, he had kept his word.

A deep smile came to her face when she realised that her judgement of him had been correct. He was indeed an honourable man. A good man, who put her well-being before his own.

She could be happy with him.

If only …

Although Charlotte exchanged the occasional meaningful glance with her husband the following morning, which sent her heart into an uproar-a delightfully exciting one-the general mood was rather subdued. Which, of course, was understandable, considering that they were heading back for the late earl's funeral.

However, it was not sadness that rested in his family's eyes, but rather the notion that they *ought* to feel sad. After all, death was a sad occasion and the departed ought to be mourned. And yet, in all honesty, they hadn't cared for the late earl when he'd been alive. Why would they now in death?

As they sat in the carriage, heart and mind didn't go hand in hand. While they could not shed honest tears for a man who had shared their blood but not their lives, they knew that it would be in bad taste to chat and laugh as they would on a journey. And so, they all remained quiet, each glancing out the window at the passing landscape.

When they had found Victoria on their doorstep that morning, Charlotte had nearly suffered a heart attack for fear her sister-in-law's husband was just around the corner waiting for the opportune moment to make his presence known. However, according to Victoria, he had not been home when she had returned the day before, and so, she had merely left him a note saying that her father had passed away and that she would return to her family's estate for a few days.

Charlotte had been relieved, and so had her husband.

Although they had agreed that something had to be done about Northfield-mostly for Victoria's sake-they hadn't had an opportunity to discuss details. However, now that they were leaving London, Charlotte hoped that Northfield would find other entertainment and forget about her ... at least for a little while.

Once they returned, she would think of a solution.

She had to.

When they arrived at Hartridge Hall, Charlotte felt as though she had been gone a lifetime. Glancing up at the looming facade, she remembered the moment she had first crossed the threshold. She remembered the unadulterated shock on the earl's face when he had been informed that she was now his daughter-in-law. But she also remembered her mother-in-law's warm welcome as well as Victoria's delight to see her brother married.

Opening the door to her old bedchamber, Charlotte shook her head, wondering how the world could have changed so drastically in so short a time. It had been all but a few weeks since she'd last slept in this bed, and yet, her life had taken a sharp turn ... or rather two.

One for the worse.

And one for the better.

Charlotte wondered which one would ultimately define her future, and although she hoped that it was the new love slowly growing between her husband and her, she knew deep in her heart that the threat Northfield presented would not simply vanish ... but rather return with a vengeance.

After all, he had always been set on seeing her fall.

That night after supper, they all sat together in the drawing room. While Victoria and her mother occupied the settee, their eyes focused on the needlework in their hands, Charlotte and Sebastian strode around the room, here and there stopping to look out the window at the darkened sky, to inspect one of the artefacts placed around the room or to gaze at one another, the memory of their kiss evident in their eyes.

It was an odd moment to feel such joy, and yet, Charlotte could barely contain herself. When her husband looked at her with such intensity, a soft smile playing on his lips, she felt like a young woman again, unburdened by her past, and her heart longed to hold on to that feeling, determined never to relinquish the treasure it had found so unexpectedly.

Once more stopping by the window, Charlotte pressed her lips together to suppress a most inappropriate smile as her husband, who had remained at the fireplace looking at a painting, abandoned his post and strode over. His sleeve brushed against hers as he came to stand beside her. His eyes sparkled with mischief, and yet, he took great care not to touch her.

Shoulder to shoulder, they stood, and Charlotte felt her heart thud in her chest as her body became increasingly aware of his presence ... so close, and yet, not close enough.

Allowing her hand to drop to her side, she kept her gaze fixed out the window as she shifted on her feet, her fingers slightly brushing against his. Instantly, a jolt shot through her, and she heard him suck in a breath before his eyes shifted to hers, an alluring smile drawing up the corners of his mouth.

When a knock sounded on the door, they both flinched.

"Excuse me, my lord, my ladies," Hartridge Hall's butler mumbled, "but you have a visitor."

"This late?" the dowager countess asked, a frown on her face as she put aside her needlework and rose to her feet.

"Who is it?" Sebastian asked, turning toward the door.

As the butler opened his mouth to reply, footsteps echoed from behind and a moment later the door swung open, revealing Victoria's husband in its frame.

Blind panic seized Charlotte.

Closing her eyes briefly, she gulped down a few breaths of air and fought down the terror that held her in its clutches with everything she had, remembering that he could not harm her if he did not catch her alone ... or reveal the truth about her.

"Northfield," Sebastian growled beside her, instinctively taking a step forward, shielding her from the threat that had entered their house.

"Good evening," their guest greeted them, a delighted smile on his face while his eyes burnt with excitement. "I apologise for the delay. I would have arrived sooner, but important business kept me in Town."

While Victoria and the dowager countess remained quiet, the expression on their faces speaking of annoyance as well as displeasure, Sebastian approached their uninvited guest. "What are you doing here?"

Feigning surprise, Northfield frowned. "I'm here to pay my respects to your late father. Truly, he was a most honourable man and will be greatly missed. I, myself, owe him a debt of gratitude, for without his diligence, I would not have such a lovely woman in my life." However, instead of looking at Victoria, his eyes travelled to Charlotte, and what she saw there sent cold shivers down her back.

Why had he come? After all, he had given her a fortnight to respond to his ... offer. Had he changed his mind? Or did he simply enjoy seeing her so miserable?

Temporarily distracted, Charlotte barely noticed the tension that rested in her husband's shoulders. Only when his gaze followed Northfield's and came to rest upon her did she notice his hands slowly balling into fists, an enraged snarl on his face.

"Is something wrong?" Northfield asked in mock concern, his gaze fixed on his brother-in-law's face, amusement lighting up his eyes. "Are you not feeling well?"

Aware that her husband was only seconds away from lunging himself at Northfield, Charlotte stepped forward and quickly slid her arm through his. "I'm tired, my dear," she said, pulling him forward and past Northfield. "Let's continue this discussion in the morning."

Although she could feel his reluctance to go in the tense muscles under her fingers, her husband allowed her to lead him from the room, his face dark and twisted with barely controlled rage. The moment the door closed behind them, he stopped, his eyes turning to her. "Are you all right?" he asked through gritted teeth as his gaze slowly grew softer.

"I'm fine," Charlotte assured him, once more taking hold of his arm and dragging him onward. Who knew what would happen if North-field decided to follow them?

"I'm sorry," he growled as they headed up the stairs. "That man should not be here, and yet, it is his right." A dark laugh rose from his throat. "After all, he is *family*."

"I know," Charlotte whispered, feeling the same sense of absurdity at the current situation. That man was the enemy; yet, they could not keep him from entering their home.

Opening the door to her bedchamber, Charlotte pulled her husband inside. "But you must not go after him," she cautioned as an old fear crept into her heart. "He is baiting you, taunting you, and if you let down your guard, he will destroy you." Coming to stand before him, she looked up into her husband's eyes. "I don't want to lose you, too."

A slow smile touched his lips as his gaze began to soften.

Reaching up her hand, Charlotte cupped his cheek, suddenly unable not to touch him. Then she bit her lower lip in a moment of indecision before she reached up and pulled him into a kiss.

When had this happened? She wondered. When had she become so dependent on the feel of his skin against hers? Mere days ago, the thought of his touch would have sent her fleeing from the room.

Hesitating for no more than a second, her husband wrapped his arms around her, pulling her closer, a low growl rumbling in is throat as he returned her kiss hungrily.

Passion ignited between them, heating her skin and stealing her breath. His lips were eager, demanding, and his hands held her posses-sively, their embrace unyielding. Instead of tender, his touch was rough, and a spark of fear began to burn in her heart as her soul remembered the power of blind, all-consuming desire with no regard for anything but its own needs.

However, before she could will herself to stop him, he suddenly released her, stepping back. Breathing heavily, he shook his head, eyes apologetic as he gazed at her swollen lips. "I'm sorry. We shouldn't do this. Not here. Not now." He took a deep breath, seeking to steady his rattled nerves. "I'm too close to losing control that I fear I cannot trust myself right now, and the last thing I want is to lose your trust in me."

Touched by his words, Charlotte nodded in agreement despite the regret that echoed in her heart. "I suppose you're right." She cleared her throat and met his eyes. "After all, there are more important matters to discuss. I had hoped it could wait until after your father's funeral, but I suppose I should have known that ... *he* ... would not allow us to bury him in peace."

"Bury him in peace?" her husband scoffed, shaking his head. "Please, do not worry about how we bury my father for it is merely an obligation for us. I know it is harsh to speak of him in such a way; yet, it is nothing but the truth." He swallowed and openly met her eyes, regret and a touch of sadness resting in their blue depths. "I never loved him as I am certain he never loved me, and the only thing I feel saddened about is the thought that a long time ago, I might have had a chance to have a father who cared about me, about who I was and not merely about the fact that I was his heir, born to uphold the family name." He took a deep breath. "But that time has come and gone, and although I regret the turn our lives has taken, nothing I do now will ever change that and I've made my peace with it. At this point, I bear him no ill-will. He is of no importance to me. The only thing I've ever been grateful to him for is that he's taught me what not to do." Grasping her hands, he looked deep into her eyes. "For the thought of living a life like his, of being cold and distant, of having those around me despise me turns my stomach. Life is too precious to waste it on unimportant matters. From now on, all my efforts shall go to ensuring the happiness of those dearest to my heart."

Smiling up at him, Charlotte nodded. "You've come a long way from the rash and unrelenting man I met only a couple of months ago." She squeezed his hands, and he smiled at her. "I'm proud of you."

He grinned, and a mischievous twinkle came to his eyes. "You know what? I, too, am proud of myself. I assure you it was not easy to let go of something that has been on my mind for the past decade, and I certainly couldn't have done it without you. You helped me see what was important, what I needed ... and what I wanted."

As his eyes burned into hers, Charlotte breathed a sigh of relief. More than anything, she wanted to give in and step into the embrace he offered, and yet, she knew that there were more important matters to take care of first. "What shall we do about Victoria?" she asked as he stepped toward her.

Instantly, he stopped, and the smile died on his lips. Hanging his head, he gritted his teeth. "I've thought about it, and I'm ashamed to say that I don't know what to do. That man," a menacing growl rose from his throat, "he may be the devil incarnate, but he is also her husband, and as such, she is bound to him for the rest of her life. There is nothing we can do, no legal argument that could declare their marriage void. Believe me, I've made enquiries."

The breath caught in Charlotte's throat as his words echoed in her head. ... *she is bound to him for the rest of her life* ...

How could she not have seen it before? It was so simple, so easy, and suddenly so clear.

A life for a life.

That thought had echoed in her mind once before ... and it had led to a terrible injustice. A tragedy.

Now, this was her chance to repay her debt.

"What's wrong?" her husband asked, his eyes slightly narrowed as they studied her face. "What are you thinking?"

Charlotte took a deep breath before she looked at him. "Nothing," she whispered as her mind raced, torn whether to tell him. Would he be supportive? How could he be?

"Don't lie to me," he replied, the muscles in his throat suddenly tense. "I can see that you've come to some kind of conclusion, and the fact that you won't share it with me suggests that it is something most unwise." His hands grasped her shoulders. "Tell me."

Knowing that he wouldn't be dissuaded, Charlotte sighed. "All right," she whispered, meeting his eyes. "However, you must promise me not to stand in my way."

His eyes narrowed. "I will promise no such thing," he declared, shaking his head, "and the fact that you would ask this of me speaks volumes. Tell me! Now!"

Charlotte swallowed. "You said she is bound to him for the rest of her life."

"So?"

"That's not entirely true," she corrected, and a determined smile came to her lips. "Don't you see? Now that your father has passed on, your mother is free again to live the remainder of her life in a way that pleases her."

A confused frown drew down his brows. "But what does-?" Then he stopped, and his eyes narrowed even more. "You're not suggesting we sit and wait for him to die of some kind of affliction, are you?" he asked, suspicion ringing in his voice and his hands tightening on her shoulders. "What are you saying?"

Meeting his gaze without flinching, Charlotte took a deep breath. "Are you certain you wish to know?"

"I think I already know," he replied, his features tense, "but I need you to say it nonetheless."

"As you said, that man is evil in every sense of the word," she began, hoping that on some level he would be able to understand. "He doesn't deserve to live and inflict pain on those around him. For as long as he's alive, Victoria will be forced to live in a world of shame and degradation."

Staring at her as though she had just sprouted another head, her husband swallowed. "Would you truly take his life?"

"He doesn't deserve mercy," she reminded him.

"I'm not concerned about him," her husband whispered, his eyes clouded as they searched her face, "but about you." He swallowed. "You speak as though ..."

This was it! Charlotte thought. Finally, the moment had come when she couldn't hide the dark side of her being from her husband any longer. Since he met her, he had only ever seen her as a victim. Now, he would have to find out that she hadn't been a victim for a long time.

Holding his questioning gaze, Charlotte nodded. "I tried to tell you this before, but you wouldn't believe me. I told you that I've done things that are unforgivable, that-"

"But you wouldn't ..." Staring at her, he shook his head. "You didn't ..."

As tears stung behind her eyes, Charlotte nodded, whispering a silent goodbye to the wonderful dream that would now come to an end. "But I did," she said, confirming his suspicions. "I took someone's life."

Chapter Thirty-Seven
ANOTHER SECRET REVEALED

U nblinking, Sebastian stared at his wife, waiting, hoping for her to tell him that it wasn't true. After all, she couldn't have. Could she? *His* wife! *His* Charlotte! She had only ever been kind-hearted and sweet, diligent in her care for his mother, his sister ... and him as well. Could this possibly be true?

"I know you don't want to believe this," she spoke when he remained quiet, not knowing what to say, "but it is true, and no amount of wishful thinking is going to change that." She swallowed, tears brimming in her eyes. "We're not equals. You're a good man, but I ..." She shook her head. "I've done something irredeemable, and this is my chance to ... make amends. Maybe this is fate. Maybe I am still alive because I was meant to deliver your sister from this marriage to a man who set me on the path to my own destruction long ago." She shrugged, blinking rapidly and tears fell from her eyelashes and rolled down her cheeks. "Although I wish it were different, I cannot change what happened. I do wish I could simply forget about the past and look to the future, a future with you. You have no idea how much I wish I could." Pressing her lips together, she wiped the tears from her cheeks. "But it wouldn't be right. I don't deserve happiness, and I'm sorry that my past causes you pain. I should never have involved you in all of this. I should never have married you, and yet," a soft smile came to her lips as she looked at him through a curtain of tears, "I cannot bring myself to regret it."

Taking a deep breath, Sebastian tried to organise his thoughts. So many things had come rushing at him in the past few minutes that he hardly knew what to think. All he knew for certain was that she spoke as though she was saying goodbye, and his heart twisted in agony at the thought of losing her. "How?" he demanded as a dark suspicion emerged from the fog clouding his mind. "How do you plan to deliver my sister?"

His wife took a deep breath, and for a moment, he thought she would drop her gaze. But she didn't. Her eyes remained fixed on his, telling him more than words ever could.

He saw pain and regret, but also love and devotion as well as a determination that almost knocked his legs out from under him.

Gritting his teeth, he tightened his hands on her shoulders as though that would keep her from walking down the path she had chosen. "I won't allow it," he growled, shaking his head vehemently.

"It's not your choice," she whispered, a soft smile playing on her lips as she looked at him. "It's mine. Mine alone."

"You're my wife!" Again, he shook his head. "I won't let you go! Whatever you did, I'm certain you had your reasons. I-"

"You truly love me, don't you?" she whispered in awe, her eyes glowing as she looked up at him. "Why else would you try to ratio-nalise what I did? No one would. Only someone in love. Someone whose mind is clouded by his heart's desire."

"Yes, I *am* in love," Sebastian growled out, his arms coming around her, pulling her closer against him. "I love you, and I know the person you are. I cannot believe-I won't!-that you did something out of malice. There had to have been a good reason for you to-"

"He was a good man," his wife whispered, grief darkening her eyes. "He didn't deserve to die." Holding his gaze, she nodded. "He was loved, too. He had a wife and a daughter. He was loved." New tears came to her eyes. "What I did was unforgivable. As much as you like to believe that, I didn't have a good reason. He was not a villain. He was not like Northfield. He didn't deserve to die."

"Then why?" Sebastian choked out as despair clawed at his heart.

"That's a long story," his wife said, averting her gaze, "but it began that night when Northfield forced himself on me. That night set everything in motion, and it has brought us here." Again, she raised her eyes, cold steel shining in them as she looked at him. "Everything I've done has led me here, and now, I need to finish it once and for all."

Staring at her, Sebastian shook his head. "I won't let you!"

She took a deep breath, and then her gaze grew softer. "Thank you for everything you've done for me. I'd forgotten what it felt like to be loved, to have someone who would stand with me. You helped me remember who I once had been. I'd thought I'd lost that part of me a long time ago, but you helped me find it once more."

Holding her gaze, Sebastian wondered about the change in her tone as well as the softness that had come to her eyes.

"It is late," she whispered, and her eyes closed briefly. "Let us speak about this tomorrow."

Sebastian's gaze narrowed.

"Lock me in my room if you don't believe me," his wife challenged, exhaustion plain on her features. "I promise I won't do anything tonight."

"And after tonight?"

She took a deep breath. "I will do what I must."

Chapter Thirty-Eight
THE ONE AT FAULT

Sebastian rose early the next morning, long before the sun did. All night he had spent tormented by the news his wife had finally shared with him, and she had been right, a part of him wished he had never known.

After assuring himself that Charlotte was still asleep, he headed downstairs, unable to keep still. Since he would not leave her alone with Northfield under the same roof, he busied himself walking around the manor.

Lost in thought, he eventually entered the library and found his sister slumped in one of the armchairs, head tilted to one side, fast asleep.

His heart tightened in his chest, and he strode over, gently brushing a strand of hair from her forehead.

She sighed then, and her eyelids began to flutter.

A moment later, she awoke with a start, eyes wide and a hand clasped to her chest. When she saw him, relief came to her face, and she exhaled deeply. "Oh, it is you. Thank God."

"Did you think it was *him?*" Sebastian growled, suddenly more than tempted to head upstairs and strangle the man in his sleep. "Why are you sleeping in a chair?"

Rising to her feet, Victoria brushed down her dress, all the while avoiding meeting his gaze. "I guess I fell asleep reading."

"Reading?" Sebastian repeated, doubt in his voice. "What book did you read? And, where is it?"

Eyes flitting about the room, now and then darting to him, Victoria stammered for words. "Well, I … it … it must be here somewhere. Maybe one of the servants returned it to the shelf."

Shaking his head, Sebastian stepped forward; his hand caught her chin, forcing her to look at him. "You slept here to escape him, didn't you?"

Sadness filled her eyes, and for a moment, she closed them. Exhaustion clung to her features, and Sebastian feared that she would sink to the floor, unable to bear the weight resting on her shoulders any longer.

"We will find a solution, Victoria," he promised, holding her gaze, hoping that she would believe him and that he would not fail her again.

"There's nothing you can do," she whispered, resignation in her voice. "He's my husband, and I'm bound to him."

As anger coursed through his veins, Sebastian shook his head. "We shall see about that." Then he cleared his throat, ignoring the confused look in his sister's eyes, he asked, "Charlotte spoke to you, did she not?"

Victoria nodded. "After that night when …" Her voice trailed off, and she lowered her eyes.

"She told you how she came to … know your husband?" Sebastian forced out.

"She did," his sister confirmed, her eyes searching his once more. "She spoke to you as well."

"Yes, I came upon her that night as she sneaked out to the stables."

Victoria's eyes widened. "She wanted to run away?"

He nodded.

"I cannot blame her," she whispered. "I would do the same if I had the courage."

Seeing the misery on her face, Sebastian cursed. There had to be a way he could protect them both without allowing his wife to sacrifice herself for his sister. "She's determined to protect you," he confessed. "She wants to free you of your husband."

A soft smile came to Victoria's face. "She feels guilty for escaping him when I am trapped being his wife. I shall speak to her. It is not her fault."

Sebastian drew in a deep breath, uncertain if it was right to speak to his sister about this, and yet, he felt he would burst if he kept it in any longer. "She told me ... she took someone's life."

His sister's eyes widened in shock. "I'm certain she didn't mean-"

"No," he interrupted. "She was quite serious. She told me she killed someone."

"Why?"

"She didn't say. All she said was that he was innocent and what she did unforgivable."

"Who?" Victoria asked, her shoulders tense as she stood before him. "Do you know who she ...?"

Sebastian drew in a deep breath. "I've lain awake all night wondering about that."

"You didn't ask her?"

"I know I should have," he admitted, "and I know she would have told me, but ..." He sighed. "I couldn't bring myself to ask her for then it would have been true, and I wasn't quite ready to accept that last night."

For a moment, Victoria closed her eyes before she met his again. "I don't know much about her past. She's told me bits and pieces, but I'm certain that most of her story still lies in the dark. However, I refuse to believe that she's an evil person. She's nothing like my husband. There's no malice in her, no desire to triumph over others, to see them weak and degraded. Whatever she's done, there was a reason. I'm certain of it."

Sebastian nodded. If only he knew what it was! However, he was certain he would never know unless he finally asked her whose life she had taken and learn the rest of her story, however painful it might be.

Feigning a headache, Charlotte took breakfast in her chamber the next morning. As much as she refused to bow her head and run like a coward, the thought of sitting across the table from *that man* brought chills to her body that reached deep inside her bones.

She had to end this. Somehow, she had to end this.

After speaking to her husband the night before, Charlotte knew that her time had finally come. She could not run from it now, but had to find a way to use it to her advantage.

One good deed to balance out the atrocity she had committed.

And then she would be free.

Hopefully.

A knock sounded on the door, and Charlotte froze.

He wouldn't dare seek her out in her bedchamber, would he?

The thought turned her stomach upside down.

The moment she realised that *that man* would have no scruples of attacking her in such a manner and in her bedroom of all places, she also knew without a doubt that her husband would never allow it. Ever since Northfield had arrived, Sebastian had never been far from her side and had, in addition, posted footmen to stand by every door ... just in case.

"It's me, Victoria," her sister-in-law called. "May I come in?"

Breathing a sigh of relief, Charlotte hurried to open the door and invited her husband's sister inside. "Are you all right?" she asked, eyeing Victoria's pale cheeks and slumped shoulders with concern. "You were as shocked about his sudden arrival as were we, weren't you?"

Sinking into an armchair by the window, Victoria exhaled deeply, her limbs seemingly heavy as lead. "I never thought he would follow me here," she said, her eyes apologetic as she looked at Charlotte. "When I came to visit for Christmas, he stayed in town, and so I thought ..."

"He came because of me," Charlotte said, no doubt in her mind about Lord Northfield's intentions. "None of this is your fault. He came because he wants to torture me. He wants to see me squirm." Shaking her head, Charlotte took a deep breath. "He is the kind of man who derives pleasure from seeing others in pain."

"I know," Victoria whispered, not even a hint of surprise or shock on her features. Instead, it was resignation that clouded her eyes and stole the smile from her face. "And yet, I am sorry. After all, he is my husband, and as such, he has every right to be here. Otherwise, Sebastian could simply send him from the house."

"Don't blame yourself. He does what he does because of who he is," Charlotte counselled, worried by the dark lines under her sister-in-law's eyes. "If he wasn't your husband, he would find another way to seek me out."

"I suppose you're right," Victoria said. Then she sat up and met Charlotte's eyes. "I came here to speak to you because I know that you believe it to be your responsibility to liberate me from my marriage. You think if you had married him then, he couldn't have married me and I'd be free today." Victoria shook her head, tears clinging to her dark eyelashes. "But you mustn't blame yourself. If it hadn't been either of us, it would have been another unfortunate woman, and none of us would be at fault. Please hear me; it is not your duty to save me."

"I know," Charlotte whispered, touched by Victoria's strength and compassion. "I know that the only one at fault here is him, and yet, there is ..." She took a deep breath. "There is something in my past that I cannot forget. I did something that I cannot live with. It plagues me every day, and I've long sought the means to redeem myself ... if that is even possible."

"And you think by saving me, you can repay your debt?" Victoria asked, her knowing eyes travelling over Charlotte's face.

"Sebastian told you, didn't he?"

Victoria nodded. "Please don't hold it against him. He simply needed to speak to someone."

"I'm not angry," Charlotte replied, relieved that Victoria knew. Maybe eventually the truth would indeed set her free.

A relieved smile came to her sister-in-law's face. "I'm glad. He may be confused right now, but he truly loves you."

Biting her lower lip, Charlotte averted her eyes. Although she knew Victoria's words to be true, she felt unworthy of her husband's love. Who was she to find happiness in her marriage?

"Please believe me," Victoria went on, interpreting Charlotte's reaction as doubt. "That day when you fled my house after my husband came home, I met Sebastian at the theatre. I drew him aside and told him what had happened. You should have seen his face. He was so scared for you." She shook her head at the painful memory. "Even before I'd said a word, the moment he saw me coming, he knew that something was wrong, and his thoughts went to you right away. He barely said a word of goodbye to Lord Elmridge and his wife. In an instant, everyone around him was forgotten, and all he saw was you."

The blood froze in Charlotte's veins. "Lord Elmridge?" she stammered as her vision blurred, and her mind conjured the moment of Leopold's death.

"Yes, he and his wife were at the theatre that night," Victoria went on, eyeing Charlotte with a mixture of confusion and concern. "Sebastian and the late Lord Elmridge grew up together and were good friends. He passed on not two years ago. Since he only had a daughter, his brother Frederick inherited the title." Her eyes narrowed. "Do you know them?"

Staring into the distance, Charlotte couldn't believe her ears, her body stunned into paralysis. Leopold Lancaster, the man whose life she had taken, had been a childhood friend of her husband's.

Closing her eyes, Charlotte knew in that moment that all hope was finally lost. Now, there was no reason for her to tread lightly in hopes that her husband might find a way to forgive her past.

This put the final nail in her coffin.

Charlotte took a deep breath then, and for an instant, familiar emotions attacked her heart-pain, regret, shame and above all guilt-before they slowly faded away, leaving behind nothing but a barren rock where her heart had once beaten in her chest. The old fog once more settled on her mind, dulling her senses and shrouding the world in a grey veil.

Once more, she would act without emotion, cold and calculated, her eyes fixed on one thing alone: retribution.

Chapter Thirty-Nine

RETRIBUTION

P acing up and down the floor in front of the drawing room, Sebastian wrung his hands. More than anything, he wanted to stride through the doors and throttle the man who was currently exchanging polite pleasantries with his mother. And yet, he knew that it would only make things worse.

Not that that man didn't deserve an untimely and most importantly painful end. He did, more than anyone Sebastian had ever known.

Not trusting himself, he hurried up the staircase and down the corridor toward his wife's bedchamber. He had to speak to her. He had to know the truth as painful as it might be. Maybe, just maybe, they would find a way to deal with this awful situation.

As he came closer, Sebastian frowned as loud knocking sounded from up ahead. He turned a corner and found a chair shoved against his wife's bedroom door, blocking the handle from turning. "Hello? Is anyone out there?" his sister's voice called from behind the door. "Hello? Charlotte?"

Pulling the chair away, Sebastian flung open the door and met his sister's gaze, her eyes narrowed in concern. "What is going on here? What happened? Where is Charlotte?"

Swallowing, Victoria shook her head, her eyes glancing up and down the corridor. "I don't know. She just left. She pulled out the chair, closed the door and walked away ... without saying a word. Oh, Sebastian, I'm terribly worried about her."

As his own heartbeat quickened, Sebastian grasped his sister by the shoulders, lowering his head to meet her eyes. "Tell me what happened. Did you speak to her? What did she say?"

"Nothing." Shock evident on her face, Victoria stared at him. "She said nothing. She simply got up and left."

Sebastian frowned. "What did you talk about?"

"About my husband and how it's not her fault that I'm married to him," Victoria explained, her eyes darting from left to right as she raked her brain for a reason that would explain Charlotte's reaction. "I don't know what happened. I don't know what I said, but ..."

"But?" Sebastian pressed as the blood in his veins ran cold.

His sister met his eyes. "You should have seen her face. There was something ... It changed. Suddenly, it was as though she wasn't Charlotte any longer. I looked into her eyes, and she was gone, replaced by something cold and ... dead." A shiver went down her back as she stared at him, fear plain in her gaze.

"Did you see where she went?" he asked, hurrying out the door, his sister on his heels.

"No, she closed the door behind her before I could follow."

As they hurried down the stairs, Sebastian scanned their surroundings, but his wife was nowhere to be seen. "Search the east wing," he said to Victoria, "but don't alert your husband. He's in the drawing room with Mother."

"I won't," his sister assured him and hurried away.

Turning down the corridor that led to the library, Sebastian called to Coleridge as the old butler came toward him. "Have you seen my wife?"

"Not today, my lord," Coleridge said, then lifted a hand to stop Sebastian as he was about to rush past him. "Excuse me, my lord, but one of the pistols in your late father's collection is missing. The case stood open. Did you remove it?"

"No, I didn't. I-" The words died on his lips as a new cold gripped his heart. *His wife!* She had taken the pistol, determined to repay the debt she thought was hers.

Frantically, his eyes searched up and down the corridor. Where was she? No shot had been fired yet, but if he didn't find her soon, her life would be forfeit.

Turning on his heel, Sebastian hurried toward his father's study and the pistol collection the late earl had been so proud of, but stopped short after only a few steps. Of course, she wouldn't be there. She had already left, pistol in hand, and could be anywhere by now. Where was she?

Northfield!

Sebastian drew in a deep breath as the pulse hammered in his chest. He may not know where his wife was right now, but he knew where she would go. After all, Northfield was her target.

Spinning around once more, he rushed down the corridor toward the front hall, the elderly butler barely keeping up with his large strides. As he burst through the arched doorway, he saw his wife up ahead, a pistol in her right hand as she stepped toward the closed drawing room doors.

Not daring to call out, lest he should alert his mother or Northfield, Sebastian doubled his efforts and reached her the very moment as her hand moved toward the door handle.

Grabbing her by the arms, he pulled her aside and pushed her back against the wall. Then he took the pistol from her, handing it to a rather wide-eyed Coleridge. "Return this," he ordered, his eyes fixed on his wife, "and speak of this to no one."

"Yes, my lord," Coleridge whispered, tension in his voice as he hobbled away.

"Charlotte?" Saying her name, Sebastian met her eyes and found them devoid of all emotion. Blindly, they looked back at him; yet, there was no recognition, no awareness. Neither could he see pain or regret, fear or terror. It was as though the woman he'd known had left; all that remained was an empty shell.

As voices behind the door grew louder, Sebastian hesitated for but a moment before he picked her up and carried her up the stairs. Back in her bedchamber, he set her down and closed the door. Then he turned to her, not knowing how to proceed.

Again, he said her name, and again, she did not respond.

Taking a deep breath, he stepped toward her, his gaze focused on her face, hoping for some sort of reaction as he closed the distance between them. Although they had grown closer as of late, she had always reacted with at least a sort of nervous anticipation when he had stepped too close, when his arms had reached for her as though she needed to gather her courage to allow him near her.

Now, she failed to react at all.

Gritting his teeth, Sebastian staked everything on one card and slid his arms around her waist, pulling her closer.

Although she blinked, the expression on her face did not change. She remained immobile, rigid, almost unaware of his presence.

At a loss, Sebastian continued to stare at her, willing her eyes to focus and see him, but his attempts were futile. Trapped in a trance, she had lost contact with the world around her. Would she ever return? Or was she already lost to him for good?

Cold fear spread through his heart, and his hands tightened on her as though he could keep her safe simply by keeping her close.

She sucked in a sharp breath.

Sebastian blinked, his eyes snapping to her face, watching. "Charlotte? Can you hear me?"

Nothing.

Had he imagined the sharp intake of breath? Was he going mad? No, there had been ... something. On some level, he had reached her, reached a part of her that lay buried deep under layers of her protective shell. She had felt his hands on her, holding her close possessively ... and a part of her had objected.

An idea rushed through Sebastian's head, and he cringed.

He couldn't! He had given her his word. He had sworn he would never break it. And yet ...

Was he simply to step back and leave her trapped in a world of her own making? Cut off from everything and everyone? Lost even to herself?

"Charlotte?" he whispered, cupping his hands to her face, his eyes searching hers. "Can you hear me?" He waited for a moment, then another, and sighed when her eyes remained unfocused. Taking a deep breath, he stepped even closer. "Charlotte, I'm going to kiss you now," he warned, hoping she would object.

But she didn't.

"I'm going to kiss you now, but if you don't want me to," he continued, his muscles tense with anticipation, "then stop me. Tell me not to. Do you hear me?"

Hesitantly, Sebastian pulled her rigid body against his, feeling her chest rise and fall with each soft breath. Then he closed his eyes, unable to bear the void look in hers any longer, and leant toward her, gently pressing his lips to hers.

Then he froze. Had the muscles in her back tightened? Or had he simply imagined it?

Encouraged, his hands pulled her closer as he pressed his body to hers, his mouth deepening the kiss.

Despite his own moral objections to his actions, warmth spread through his middle. Her skin felt warm to the touch, and her lips tasted sweet like honey and marmalade.

Her arms came up then, the palms of her hands pressed against his chest, and Sebastian rejoiced. Tightening his hold on her even more, he dared her to react, hoping she would push him back and even slap his face for taking such liberties.

For a moment, her hands seemed to strain against him before they gave up their post and moved upward onto his shoulders.

Surprised, Sebastian stilled.

Then her arms came around his neck, pulling her closer against him, and she opened her mouth, returning his kiss.

Forgetting the world around himself, Sebastian decided to live in the moment.

Chapter Forty

TOO LATE

Hands touched her, moved over her body, and Charlotte felt an old panic spread through her soul.

The fog that had settled on her mind slowly receded; the harsh light of the world around her pierced her skull, sending jolts of pain through her body.

Lips brushed against hers, and Charlotte tensed, remembering pain and degradation.

Then she hesitated though. Something was different.

The mouth on hers did not crush her lips, bruising them in an onslaught of desire. Neither were the hands that held her rough and painfully intimate. Instead, she felt cradled in his arms, held tightly but gently, safe and protected from the memory that had haunted her for so long.

Sebastian.

His name echoed in her mind and heart, and a smile came to her soul.

Enjoying his soft caresses, she lifted her arms, and her hands encircled his neck as she pressed herself against him, savouring this perfect moment. Her mouth opened, and she kissed him back.

For a moment, he stilled as though hesitant before his own desire broke free, and he returned her kiss with a passion so unfamiliar, and yet, so tantalising that Charlotte almost forgot to breathe. Clinging to him, she marvelled at the delicious sensations that shot through her body and relinquished all control.

For a seemingly never-ending moment, Charlotte allowed herself to feel, to enjoy, to cherish and treasure his touch, her body humming with pleasure, until the tip of his tongue brushed against hers.

Instantly, an old panic leapt up in her heart, freezing her limbs.

And yet, his touch was anything but repulsive. It felt nothing like the sickening sensation that had almost overpowered her that night long ago. His touch remained gentle and considerate, far from the forceful attack she'd experienced.

And yet, doubt remained. Would he stop if she asked him to? Or would he disregard her wishes and force her into submission?

Although her mind readily spoke out in his favour, her soul still ached with fear, demanding confirmation. Too painful were the memories that still lived there.

Loosening her hold on him, she retreated, pulling away, hoping, praying that he would understand.

As she stepped back, he followed, his mouth capturing hers once again.

Instantly, Charlotte tensed, her hands coming up to block his path. Would history repeat itself?

The second her hands pressed against his chest, his lips stilled and he lifted his head, his deep blue gaze finding hers. Panting, he searched her face, seeing the tension that lingered in her eyes as they begged him to stop. "I'm sorry," he whispered, his voice hoarse and repentant. "I suppose when you kissed me back, I got carried away. I'm sorry."

Joy came to his face then, and his eyes roamed hers with such delight that she smiled back at him.

Lifting his hand, he reached for her, but then stopped. "May I?"

Swallowing, Charlotte nodded.

As the knuckles of his hand gently brushed over her cheek, she closed her eyes, enjoying the softness of his touch.

"I was truly scared there for a moment," he whispered, and her eyes opened. "I thought I'd lost you. I looked at you, and," pain edged into his face, he shook his head, "you were gone. What happened?"

Taking a deep breath, Charlotte held his gaze, trying to remember. "I'm not certain," she whispered. "I remember speaking to Victoria, and then ..." Her voice trailed off as elusive images drifted before her eyes, like a dream she couldn't quite grasp.

When she hesitated, he said, "I found you downstairs on your way to the drawing room, a pistol in your hand."

Charlotte's mouth opened in shock before the images cleared, filling in the blanks. Then she swallowed and met his eyes, not knowing what to say.

"Did you truly intend to kill him?"

Charlotte sighed. "He deserves it."

"I know he does," her husband agreed, and yet, his face remained tense. "But despite what you believe, you do not deserve to hang for it."

Charlotte swallowed, almost feeling the noose tighten around her neck. "How do you know?" she whispered, feeling tears sting her eyes. "I told you what I did, and yet, you believe me to be innocent. Why?"

He shrugged. "Maybe I'm selfish, but I can't imagine being without you ever again." He reached out and pulled her into his arms, his eyes pleading as he looked down at her. "We'll find another way. Please don't do this. Promise me that you will not try again. You'd ruin your life ... as well as mine."

Shaking her head, Charlotte closed her eyes, feeling tears run down her face. "My life is forfeit," she whispered, then looked up at him, her vision blurred. "In truth, I died a long time ago ... or at least I should have. I cannot go on pretending to have a life. The mistakes I've made have led me here. This," she swallowed, nodding her head, "is the way it's supposed to be. This is my chance. If I can give my life to protect your sister as well as her baby, then that is a trade I'm willing to make."

"I'm not," he growled, his hands tightening around her protectively.

For a moment, Charlotte couldn't help but smile. She had been so certain that she would never know what it felt like to be loved. And now, here she was, married to a man who had truly come to love her. Now, when it was too late.

"No one in this world is free of mistakes," he continued, his eyes imploring her to believe him, "of having done wrong. Some worse than others, yes, but at some point, you need to find a way to forgive yourself and move on. It is time to let go of the past and look to the future."

Oh, how I wish I could! Charlotte thought, knowing that there was only one way she could make him leave her side and allow her to pay her debt.

Her insides cringed as she dimly recalled Victoria's words. *Sebastian and the late Lord Elmridge grew up together and were good friends.*

"I took someone's life," she reminded him, watching his eyes cloud with pain and regret before a solemn determination pushed them away.

"That was a long time ago," he replied, nodding his head as though trying to convince himself.

Taking a deep breath, Charlotte steeled herself for what was to come. "That is always easy to say when you speak of a faceless someone with no name, no family. The loss, the pain is not as severe as when you can truly picture the colour of his eyes, the smile that came to his lips when he saw his wife enter a room or the love that shone in his eyes when he gazed upon his daughter." As her teeth began to chatter, Charlotte clenched her hands, holding on desperately to what little control she had left. "What you feel is a sense of regret that someone lost his life," she continued, seeing uncomfortable tension come to his shoulders as he came to realise that he couldn't sway her from her path. "But everything changes when the one who was lost receives a face and a name, when he becomes more than just a casualty, a headline in the paper, when his life receives a deeper meaning." Swallowing, she looked up at him. "Do you wish to know who he was?"

Chapter Forty-One

AWAKENING

Holding his breath, Sebastian stared at her. Somehow, he knew that she was right. There was something in her eyes, something in the way she looked at him that told him that once he knew, everything would be different.

Right then and there, he could not imagine it to be true, and yet, the certainty in her eyes scared him nearly witless and he almost bolted for the door, afraid to hear what she had to say.

Afraid that she would be truly lost to him.

"Tell me," he whispered instead, every single muscle in his body tense to the point of breaking. Although he dreaded to know the truth, he also knew that if they were to have a chance-as slim as it might be-that this was the only way. He had to know, and he could only hope that the truth would not shatter him.

She swallowed then, and the tip of her tongue snaked out to wet her lips. Her eyes met his, and unfathomable pain and regret rested in them as she opened her mouth. "It was your friend," she whispered, and his heart stopped, "Leopold Lancaster, the late Marquess of Elmridge."

Staring at her, Sebastian felt the weight of her words crash into him like blows to his body, and he staggered backwards, his knees suddenly weak. The air was knocked from his lungs, and his stomach turned, threatening to expel its contents. "Leopold?" he gasped, hoping it wasn't true, and yet, knowing that it could not be otherwise. "You? That was you?" he demanded, rage burning in his heart as the pain of his friend's loss hit him with such force as though he had just died in his arms.

"Forgiveness is far from easy when the loss is your own," she whispered, her tear-streaked face the picture of misery, and yet, he could not bring himself to care.

Instead, his insides burned with uncontrollable rage, only held in check by the need to understand why anyone would kill a man as honourable and kind as his friend had been. "Why?" he forced out through gritted teeth. "Why him? He never hurt you, did he?"

"No."

"Then why him?" he growled out, his hands clenched, and he took a step back, lest he lunge himself at her. "He was not the one who ..." He shook his head, the thoughts in his mind running rampant. "You're right if anyone deserves to die, it's Northfield. Why not him? Why did you not go after him?"

"I never went after your friend," she whispered, fresh tears spilling down her cheeks. "It was an accident, a horrible accident, but it was my fault. He took the poisoned drink meant for another man."

Sebastian stilled, staring at her. "Northfield?"

"No," his wife said, taking a deep breath. "His brother, Frederick."

Again, the world turned upside down that Sebastian could barely keep his feet under him. Shaking his head, he stared at her. "That doesn't make any sense. Why would you want to kill either one of them? I've known them my whole life."

"As have I," Charlotte whispered, holding his gaze.

Sebastian blinked, and a distant memory of a little brown-haired girl flashed before his eyes as she had raced around the gardens, always trailing behind young Frederick and his friends. What had been their names? Oliver and...Kenneth!

"Charlotte," he whispered as the last piece of the puzzle fell into place. Although he had learnt her true name a matter of days ago, it had not been familiar and Sebastian had not had the opportunity to make enquiries into who she had been.

Now, he knew.

And yet, he still didn't understand. "Tell me what happened," he growled out, taking another step back, unable to bear the pained look in her eyes. She did not deserve his pity, or his compassion, not after what she had done.

Shaking his head, Sebastian swallowed, realising that everything was indeed different now. She had been right. He could not forgive her for what she had done, and neither did she deserve to forgive herself.

A knock sounded on the door. "Sebastian? Charlotte? Are you in there?" came Victoria's voice.

"Not now!" Sebastian snarled, regret filling his heart at his harsh tone. "Please leave," he added, then raised his gaze to his wife once more. "Tell me what happened."

Taking a deep breath, his wife turned away from him, her eyes focused out of the window at the horizon in the distance. "It all began that night about four years ago at Lord Radcliffe's ball." Her hands clenched, and a shiver shook her delicate frame.

"Northfield?"

She nodded, and another tear ran down her cheek. "I don't think I can put into words what that night did to me. And yet, it still got worse. When I told my parents what he had done, they said it was my fault. My father said I had allowed him to compromise me and insisted I accept his marriage proposal." With tears in her eyes, she looked at him. "My father called him a decent man for offering for me after what had happened, for not trying to evade his responsibility."

Sebastian swallowed, his throat tightening with the pain and despair that hung in the room like a heavy fog.

"I didn't know what to do," she continued, turning her gaze back out the window, reliving the moments of her past that had changed everything. "I knew I had no choice, and yet, the thought of marrying him felt like a death sentence." For a moment, she closed her eyes and a soft smile came to her lips. "And then Kenneth saved me."

"He asked you to marry him instead," Sebastian said when she remained quiet.

"He did." Her chest rose and fell with a deep breath as she stared out the window. "We grew up together. He was the brother I never had, and I loved him fiercely, followed him everywhere like the little sister he didn't want. More than once he snapped at me to leave him alone," she chuckled, shaking her head, "but I didn't. I always felt most alive by his side, and over time, we grew closer."

Stepping back, Sebastian leant against the wall, his head rolling back, and closed his eyes, listening.

"He was the only one who saw that something was wrong," she whispered, "the only one who didn't blame me, who stood by my side, willing to sacrifice his own happiness to protect me." As her teeth began to chatter, she closed her eyes, arms wrapped around herself as shivers shook her. "And then he was gone."

Again, silence hung about the room, and although Sebastian felt reluctant to hear more, he knew he needed to know. "You said he died in the war," he prompted, urging her to continue.

Brushing a tear from her face, she took a deep breath. "He did," she confirmed. "Frederick had always been the one to seek out adventures, and Kenneth had always followed in his path. When Frederick had gone off to war, Kenneth had followed as he always had."

"Why didn't he at least marry you first?" Sebastian asked. "He must have known that there was a chance he wouldn't return."

"Everything happened very fast. Frederick had been speaking of joining our forces on the continent for a while, but then one day, he was simply gone. Without saying goodbye, he had left." Again, her shoulders tensed, and her fingernails dug into her arms as she held herself tightly. "Kenneth was frantic with worry, knowing how fearless Frederick could be, and before I knew what had happened, he had left as well." She closed her eyes, and he could see the reluctance to go on on her face. "The day I learnt of his death, I lost my baby."

Sebastian sucked in a sharp breath, his resolve not to feel for her crumbling before his eyes.

Her lips quivered, and she swallowed the sobs that threatened to spill from her mouth. "I was devastated. Losing Kenneth and then losing my child, I ... I broke down and sobbed for days." Her fingers dug into her flesh, and the sinews on her hands stood out white.

"Although I mourned the loss of my child, I was also relieved because it was a constant reminder of that night. Torn, I didn't know what to think or feel. What was right? What was wrong? I couldn't tell. I felt it all, and yet, nothing felt right and nothing felt wrong. It all lost meaning." Turning around, she met his eyes, and the despair he saw there almost brought him to his knees. "You have no idea what it feels like to be torn apart from the inside."

Forcing the growing sympathy for her from his heart, Sebastian held her gaze unflinching, an open accusation in his eyes.

As though in answer, she nodded. "None of this can excuse what I did. All I can do is attempt to explain why it happened."

Gritting his teeth, Sebastian swallowed. "Why did you try to kill Frederick?"

Licking her lips, she turned to the window once more as though she couldn't bear to meet his eyes as she dragged the past into the light of day. "When Kenneth died, ... it changed everything. I was no longer safe. Northfield renewed his proposal, and my parents insisted." Closing her eyes, she shook her head. "And this time, there was no one to save me. The only one who'd always been there for me had just died. I was all alone, and they were coming at me from all sides. I felt cornered, and then ...," she shrugged, a hint of bewilderment marking her face, "suddenly, all the pain and fear went away, replaced by a terrible hatred. It drowned out the pain and banished the fear from my heart. It made me strong. Although a part of me knew that it was wrong, I clung to it." Tears now ran freely down her face. "I couldn't bear it any longer. I was tired and terrified, and the weight of this life felt like it would crush me any moment." Closing her eyes, she shook her head. "So, I clung to the hatred that grew in my heart, and it made me do terrible things." Again, her eyes shifted to his, pleading with him not to forgive, but to understand. "I wish I could say it hadn't been me, but it had. Deep down, I knew it had been me."

When he didn't respond, didn't even blink, she dropped her gaze and turned back to the window. "After all the grief and pain and fear, it was easier to hate. It was such a relief, and so I hated him, hated him for taking everything from me, for killing Kenneth." She swallowed, hanging her head. "The night Leopold died, I spoke to Frederick on the terrace, and when I looked in his eyes, I saw guilt. He, too, thought that he had killed Kenneth, and it broke my heart all over again."

Again, she looked up and met his eyes. "After speaking to Frederick, after learning how Kenneth had died, I'd meant to kill myself that night."

The breath caught in Sebastian's throat, and his heart twisted in agony at the thought of how close he had come to losing her. And yet, he would never even have known, for she would never have entered his life to begin with ... if she had died that night instead of Leopold.

"That's why I had the poison," she continued. "I didn't set out to harm Frederick, but the look in his eyes changed everything." Again, her fingers dug into her arms. "When I saw Leopold take the glass from Frederick, I froze," closing her eyes, she shook her head, "and before I could stop him, he had downed it. And then he was dead ...; I hated Frederick even more. After that, I lost all thought, all reason. I walked as though in a fog. I spoke and listened, and yet, nothing mattered. Life and death lost all meaning. The only thing that remained was my hatred. And so, I tried again, and again. I failed. Then I saw the love he had for his wife, saw the life he was building for himself, the life I had always wanted but now never would have, and I couldn't bear it. Deep down, I was so enraged that I wanted to make him suffer just like I did by taking everything from him he cared about." She drew in a shaky breath. "Fortunately, she survived. She and the baby."

With each word she spoke, Sebastian found his emotions had become more and more dulled. It was as though his body could no longer deal with the sheer mass of their onslaught and abandoned all hope to differentiate and process. "His name is Leo," he whispered, unsure why he felt the need to tell her.

Her eyes rose to his, and for a moment, she simply looked at him before a soft smile came to her lips. "That is good," she whispered in return.

"What happened then?" Sebastian asked, unable to hold the weight of her gaze any longer. "How did you end up at Farnworth Manor?"

"When Frederick learnt what I had done, he returned me to my parents." She shook her head. "I don't know why he did not demand retribution. I had hoped he would. I had counted on it. And when he let me live, I didn't know what to do. My soul felt as though it had died." Again, she met his eyes. "How do you live when you are dead inside? I didn't know, but I didn't need to. My parents had me locked away at Winham Institute, and for a long time, I remained dead. I didn't feel. I didn't think. I just breathed. In and out. In and out. Day after day." She took a deep breath. "Until the day of the fire."

"The fire?"

"I don't know how it happened. I don't know how I got out. All I know is that it ... it woke me." A touch of disbelief came to her eyes, and she shook her head. "And slowly I returned to the surface. The soul I thought had been dead awoke. It was tattered and bruised, barely functional, but it was there." Shrugging her shoulders, she met his eyes. "And so, I left. I simply walked away."

Chapter Forty-Two

A PREDATOR ON THE PROWL

R elief filled Charlotte's heart as she finished her story, and the weight that had threatened to crush her for so long a time vanished as though it had never existed.

Only it had come at a price.

Meeting her husband's gaze, Charlotte knew without a doubt that she had lost him. He could not forgive her for what she had done, and she would never ask him to. The life she had found had never been hers to keep. Deep down, she had known this all along.

And yet, the pain in her heart knew no right or wrong, it simply was.

Drawing in a deep breath, she squared her shoulders and took a step toward him.

Instantly, he tensed as though her presence physically hurt him.

Standing back, she met his eyes. "Now, you know. Now, you can understand why I must do this. It is only right." She nodded at him encouragingly. "I stole a man's life, and as much as I wish I could, I cannot give it back. Not even in exchange for my own. But if you let me do this, then I can give your sister back her life and save her child from growing up in the care of a monster who only looks like a man. A father who would undoubtedly turn him into an image of himself."

Gritting his teeth, her husband glared at her, his eyes dark as though a storm was brewing. He shifted from one foot to the other and back again as he inhaled deeply, indecision marking his face.

"Please," Charlotte pleaded. "You yourself admitted that he does not deserve to live, and now, you know why I don't either. So, please, let me do this. Let me free her from the man who turned me into a monster before he does the same to her."

Long moments passed as they looked at each other, their eyes open to a new reality, a reality neither one of them wanted, a reality that had shattered everything they had hoped for. And yet, Charlotte could not regret the turn her life had taken. Had she not met and married the man before her, then Victoria would have been lost. Now, she had a chance, but only if Charlotte could gain her husband's permission to help her.

As his jaw clenched and unclenched, he stared at her as though trying to see the person she had just revealed herself to be. Then he swallowed and slowly shook his head.

Charlotte's heart throbbed painfully in her chest. "Please," she whispered as tears came to her eyes as much for Victoria's sake as her own. She needed this; she had to make him understand. "Let me do this. One good deed. Just one. Please."

His eyes hard, he opened his mouth when a knock sounded on the door.

They both flinched, having forgotten the world around them.

"Sebastian?" Victoria's voice drifted through the door. "Is everything alright? It is time to leave. Are you coming? What should I tell Mother?"

Hanging his head, Sebastian closed his eyes. "The funeral," he mumbled, then raised his gaze to look at Charlotte. "Tell Mother we'll be there," he said to Victoria, his eyes still fixed on his wife.

"Alright." After a moment, they heard Victoria's footsteps hasten down the hall.

His eyes burned into hers as he stepped forward. "You will not say a word of this to anyone," he hissed, his face contorted into a snarl. "You will play your part as I will play mine. Do you understand?"

Taking a deep breath, Charlotte nodded.

"Good." Again, he took a step toward her, his head bending down, closing the distance between them as his eyes held hers. "And don't even think about going after Northfield. Not here. Not now. Have I made myself clear?"

Again, Charlotte nodded, despair constricting her throat as she watched him turn on his heel and stride from the room without another word. Of course, she couldn't blame him, and yet, she couldn't help but wish for a different outcome.

The funeral passed in a daze. With their eyes clouded and their faces tense, they portrayed without difficulty the image of a grieving family. Nevertheless, Charlotte could feel the anger that radiated off her husband as he stood beside her before his father's grave. Victoria, too, knew that something was wrong, her gaze occasionally drifting to her brother and sister-in-law, a burning question in her eyes. The only one who seemed to take any kind of pleasure from these dreary proceedings was Northfield.

Although he didn't smile, there was something in his eyes as they came to rest on Charlotte that spoke of amusement. She squirmed under his gaze as it drew forth the memories she so loathed, memories that seemed to please him greatly. His eyes shifted from her to her husband before they narrowed, easily detecting the change in their relationship, and the corners of his mouth twitched.

After the funeral, they returned to the manor, and Sebastian informed his family that they would be returning to Town in the morning. Frowning at her son for a moment, his mother merely nodded and then left to make arrangements, escorting Victoria upstairs as she had begun to feel lightheaded.

Not even looking at his wife, Sebastian then strode from the room, calling for Coleridge.

With a sinking heart, Charlotte watched him leave before she remembered that she wasn't alone after all. Turning around, she met Northfield's gaze.

"He seems greatly displeased with you, my dear," he whispered, a smirk on his face as he strode closer. "Not protective in the least."

Although his words were merely an observation, the threat in his voice resonated in her ears, and Charlotte took an involuntary step backwards. "Don't call me *my dear*," she hissed, trying her best to sound confident as her body began to tremble with the memories his proximity elicited, "and stay away from me."

A smile came to his face, obviously pleased with her reaction. "What will you do if I don't?" he asked, his breath brushing over her skin as he came to stand before her. "Will you scream for help? I doubt it."

As her teeth began to chatter, Charlotte ground them together, forcing herself to hold his gaze. "You cannot intimidate me anymore," she forced out, but her voice sounded strangled. "I've already lost everything I held dear. There's nothing you can do to me anymore."

At her words, his eyes lit up and a smile came to his face. "Shall we test that theory?" he challenged, his hands suddenly reaching for her.

As his arms came around her, his body pressing her against the wall, Charlotte's soul screamed out and her stomach turned. A part of her could not believe what was happening, but still she fought him with everything she had as his mouth closed in on hers.

And then he was flung backwards.

Panting, Charlotte stared at her husband, a murderous gleam in his eyes, as he advanced on Northfield scrambling to his feet.

"My apologies," Northfield mumbled, brushing down his coat, his face quickly reclaiming a look of bored indifference. "I was merely-"

"I will kill you!" her husband growled, circling his opponent like a predator on the prowl.

Northfield swallowed but held his ground.

Knowing she could not allow her husband to ruin his life for her of all people, Charlotte acted on instinct. In the blink of an eye, she stood beside him, laying a careful hand on his arm. "Please don't," she whispered, praying that he would listen.

At her touch, he flinched, his eyes darting to her face.

"It's not your place." Shaking her head, she implored him. "Think of Victoria and your mother. Don't do this. They need you."

He drew in a painful breath, and the dark in his eyes remained. However, some of the tension left his body as he nodded to her almost imperceptibly. Then he turned his attention back on Northfield. "I want you out of this house," he growled, approaching with measured steps. "Now." His eyes narrowed, and this time it was Northfield who took an involuntary step back. "And if you ever dare lay a hand on her again," her husband snarled, "I shall hunt you down and kill you where you stand."

Holding her husband's murderous gaze, Northfield's eyes narrowed and hardened. At that moment, Charlotte knew that her husband had just then gained an enemy. An enemy who didn't fight fair. An enemy who couldn't be intimidated into submission. An enemy who would lie in wait, patiently anticipating the moment he could exact his revenge.

As he had with Kenneth.

Upon receiving his letter after his death, Charlotte had finally understood the whole truth ... as useless as it had been in that moment.

Without saying a word, Northfield spun on his heel and left, and her husband turned to face her. "Are you all right?" he asked, his voice hard as though he did not care.

Charlotte nodded. "Thank you."

He cringed at her words and took a step back. "There's no need. After all, it was my fault. I should never have left you alone with him." Then he turned and strode from the room, and all Charlotte could think of were his arms holding her tight, keeping her safe.

Chapter Forty-Three

A BROKEN SOUL

The moment the carriage drew to a halt in front of their townhouse, Sebastian got out and left, walking down the street without a look back. He could only imagine the confused expressions on their faces as they stared after him until he heard someone call out his name. Had it been Victoria or his mother? Or his wife even?

Sebastian shook his head. He didn't care. He needed to get away. He needed to think, and he couldn't find a clear thought in his head when they looked at him, their eyes full of concern and confusion.

And so, he walked. He didn't see where he went, all he knew was that he needed to get away and so his legs kept moving until the sky began to grow dim and the cold air began to chill his bones.

Hidden in the shadows that spread over the darkening world, Sebastian found himself standing across the street from a mid-sized townhouse, its facade familiar to his eyes.

At first, he frowned, unsure why his legs had carried him there when a carriage drew up to the kerb. A carriage that carried the coat-of-arms of a gentleman who didn't deserve the word.

"Northfield," he growled under his breath, forcing his limbs to remain still when all he wanted was to rush across the street and throttle the man where he stood.

But he didn't.

He watched as Northfield climbed the stairs to the front door and was immediately permitted inside. Who lived here? Sebastian wondered, raking his mind, trying to remember as the chaos in his head seemed to increase.

And then it clicked. He remembered the last time he had been here.

Visiting his sister for the first time after her wedding, he had returned to his carriage, only to spot his new brother-in-law's carriage drive around the corner and down the street. On a whim, he had instructed his coachman to follow, and this is where they had come.

Later, he had found out that the woman who lived here was North-field's mistress, and his heart had broken over his sister's lot all over again.

Desperate to leave behind the pain he always saw in her eyes, Sebastian had gone to visit his friend at Farnworth Manor.

Where he had met Lotte.

Charlotte.

Standing out in the street, Sebastian looked up at the lit windows and couldn't help but wonder about the nature of people. How could Northfield be so cold and unfeeling? Did it truly not touch him to see someone else in pain?

And then there was Charlotte.

Yes, she had committed an unspeakable crime, and yet ... and yet, deep down, a part of him could understand how it had happened. But did that mean he ought to forgive her?

Closing his eyes, Sebastian shook his head. Then he turned around, hailed a hackney coach and instructed the coachman to take him to his sister's townhouse. After all, he knew beyond the shadow of a doubt that her husband would not be there.

After mulling everything over in his mind, he found he needed to speak to someone, and his sister already knew ... at least most of it.

"Sebastian!" she exclaimed upon finding him in her drawing room. "Wherever did you go? We were terribly worried." Drawing him into her arms, she held him close for a long moment, and Sebastian drew in a deep breath, welcoming the warmth of her embrace.

"I simply walked around," he said, meeting her enquiring eyes. "I had to think."

"All day?" she asked as she took his hand and pulled him down onto the settee next to her. "Tell me what happened."

In a few words, Sebastian explained what had transpired between him and his wife after he had found her with a pistol in her hand ready to kill Northfield. As he spoke, Victoria's eyes grew wide, and tears appeared in their corners as he spoke of Leopold's death.

"I don't know what to do," he whispered, shaking his head. "At first, I was so ... angry," gritting his teeth, he inhaled deeply through his nose, seeking to calm himself. "I still am. Every now and then, I feel enraged. It grabs me, and all I can think about is Leopold's lifeless body. But then ..."

"But then you remember that you love her," Victoria finished for him, and he looked up at her and nodded.

"I know I cannot ignore what she did," he continued, trying to find the words to explain the chaos in his head, "but at the same time, my heart almost desperately wants to forgive her. But I can't. Nothing would be more wrong." He shook his head. "Is it even my place to forgive her? Yes, Leopold was my friend, but there are others who were closer to him. Don't they deserve to know? Is it not my duty to tell them where she is? After all, they believe her dead." Turning pleading eyes to his sister, Sebastian begged, "Tell me what to do."

Victoria took a deep breath and closed her hand over his. "I cannot do that. It is not my place to tell you what to do, but I can tell you what I think."

He nodded his head vigorously.

"Despite what you've told me," his sister began, "I believe that Charlotte is a good person, who would never intentionally harm another ... not without good cause."

"But she did!" Sebastian insisted. "She killed Leopold. She tried to kill Frederick. They never harmed her. What good cause could she possibly have had?"

"None that you can understand," Victoria replied, her eyes overhung with sadness. "Do you have any idea what it does to your soul to be broken into a million pieces?" She swallowed, and a slight tremble shook her hand still resting on top of his. "Having to submit your life ... your body to a man who you feel repulsed by, who does things to you that can never be forgotten or ignored."

Holding his breath, Sebastian stared at her, wishing she would not continue.

"Now and then, I hardly recognise myself in the woman I've become," she whispered, then placed her other hand on the slight curve of her belly. "In the beginning, I hated this child." Lifting her eyes to his, she nodded. "I was disgusted by the thought of it growing inside of me. Of course, I knew it to be wrong, and I felt ashamed. What mother would hate her own child?" Tears glistened in her eyes. "Although I knew the child to be innocent, a precious little life like all the others, I couldn't love it because to me it was a mere representation of what he did to me."

Sitting beside his sister and seeing her misery pour down her cheeks, Sebastian had never felt more helpless. Torn between the desire to end her husband's life and ease Victoria's pain, he felt unable to do either. As his emotions ate him up from the inside, he simply sat there and stared at her.

"I can see how you feel," she said, nodding her head. "The pain, the anger, the confusion. It is all there, written on your face, and yet, ..." licking her lips, she met his eyes, an apologetic look resting in them, "for me and Charlotte, it is a million times worse."

Her words hit him like a punch to the gut.

"What do you do when you're trapped in a life that crushes you a little more every day?" she asked, brushing the tears from her face. "Eventually, you won't be able to withstand the pressure and give in. Believe me, it takes a lot of strength merely to rise in the morning." Searching his eyes, a sad smile came to her face. "You wanted me to tell you the truth, remember? Again, and again, you have asked me to confide in you, but you never truly wanted to know, did you? Do you regret that I told you?"

Sebastian closed his eyes briefly and took a deep breath. "Yes. No," he whispered. "Although it pains me ... so much," tears stung his eyes,

"I can't not know. You're my sister, and I love you. If you cannot confide in me, then in whom?" He shook his head, drawing her hand into his, holding it tight.

"And what about Charlotte?"

"I don't know." Shrugging, he hesitated. "Can I ask you something?"

Victoria nodded.

"Have you ever," he began, eyeing her closely, hoping he wouldn't offend her, "wanted to kill your husband?"

Holding his gaze, she nodded.

Sebastian's eyes widened as he saw the gap between Charlotte and his sister grow smaller.

"But I won't," she said when he remained quiet.

"Why not?"

"Because I have you and Mother," she said, and a soft smile tugged at the corner of her mouth, "and Charlotte, too. Especially Charlotte." She nodded. "You, all of you, helped me to find my way back to myself. I've even come to love my child," again, she placed a gentle hand on her belly, "not as a mother should, but a little. And I'm hoping that one day, I will truly see him for himself alone and not for who his father is." She swallowed, and her eyes grew serious once more as she looked at him, her eyes imploring. "Only Charlotte didn't have that. She was abandoned, alone. There was no one to fight for her, to guide her through all those contradicting emotions that threatened to tear her apart." She nodded, and a touch of awe came to her eyes. "To me, it is truly amazing that after everything that happened to her and everything she lost, she was still able to return to her old self. I don't know if I could have." Holding his gaze, she shook her head. "I doubt it."

Chapter Forty-Four
TO SEE A GHOST

Early the next morning after a wakeful night, Sebastian called for the carriage and had the coachman take him to Frederick's townhouse, grateful that during the Season people generally stayed in Town and were, thus, far easier to call upon.

Waiting in the study after the butler had gone off to alert his master to his rather early visitor, Sebastian found himself pacing the length of the room, his mind busy sorting through all that needed to be said, trying to determine the best way to say it. After all, the rest of the world believed Charlotte to be dead.

And the rest of the world included Frederick and his wife.

When the door finally opened, Sebastian's heart leapt into his throat, and he turned to greet his friend's brother as well as the new marchioness with shaking hands. "Good morning. Please forgive my early visit. However, what I have to say cannot wait."

Seeing the tension on Sebastian's face, Frederick's eyes narrowed. "Is something wrong? You look as though you've seen a ghost." Escorting his wife to the settee, he gestured for Sebastian to sit in the armchair by the window and took the seat opposite him.

"I suppose that's a fitting description," Sebastian mumbled, taking a seat, "under the circumstances."

"What circumstances?" the marchioness asked, her kind eyes drifting back and forth between her husband and their untimely visitor.

Sebastian swallowed, wringing his hands. "This is about Leopold," he began, and their faces darkened. "Rumour said that he died of poison, but as far as I know no one ever discovered who had done it." He glanced from the marchioness to her husband. "I came to enquire if there were any news."

The marchioness drew in a deep breath and her gaze travelled to her husband, who sat rigid in his chair, his eyes focused on Sebastian. For a long moment, he remained still before his gaze narrowed and a frown drew down his brows. "Why do you ask?"

Sebastian exhaled the breath he'd been holding as he saw the suspicion on Frederick's face. "You know who did it, don't you?" he said, not knowing how else to begin. "Tell me."

Frederick's shoulders tensed, and he glanced at his wife, a silent communication passing between them before he returned his attention to Sebastian. "I do not know what you speak of."

Sebastian shook his head, and the ghost of a smile flashed over his face. "She killed your brother, and yet, you protect her. Why?"

With his eyes trained on Frederick, Sebastian saw him fall apart as utter shock claimed his expression. Staring at Sebastian, he gulped down a couple of breaths before asking, "How do you know?" Then his gaze drifted to his wife, who seemed equally stunned, her hand reaching for his, pulling it into her lap.

Holding Frederick's gaze, Sebastian said, "Because she's my wife."

"Charlotte," the marchioness gasped, her eyes wide, uncomprehending. "Charlotte is your wife, but..." She turned wide eyes to her husband. "We thought ..."

Frederick swallowed, then leant forward and scooted to the edge of his seat, his eyes unblinking. "She died," he gasped. "Less than a year ago."

Sebastian shook his head. "No, she didn't. She escaped the fire."

Shaking his head, Frederick rubbed his hands over his face as his mind tried to process such unexpected information. "And she's your wife? How?"

In as few words as he could, Sebastian told them how he had met Charlotte as Lotte at his friend's estate and whisked her off to Gretna Green less than a fortnight later.

"And she told you about Leopold?" Frederick asked, his eyes still clouded with grief whenever he mentioned his brother's name. "She told you what she did?"

Sebastian nodded. "She did."

"Then why are you here?"

Sebastian shrugged. "I'm not sure. I came because ..." He looked up into their kind faces and hoped that somehow they could tell him what to do. "Did you forgive her for what she's done? How could you do it? Suddenly, when I look at her I feel ..." His hands balled into fists as words failed him.

"You love her," the marchioness whispered, a pleased smile coming to her face. "I'm glad she's found you."

"You are?" Sebastian asked, unable to comprehend how she could think so. "Does it not pain you to know that the woman who killed Leopold is ...?"

"Alive?" Frederick asked, then he nodded. "A part of me does feel pain at the thought of her, at the thought of what she did to Leopold, at the thought of his loss, yes." He swallowed, then rose from his chair and sat down on the settee beside his wife, pulling her right hand into his and holding it tightly as though only her touch gave him the strength he needed to continue.

Watching them, Sebastian felt an ache in his heart as he remembered his own hopes and dreams for a future with the woman he loved. "Then how can you forgive her?"

"Maybe because I know only too well how pain and loss can force you down a path that you wouldn't otherwise have chosen," Frederick said, his voice thick with regret, and his gaze shifted to his wife, who smiled at him encouragingly, her soft eyes assuring him that she would remain by his side ... no matter what.

For a moment, silence hung over the room before Frederick returned his gaze to Sebastian. "What she did was wrong. Of course, it was. And the part of me that only knows the loss of my brother, the part of me unwilling to see that there is a cause for every consequence will never be able to forgive her. It hates her with a burning rage." His jaw clenched, and he drew in a deep breath. "I'm not proud of this feeling for I know she does not deserve it."

Sebastian licked his lips and leant forward, eager to hear how Frederick had achieved this balance he saw on his face despite the warring emotions within him.

"The war changed me," Frederick whispered as though revealing a secret. "It changed how I saw the world and the people in it, but mostly it changed how I saw myself. I felt completely uprooted as though I was taking my first steps in the world and didn't know how to feel and think, who to hate and love." His hands tightened on his wife's. "Life was torture, and I admit that I longed for death, for I thought I could bear it not a moment longer."

Shocked beyond comprehension, Sebastian remained quiet, simply watching the honesty of Frederick's words play across his face.

Lifting his gaze, Frederick met his eyes. "I'd be dead today," he said, his voice suddenly strong, ringing with conviction, "if it weren't for Ellie." Turning his head, he smiled at his wife, who reached out her other hand and gently cupped his cheek, letting it run down his arm until it came to rest on top of their already linked hands ... where it belonged.

Forcing his attention back to their guest, Frederick drew in a deep breath. "After returning from the war, I was a different man. There was darkness in my heart that threatened to engulf me day after day. I could barely keep it at bay and felt certain I'd succumb to it before long." He nodded, his gaze clear. "And I would have, had my wife not been there to fight by my side. I would have been lost, for alone I could never have triumphed."

Remembering Victoria's words, Sebastian closed his eyes. Charlotte had been alone to fight the darkness that threatened to engulf her, and it had. It had changed her, forced her down a path she hadn't willingly chosen. And yet, she had returned.

"The night of the fire at Elmridge," Frederick continued, "the night I finally realised what had happened to her, she was a raging woman with no resemblance to the friend I had known." Shaking his head, he sighed and lifted his gaze to Sebastian. "I believe with every fibre of my soul that the woman she is at heart would never have hurt Leopold. Grief, loss and pain changed her until very little of her true self remained." He swallowed, an apologetic look in his eyes. "She must have loved Kenneth very much. Until that night, I hadn't realised how much."

Sebastian cleared his throat, remembering that there was a part of Charlotte's story of which they were not aware. Taking a deep breath, he told them of Northfield and his attack on her. He spoke of the baby and how she'd lost it the day she had learnt of Kenneth's death.

With each word, their faces grew paler and their eyes wider. The marchioness had tears in her eyes as she looked to her husband, and Sebastian could see the compassion she felt as she contemplated the many blows of fate Charlotte had had to endure. Frederick's face, though, grew angry as he listened, and when Sebastian had finished, he rose to his feet and stomped around the room. "Curse that man," he growled. "I should have known that something was wrong. I should've seen it. I ..."

"Kenneth did," Sebastian said, wishing he could have met the man who had been willing to sacrifice his own happiness to protect Charlotte. "He wanted to protect her. He did everything he could."

Frederick's hands balled into fists as he suddenly stood stock still in the middle of the room, his eyes staring into the distance, remembering a past moment. "He followed me," he whispered then. "He was angry that I had left without speaking to him, and he came to bring me home." He shook his head, regret filling his eyes. "I refused, and so he stayed ... to protect me."

Silently, his wife moved to his side, wrapping her arms around his, her cheek resting against his shoulder.

Frederick took a deep breath then, his eyes shifting to hers, and the ghost of a smile flashed over his face. Then he cleared his throat and met Sebastian's confused gaze. "When he came after me, he demanded to know why I would leave him a letter instead of speaking to him in person. I didn't know what he was talking about. He told me he had received a letter, which implied that I sought to kill myself on the battlefield." Shaking his head, Frederick furrowed his brows. "I couldn't believe it. After all, I had sent no such letter. But Kenneth refused to believe me until ... he suddenly grew thoughtful. He pulled out the letter and showed it to me, and that's when he realised it hadn't been my handwriting. I suppose he hadn't noticed it before because he had been too concerned. He began to pace the floor, cursing under his breath, until he suddenly stopped and growled out one word."

A cold shiver ran down Sebastian's back as he waited for the confirmation of the awful suspicion that had settled in his stomach like a heavy lump.

"Northfield," Frederick spat, his lips contorted in a snarl, as his body tensed with understanding. Gritting his teeth, he closed his eyes briefly. "He sent the letter to get Kenneth out of the way." His eyes travelled from his wife to Sebastian. "I didn't know. I told him to go back to her, and he said he would. He wanted to leave the next day, and then ..." Again, he closed his eyes and drew a deep breath into his lungs.

"Unbelievable," Sebastian muttered under his breath. Rising from his seat, he, too, began to stalk around the room, unable to keep still. "I had thought him a man of questionable character, but this," he shook his head, "this is beyond what even I could have imagined."

Frederick nodded, determination marring his features. "Something has to be done about him. We cannot allow him to continue in this manner."

Scoffing, Sebastian shook his head in disbelief. "As I was out of the country as it happened, I'm not sure if you're aware of this, but," he looked from Frederick to his wife, "he is my sister's husband."

A guttural growl escaped Frederick as his wife gasped.

"Charlotte is determined to free Victoria from her husband," Sebastian continued, feeling relieved to share this enormous secret with another.

"How?" the marchioness asked, a concerned gleam in her eyes.

Sebastian swallowed. "She wants to kill him."

Frederick shook his head. "They'd hang her for it."

"I know," Sebastian replied, fear gripping his heart. "But she feels it's the only way for her to repay her debt, the only way for her to make amends for taking your brother's life."

Frederick swallowed, his lips pressed into a thin line as he stood silent for a moment. Then he shook his head in vehemence. "No, we will not sacrifice Charlotte," he said, determination ringing in his voice. "I failed to protect her then, but I will not now." His wife nodded, her arms holding his more tightly. "She is a victim as was Kenneth, and I will make sure Northfield will pay for what he's done to both of them," he swallowed, "as well as to Leopold."

"How?" was all Sebastian could say as his blood hummed in his veins.

A devilish grin came to Frederick's face. "Oliver will know."

Chapter Forty-Five

THE IMPOSSIBLE

Upon enquiring after her husband's whereabouts the next day, Charlotte was informed that he had called for a carriage early that morning and hadn't returned since.

Pacing the downstairs parlour, Charlotte wondered where he had gone. After he had disappeared for most of the previous day, only returning long after the sun had set, she had hoped to be able to speak to him the next day. Where had he gone? And why?

A nagging fear settled in her stomach as she pictured her husband out in some secluded spot in Hyde Park, facing Northfield, a duelling pistol in hand.

Shaking her head, she pushed that thought aside. No, he wouldn't. He was not fool enough to call out Northfield. And yet, he had been rather enraged to find his sister's husband attacking his wife only moments after his father's funeral. Could she still count on his word not to do anything rash? Was he still ruled by rational thought? Or had his desire for revenge gotten the better of him?

Guilt joined the fear that lived in her heart as she thought about what losing him would mean to his family. They would be devastated, to say the least.

And what about you? Her heart whispered. *What would you feel aside from guilt?*

Cringing at the mere contemplation of his loss, Charlotte closed her eyes, finally admitting to herself that she, too, would be devastated ...

... and heartbroken

... and inconsolable

... and close to despair.

Yes, losing him would break her heart like nothing ever had.

After all the darkness she had waded through the past few years, she could not imagine ever being without his warmth and compassion, his comfort and ... yes, his love ever again. After all, he did love her, did he not? More than once he had said so, and her heart had rejoiced at hearing those precious three words.

And yet, she had not reciprocated.

Why? Her heart wondered.

In that moment, she couldn't think of a reason. Everything had felt so simple ... and yet, so complicated.

Again, Northfield shot to the front of her mind, and Charlotte groaned.

Nothing was simple. Nothing had been simple ever since that fateful night long ago. Yes, everything had been set into motion when Northfield had forced himself on her, but then it had been Charlotte herself who had made the wrong choices ...

... and become a monster no one could possibly love.

And yet, someone did.

For a moment, she thought of Victoria as her feet continued to carry her around the room, unable to keep still. Although her sister-in-law had suffered a most similar atrocity, Charlotte couldn't help but realise that despite everything, Victoria had remained true to herself. She was still as kind and compassionate as before her marriage. Never had she strayed from a just path to forget or not to feel.

Charlotte admired her greatly, wishing she herself had had that kind of inner strength.

The front door closed, and Charlotte's head snapped up as the soft echo drifted from the hall to her ears.

For a moment, she stood stock still, debating with herself how to proceed. However, without knowing whether her husband had indeed returned, all further planning would be moot.

As she strode toward the door, determined to find out, it suddenly swung open, revealing Sebastian in its frame.

Stopping in her tracks, Charlotte stared at him, taking note of the dark circles under his eyes as well as the tension resting in his shoulders.

"There you are," he said, his eyes meeting hers without judgement or accusation, and Charlotte's heart beat a little faster.

"I'm glad you've returned," she whispered, taking a careful step toward him. "I was worried. I'd thought ..."

Gathering her meaning, he shook his head, a hint of regret coming to his features. "I apologise for leaving without a word." He took a deep breath. "But I needed to think."

"I understand."

For a moment, he held her gaze, and Charlotte thought to see an old light spark briefly as though he, too, wished that things could be different. "Would you accompany me to my study?" he asked then. "There is something we need to discuss."

"Of course," Charlotte replied, her voice shaky as she spoke, and yet, her legs carried her down the corridor without a hitch, despite the slight tremble that shook her frame. What would he say to her? She wondered. Would he agree to her request and allow her to see his sister safe?

Now that the fog had retreated, was she even still capable of doing so? Charlotte wondered in a moment of uncertainty.

Opening the door to his study, her husband bade her to enter and then closed the door behind them.

Crossing the large carpet covering the floor, Charlotte stopped on her way to the armchairs facing the massive desk when she caught a movement out of the corner of her eye.

To her surprise, a man stood by the window front, gazing out onto the street. Even with his back turned, a sense of recognition washed over her, and Charlotte squinted her eyes.

Then he turned.

As her jaw dropped open, Charlotte's hand involuntarily went to her throat. "Frederick," she gasped, and the world around her began to sway dangerously under her feet.

In an instant, her husband was there, his steady arm holding her upright as he urged her to sit.

"Charlotte." Holding her gaze, his eyes searching, Frederick drew in a deep breath. "It is good to see you," he said, a slight tremble in his voice. "The last time we saw each other, I feared for the worst." He swallowed. "And when I received news of your death, I grieved for you."

Staring at him in shock, Charlotte couldn't believe her ears. Had she strayed into a dream? She had to have for this couldn't possibly be real. How could he speak to her with such compassion after what she had done to him? To his wife? To his unborn child? Most of all, to his brother?

Shaking her head, she licked her lips, trying to express the confusion that raged in her heart and mind. Her mouth opened, and the only word that tumbled out was, "How?"

Stepping forward, Frederick took the seat opposite her, his eyes momentarily darting to Sebastian, who stood behind her, his hands resting on her shoulders. Frederick swallowed then and met her eyes, drawing in a deep breath as though needing to fortify himself. "I killed men, too," he began, his tone dark, full of regret and disbelief. "Brothers and fathers, sons and husbands. I did it in the name of my country, and somehow that is to absolve me of my responsibility." Lips pressed into a thin line, he shook his head. "I don't think it does, and yet, I have to live with it."

"But," Charlotte began, "he was your brother. I ..."

"And you were my friend," Frederick said, his eyes holding hers, willing her to believe him. "You *are* my friend. I have come here today to offer you my help. Better late than never."

His help? Charlotte frowned. *How could he look at her with anything but disgust and repulsion?*

"I wish to help you and Victoria," Frederick continued, his gaze briefly shifting to her husband.

At the mention of his sister, Sebastian's hands tightened on her shoulders, and Charlotte drew in a deep breath. Could this truly be happening?

"Northfield needs to be stopped," Frederick said, and anger sparked in his eyes. "He killed Kenneth just as much as Leopold."

Shaking her head, Charlotte stared at her childhood friend, and tears came to her eyes as she saw his unwavering willingness to protect her. "I missed you." The words left her lips before she'd consciously decided to share them.

A soft smile tugged at the corner of his mouth, and Frederick nodded. "I missed you, too. I apologise for not seeing your distress. I should have acted sooner. If I had, then ..." He shrugged. "All I can do is try to set things right now."

Biting her lip, Charlotte averted her gaze. "There's only one way," she mumbled, trying to find the right words to convince Frederick of her rightful course.

"Yes, there is," her friend replied, his voice strong and adamant.

Lifting her eyes to his, Charlotte found him shaking his head.

"You will not sacrifice yourself," he ordered. "I will not allow it."

Charlotte opened her mouth in protest. "But-"

"That is not who you are," Frederick insisted.

Touched, Charlotte smiled at him. She had forgotten what it was like to have others to call upon. "But he is a peer," she said nonetheless, knowing that her way was the only one open to them. "No one can touch him. People owing money go to debtor's prison, but the law does not seek to punish those who destroy lives the way Northfield did and still does."

Taking a deep breath, Charlotte glanced at her husband, his face stony as he stood behind her. Then his gaze shifted to her, and he took a deep breath. "We will think of something," he assured her, his voice gentle, almost soothing. "We will. Believe me."

"Actually," Frederick said, rising from his seat, a broad grin on his face, "Oliver already has."

Chapter Forty-Six

A RATHER UNCONVENTIONAL PUNISHMENT

"Whose house is this?" Charlotte asked from the driver's seat of the carriage, glancing up at the looming townhouse wrapped in silence as the moon glistened overhead, casting an eerie light on the deserted street.

Standing hidden beside the carriage's front wheel, her husband cleared his throat, and even in the dark of night, Charlotte could see the disapproving frown that came to his features. "His mistress lives here," he finally said, disgust tinging his voice as he glanced past her toward the closed front door.

"I see," Charlotte mumbled, her gloved fingers running over the rough leather of the reins in her hand. Wrapped in a black cloak, a large hat pulled deep into her face, she sat, waiting in the dark, her left foot restlessly tapping against the footrest.

Behind her, inside the carriage, Frederick Lancaster, Marquess of Elmridge, and Oliver Cromwell, Earl of Cullingwood-Kenneth's childhood friends as well as her own-lay in wait while her husband stood by her side, unwilling to leave her alone-just in case. After all, at first, he had straight-out refused her request to accompany them, deeming it far too dangerous. However, Frederick had understood her need to see this through to the end and had gently urged his late brother's friend to give his permission.

"How much longer?" Charlotte whispered, her nerves strained beyond comprehension.

Her husband scoffed. "How am I to know?"

Drawing in a deep breath, Charlotte forced her restless foot to still. It would be a long night, and the last thing any of them needed was for her to give away their plan before it could be executed.

"Where did Oliver find the carriage?" she enquired before she could stop herself.

Beside her, his head bobbing up next to her knee, Sebastian grinned. "Do you regret that you came? Would you rather I take you home?"

"Nonsense!" Charlotte hissed, annoyed with herself for not listening more closely when Oliver had shared the details of his plan with them the day before. Back then, her nerves had been far too rattled once she'd understood what he had in mind. Never in her wildest dreams would she have thought that her old friends would assist her in such a determined way, their eyes looking at her as though nothing had happened.

Upon seeing Oliver for the first time in years, Charlotte had been shocked speechless when he had bowed to her, his usual good-natured smile on his lips as well as a touch of mischief in his eyes. Then he had winked at her as he had countless times before, and she had nearly fainted.

"With Oliver, one never knows," her husband whispered beside her. "As far as I remember even as a young boy, he was usually the one up to no good." He coughed quietly, a hint of disapproval in his tone. "I didn't ask," he finally admitted, and Charlotte wondered what secrets lay hidden behind her old friend's good-natured smile.

Maybe it would be best for her not to ask him to explain.

Beside her, her husband sucked in a sharp breath. "There," he whispered, and Charlotte turned her head toward the townhouse, her heart hammering in her chest.

Slowly, the door slid open.

Before she could see anything though, Charlotte jerked her head back to the front, praying that Northfield hadn't noticed anything out of the ordinary. Beside her, she heard her husband's soft knock on the side of the carriage, informing those within that the moment of truth had finally come.

As the muscles in her body tensed to the point of breaking, Charlotte caught movement out of the corner of her eye as Northfield walked down the front stoop toward his waiting carriage. Praying that he wouldn't speak to her or notice the freshly painted coat-of-arms on the side of the carriage that resembled his own to a fault-how had Oliver done this?-Charlotte held her breath.

"Home, Wilson," Northfield's commanding voice spoke as though to no one of importance.

Freezing in shock, Charlotte barely managed to nod her head in acknowledgement before he climbed up the lowered step and vanished inside the carriage through the open door.

All had been done exactly as always, and Northfield had been none the wiser.

At least until Charlotte heard the muffled sounds of a struggle from inside the carriage.

Instantly, her husband rushed around, obscured the freshly painted coat-of-arms with black paint and peeked inside.

"Go!" Oliver's voice called out, pulling the door closed.

Then her husband swung himself up onto the driver's seat beside her, grabbed the reins from her numb fingers and urged the horses down the deserted street.

Slightly annoyed with his attitude, and yet utterly grateful for it, Charlotte clung to her seat as her husband guided the carriage skilfully through the night. Slowly, the streets grew narrower and darker as they left behind the well-lit neighbourhoods of the upper class. Salty sea air touched her nostrils as the wind swept over her face, and she remembered where they were headed.

When the docks came in sight, a cold shiver went down Charlotte's back and she instinctively grabbed her husband's arm, drawing herself closer to him.

Pulling the carriage to a stop in front of a large ship, docked in the farthest corner of the port, its gangplank lowered, he looked down at her and the corners of his lips curved up into a smile. Then he pulled her closer, his hand settling on hers, giving it a gentle squeeze.

"Moon over your wife later," Oliver chided, a chuckle in his voice, as he looked up at them from beside the carriage. "There's work to be done. The fellow is heavier than he looks. Give us a hand, will you?"

Jumping down from the driver's seat, Sebastian assisted Charlotte down before he turned toward the interior of the carriage, a grimace of disgust on his face. "Why don't we just toss him in the water?"

"Because that is not the plan," Oliver chided, clicking his tongue, as he stepped out of the carriage, holding Northfield's feet.

Even seeing him unconscious made Charlotte shudder, and her hands clenched into the fabric of her thick cloak. This was it! She kept thinking. Finally, he was getting what he deserved.

As Frederick came into view, his arms wrapped around Northfield's chest, Charlotte noticed the absence of the man's fine clothing. Instead, he wore worn breeches, a stained shirt, a most likely moth-infested overcoat and scuffed boots. He looked every bit the penniless wastrel!

"This yer man," a rough voice spoke out from behind, and Charlotte spun around. A sailor-or rather a captain, judging from the hat he'd donned-stood a few steps from the gangplank leading up to the large vessel docked behind them.

"What gave him away?" Oliver chuckled, handing Northfield's lower half over to Sebastian and then strode toward the captain. "Are we clear?" he asked, his watchful eyes meeting the captain's.

"Aye, we're clear."

A pleased smile on his face, Oliver nodded, then withdrew a small purse from inside his overcoat and handed it to the captain. "A one-way trip. No returns."

"Returns cost extra," the captain grinned, revealing teeth that shone yellow in the dim light on the docks. Opening the string on the purse, he began to count and his grin grew wider. Then he gestured toward two sailors waiting on deck.

Upon their captain's signal, they hurried down the gangplank and took hold of Northfield, carrying him aboard without a word.

The moment the man who had haunted her life for the past four years vanished from their view, Charlotte's knees buckled and she sank down until strong arms caught her. Looking up, she found her husband's concerned face hovering above her as he pulled her against his chest, holding her tight. "It's over now," he whispered into her hair, then placed a gentle kiss on the top of her head. "It's over."

Closing her eyes, Charlotte buried her face in his coat, clinging to him like the lifeline he had been for her almost from the very moment they'd met. Never in her life had she felt safer ... or more loved. But could he forgive her?

"Do you think he'll like the land down under?" Frederick asked, a hint of gratification in his otherwise serious voice.

"I rather doubt it," Oliver answered, another chuckle leaving his lips. "Although Captain Reed is a gentleman of the finest breed," he mocked, "the conditions under deck are rather harsh and far from what the dear baron is used to. In addition, I suppose he'll object to convicts for company." Then he shrugged, his gaze shifting to Charlotte and a reassuring smile came to his face. "Fortunately for us, he won't have a say in the matter ... in any matter, ever again."

Returning his smile, Charlotte nodded, grateful beyond her wildest dreams. Never would she have dared to contemplate such an outcome. Never had she believed that Northfield, untouchable by the law, would ever live to see his deeds punished ... even if it was a rather unconventional punishment.

And yet, it seemed fitting beyond reproach.

The man who had committed countless atrocities in his pursuit of wealth and reputation was now doomed to live the life of a convict, far from home, in a place that would teach him that his precious title mattered very little when it came to the raw nature of survival.

Charlotte could only hope that he would learn from the experience.

Deep down, however, she doubted that he would.

However, that wasn't her problem.

It was his ...

... and she couldn't care less.

Leaving the docks-as well as Northfield-behind, Sebastian noticed the way Charlotte sat slumped in her seat. While Oliver had taken over the reins, the rest of them had retreated inside the carriage, relieved to be on their way home, most of the events of that night finally behind them.

Later, Oliver would get rid of the counterfeit carriage and then return to the tavern where Northfield's driver was currently celebrating his unexpected wins in a gambling hall the night before with women and liquor. Come morning, he would wake on the shores of the Thames, his master's carriage sunk to its bottom, with no recollection of how he or the carriage had gotten there.

"Are you all right?" Sebastian whispered to his wife, aware of Frederick's gaze resting on Charlotte, his brows drawn down in concern.

At his voice, Charlotte's head snapped up and she blinked, momentarily confused. Then she nodded. "Yes, I'm fine." For a moment, she kept nodding her head as though she couldn't stop herself, as though she needed to remind herself that it was true.

Regretting the earlier harshness of his tone, Sebastian gritted his teeth, inhaling deeply through his nose, and met Frederick's gaze.

His dark eyes seemed clouded even in the dim interior of the carriage. However, instead of the edge of pain and loathing Sebastian would have expected to find within them, they seemed to glow with compassion as well as a sadness that Frederick understood in a way Sebastian couldn't fathom. And for the millionth time since seeking Frederick's counsel, Sebastian wondered what it was that seemed to connect his late friend's brother to his wife ... despite the circumstances.

Was it simply the edge of death from which they had both retreated?

Did they see the world differently now after the darkness they'd lived through?

Had they gained a greater understanding of heart and mind that eluded him?

A jolt of jealousy coursed through him, and Sebastian cringed involuntarily. Would he ever be able to understand his wife as well as Frederick?

Beside him, his wife inhaled deeply, and her shoulders drew back, straightening her spine. Her eyes moved upward from the darkness of the carriage's floor and came to rest on Frederick. Again, she drew in a deep breath and then opened her mouth.

Only no sound came out.

Swallowing, she licked her lips, her eyes unwavering, and once more she opened her mouth to speak.

"I know," Frederick said, nodding his head in understanding before she had even uttered a single word. His eyes held hers, and he drew in a deep breath as though needing to steady himself.

"I'm sorry," Charlotte whispered, her voice breaking as a sob tore from her throat. Tears streamed down her face, and her hands clenched, her fingers digging into the fabric of her skirt. "I ..." At a loss, she merely nodded her head.

"I know," Frederick said once more, not even the slightest hint of doubt on his face about what she was saying.

"I wish ..."

"Me, too," he whispered, a sad smile tugging on his lips. "With all my heart."

Another sob tore from Charlotte's throat, and Sebastian tensed.

Although his heart urged him to comfort her, his mind still objected to such a show of mercy. After what she had done, did she deserve comfort? The rational side of him demanded.

His heart, however, only saw her misery, her honest regret, and knew without a doubt that she could not be counted among the evil-doers of the world. She'd made a mistake. An awful, grave mistake.

But she had not been herself at the time.

Should he not forgive her when even Frederick had? Was it not his duty as her husband?

Looking up, he met Frederick's gaze, which was fixing him with an intense stare as he was trying to communicate with him in the same way he seemed to be able to so effortlessly with Charlotte. His brows rose as his gaze shifted to Sebastian's wife before it returned to him, urgency resting in their clouded depths. Then he nodded his head.

Taking a deep breath, Sebastian lifted his arm as though a

puppeteer was controlling him and placed it around his wife's shoulders, pulling her closer.

Sebastian wasn't certain what he'd expected. But she turned to him then, burying her face against his shoulder, her fingers digging into his coat as she pressed herself against him, her tears wetting his shirt.

A soft smile came to Frederick's face then, and he nodded in approval before leaning back in his seat, his jaw relaxed where before it had been marked by concern.

Feeling Charlotte's soft body moulded to his own, her frame shaking as the pain of the past streamed down her face, Sebastian knew that it was only a matter of time before his heart would overrule his mind.

Closing his eyes, he felt relief wash over him as the future he had dreamed of slowly came back within his reach. He had thought hope was lost, and yet, all that had happened had merely brought them closer together. If this hadn't been able to break them apart for good, then nothing ever would.

And that thought comforted him more than anything he had ever known.

The carriage drew to a halt then, and he heard Oliver jump to the ground a moment before the door was flung open, revealing the man's smiling face. "My lady, my lord," he grinned, looking from Charlotte to Sebastian, "may I escort you outside?"

Offering Oliver a half-smile, Sebastian gently disentangled himself from his wife and stepped out of the carriage. Then he held out his hand to help her down. The moment her feet came to rest on the pavement beside him, she snuggled back into his arms.

Joy bloomed in Sebastian's heart as his arms wrapped around her, holding her tight. Looking up, he met Frederick's smiling eyes and knew that everything would be all right.

"Be good to each other," Frederick whispered, pulling the door closed as Oliver returned to take the reins. "Love is the greatest gift any of us can ever hope to find; don't waste it," he implored as the carriage drew away from the kerb.

Chapter Forty-Seven

BON VOYAGE

Charlotte's fingers trembled as her eyes flew over the few words written on a simple, white sheet of paper. There had been no calling card in the envelope, nor was the sheet signed or addressed to a particular person.

And yet, Charlotte knew exactly who had sent it.

As did her husband.

A wide grin on his face, he stood before her, the pulse in his neck quickening as the implications of those few words slowly sank it.

Bon voyage.

"He's truly gone, isn't he?" Charlotte whispered as though speaking too loudly would turn the ship around and bring him back to England's shores.

Her husband's head bobbed up and down as he took her hands in his, the small sheet of paper gliding to the ground, its purpose fulfilled. "Gone for good," he whispered as though he feared the same as her. "Good riddance."

Seeing excitement sparkle in his eyes, Charlotte found herself step forward without thought and her arms wound around his neck, pulling him into an embrace. "I haven't felt this free in a long time," she whispered, feeling his hands slide up and down her back.

Instantly, her senses sharpened and her breath caught in her throat as his nearness overwhelmed her, pouring into every fibre of her body. Although his touch no longer scared her, it still amazed her how quickly it could change how she felt, how unexpectedly it could conjure new feelings and discard old ones. "I love you," she whispered then, and his answering smile made her forget the world around them.

At least, until ...

"Victoria," Charlotte gasped before she would lose all hold on reality.

Pulling back, Sebastian looked at her, his brows quizzical. "Excuse me?" he asked, a touch of humour to his voice.

"I'm sorry," Charlotte said, biting her lower lip as a touch of red darkened her cheeks. "All I wanted to say was that," she took a deep breath as his eyes burnt into hers as though seeing all the way into her soul, "we should go and speak to Victoria. She deserves to know, don't you think?"

Reluctantly, her husband nodded. "You're right." He pulled her toward the foyer, a devilish twinkle in his eyes. "The sooner we leave; the sooner we'll return."

Heat seized Charlotte at the expression in his eyes, and she was grateful for the short carriage ride to reclaim her composure.

Seated in Victoria's parlour not fifteen minutes later, Charlotte didn't know where to begin.

All but two days ago, they had changed all their lives by putting Northfield on a prisoner ship bound for Australia, a ship where he belonged ... if not in the eyes of the law.

How much were they to tell Victoria? Would she want to know everything that had happened? Or would it be enough for her to know that her husband would never return?

"I'm so relieved," Victoria exclaimed, a deep smile on her face, "that you've managed to work things out. Quite frankly, the two of you simply belong together, and it pained me greatly to see you both so sad."

Again, heat rose in Charlotte's cheeks at her sister-in-law's observation. However, her own embarrassment subsided as she saw that her husband's face, too, sported a rather rosy touch.

Clearing his throat, he reached for his teacup. "Who told you we've worked things out?"

Victoria grinned. "No one," she whispered as though in confidence. "However, it is written all over your faces. Happiness suits you, dear Brother. You, too, Charlotte." A touch of regret came to Victoria's eyes as she spoke, and a sigh escaped her.

Opening her mouth to give Victoria peace of mind, Charlotte found herself interrupted as the dowager baroness, Northfield's mother, suddenly swept into the parlour, her brows drawn down in displeasure. "Where is he?" she demanded, glancing around the room.

As the breath caught in Charlotte's throat and she cast a worried glance at her husband, Victoria merely frowned. "Who do you speak of?"

"My son, of course," his mother retorted as though it should have been obvious. "He was to accompany me to Lady Chamberlain today."

"I have not seen him," Victoria answered, eyeing her mother-in-law wearily. "Maybe he simply forgot."

The dowager baroness huffed. "My son does not forget something as important as an agreed upon engagement. After all, the family's reputation is at stake." Her eyes narrowed as she regarded Victoria. "I assure you I am very cross with him."

"As you have every right to be," Victoria assured her, then glanced at Charlotte and Sebastian, seeking help.

"This is utterly strange," the dowager baroness proclaimed. "After all, my son has infallible manners. This is indeed most strange."

Gritting her teeth, Charlotte suddenly found herself overcome with laughter. Even more so when her husband met her eyes, and she had to turn away to keep from laughing out loud.

Seeing their faces, Victoria frowned. While listening to her mother-in-law praise her son, again and again uttering how exceedingly strange such behaviour was for him, Victoria studied them through narrowed eyes.

Taking a deep breath, Charlotte met Victoria's gaze openly before she glanced at the dowager baroness pacing a hole into the Persian rug and then nodded her head almost imperceptibly.

For a moment, the frown on Victoria's face grew even deeper before her eyes suddenly snapped open and her jaw dropped. A gasp escaped her lips, and she instantly clasped a hand over her mouth.

"Are you all right, Dear?" the dowager baroness asked, eyeing the rest of them curiously.

Victoria swallowed. "Quite all right," she whispered, sounding breathless. "I fear the tea is hotter than I expected." She looked at Charlotte and Sebastian. "I do apologise for this oversight."

While Charlotte and Sebastian merely nodded their heads, the dowager baroness started into a lamentation about the great difficulty of finding sufficiently skilled staff before finally taking her leave.

When the door closed and they were alone in the parlour, Victoria scooted to the edge of her seat, her eyes wide with anticipation. "Tell me at once what's happened!" she demanded, the pulse in her neck racing.

Exchanging a knowing look with her husband, Charlotte smiled. "We promised to liberate you from your marriage," she said, "and today we're pleased to report ... that we have succeeded."

Staring at them, Victoria swallowed. "Truly?" she whispered, hope and dread waging a war within her heart. "Is he truly gone?"

Charlotte nodded and then looked at her husband.

"He is, Sister," Sebastian confirmed. "Never to return."

"But ... but ... how?" she gasped, her cheeks pale as she gasped for air. "How did you ...?"

Sebastian shook his head. "That doesn't matter," he said, an affectionate smile on his face as he looked at his beloved sister. "All that matters is that he is gone, and you're free."

"Free?" Victoria whispered as though to herself. Her gaze unseeing, she lifted her hand and gently placed it on her belly. Then she closed her eyes, and a deep smile came to her face. "Now, you're all mine," she whispered, "and I promise I shall do what I must to love you the way you deserve."

Epilogue

England, spring 1808 (or a variation thereof)

One day earlier

His head pounded as it had never had before, and through the fog that clouded his mind, Philip Stanton, Baron Northfield, tried to remember where he had been the previous night and how he could have allowed himself to become this inebriated, warranting such a headache the morning after.

Try as he might, he couldn't recall.

Opening his eyes, he groaned as the dim light touched his senses and a blinding pain shot through his head. Reflexively, he pressed his hands to his temples and rolled over, rough wood scratching his face. Where the bloody hell was he? And what on earth had happened?

"Look here," a voice nearby slurred drowsily, "he's coming to."

"Shhh," another warned, a growl rumbling through the air. "I'm trying to sleep here. Best ye can do."

Gritting his teeth, Philip turned his head away, waiting for the pain to subside. Had he passed out in some tavern? Frowning, he would have shaken his head if he'd dared. Impossible! Not since his youth had he set foot in lower establishments. After all, he had a reputation to maintain!

Again, his cheeks scratched over the rough wood beneath him, and he winced as a splinter dug into his skin. He cursed silently before his stomach suddenly flipped and a new queasiness came to his insides.

The floor was moving.

Was he still drunk?

"What'd you do?" someone asked relatively close by, and a previously unknown stench assaulted his senses.

Cracking open an eye, Philip carefully glanced at his surroundings. However, all he could see as the light attacked his eyes were wooden walls, boards everywhere as well as iron bars, behind which men sat on the rough floor, their faces stained with dirt, their eyes downcast.

"What'd you do?" the man beside him repeated, eyeing him with mild curiosity as he continued to scratch himself every place he could reach.

Lice! Philip thought and instinctively drew back as far as he could. "What do you speak of?" he demanded, unable to believe that what he was seeing was real and not some kind of nightmare.

"Are you daft?" the man laughed. "I'm asking what got you on this ship?"

"Ship?" Philip repeated stupidly.

"Aye, to Australia." The man shook his head, then glanced over his shoulder and a moment later, more voices joined in his laughter.

"Australia?" Philip repeated as a cold shiver slowly slunk down his spine. "A ship to Australia?" he whispered, and then sudden realisation dawned.

A convict transport!

How had he gotten here?

Frantically, looking about as fear clawed at this heart, he pushed himself to his feet, one hand holding to the iron bars to keep from falling. "I demand to speak to the captain immediately."

More laughter echoed through the dim hull. "The likes of us do not get to make demands," the man beside him sneered, then shook his head and eyed him with a hint of disgust. "Get off your high horse and realise how far you've fallen."

Philip swallowed. How far indeed?

As far as he possibly could have was the answer.

But how?

Who had done this to him?

Shrinking back into a corner of his cell, Philip rested his head on his knees and closed his eyes. Shaken to his core, he tried not to give in to fear, but instead vowed to discover who had dealt him this blow and return it a thousand-fold.

Today, he had been defeated.

But tomorrow, he would return ...

... and he would not show mercy.

About nine months later

Sitting in the drawing room of Hartridge Hall, Victoria looked down at her little son, barely three months old, but already holding up his little head as he lay on his stomach at a safe distance from the smouldering fire in the hearth. His little arms and legs moved as though he was trying to swim, and a proud smile drew up the corners of her mouth.

Her son!

Shaking her head, Victoria sighed. Oh, how much she loved him! Some days, she felt certain her heart would burst with the sheer joy of having him in her life, of holding him in her arms and having him look up at her, his little fists waving as though he couldn't wait to see what life had in store for him.

"Philip is a true delight," her mother exclaimed, her own face aglow with the same enchantment that rang in Victoria's chest.

"He is my pride and joy," she mumbled, realising that the sound of her son's name no longer stung.

After her husband had *disappeared* and his carriage had then been found in the Thames, Victoria had finally believed that he was gone from her life for good. Although to this day, she did not know-nor did she wish to-what had happened to him; she finally felt safe.

Only her mother-in-law's lamentations as well as society's expectations had finally worn her down, and she had agreed to name her son after his father. At first, she had cringed every time someone had spoken his name, unable to utter it herself. However, over time, the name had reminded her less and less of her husband and more and more of her son. It no longer spoke of cruelty and shame, but of joy and unadulterated happiness.

Glancing up, Victoria smiled as she saw her brother and sister-in-law step toward the drawing room, both deep in conversation with one another, their eyes sparkling as they spoke. Sebastian stopped then in the door frame, his gaze almost imperceptibly glancing upward at the mistletoe placed there as he held out his hands to his wife.

Smiling, Charlotte took them, not yet aware of his intention, her eyes gazing up into his, love making her face glow.

As always, the closeness and affection between them drew a sigh from Victoria's slips, and she wondered if she would ever find someone who would look upon her the way her brother looked at his wife.

After her marriage, she doubted it very much, doubted that she could ever allow herself to be intimate with a man ever again-emotionally as well as physically. However, whenever she looked at her sister-in-law, she was reminded of the fact that Charlotte, too, had suffered greatly in her past and had overcome her fears, finding love when she'd least expected it.

Maybe there was still hope.

Wasn't there always? If one only looked hard enough?

Since her brother's marriage had not been binding because the marriage certificate did not show the bride's true name, Sebastian—unbeknownst to society—had whisked his wife to Gretna Green once again to claim her as his own for all eternity. Then, with Lord Elmridge's assistance, they had called upon Charlotte's parents, who had been shocked—to say the least—to see their daughter alive.

Although Victoria could see that their betrayal would never be forgotten, Charlotte had allowed them back into her life, and they'd readily assured their assistance to resurrect her from the dead.

Finally, Charlotte could breathe again ... and love without fear.

"A kiss is in order," Victoria's mother chuckled, looking from her son to her daughter-in-law. "I hope you weren't fool enough to lose yet another bet to your lovely wife, my son."

Grinning, Sebastian turned to Charlotte, and a wordless exchange passed between the two of them that made Victoria's heart ache with envy. Oh, how she wished she had someone who knew what she thought merely by looking at her!

Watching her brother pull his wife into his arms, seeing the eagerness with which Charlotte stepped into his embrace, Victoria sighed yet again.

If life had taught her anything at all, it was that anything was possible.

Smiling down at her precious son, she knew that no matter what the future held, her family would be by her side, and their support would give her the strength she needed to claim love ... whenever it chose to find her.

THE END

Thank you for your enthusiasm for *Ruined & Redeemed*!

Now, witness Oliver, our gallant Earl of Cullingwood, as his life takes an extraordinary turn. Captured by a French privateer, he finds himself face to face with a remarkable woman—most unexpectedly as you can imagine.

Violet stands as her father's legacy, a tempest of bravery and brilliance, drawing Oliver into a maelstrom of forbidden affection. Their course is set amidst tumultuous oceans and societal expectations, compelling Oliver to contemplate a gamble on love against all odds. Will he brave the storm for a future with Violet, or will he watch her vanish into the horizon?

Their odyssey for love and liberty will carry them from the high seas' wild freedom to the opulent whirl of London's grandeur. Step aboard with me and prepare to be swept away by an epic romance where destiny pairs the most unlikely of hearts in *Condemned & Admired - The Earl's Cunning Wife*.

Read on for an excerpt!

Read a Sneak-Peek

Condemned & Admired
The Earl's Cunning Wife

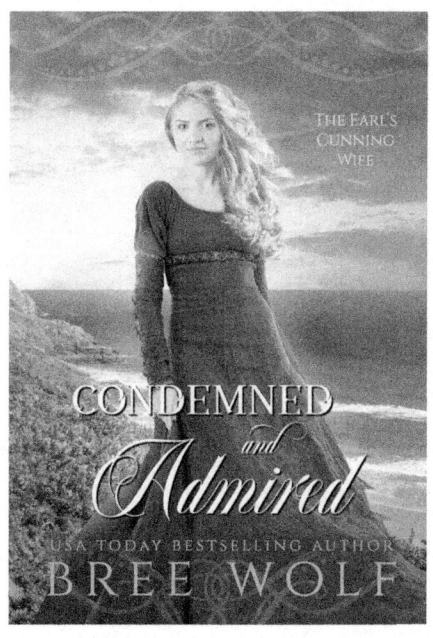

Prologue

Norfolk, England 1796 (or a variation thereof)

Twelve Years Ago

"Violet, Sweetheart, wake up."

Snuggling deeper into the pillow, six-year-old Violet Winters, daughter to Viscount Silcox, tried to hold on to the sweet oblivion of slumber. Still, her mother's gentle but insistent voice reached her little mind, tickling it awake and chasing away the last remnants of sleep.

A deep yawn opened Violet's mouth, and she rubbed her hand over her eyes. Blinking into the night's darkness, she looked up at her mother sitting on the side of her bed, a heavy woollen cloak wrapped around her shoulders and a small bundle sitting in her lap. Her golden hair–the same colour as Violet's–was hidden under the black cloak and her blue eyes seemed dark in the dimness of the room. "Mummy?" Violet squeaked, her voice sounding too loud in the silence that engulfed them.

"Shhh," her mother whispered, putting her right index finger to her lips, her eyes darting to the door in her back as though she expected someone to happen upon them at any moment.

A frown drew down Violet's brows as she saw the strain on her mother's face. Something was wrong! Even at the innocent age of six years, Violet could see that the slight tremble in her mother's hands was not due to the chill of the season. Nor could the way she glanced over her shoulder every few seconds be attributed to anything harmless.

Violet swallowed as she recognised the hint of fear that rested in her mother's eyes. "What's wrong, Mummy?"

A soft smile came to her mother's face as she brushed a gentle hand over her daughter's head and then cupped her cheek. "Everything's fine," she whispered, leaning close as she kept her voice down. "We're going on a little adventure."

"An adventure?" Violet glanced toward the windows where heavy curtains shut out the night. "But it's still dark."

Squeezing her daughter's hands, Alexandra Winters, Viscountess Silcox, nodded. "Precisely," she whispered, and for the first time, Violet thought to see a touch of excitement under the fear that clouded her mother's eyes.

"Come, you need to get dressed." Pulling back the blanket, her mother reached for a dress and a cloak lying over the back of Violet's bed. "But quietly. We must not make a sound, but be as quiet as mice, do you understand?"

Although Violet could not imagine why her mother urged her out of bed in the middle of the night, she nodded and quickly did as she was bid. After all, Violet's little heart felt nothing but unconditional love and trust toward her mother. Always had she wiped away her daughter's tears. Always had she comforted her on stormy nights. Always had she whispered words of love and promise in her ear.

No, there was not a single doubt in Violet's head as she pulled the cloak tightly around her small shoulders and then followed her mother out into the corridor.

Still, her heart beat loudly and the fingers of her right hand curled almost painfully into the woollen cloak while the other rested safely in her mother's.

Like shadows, they rushed down the dark corridor, past closed doors and then down one of the servants' staircases in the back of

Silcox Manor. Everything looked different at night, with the sun locked away tightly, and nothing but the silvery light of the moon touching the world. There were no sounds of rushing footsteps—none but their own—nor any voices whispering nearby. Only the wind howled around the house as it blew in from the sea and swept over the cliffs to the east of her father's country estate.

All her life, Violet had lived here, in a house full of servants with her mother by her side. Her father only occasionally visited them and insisted that his wife accompany him to London for a few weeks each year during the season. These weeks were the most awful of Violet's life.

Away from her mother.

Alone and unwanted.

Despite her young age, Violet knew very well that her birth had been a disappointment to her father as was the fact that no further child had been born these past six years. Her father wished for nothing more than a son.

An heir.

He had no use for a daughter, and he did not try to hide his resentment.

Early on, Violet had learnt that her father was not one to turn to with the joys and sorrows of life. Instead, her little heart had turned to the woman who never failed to look at her with love and devotion shining in her blue eyes.

Alexandra Winters, Viscountess Silcox, was her daughter's whole world...and Violet would have followed her into hell if she had asked.

Unlocking the heavy door, her mother looked down at Violet, a slight smile playing on her lips, and squeezed her daughter's hand. "Are you ready?"

Violet nodded. "Where are we going?"

"On a ship."

"A ship?" Violet's little heart skipped a beat. "You mean, like Gulliver's Travels?"

Her mother sighed, momentarily leaning against the door. Then her dark blue eyes turned to her daughter. "I do not know what awaits us, my sweet child, but I am certain that we will find happiness out there that is denied us in here." Then she drew in a deep breath, pushed open the heavy door with a slight grunt and pulled her daughter out into the night toward a new life.

Before they had even taken more than two steps, the wind rushed toward them, brushing over their cheeks and stealing under their hoods, pulling strands of their golden hair loose. Her mother's hand tightened on Violet's as she leaned into the wind and headed down the small path leading down toward the cliffs and the beach below.

Violet could hear the howling of a nearing storm, and even in the dark she could make out heavy clouds drifting in from the sea. Beside them, Silcox Manor loomed like a giant in the night, and Violet could not help but feel relieved with each step they took toward their adventure and away from the prison that had been their home.

With her mother's hand wrapped tightly around her own, Violet followed her down the small path snaking toward the beach, her little feet stumbling over rocks here and there. Still, her mother's grasp never wavered, catching her when need be.

Heading down the slope toward the beach, Violet glanced apprehensively at the tall boulders that seemed to have risen out of the earth and cast dark shadows even in the dim light of the silvery moon overhead. Her heart thudded wildly, and she did her best to remind herself that they were not monsters come to devour her, but merely tricks her mind played on her in the dark.

Still, when her eyes caught movement among the shadows and then something jumped into their path, a terrified shriek tore from Violet's lips.

Fortunately, it was drowned out by the howling of the wind.

Clinging to her mother, Violet stared at the shadow as it moved closer and then stepped into the light of the moon. Only then did her heart slow down as she saw that the monster was not a monster after all, but a man.

A man dressed almost completely in black were it not for the white shirt peeking out from under his vest and tailcoat. His dark hair was half-hidden under a sea captain's hat, and his eyes shone steel grey in the light of the moon. A sword dangled from his hip, and he moved with cat-like stealth. Everything about this man seemed dangerous, threatening.

Everything but his eyes.

For they looked at Violet's mother with such longing and devotion that the little girl soon forgot to be afraid. Instead, curiosity filled her as she observed the way he took her mother's hand, his thumb gently brushing over her knuckles as his gaze held hers. "Are you all right, ma chérie?" he asked, a strange lilt to his voice. "Did anyone see you?"

"I do not believe so," her mother replied, a soft smile on her face as she looked at him...and for a long moment, neither one of them said a word, the world around them all but forgotten.

Squeezing her mother's hand, Violet looked up at them, surprised by the glow that had come to her mother's face. "Mummy?"

Her mother swallowed, then blinked as though waking from a dream. "This is my daughter," she said, looking down at Violet and pulling her closer into her arms. "Violet."

The man nodded, and his eyes drifted down to her. "*Bon soir, Violette,*" he addressed her, a gentle smile coming to his lips as he knelt down in front of her. "Have you ever been on a ship?"

Violet shook her head. "Are you a pirate?" she asked, surprising even herself by asking that question.

The man laughed. "Not quite, *ma petite.* My name is *Antoine Duret,* and I am a privateer, sailing under a French flag." He glanced up at her mother, and the corners of his mouth curled into a smile. Then his eyes returned to Violet, and once more, she could see the depth of his emotions plainly on his face. "I've come to steal your mother away." Again, he smiled as though his heart's desire had just been fulfilled. "Your mother and you." Then he held out his hand to her. "Will you come with me?"

Glancing up at her mother, Violet could see that her eyes were glistening with tears. Still, her face held neither fear nor sorrow, but hope and trust instead. And in that moment, Violet knew beyond the shadow of a doubt that her mother had found someone to love.

Someone who loved her just the same.

And despite being only six years of age, Violet knew how precious that was.

After all, didn't her mother always say that love was the one thing not even the rich could buy?

Taking a deep breath, Violet slipped her hand into Antoine's and his fingers closed around hers warmly, the same way her other hand rested in her mother's. Perhaps this man who had come for them in the dark of night could not only love her mother, but Violet as well.

As Antoine guided them down toward the beach, Violet wondered if she would ever know the love of a father, if she would ever know what it felt like to be looked upon with pride.

Violet could only hope so.

Let the adventure begin.

About Bree

USA Today bestselling and award-winning author, Bree Wolf has always been a language enthusiast (though not a grammarian!) and is rarely found without a book in her hand or her fingers glued to a keyboard. Trying to find her way, she has taught English as a second language, traveled abroad and worked at a translation agency as well as a law firm in Ireland. She also spent loooong years obtaining a BA in English and Education and an MA in Specialized Translation while wishing she could simply be a writer. Although there is nothing simple about being a writer, her dreams have finally come true.

"A big thanks to my fairy godmother!"

Currently, Bree has found her new home in the historical romance genre, writing Regency novels and novellas. Enjoying the mix of fact and fiction, she occasionally feels like a puppet master (or mistress? Although that sounds weird!), forcing her characters into ever-new situations that will put their strength, their beliefs, their love to the test, hoping that in the end they will triumph and get the happily-ever-after we are all looking for.

If you're an avid reader, sign up for Bree's newsletter on **www. breewolf.com** as she has the tendency to simply give books away. Find out about freebies, giveaways as well as occasional advance reader copies and read before the book is even on the shelves!

Connect with Bree and stay up-to-date on new releases:

facebook.com/breewolf.novels

x.com/breewolf_author

instagram.com/breewolf_author

bookbub.com/authors/bree-wolf

amazon.com/Bree-Wolf/e/B00FJX27Z4

Printed in Dunstable, United Kingdom